BROKEN RIVER

SHATTERED SKY

To order additional copies of *Broken River, Shattered Sky,* by William Noel, call 1-800-765-6955.

Visit us at www.reviewandherald.com for information on other Review and Herald® products.

WILLIAM NOEL

BROKEN RIVER SHATTERED SKY

REVIEW AND HERALD® PUBLISHING ASSOCIATION
HAGERSTOWN, MD 21740

The author assumes full responsibility for the accuracy of all facts and
quotations as cited in this book.

Texts credited to NIV are from the *Holy Bible, New International Version.*
Copyright © 1973, 1978, 1984, International Bible Society. Used by permission
of Zondervan Bible Publishers.

This book was
Edited by Penny Estes Wheeler
Cover photos by Photos.com
Cover design and illustration by Ron J. Pride/square1studio
Typeset: 11/13 Veljovic Book

PRINTED IN U.S.A.

08 07 06 05 04   5 4 3 2 1

R&H Cataloging Service
Noel, William Fred, 1955-
     Broken river, shattered sky

     I. Title.

ISBN 0-8280-1773-5

DEDICATED

To my loving and faithful wife, Anita.

Perhaps the only person in this world who understands the creative gift God has given me, she is still able to keep loving me when I must escape to the corners of my imagination to form and play with characters who exist only there and on my hard drive.

ACKNOWLEDGMENTS

Many people have made contributions to this book, both large and small. It grew out of an argument with my brother, Ted, who was working on a theological treatise about Bible prophecy and the second coming of Jesus. I argued that if he wanted his book to be popular, it had to be a novel, because spiritual novels are far more popular than the form of book he was writing.

After several rounds of our discussion, he finally said, "You're the creative writer between us. Why don't *you* write it?" Suddenly I couldn't resist. God gave me the inspiration, and the creativity began flowing. Many times Ted served as a sounding board to evaluate ideas and to clarify my understanding of the underlying theology.

One question I am often asked is which of my characters are based on real people and which are invented. The answer is that each is some degree of both. Characters are servants of the plot, and they take on the characteristics needed to create and illustrate the story. From time to time along the way I have realized that I have unconsciously modeled significant aspects of my characters after real-life people I have met or currently know. Who they are and what aspects of their lives I have borrowed will remain my secret.

One person who deserves great thanks is my editor, Penny Estes Wheeler. As a breed, we writers are very protective and take very personally any threat of change to our work. I've been writing for more than 20 years and have also been an editor, so I knew it was a necessary step. Even so, it was with great fear that I turned my work over to her for editing. I need not have feared. I have respected Penny's skills as a writer for years, and I quickly discovered in her a fellow creative who was a true partner. At times I felt as if we were almost reading each other's minds. Though I think I did a good job of creating Hope Lancaster, the manuscript still required Penny's outstanding skills to turn Hope from a good character into a great one.

Most of all, credit goes to God for giving me the creativity, the love for good dramatic stories, and the specific inspiration for this book on a day-by-day basis as I wrote. I grew up hearing and reading the great dramatic stories of the Bible. That stimulated a creativity and imagination in me that soon came into conflict with a religious upbringing that typically labeled fiction as sinful. At the same time I fell in love with personal testimonies of God's power to transform lives. I found resolution in the parables of Jesus—stories that were obviously made up, yet realistic and powerful teachers of eternal and everyday truths.

The result is that you, the reader, can sit back and enjoy a good story that I hope will draw you into a closer relationship with, and greater love for, God.

CHAPTER ONE

Hope Lancaster kept her eye straight into the lens until the red light atop the TV camera went out. "We're in commercial!" the studio floor director announced. "Back in 90 seconds." Still Hope held her smile, gazing steadily into the camera for a two-count just to be sure no viewer would see her when she turned her attention away.

"OK, I've got the story about the barges running aground in the river, then I segue into the weather. Right?" Hope asked after glancing down at the printed outline of stories for the evening's 6:00 newscast. The question was aimed at the director, who sat in the control room across the hall from the studio.

"That's right. We're doing fine." Hope heard the director's disembodied voice through a tiny earphone tucked invisibly in her right ear. She picked up a pen and drew a line under the story even as she and her coanchor, Alan Ferrell, both reached under the news desk for something to drink. For Hope it was a bottle of water, for Alan a caffeine-laced soda.

"You're always drinking those things. When are you going to develop a taste for the natural stuff?" she teased.

"I think I'm allergic to plain water," Alan shot back. "No taste. No calories. No caffeine. I no drink it."

"We're back in 20 seconds!" the floor director announced. Alan and Hope double-checked their paper outlines, then assumed their smiling camera faces as they straightened their postures, eyed the cameras, and waited for an unseen technician to align their next story on the teleprompter. The teleprompter was a large apparatus consisting of an upward-facing television and a mirror mounted at a 45-degree angle. A person standing in front of it could read the text projected on the television while the camera looked through the mirror. That way Hope and Alan could read their copy and appear as though they were actually talking to their viewers.

"Back in five . . . four . . . three . . ." The floor director counted down the seconds with his fingers, shifting to silent hand signals for the last two seconds. The "one" signal was his index finger held aloft, then pointed sharply forward at the anchors, telling them to proceed.

"Barge traffic on the Mississippi River coming into the port of Memphis was blocked for five hours today when several barges ran aground on a sandbar," Hope read. "Mindy Chernoff is in the newsroom and has the story."

The monitor changed to the reporter in the newsroom who described the scene. Video shot from a helicopter showed the barges surrounded by tugboats straining to pull them off the sandbar. "A spokesman for the U.S. Army Corps of Engineers said they monitor the height of that sandbar and from time to time must dredge the area so that barges and tugboats can cross it. Apparently it has been growing at a faster rate than what they expected. Back to you, Hope."

"We've got some pretty ominous weather approaching from the west. For the latest on that, let's go over to Walter Smartt in the weather center," Hope announced.

Walt "the Weather Guy" Smartt did his broadcasts from the weather center, a glassed-in section of the newsroom with a green wall on one side. Standing in front of the green, he looked to on-site observers as though he was performing a pantomime and pointing to unseen things in space. However, a computer in the control room subtracted out that particular shade of green and replaced it with a picture of whatever he described. By keeping his eyes on a monitor just outside the camera's view, he was able to position his hands to point at just the right place in the picture.

"That's right, Hope," he answered her even as he began his report. "You can see what's happening here on this satellite view. This storm system runs from all the way down here in the Gulf of Mexico, south of Louisiana." Walt the Weather Guy bent slightly and pointed downward toward his lower right. "These storms extend all the way up here into southern Missouri"—he swept his arms upward—"and we've already received reports of high winds and even a few tornadoes on the ground here, here, and here." With each "here" he pointed to a brightly colored blob of thunderstorm.

Smartt clicked the mouse tucked into one hand, and the picture behind him changed. "Let's take a closer look at what's heading for us on our exclusive channel 3 Sky Eye Radar. Keep your eyes on this series of storm cells. Watch how fast they've grown over the past three hours. We're not looking at routine thunderstorms, folks. Here, here, and here"—he pointed to three places bunched close together—"we're looking at supercells. And these two here and here"—he paused for emphasis—"we'll be keeping a really close eye on for you, because they could merge into what is called a 'megacell.' A supercell is bad enough, folks, but a megacell is real trouble."

Smartt turned toward the camera. "Folks, I've got to be honest with you. This is the strongest severe-weather system I've seen in many years, so my advice to you is to keep your TV tuned right here to channel 3, and if trouble develops we'll break into our current programming to let you know what's going on just as soon as it happens."

Commercials, the sportscast, and a closing news story followed. "We're clear," the director declared 20 minutes later over a loudspeaker hidden somewhere above the studio lights. A camera operator removed his headset, hung it over one of the side handles used to move the camera, and began rubbing his ears. Both Hope and Alan removed the custom-fitted earphones and unplugged them from under the desk. Next they removed and disconnected their microphones. Now they could leave the studio.

"Good job," Alan praised as he and Hope walked into the newsroom. "I'm ready to go home and have dinner."

"Same here," Hope sighed.

"I hate to tell you this, but nobody's going home for a while," the news director announced from two desks away. "You heard what Walter said about that storm system. I'm putting everybody on storm watch. Everybody stays until it's over, so we can go on the air on short notice." He pointed across the room to

11

one of the video editors. "David over there is taking supper orders. Just tell him what you want. Anything short of fine china and candlelight."

The thought of fine china and candlelight in the fluorescent-lit, cubicled newsroom with desks strewn with candy and chip wrappers, empty soda cans and Styrofoam coffee cups, made Hope laugh inside. Her mouth turned up in a one-sided grin that happened habitually when she was just short of laughing out loud. The news director's announcement was his way of reminding everyone not to abuse their expense accounts. At the same time she felt her stomach sagging. It was just that Dave, the guy taking food orders, used to work for a pizza delivery chain and was far more likely to order from his old employer than from a nice restaurant with a take-out service. It also was the thought of not seeing her husband after a long day or getting a good-night hug and kiss when she tucked her 6-year-old daughter into bed.

Shaking her head to clear the disappointment, she settled into the canvas-covered deck chair and reached for the phone.

Mark answered on the second ring. "I'm sorry to hear that, hon. I guess Jennifer and I will have to make supper on our own."

"There's plenty in the fridge to pick from, so no fast food and no calling for pizza, OK?"

He laughed. "Yes, ma'am. But what do you suggest?"

"You could do something easy, such as opening a can of soup and making grilled cheese sandwiches. Jennifer likes that. And of course there are grapes and apples and, I don't know, other fruit."

"Sounds good. Oh, Jennifer wants to talk to you."

Hope spent the next minute creating a funny story out of her need to remain at the studio, and her daughter was laughing when they signed off. "I love you, sweetie," Hope said.

"I love you better," came the routine reply, and they both laughed.

After overhearing coworkers ordering pizza, Hope and three others opted for walking two blocks down the street to an Italian eatery frequented by station employees. An hour later they were back in the newsroom reading wire service reports of storm damage in Arkansas at the western edge of the station's broadcast area. As the storms rolled ever closer across the miles they began hearing reports over the police scanners that were monitored in one corner of the newsroom.

On the other side of the newsroom, in a glassed-in area, Walter Smartt and his trio of supporting meteorologists pored over their radar images and printouts from the National Weather Service. As the minutes passed, Hope saw mounting tension in their brisk movements, clipped replies to questions, and the strained intensity on their faces.

The only questions were where funnel clouds would sweep and how severely the area would be damaged.

The news director huddled with the producers, who in turn dispatched camera crews to various locations. Two men headed west across the expansive Mississippi River to locations in eastern Arkansas. Other crews spread along a line crossing Memphis from north to south, and a few were located east. All those who could work, even part-timers, were on the clock. An eerie quiet settled over the newsroom as the crews departed, leaving the anchors, a few editors, and the news director to look at one another and wonder what the passing hours would bring.

Hope again called home. "Hello, Jennifer!" she cheerily greeted her daughter. "How's my sweet girl?"

"I'm OK. When are you coming home?"

"I don't know. We're on storm watch."

"Daddy and I were watching Walt the Weather Guy on the news and"—she lowered her voice—"to tell you the truth, Daddy looks worried."

"Well, that's why I'm here at the station. If it gets bad, we have to be ready to go on the air to let people know where the storms are so they can take shelter. Now, do you remember where to go in case of a tornado?"

"In the closet under the stairway. And close the door tight," Jennifer answered cheerfully. "And take a flashlight, too."

"That's right. And what else?"

"Take the little TV in there so we can watch the weather reports on channel 3."

"Right. And what else?"

"Take pillows and blankets. And if a tornado comes, cover up really good so we won't get hurt." Jennifer spoke in a surprisingly mature manner.

"That's my girl. I'm really proud of you, and I wish I could be there to tuck you into bed. I hope you understand."

"I wish you were here too," Jennifer said softly.

"I know," Hope sighed. "But it's time for you to go to bed. I want you and Daddy to have worship before you go to sleep. Trust Daddy to watch the weather for you and take care of you, OK?"

"Yes, Mommy. I love you, Mommy."

"I love you, too, sweetheart. Night-night."

"Night-night, Mommy."

Mark came on the phone. "I'll tuck her into bed and call you back in a few minutes."

Father and daughter knelt beside her bed, and Jennifer prayed first. "Dear Jesus, we know there are some really bad storms coming our way, so please keep the bad storms away from us. Keep us safe tonight, and bring Mommy home soon. Amen."

Mark hugged his little girl and tucked her into bed, checking to make sure she was comfortable. Then he sat on the side of her bed and stroked the long brown hair away from her face. "It's my turn to pray. Dear Jesus, thank You for this precious daughter You have given me. She has been a source of great joy to her mother and me. Now please keep us safe tonight and help us to trust that, whatever happens, You are with us, and our salvation is secure in You. Amen."

Mark looked down at his daughter, her eyes closed as she drifted off to sleep. *You have truly blessed me, Lord!* he prayed silently. *I have everything: a beautiful wife, a loving daughter, a nice home, a good job. Most of all, I have Your promise of salvation.*

Returning to the family room, Mark retrieved the TV remote control from a lower shelf on a bookcase before settling into their large leather sofa. A few clicks later he found channel 3, where a popular evening drama was surrounded by a window warning viewers about the approaching severe weather. Still, the story line captivated him.

Six miles away at the channel 3 studios, Walter Smartt rocketed out of his chair, almost crashing into a desk outside the glass doors of the weather center. "Go live!" he yelled across the room to the news director. "We just got a huge hook echo on the radar over west Memphis. That's our first tornado!" Just as quickly he spun around and planted himself in front of the green wall, then checked to make sure his wireless microphone was turned on.

"Control room! How long before we're live?" he demanded.

"Ten seconds," someone answered.

"That's too long. We've got lives in danger here, folks," Smartt muttered impatiently. "Let's go!"

Smartt had trained his team well enough that he didn't have to give orders. They knew he wanted the radar image superimposed on the green screen behind him. They also knew to be ready to add other things such as close-up radar views and street-level maps so that people would know if they needed to take cover.

"We're live," someone announced as the "on air" monitors throughout the building shifted from the drama to a "Special Weather Announcement" slide, then a live view of Walter Smartt standing in front of the radar picture.

"We interrupt this program to bring you breaking weather information," Smartt said calmly. His smooth voice was a marked contrast to his manner of seconds before. "The severe weather system approaching our viewing area from the west is showing a strong hook echo in one of the supercells. A hook echo tells us that a tornado is forming in the area. We don't know yet if it's on the ground, but this storm is so big, so strong, that it's just a question of time before that happens."

One of the other meteorologists stepped beside the camera where Walt would see him. He held out his right fist with the index finger extended, then circled it downward toward the open palm of his left hand.

"I've just been told that the tornado is on the ground," Walt declared. "I repeat, the tornado has put a funnel cloud on the ground."

Walt turned to study the monitor radar picture for a moment. "Wait a minute, folks. This is happening fast. It looks like we're getting a second hook echo out of this first storm, and we've got smaller hook echoes out of this storm . . . and this one, too." He struggled to keep a tremor out of his voice as he pointed at the two other large thunderstorm blobs on the radar image.

"Let's go to a close-up of this supercell," Smartt commanded. Out of the camera's view one of the other meteorologists clicked a computer mouse a few times, and the image on the screen changed as the radar line swept across the storm. "What we're looking at here, folks, is called 'storm relative velocity.' The radar computer colors the winds moving away from the radar in the blue and green shades and the winds moving toward the radar in the red and yellow shades. Each color indicates a velocity range, and the contrast tells us how fast the winds in the funnel cloud are spinning. Judging by this contrast, this storm is at least a Force Four, if not a Force Five.

"Folks, Force Five is the top of the Fujita scale. That's as severe as they come. The winds can be more than 200 miles an hour." His voice grew commanding. "If you're anywhere near this storm it's definitely time to stop watching me and get into a sheltered place. Get in an inside room—one with no windows—so you'll be protected from flying glass. Get into the strongest part of the house. If you have a basement, get in it. It could be just a closet. *Just get in it.* If you're in a mobile home, *get out,* and get into the lowest place you can find."

The picture shifted to a close-up of the particular storm, and Smartt began detailing where the storm was and the direction it was moving.

From their separate locations, both Hope and Mark watched intently to see if that particular storm was headed their way. No, it would pass north of Memphis. That was small relief for Hope, for it still meant she could be in for a very long night of live reporting.

Smartt shifted his attention to a storm just to the south of the one producing the tornado that raged along the ground. "I'm really, really concerned about this storm, folks," he declared. "If you were watching our 6:00 broadcast, this is the megacell I told you might form as two supercells joined together. Let me show you just how big, how powerful, this storm is."

The picture changed to a split screen. One side showed a close-up of the storm and its expected track. The other was a radar cross section of the storm cloud. "The storm producing the tornado that's already on the ground tops out at 46,000 feet. That's a very strong storm. But this megacell tops out at 54,000 feet, and folks, *it's still growing.* Plus the cell is almost 20 miles across. That means it could produce a tornado anywhere. It could even produce several tornadoes at the same time. And because there is so much energy trapped in this supercell, I don't expect any of those tornadoes to be less than a Force Five. That's strong enough to take a giant oak tree and reduce it to a twisted stump. Or blow down even the best-built house without leaving a trace. This is one *very* intense storm, and it's headed right at Memphis, folks. It'll be here in about 45 minutes, so you have time to get ready for it."

Outside, Hope heard the tornado warning sirens begin their mournful wail. The storm would cover a large area of the city, so the risk was very great. And her home, with her husband and daughter, was directly in its path. A knot twisted in her stomach.

"Alan! I want you ready to report from in here. Hope! It's time to get hooked up on the set. Let's roll, folks," the news director barked. "We'll be getting live reports from the field soon, and I want to be ready. I'll give it to you on the intercom as it comes."

Hope made a quick stop in the restroom, then walked through the studio dressing room long enough to check her makeup in its mirror. She retouched her lipstick while walking toward the news desk. From a darkened area the halogen studio lights came up with a loud *click*. Hope settled into her chair and popped the intercom earphone into her ear. A sound technician helped her hide the tiny microphone in the front of her blouse before slipping her arms into the matching designer suit coat and buttoning the front. Mostly she would wait. But she knew from experience that when things happened they happened quickly. Everyone would be working without a script; everyone had to think on their feet.

Mark watched the approach of the storm with grave concern. He gathered a flashlight, blankets and pillows, and the battery-operated TV and put them in the closet under the stairway. Before turning to go upstairs, he paused to look westward through the large glass panes on either side of their front door. Though much of the storm cloud was obscured by darkness, what he saw almost took his breath away. In the distance the top of the megacell glowed with continuous lightning. Occasionally streaks of bright-red flame flew through the glow. He stood mesmerized for several moments, then with a panic realized the cloud would be on them in mere minutes. It was time to retrieve Jennifer and head for the closet.

Jennifer barely awoke as Mark yanked back her covers and snatched her from the bed. She settled sleepily into her father's embrace as they went down the stairs and settled on the closet floor. Mark had tossed out some coats and empty gift boxes to make room for them. A folded blanket provided a seat, while pillows comforted them against the wall. Since the TV wasn't attached to the cable system he had to manually tune it to channel 3. Interference from the storm and the antenna provided a snowy yet understandable picture.

"We have two . . . no, three distinct hook echoes in this storm," Smartt announced. "It's been years since I last saw this many tornadoes from a single storm. OK, the first one down here on the south end is crossing the Mississippi, so let's go to a street-level map and see where you need to take cover."

The street-level map came up. An unseen hand placed a computer cursor on the center of the storm and drew out a line along which the storm was expected to travel. An instant later a list of streets and other landmarks appeared with the storm's expected arrival times superimposed in bright letters.

Hope looked intently at the image on the monitor buried under the glass top of the news desk. The deadly line stretched directly across the neighborhood where she lived. Mark saw the line too.

Hope reached under the desk for a telephone and punched her home number. *Please, Jesus, keep them safe,* she prayed silently as she waited for the connection. Time seemed to stretch into eternity before she heard the phone ringing.

The downstairs phone was located just around the corner from the hall closet where Mark and Jennifer were sheltered. He debated going out to answer. But Jennifer was asleep in his arms, and getting up would surely awaken her. *It's probably some telemarketer,* he thought, *calling from six states away.*

Five rings. Six rings. "Please answer," Hope said urgently. Seven rings. Eight.

"Isolate camera 2," the director in the control room ordered. That meant the camera aimed at her would be recorded separately from all other inputs, but in that moment she cared only about the safety of her husband and daughter. At last she hung up the phone, bravely trying to keep a neutral camera face. Still, the tension showed.

Mark heard the wind whistling around the house change from a breeze into a howl, then an angry roar. It sounded as if a railroad locomotive was roaring across the lawn. *So this is what a tornado sounds like,* he thought.

The house shook. Mark felt the walls shift, and the air pressure changed so sharply that his ears popped. Jennifer awoke with a cry of pain. "My ears hurt," she whimpered.

"Swallow. Pinch your nose and swallow hard," he ordered.

Panic rose in Jennifer's voice as she awoke fully and realized both where they were and the horrible sound outside that drowned out the TV. "Daddy! I'm scared!" she cried, throwing her arms tightly around her father's neck.

Mark pulled the blankets and pillows around them as they felt the walls shifting slightly in the wind. Just when it seemed the winds were abating, a loud crash reverberated through the walls, followed by a second and third sound of shattering windows. Then just as quickly as the winds had risen, they slowed to a breeze filled with driving rain.

H ope's attention was so tightly riveted to the radar image on the monitor screen that she forgot about keeping up a camera face or watching the teleprompter for cues that a story was coming her way. Nor did she notice—or care—that the camera focused on her was still running, recording every breath and expression of fear. Fortunately, most of the action was coming from the weather center, so there was no need for the director in the control room to switch to her.

But the director, watching from the control room, saw the tension on her face and decided to keep her off the air for the time being. "Alan, we've got a live report from Terry Kilburn over in Simsboro. We'll go to you live as soon as Walt gets done with this latest update," he ordered over the intercom. "Walt, try to wrap it up in 10 seconds.

"Stand by, Alan," the director called. Alan sat up straight in his chair and locked his eyes on the camera posted on a tripod just a few feet in front of his desk.

"Now let's go to Alan Ferrell in the newsroom," Walt declared as he turned away from the map and looked straight into the camera.

"Thank you, Walt. We've got a live report coming in from channel 3 reporter Terry Kilburn over in Simsboro, Arkansas." The picture changed to show the wind-battered reporter standing in front of a high mound of rubble that apparently had been some sort of commercial building. Red and blue strobe lights from emergency vehicles added to the halogen-white glow of headlights illuminating the wind-twisted sheet metal and broken glass behind him. "Terry, what's happening where you are?"

"Alan, what we can tell you is that this storm cut a swath at least a quarter mile wide through this crossroads town, right through the middle of it, in fact. Um, what the local sheriff's deputies are telling me is that this building behind me used to be the local hardware and farm supply store. As you can see, it's a total loss. I have the store's owner, Marjorie Comiskey, here with me."

Terry took a step to his left to bring the store owner into the picture. "Tell me, Marjorie, how much damage has the storm done here to your store?"

The gray-haired woman shook her head. "Oh! It's . . . it's a total loss." Her voice was shrill as she turned to look at the rubble. "Just look at this! It's gone! We're just thankful it didn't take out our home just a couple hundred yards down the road."

"Where were you when the storm hit?"

"At home. We were watching the storm warnings on channel 3, and we got into our storm shelter when Walter Smartt told us to. That was one time I didn't mind going down there with all those black widow spiders that live in there. I think God told 'em that we needed to be in there right then, and they left us alone."

"What would you estimate is the value of your loss here tonight?" Terry asked.

Marjorie shook her head. "Hard to say right now, 'cause we don't know what's under the roof where it's collapsed or if there's part that hasn't been damaged. I'd say at least a couple hundred thousand dollars. At least."

"Back to Walt," the director ordered. The picture cut to Walt Smartt standing in front of the radar image showing the storm's track across the map.

"We're back live here in the weather center, folks," Walter Smartt said after the picture switched to him. "Here's the line that storm that went through Simsboro has taken. Judging by the first reports we received, it touched down about six miles west of the town. This is the same storm that's cut a path across the city of Memphis and is continuing east-northeast-ward at 35 to 40 miles an hour."

Walt continued with his updates, including the expected track of two other tornadoes reported to be on the ground in the station's viewing area. The report from a field crew about the damage caused by one was also given to Alan.

The phone under the news desk rang. Hope's eyes barely moved from the radar image on the monitor under the glass-topped news desk as her right hand retrieved the phone. "This is Hope Lancaster."

"Hope, I know that's your neighborhood," the news director spoke. "I've got a crew chasing that storm, and I've given them orders to check your house as soon as they can get there. I'll let you know when they report anything."

"Thanks," Hope answered, her eyes still glued to the screen. She blinked rapidly as she hung up the phone, then felt around under her desk for the box of tissues hidden somewhere around her knees.

~ ~ ~

"I'm amazed the power's still on," Mark said to himself as he and Jennifer cautiously crept out of the closet. Immediately their eyes were greeted with a sea of broken glass from one of the tall panes beside the front door. Pieces of glass were impaled in the wall around the closet; small fragments crunched under his shoes. Mark picked up the little girl to protect her bare feet. A similar scene greeted them in the family room where the large picture window looking into the backyard was shattered. More glass shards were impaled in the back of the leather sofa and strewn across the carpet along with a mixture of pine needles and assorted other debris.

Just then the lights went out. Mark stopped short, almost tripping; then, still carrying his daughter, he carefully eased his way into the kitchen. Rogue lightning provided temporary light, and he opened a drawer and felt for a small flashlight. He used that small beam to find his way back to the closet, where he picked up the larger one he'd taken there as part of their storm preparations. Then they made their way up the stairs to Jennifer's bedroom, and he helped her dress in the semidarkness. "But I don't want to wear shoes," a tired girl protested.

"I don't want your feet getting cut on any of that broken glass," Mark told her. "You're wearing shoes!"

Back downstairs, he was surveying the damage when someone pounded at the front door, then yelled through the broken window. "Is everybody OK here?"

Mark recognized the voice of Kyle Martin, a neighbor from directly across the street. Kyle wore a rain suit, and his face was streaked by droplets. "We're OK," Mark called back. "We've got some broken windows, and I'm sure some other damage. But that's all I can see right now."

"That's good to hear," Kyle shouted over the wind. "We're checking on all the neighbors. Looks like things are a lot worse down the block. There's enough debris in the street that the fire department can't get in, so we're rounding up all the gas-powered tools we can to help down there. Think you could help some?"

Even before he'd finished the question, Mark opened the front door to let him in. "Look, I've got a generator out in the garage that's all fueled up. I've got a chain saw and lights and stuff. If Connie can watch Jennifer, we can take everything down there and do whatever we need to do."

The generator was on a wheeled cart with boxes holding a trio of floodlights and extension cords. The men worked without words, tossing a chain saw, gloves, and hand tools into a wheelbarrow, then struggled to open the electrically operated garage door manually. Through all this, Jennifer stood to the side, watching with wide eyes.

As they got the door open, Connie appeared through the darkness behind a moving beam of light, under a wind-buffeted umbrella. Jennifer took her hand, and the two disappeared across the street. Mark ran back to retrieve a raincoat from a hook inside the mudroom and jogged down the street after Kyle.

Four houses away, that house was missing its roof. The next homes on each side of the street were missing much of their upper floors. Mark played his flashlight across the houses beyond them—twisted, shattered piles of wood and glass. Wind whipped his raincoat, and rain slashed his face. The beam of light from his hand was feeble in the dense darkness. Debris from these homes and an unknown number of others blocked the street. Firefighters carrying hand lanterns clustered around one half-standing home while bare-handed neighbors dug frantically into the rubble where someone was trapped.

Moments later Mark had the generator running and the floodlights in the hands of willing helpers. He pulled on gloves and safety glasses, then yanked on the chain saw's starter cord. It coughed. Another pull. A sputter. A third pull, and it roared to life.

The sound of the idling chain saw caught the attention of the rescuers who moved out of the way. It took nearly 20 minutes of careful cutting to remove enough of the broken wall that physical contact could be made with the man trapped below. Paramedics moved in to help clear a path along which he could be slid from under the pile. With each motion the man screamed shrilly. Then he was strapped onto a stretcher; a back and neck brace kept his spine rigid. Volunteers lined up on either side to help carry him to an ambulance waiting a block down the street. Somewhere along the way a set of TV lights pierced the blackness and tracked the victim's insertion into the waiting vehicle.

A fireman asked Mark if he could bring his equipment to a second house where victims were trapped. "Of course," he replied. "Where?"

The rescue squad had set up lights powered from a generator on a nearby truck. Mark stepped in to help, but the chain saw sputtered, stopped, and wouldn't start again. Out of gas. In the same moment he felt his muscles go limp from the hours of fear and exertion, so he stopped to take a break. A bathtub lay overturned across the sidewalk in front of the house, the faucet end resting in the street. Mark slapped small debris off the bottom of the tub with his gloves and cleared a place to sit down. Seconds later a man wearing a Red Cross windbreaker offered him a steaming cup of coffee. Someone wearing a coat with "Rescue Squad" in reflective letters on the back arrived with a fuel can and filled the tank on the chain saw. Then he picked up the saw and walked toward the house.

Some time later Kyle sat down beside Mark. Neither man spoke. They sat silently in the rain and darkness, hardly hearing the shouts and cries in the distance.

At last Kyle spoke. His voice was flat.

"They're all dead," he said. "The Andersons. All four of 'em."

"No way!" Mark gasped.

Kyle shook his head. "The fire captain just told me. They were all together in a downstairs room. It looks like the place just collapsed on 'em, and they got crushed. They might've been in the safest place in the house, but the storm was so strong they didn't have a chance."

Mark took a deep breath, and a chill ran up and down his spine as he realized how close death had come to visiting his house. He shook his head, unbelieving. "It came so close. I mean, five houses farther south . . . it could've been Jennifer and me."

"I just saw them at church Sunday. Evan, their boy, he's in my Sunday school class," Kyle said. "Well, he was . . . I guess . . . now."

"So close," Mark said, his voice barely audible among the rumbles of the generators and the shouts of the rescuers working to retrieve the bodies. "It came so close."

~ ~ ~

"How much longer till they get to my neighborhood?" Hope implored the news director.

"They're trying to get in there right now. There are several houses in the first block off the highway that got smashed really bad. They're setting up a live shot there and should be on the air in a few minutes. They say the area where your house is doesn't look too bad, but it'll be awhile before they can actually check."

Hope placed the phone back on its cradle. A producer came on the intercom to announce that a crew was ready to do a live shot. The teleprompter operator typed up an introduction line for Hope, who put on her bravest camera face.

"Go to Hope on camera 2. We're on 2," the director ordered from the control room.

"We're told that reporter David Williams is, well, I'm not sure where. David, how about telling us where you are?" Hope said mechanically.

The picture on the monitor showed a reporter with rain-soaked and windblown hair standing in front of a scene of devastation. A chain saw and other power tools rumbled and roared in the background as a mix of emergency workers and neighbors dug into the rubble. "I'm in front of a house on Dexter Avenue here in south Memphis where rescue workers have just confirmed to channel 3 news that four people have been killed. Apparently the four had taken shelter in the lower part of the house when the tornado hit. But the wind was so strong they didn't have a chance . . ."

An involuntary shudder rushed down Hope's back as the picture appeared before her. "David, can you give us some more information about how many houses in the area have been destroyed or damaged?" she asked.

"Sure, Hope." David turned to look around the area. "I'd say there are at least eight houses on this street alone that are totally destroyed. Most of the homes in this area are two-story and of those, eight, maybe 10 homes are just piles of rubble, some of them all the way down to their foundations. On either side of the tornado's path the damage is less as you get farther away. We haven't been able to go past this immediate area yet, but we'll walk on down the street as soon as we can. Hope, I know your house is down there, and we're going there next. We'll get back to you as soon as we've taken a look."

"Thank you, David," Hope said as the camera came back to her.

"Hope, hand off to Walt," the director commanded.

"Now to the weather center, where Walter Smartt has an update for us on the storm's progress." She held her gaze on the camera for a two-count after the red light went dark, then reached for the phone under the desk and dialed the news director's extension. "I don't know how much longer I'll hold up here," Hope told him. "Can you get the 10:00 anchors in here?"

"I'm working on it. Gimme about five or 10 minutes and we'll have you outta there," he promised.

Seven minutes later the 10:00 anchors walked through the door. Hope yanked her intercom and microphone connections out of their connector jacks as she rose from her chair. But the phone rang just then, and she instinctively reached to answer it.

"Hope? Good news!" David Williams fairly shouted above the noise of a rescue in progress. "I've found your husband. He says there's light damage to the house. Some windows broken out, that sort of thing. Nothing major that he knows about. And your daughter's fine. She's with neighbors while he's out here helping. He's been working over here at the house that has the four fatalities."

"Oh, David! Thank you! Next time I see you, I owe you a bear hug." Hope felt tears warming her cheeks. "I'm out of here," she fairly shouted as she headed for the door.

26

By the time Hope turned onto Dexter Avenue, the city had been able to get some heavy equipment into the area and push the larger debris off the street. What on a normal night would have been a well-illuminated path was wrapped in total darkness, pierced by her Honda's headlights and the floodlights on emergency vehicles. Unidentified bits and pieces of debris ate at her tires as she slowly drove along the street. To the sides she saw clusters of neighbors consoling and commiserating with one another as they aimed dimming flashlights at the wreckage. A Red Cross van was parked at one place distributing food to the emergency workers who still dug in the wreckage of one house. It was there she saw the crew that she'd introduced on the air only minutes before. Then she saw her husband and another man pushing a cart and a wheelbarrow up the street. Reaching her home, she parked as quickly as possible, leaped out of the car, and fairly flew into Mark's arms as he walked up the driveway.

"Mark! I was so worried about you. I'm so glad you're OK," she cried after a tight embrace and a kiss. "I was so scared. I was watching the live radar as the tornado came through here. Oh! I'm so relieved! Where's Jennifer?"

"She's with Connie," Kyle answered as he let go of the generator cart. "I'm surely glad you had these tools, Mark, and especially that generator and those lights. They were a big help."

The group found a flashlight for Hope and together inspected the house the best they could. The couch in the family room and at least one other piece of upholstered furniture would have to be replaced. Several items had scratches but looked repairable. The walls just inside the front door would need to be refinished and repainted. After the windows were replaced, the job would be mostly cleanup. Of course, it would be morning before they could check the roof for missing shingles.

"I'll call our insurance agent first thing in the morning," Mark told her.

"Let's hope you don't get a busy signal," Hope observed with a wry smile, the first one she'd had in what seemed since forever.

"Nah. After a disaster like this, they'll probably have a team working at sunrise. Who knows? They might wake you up in the morning."

They walked back downstairs. "Let's go get Jennifer and see

if we can get some sleep," Hope said. "I know they'll want me in early tomorrow." She paused and turned to take her husband's hand. "I'll tell you what. I sure could use a cup of SleepyTime tea to help me relax for bed."

"Without electricity you'll have to pass on that tonight," Mark observed.

"Naw. If you've got the tea, come on over, and we'll brew it up over our camping stove," Kyle offered. "And if the power's still off come morning, come on over for breakfast, too."

"Thank you, Kyle." She smiled at him through the semidarkness. "You and Connie are such sweethearts. Let me find the tea, and we'll be right over."

"You know, I'm so keyed up right now I think I could drink a gallon of SleepyTime tea and still not go to sleep for two days," Mark told Hope as they headed to the kitchen.

THREE

Watch out, Daniel!"

Susan Morris put down the large bowl of tossed salad she was carrying and plucked her toddler grandson off the kitchen floor. "Where do you thing you're going? I almost stepped on you." Still holding the little boy, she turned toward the dining room.

Carla, Susan's daughter-in-law, placed the serving dish she was carrying onto the large dining room table and reached to take her explorative child from his grandmother's arms. "Gam-ma. Gam-ma," he chanted as Susan took him.

"That's right. I'm Grandma," Susan cooed back to Daniel as she tweaked his cheek. "You're Grandma's pwesious widdle boy. Yes, you are!"

Daniel wriggled, and his little face crumpled. "I think he's hungry. How long till we eat?" Carla asked.

Susan made a quick visual survey of the table, now almost completely set for Sunday dinner. "Just a couple minutes. The rolls are ready to come out of the oven. The salad and roast and veggies and mashed potatoes are all on the table. Dessert's in the fridge. All that's left to do is mix up the fruit punch, so—two, three minutes." Susan grabbed a bread stick from a nearby serving dish and handed it to Daniel, who began trying to bite off a chunk.

First Sunday was well under way at the home of Hope's parents, Aubrey and Susan Morris. The traditional family gathering had begun years before, when Hope first went away to college. By parental edict the rule became: if you were within 100 miles of the house on the first Sunday of the month, you came home for church and lunch. Never mind that Hope was attending Vanderbilt University in Nashville, three and a half hours' drive away. She usually came home sometime on Saturday and spent the night, returning to Nashville after Sunday services at her father's church and, of course, Sunday dinner with the family.

The group around the table had grown as Hope's younger siblings, brother David and sister Allison, each took their turns leaving home, then marrying and having children. Including grandchildren, the head count was currently 11—eight adults, two toddlers, and Jennifer. Well, 12, if you counted the little one proclaiming his approaching arrival in Carla's ballooning belly.

The adults took chairs around the large dining room table, with toddlers Daniel and Stephanie enthroned in high chairs nearby. Jennifer sat on a stool by her grandmother. Aubrey Morris, patriarch of the clan, called everyone's attention and led the family in a blessing worthy of the Southern Baptist preacher that he was, including references to Bible promises and being thankful for the divine protection that each had experienced in the previous week's storms. Finally he thanked the Lord for the food spread before them and pronounced the much-anticipated "Amen."

"You had quite a series of storms through here the other night, didn't you?" Jeff, Allison's husband, asked. "They went just north of us down in Clarksdale."

"It's been a good many years since I remember that many storms in the same night," Susan answered. Eyes closed for a moment in thought, she asked, "What did the weather service say was the final count? Seventeen tornadoes on the ground at one time within a 200-mile area?"

Allison nodded and swallowed before speaking. "The part I remember was Walt the Weather Guy on channel 3 saying that there were four on the ground here in the Memphis area at the same time. Now, that was scary!"

"We had four fatalities in our church alone, and what, more than 40 total?" Aubrey asked, scooping up a serving of broccoli au gratin. "Then there were all those people made homeless when that apartment complex was wiped out. You know, the Red Cross is still using our church fellowship hall as a shelter. Would you please pass the mashed potatoes?"

"As of Friday afternoon it was 32 killed, with more than 200 injured," Hope updated her father. "I'll tell you what. I never want to go through another night like that in my life. I mean, being there in the studio and watching on the radar as the storm goes across your neighborhood. I've never been so scared. I was afraid two of the fatalities were going to be Mark and Jennifer."

"We're all very thankful the Lord protected them," Aubrey declared, looking around the table.

"I enjoyed your sermon this morning, Dad," Allison told him. "You gave me something to think about when you said that such storms as we had this week are a sign that the return of Jesus can't be far away."

"Could happen any day," Aubrey nodded as he forked his first bite of pot roast. "All these storms, the earthquakes, the famines—the other natural disasters around the world—they're just signs that Jesus is about to return. I expect it'll be very, very soon that we're snatched away in the Rapture. Then it'll be tribulation time here. I'm so glad I'll be watching it from heaven instead of being in the middle of it, 'cause it's gonna be a hard time for unrepentant sinners."

"I was listening to a radio preacher the other day," Jeff interjected. "I think he's the pastor of a large church in Dallas. His view is that the Rapture can't be more than a few months away, considering the state of the world economy, all these disasters we're seeing around the world, and such." He looked at his father-in-law for affirmation. "He made a really convincing case that's making me rethink my priorities. I'm thinking, *If I won't be around to enjoy that next promotion, why bust my back to go after it?*"

"Our pastor over in west Memphis had a similar sermon just last Sunday before the storms came through," David put in. "That storm system seemed like a fulfillment of prophecy to me. All the way through I was thinking and praying, *'Lord, it's time to come get us!'*"

Aubrey eyed his son across the length of the table with a smile. "So when are you going to quit working in a car parts factory and start preaching?"

"I don't feel the Lord calling me that way, Dad. I think He

31

wants me right where I am so that I can keep leading the guys on the factory floor to Jesus. Just two weeks ago I led another sinner to accept salvation."

"That's wonderful!" his mom exclaimed. "If you're doing the Lord's work where you are, then stay where He wants you, son. That's what I say."

"Could someone pass me the salad dressing? The light Italian," David requested. "You know what frustrates me, Mom? About six months ago I led a man to Christ, and he's really studying the Bible. I mean, I thought I knew the Bible, but this guy is coming up with all sorts of things that I can't answer."

"Like what?" Aubrey asked.

"Well, he doesn't believe in the Rapture anymore. He says the Bible doesn't teach it. He says Jesus is coming back only once more, that it will be visible, and that there'll be no more second chance for sinners to repent. You know, like what we believe will happen after the Tribulation, except that he believes there won't even be a seven-year tribulation."

"Now, the Bible's pretty clear on that point," the preacher declared. "Take Titus 2, verse 13, where it talks about the blessed hope and then the Second Coming. The blessed hope is the Rapture, which is followed by the Second Coming. The Rapture is secret, and all the righteous are taken to heaven. Then comes the seven years of Tribulation, when the Antichrist power is revealed and the temple gets rebuilt. Then comes Jesus' final return, the one where He comes in all the glory of His Father and all the angels."

"Not according to this guy. You know what he showed me the other day?"

"What?" two voices chorused from different directions.

David took a steaming popover from the cloth-lined bowl in front of him and held it as he gestured with his words. "We were having a discussion about Luke 17 where it talks about the time of the coming of Jesus being the way it was in the days of Noah. Life was going on normally when suddenly the Flood came, and everybody who wasn't in the ark was drowned. Now, we've always believed that it's the folks who are taken who will be saved, because they'll be taken away in the Rapture, right?"

Heads around the table nodded.

"That's right, of course," Aubrey asserted.

"Well, this guy suggested that the verse there in Luke 17 is saying life will be going on normally when all of a sudden Jesus comes, and the wicked are destroyed. Then he pointed me back to the story of the Flood—who got saved and who got destroyed." Food forgotten for the time, David leaned forward toward his dad. "Now, we believe that those who are left behind get a second chance to be saved, right?"

Heads nodded again, and food-filled mouths mumbled agreement.

"Well, listen to this. The story in Genesis doesn't actually say that. I looked it up. Genesis says that the people who were in the ark got left behind and they were saved, but the people who were taken away were all destroyed. They never got a second chance to be saved." David's face was puzzled. "It looks like we're reversing the story when we use the story of the Flood as a model for the Rapture, and it looks like we're making it say something it doesn't say. So this guy at work says he'd rather be left behind, because he says the Rapture's a false doctrine."

"Some people just don't understand, do they?" Carla said sadly. "You really need to be working on him."

David nodded and swallowed. "I'm working on him as hard as I can. But you know what he challenged me with just yesterday?"

"What?" Susan asked.

"He challenged me to find the Secret Rapture anywhere in the Bible, to show where Jesus said His return would be unseen, unheard, and anything less than totally cataclysmic for the entire world. And you know what? So far I haven't been able to find even the word 'rapture' anywhere in the Bible. What's worse, I can't find any description by Jesus or anybody else in the New Testament to refute what this guy's telling me. I mean, we pull together a lot of texts and say the Rapture's going to happen that way. And I *believe* it, of course. But I can't find a text—I mean, not a single one—that comes out and says in so many words that Jesus will come secretly. Not a one."

Aubrey's fair-skinned face was red. He took a long swallow of his juice. "Son, you've got to watch out for people like him. He's like the Judaizers the apostle Paul talked about, people who would have you obeying the old law that was done away with at the cross instead of living under grace. Keep studying, and I'm sure you'll see that what you've been taught all these years is correct and that he's the one who's deceived. I just want you to be careful so that you're not the one being deceived by him."

"Well, that's part of the problem, Dad. Everything he's showing me about the Rapture and the Second Coming from the Bible is different than what I grew up believing."

The lines around Aubrey's eyes hardened, and the veins in his neck grew more prominent as he looked down the table at his son. The fork slipped from his hand and clattered against his plate. "Son, would I teach you anything wrong? anything that wasn't in the Bible?"

"No, sir. I mean, I believe you're sincere. It's just that what I'm reading in the Bible is different than what you taught me growing up, so I'm really having a hard time deciding what to believe."

"Son, a lot of scholars over a lot of years have accumulated a lot more knowledge than that man has, and a lot of them were my teachers when I was working on my Doctor of Divinity degree back at Dallas Theological Seminary. They believe in the Rapture because it's in the Bible, and you should, too."

Susan, always the peacemaker, squirmed in her chair and wished for some way to change the topic. "Mark, how are things at your work?" she inquired.

"For me, pretty good. I'm in product development, so my team and I are covered up with work. But with the economy down, sales have dropped. Last week about 20 people in production and sales got laid off, but my group looks pretty solid," he told her. "Thursday I'm flying out to Las Vegas for the software show. We've got a big booth, so we're sending about two dozen people. We'll be introducing our newest package of services and products then, so we think sales will start picking up soon."

"That's good; that's great," Susan murmured, reaching across to squeeze Hope's hand. She opened her mouth to speak, but Jeff didn't notice. He was looking at David and nodding.

"You know," he said, "I'm having an experience in my office similar to what David's having at his work. We've got a woman who's attending a series of prophecy meetings over at the Holiday Inn. She comes in practically every morning all charged up about the things she learned the night before. She's quit believing in the Rapture too," he said, almost in disbelief. "She says it's all a clever deception by the devil to keep people from following Jesus."

"Deception by the devil? Now I've heard everything!" Aubrey snorted as his right fist and the butt of his knife hit the glass tabletop. "I am a sincere, Bible-believing Christian and a minister of the gospel of Jesus Christ. I would never lead you or anyone else astray like . . . like whoever it was that woman was listening to at those meetings wherever. It's just not true, son. First there'll be the Rapture, then the Tribulation, *then* Jesus comes back visibly."

Little Stephanie was pounding her tray with a plastic spoon, and Susan reached across to her with a cracker. She didn't look at her husband. "Uh, Mark. The other day you said your company was concerned about people in such places as China pirating your software. How big a problem is that?" she asked.

He was glad for a change in the subject. "It's not hurting our sales right now, because we're not directly marketing in China. What it's doing is preventing us from expanding into China, because companies over there are adopting our software into their own products and capturing the market before we can get there."

"I saw the other day that two software companies were merging," Carla put in, catching Susan's eye. "Or was it that one was buying out the other? Anyway, what's the chance your company will be able to avoid getting gobbled up by one of those megacompanies?"

"The owner says he's already turned down several offers, so it seems pretty clear that he wants to stay independent. But you never know." Mark shrugged. "You just never know these days. It could happen in the blink of an eye."

"'Bout the same speed as the Rapture, right?" Carla asked with a smirk.

Mark laughed. "Considering how long it takes me to hear about things at work, I'm afraid I might get left behind."

Carla leaned forward. "Will this be your first trip to Vegas?"

"No, not at all. I've been to software shows there the past three years," Mark replied. "The place is pretty impressive the first time you go. The night lit up like day, the casinos, and all. But after about the second time it's just a flashy, glitzy place. You go. You do your business. You go home," he said with a laugh. "Now, some of the stage shows are pretty impressive. My favorites are the magic shows."

Aubrey looked beyond Mark to Allison. "You're being awfully quiet down at your end of the table," he said. "How are things with you?"

"Uh . . . OK . . . I guess."

"Is there something you want to tell us?" Susan asked, lifting Stephanie out of her chair and wiping her food-covered chin with a napkin. "You look as though you've got something weighing on your mind."

Allison chewed as eyes moved in her direction. "Ummm . . . well, I was just trying to stay out of it."

Aubrey fixed his gaze on his daughter at the far end of the table. "Allison, you've always been a reasonable person, so tell me: Do you still believe in the Rapture?"

"I haven't seen a good reason to stop believing in it, Dad."

"At least my youngest child isn't being led astray," he observed with some relief.

Allison opened her mouth to say something, then decided against it. She picked up her juice glass and swirled the ice in the dark liquid. Jennifer asked for another popover. Someone else started the salad back around the table. Allison decided to go ahead with her thought.

"Daddy, do you remember the Alderton family that used to attend our church?" she asked.

"Well, yes. They stopped coming some months back. Why do you ask?"

"Well, I bumped into them—Guy and Donna—the other day in the grocery store and had a really nice visit with them."

"That's nice, Allison," Susan said. "What's new with them?"

"Well, you do know why they don't come to church anymore, don't you?"

" 'Bout all I heard was that they'd stopped believing," Aubrey offered. "A couple of the elders went to visit them but couldn't convince them to give up some crazy things they'd gotten involved in. At least that's what I recall."

Allison's fingers twirled a strand of hair against her cheek. Her voice was low. "They told me that they're Bible-believing Christians now."

36

"Now?" several voices echoed.

"Yes—now! And what's more, they said that they've joined God's true church. That's what they called it. And you know what else they told me?"

"What?" several voices asked.

"They don't go to church on the Lord's Day anymore! They're going on Saturday. They say that at the end of Creation week God rested and actually made the seventh day of the week holy."

Little Daniel banged his plastic plate on his tray. Aubrey snorted, and Susan laughed out loud.

"Didn't I say something a minute ago about people claiming that you still have to keep the old law?" Aubrey demanded.

"But Daddy!" Allison protested. "They're really, really sincere."

"Sincerely wrong, I assure you!"

"Mark, did you ever go into the casinos in Vegas?" David changed the subject, and Mark took the bait and ran with it.

"It's like, how do you avoid the casinos? I mean, they're right next to the hotel check-in desk, and almost every place in Vegas has slot machines. At some of the hotels you literally have to walk through the casino to check in or out."

"You're not answering my question," David teased. "How much money have you left in Vegas?"

Mark held up his hands. "I confess. On my first trip I just had to check out one of the casinos. I spent about $40 trying out the slot machines and a blackjack table, and lost two thirds of it, I think. Didn't seem like great odds of winning to me, so I quit bef—"

A low rumble captured everyone's attention as the juice in their glasses quivered and the walls of the house shook around them. Instinctively Susan put her arm around Jennifer while someone else snatched up Daniel from the floor. Several heads turned to look out the windows. The swings on the set recently installed for the grandchildren to enjoy swayed perceptibly. Leaves on the backyard maple trees trembled. Then before anyone could cry out it was over.

"What was that?" eight adult voices exclaimed in unison. The only one who had paid no attention was Stephanie, who peered over the side of her high chair to see if someone had kicked a

37

leg. Then she searched the faces of the grown-ups before deciding there was no reason to cry out in fear.

"That was an earthquake," Mark exclaimed softly. "That felt and sounded just like a little one that happened the last time I was out in Silicon Valley. Only a lot shorter."

"But we don't have earthquakes here," Susan said in disbelief.

"Was somebody saying something a few minutes ago about signs of Jesus' return?" Aubrey asked, wiping his brow with a wrinkled napkin. "Earthquakes in diverse places are one of those signs."

"I wonder if there's anything on CNN about it," someone wondered aloud. Immediately chairs were pushed back from the table and half-eaten plates of food abandoned in favor of positions in front of the large-screen TV in the den. Aubrey keyed the remote control, and a commercial leaped onto the screen.

"Is that CNN?" David asked.

Aubrey checked the remote control and pushed the channel numbers again. The picture remained the same. "Yep, that's CNN. Just time to pay the freight." A second ad followed, then a program promo, and another commercial.

Then the group waited impatiently through several minutes of a prerecorded political discussion debating the latest developments in the war on terrorism followed by two more minutes of commercials. At last CNN's Breaking News slide appeared, followed by the face of the news anchor. He was reading from printed copy just handed to him instead of off the teleprompter.

"This is Gino Manconi in the CNN newsroom in Atlanta," he declared with just a hint of an Italian accent. "We'll return to the program in progress in just a moment, but first this breaking news item. The National Earthquake Monitoring Center in Pueblo, Colorado, reports that just moments ago a magnitude 3.4 earthquake occurred about 25 miles north of New Madrid, Missouri. This quake happened in the New Madrid Fault." A graphic replaced the view of the anchor. "The New Madrid Fault runs across and near the Mississippi River and is named for the town nearest its center, New Madrid, Missouri."

Manconi paused to listen to an instruction in his earphone. "Umm . . . to repeat, the National Earthquake Monitoring Center in Pueblo, Colorado, reports that about 12 minutes ago a magnitude

3.4 earthquake was detected in the New Madrid Fault. The epicenter was located . . . uh . . . about 25 miles north of New Madrid, Missouri, and . . . umm . . . just west of the Mississippi River."

The picture changed to show that the anchor had been joined by a female partner who added her voice. "A magnitude 3.4 quake is generally not considered severe enough to do major damage. I was through several of that severity or slightly worse when I was stationed at the Los Angeles Bureau. Mostly what they do is get your attention," she said. "They'll wake you up at night. That sort of thing. What is unusual about this quake is *where* it happened. The New Madrid Fault has been quiet for a long time, but a century ago it was one of the most active in North America. If I recall my history correctly, there were so many quakes in that area during that time that a number of times the quakes actually rerouted the course of the Mississippi River. We'll have to check on exactly how long it's been, but there have been no significant quakes in this area for quite some time."

"We'll pass along any developments as they come in," the male anchor declared before returning viewers to the program that had been interrupted for their report.

"Quakes actually rerouted the Mississippi River?" Carla asked in disbelief.

"Sure did," Aubrey said. "Just the other day I was reading a magazine article about searching for lost gold. Shipwrecks and things like that. Do you know where one of the largest lost gold treasures in the history of North America was found?"

Heads shook; shoulders shrugged.

"In a farm field north of St. Louis and about 35 miles west of where the Mississippi River is today. A steamboat carrying the gold was left marooned when the river changed course after one of those earthquakes. At first the area was a lake, then a swamp, then it dried up, because the river had moved 35 miles! Can you believe it? Thirty-five miles!" Aubrey shook his head from side to side.

"Well, I don't feel the earth moving under my feet anymore, but I still hear my stomach saying, 'Feed me!'" Susan proclaimed, "so I'm headed back to the table. Is anybody ready for dessert?"

"How long have we lived here in Memphis?" Aubrey asked his wife as they settled back around the table.

Susan lifted her eyes, mentally calculating. "We'll be coming up on 28 years next month."

"And you grew up here. Can you remember an earthquake happening here in your lifetime?"

"Not that I can remember. Why?"

"Then if we haven't just seen a sign of the end, I don't know what we've witnessed," Aubrey declared. "And in case anybody needs more convincing about last-day events that are about to unfold, I'm going to recommend that you read the new book out by Reverend David Robertson. The title is *Steps to the Temple*. I just finished it last night."

"That's a curious title. What's it about?" Allison asked.

"Well, he talks about a lot of things that are going to happen in the last days before the Rapture: earthquakes like we've just had here, other natural disasters, and such. He points out that they're all signs that the Rapture is about to happen. What's more, after reading that book I'm beginning to think I'm going to live to see the Temple rebuilt in Jerusalem."

"David Robertson?" Allison said thoughtfully. "Is he any relation to the TV preacher?"

Aubrey nodded. "His son."

"How soon does he think it's going to happen?" Carla asked.

"Soon. Very soon. That means we could be seeing the emergence of the Antichrist in the next few weeks or months, because it's the job of the Antichrist to bring about peace in the Middle East before Jesus can return."

CHAPTER FOUR

Why couldn't I go with Daddy to Las Wake-us?" Jennifer whined as her mother began navigating the traffic out of the Memphis International Airport. "Why couldn't we go out and see the plane he got on like we did before?"

"Airport security," Hope answered, smiling at how her daughter had fractured the city's name. "Everything changed once the terrorists attacked our country."

"What's a terrorist?"

Hope took a quick glance in her side mirror, then twisted her head around to check traffic before changing lanes. "A terrorist is a bad person who hates our country and does mean things to make us all afraid."

"Are you afraid, Mommy? Are you afraid of terrorists?" Jennifer asked.

"Well, yes and no, I guess. No, I'm not afraid, because they haven't attacked here. Yes, because you never know where or when they're going to attack again."

"Did cousin Lisa die fighting terrorists?"

The question hit Hope in the stomach. She swallowed repeatedly, trying to push down the lump that filled her throat. "No, darling. She was killed by the terrorists. She was on one of the planes that the terrorists hijacked and flew into the World Trade Center."

Tears filled her eyes as she thought of that terrible day and of her cousin who looked so much like her that they were sometimes mistaken for twins—her cousin who'd been one of her dearest friends. She did not think of Lisa as often as before, but hearing her name out of nowhere slammed her with pain as intense as that she'd felt on the September day she'd learned that Lisa had died somewhere around the eightieth floor.

Mother and daughter rode in silence, Hope concentrating on navigating the heavy traffic. A few miles later she heard Jennifer's whimper. "Mommy, my ear hurts. I don't feel good."

Exiting the interstate, Hope turned onto a busy six-lane-wide thoroughfare. At the next red light she shifted into park and twisted her body to reach back and feel Jennifer's forehead. "Honey, you're burning up. I think we'll go to the clinic instead of going home."

The light changed. Behind Hope the driver honked before she could shift the car back into drive and hit the gas. She looked around to see what cross-street they were passing and to determine what route to take to the clinic, which was on the other side of the interstate. Fortunately her cell phone was set up for hands-free, voice-activated use. "Phone, call Dr. Chapman," she commanded.

"Calling Dr. Chapman," the phone replied with a feminine but mechanical voice. Hope heard a series of dialing tones, then several rings.

"Pediatric clinic," a polite voice answered.

"Hi, this is Hope Lancaster, Jennifer's mom. She says her ear hurts, and she's running a high fever. How soon could you see her?"

"Let me check and see when we can work her in," the voice replied before putting her on hold. Hope found a place to turn around and made the U-turn before the call was resumed. "How soon could you be here? If you don't mind waiting a little, we can work her in. Can you be here in, say, 20 minutes?"

"Uh, sure." Hope replaced fear in Hope's voice. "We're in traffic just a few minutes away, so we'll be right there. Ten minutes tops."

"Great. We'll see you when you get here. Who is her regular pediatrician?"

"Dr. Chapman."

The receptionist paused. "Ma'am, Dr. Chapman is out sick today, but we have four pediatricians working this morning. One of them will work her in."

"OK. Thanks. We'll see you in a few minutes." Hope pushed a button to end the call.

"Mommy, am I going to have to take that pink medicine that tastes like strawberries again?"

"I don't know. Maybe."

"I don't want it. I don't like it. It's yucky!"

"Let's ask the doctor about it, shall we?" Hope hated arguing with her daughter. Jennifer would just have to take the medicine if the doctor prescribed it.

"Does this mean I don't have to go to school?" Jennifer asked.

"Is that a wish I'm hearing?"

"I just want to be with you, Mommy."

"I guess I'll have to call work and tell them I'm not coming in," Hope murmured to herself. She let her mind wonder if Jennifer's sudden fever had been brought on by her daddy leaving and the talk of terrorism. "Phone, call channel 3," she commanded.

A moment later an automated answering system replied.

"Extension two-four-seven," Hope spoke, and the phone translated her numbers into dialing tones.

"News Department. Bob Kroll," rumbled a gruff male voice.

"Bob, this is Hope. My daughter's gotten sick. She can't go to school, and the day-care provider won't take her if she's sick. Can y'all get along without me today?"

"Hmmm," came the slow reply. "Let me look over the status board." A long pause. Hope steered around a stalled car, her ear tuned to her daughter's labored breathing. "Is there any way you could come in just ahead of the newscast and take care of it?" Bob asked. "Around 4:00? I can give your field reports to someone else."

"Maybe I can get my mother to watch her for a couple hours." She thought quickly, running what she knew of her mom's day through her mind. "OK, unless you hear otherwise I'll aim to see you about 4:00. If that won't work, I'll let you know as soon as I can."

"Good. And I hope your daughter gets better. My youngest is down with an ear infection right now. What's yours got?"

"Seems like the same thing. Must be the bug that's running around their elementary school," Hope told him.

Thirty minutes of studying old magazines in the toy-filled

waiting room was followed by 20 minutes of staring at the walls in an examining room before a physician finally arrived. Jennifer ignored the toys and leaned against her mother's side rather than color in the little coloring book she'd been given when they registered. Hope thought that her temperature had risen noticeably by the time the unfamiliar doctor opened the door.

"Hi, I'm Dr. Krishnasami," the petite Indian woman said softly as she extended her hand to shake Hope's. "I'm sorry you had such a long wait, but now let's see what we have here." She turned to the child. "Hello, Jennifer. Dr. Chapman's not here today, and he asked me to take a look and see what's bothering you. May I look at you?"

Jennifer listlessly turned her eyes toward the stranger as she took the otoscope from its wall mount and snapped it onto a black speculum to look in the little girl's ears. Then came a peek down the throat and a few moments listening to her chest sounds. A quick probe of her abdomen concluded the exam.

Dr. Krishnasami began writing on the chart. "She has fluid behind both eardrums. There's no sign of tonsillitis or other infection, so I think we're just dealing with a bad ear infection. Does she take liquid medicine well?"

"She was telling me on the way over here that she doesn't like the pink stuff that tastes like strawberries."

Dr. Krishnasami smiled. "Amoxicillin? OK, we'll give her something else. Since she has an infection in both ears I think we ought to use something a bit stronger. Do you think she would chew a tablet?"

Hope nodded. "We can try it. What do you have in mind?"

"I'm writing her a prescription for Augmentin. She'll take one tablet four times a day. It's cherry-flavored. Let's schedule her for a recheck in two weeks." The doctor ripped the prescription off the pad, handed it to Hope, and stood to leave. "You get better now, OK?" she said with a pat on Jennifer's knee, and was out the door.

~ ~ ~

Susan Morris happily rearranged her afternoon schedule to care for Jennifer so Hope could go to work. Hope walked through the door into the newsroom at 3:30. Within minutes she

44

was doing voice-overs for news reports and writing the script for the 6:00 newscast. At 7:00 she was picking up her daughter and by 7:30 had her resting in her own bed at home.

The house felt strangely quiet and empty with Mark away. Hope watched her daughter sleeping and gently brushed a wisp of hair from across her eyes. With just the touch of her fingertips she knew Jennifer's temperature was higher than it had ever been before. She rose quietly and trod the thick hall carpet to the bathroom, where she searched through a cupboard for the digital thermometer. A moment later Jennifer barely stirred as she placed the sensor in her left ear. It showed 103.3.

"It's been three hours since her last dose of Motrin. I guess it won't hurt to give her the next dose a little early," she said to herself. Back in the bathroom she sorted through the medications in the cupboard and found the proper bottle. She read the directions and dumped one pill into her hand. After filling a cup with water, she trod quickly back to the bedroom, where she awakened her daughter.

"Mommy, my throat hurts," Jennifer wailed as her mother helped her sit up.

"I know, honey. This medicine will help you feel better," Hope replied as she held out the cup and pill for her to swallow. Hope drew her daughter close and wrapped her arms around her.

"I wish Daddy was here."

"I wish too," Hope replied tenderly. "But I think you'll be all well by the time he comes home. Won't that be nice?"

"Why did Daddy have to go away?"

"Business. Sometimes when you work for a company you have to go meet the customers."

Jennifer looked at her mother. "When I grow up, I don't want to be in business. That way I won't ever have to go away," she declared with quiet determination. "That way I won't ever have to leave my child alone when she gets sick."

Hope felt a lump of emotion rising in her throat. "You go back to sleep now, honey. OK? You'll get better faster if you're sleeping."

Jennifer lay back down, and Hope pulled the covers up around her. She felt the child's forehead and decided that maybe, just maybe, the medicine was bringing her fever down a little. Or was it just wishful thinking?

Mark answered his cell phone on the second ring. "Mitchell Software Developers. This is Mark Lancaster," he replied professionally.

"Hello, Mark Lancaster. This is your wife speaking. May I please speak to my husband?"

Mark's laugh helped Hope smile just a bit. "What's wrong, honey?"

"How'd you know?"

"The tone of your voice. Something's bothering you more than just missing me. Is Jennifer OK?"

"You get right to the point, don't you?" Hope answered. "Jennifer's got a double ear infection. She started complaining on the way home from the airport and she already had a fever, so I took her right over to the clinic. We got this Indian doctor I'd never met before, and she said it was probably just an ear infection. But I'm not so sure. I mean, 103.3. She's never had a fever that high with an ear infection."

"Well, I guess there's always a first time."

Hope took a deep breath. "Maybe you're right. Well, that's the news from the home front. What's the news where you are?"

"Oh, we're really busy. The first couple hours we were doing final setup of the booth. We've got more than a thousand square feet, so it's taking two dozen of us to cover it well. I think we should've brought more people. By tomorrow our legs and backs will be aching from standing on that hard floor, even though we've got a carpet. We're making some good contacts, so I'm hoping it will be worth the effort."

The couple chatted for another few minutes before Mark protested that he had to get back to wining and dining the customers he was with.

"What's that music I hear in the background? Where are you guys?" Hope asked.

"We're in the dinner theater here at the hotel. The evening show starts in a few minutes."

"What show is that?"

"Siegfried and Roy. You know, the magicians that use the big tigers and lions and other wild animals in their show."

For just an instant a flash of jealousy tightened Hope's jaw, then she stopped herself. Mark worked long hours with a lot of stress. He needed to get away, and this was business. "I wish I could be there and see it with you," she told him.

"Maybe we should plan to spend our next anniversary here. What do you think of that?"

"I'd love it. Right now I'm thinking about sleeping alone in that big bed, with a sick daughter across the hall. I just hope I'll be able to get some sleep tonight."

Come morning, Jennifer was somewhat cooler and managed to hold down some fruit-flavored gelatin. Susan Morris had volunteered to let Jennifer stay with her so Hope could go to work. She hugged her mother before departing. "Thanks, Mom. You don't know how much I appreciate this."

"Hey, I remember delivering a little girl named Hope to her grandmother's more than once," Susan replied. "I'm just thankful I can help."

Hope gave her daughter a hug before turning to leave. "You'll be good for Grandma now, won't you, Jennifer?"

"Yes, Mommy," she answered, hugging her special blanket and teddy as she lay down on the couch.

~ ~ ~

"Did you see who Gene was talking to a few minutes ago?" an excited coworker asked Mark before someone else walking past their display could decide to interrupt their conversation with a question.

"No, who?" He was idly leafing through their brochures, looking for typos.

"Lisa Ferrar, owner of Featherweight Software."

"Ferrar? I don't recognize the name," Mark puzzled. "Featherweight? I've heard of 'em but don't know much about 'em. What's so significant about Gene talking to her? I mean, other than the fact that he's single and she's gorgeous."

"Well, you know how many deals get done here at this show. She's reported to be the newest software billionaire and on the hunt for new companies to acquire."

"Why would she be interested in us? We write customized software for other companies." He put the slim, colorful tri-folds back in a holder.

"Could be she wants to expand or diversify her holdings. Or maybe she wants our talent."

"Somehow I'm having a hard time sharing your excitement." Mark frowned. "When software companies get bought, they get torn apart and eaten up. I have a hard time getting excited about that."

"Yeah, but what I hear is that she pays them a huge amount of money first."

"Really?"

"OK. Think of it this way." The coworker illustrated with enthusiastic hand gestures. "We each own stock in the company, right? It's private stock that's got a book value of $1 a share. Gene gave it to us as a perk because we hired on when the company was small, and he couldn't pay us much. So let's imagine this Ferrar lady from Featherweight buys the company for, say, $10 a share. Mark! We could make enough money off the deal to retire before either of us turns 35!"

Mark looked at his coworker. "You're nuts!"

"You're not excited."

"Disbelieving."

"Why?"

Mark thought for a moment. "I guess I just never thought about it. I've been so focused on writing this new business package I never thought the company's future was in any other direction."

CHAPTER FIVE

It was a mother's instinct that roused Hope from her sleep. She stepped softly, almost silently, in the deeply padded carpeting as she crossed the hall to their daughter's bedroom. The glow of moonlight through the window softly illuminated the room and bathed her face in an ethereal glow. Tenderly Hope placed her hand on the child's forehead. It no longer felt feverish. At last!

Relief flooded Hope's soul as she soaked in the peace of the moonlit room and sleeping child. She didn't move. She hardly breathed. Though aware of her bare feet in the soft carpet and the tick-tick of the second hand on her daughter's clock, she simply watched her child. *Thank You, Lord. She is so beautiful, and I get so scared when she's sick.* At last she returned to bed and cuddled up close to her husband. Ah, it felt so good to have him home again! Just having him away was bad enough, but caring for Jennifer with her double ear infection and working had drained just about every drop of emotional energy from her personal reservoir.

Mark rolled onto his side with his back toward Hope. She pulled herself closer and slid an arm across his waist and her hand up onto his chest where she could feel the beating of his heart. That steady energy gave her strength and lulled her back into peaceful sleep. All too soon the alarm clock sounded, and they were into the activities of a new day.

After their first good-morning kiss and a trip to the bathroom to scrub her face and brush her teeth Hope settled into a comfortable chair as Mark did the same in the opposite corner of their bedroom. For Mark it was an office-style chair in front of his desk where he could spend time reading his Bible by the light of an artfully styled desk lamp. For Hope it was a padded rocking chair, the same one in which she had nursed Jennifer and rocked her to sleep on countless occasions in the first year of her life before returning to work.

On a typical morning they would each read for about 30 minutes before kneeling together beside their bed to pray. This morning Mark asked God for wisdom to know the right way to handle a new situation at work. Hope rejoiced that their daughter's fever had broken and that she was on the road to recovery. Then Mark was off to the shower as Hope shuffled down the stairs in her fluffy slippers to start cooking breakfast. Somewhere along the way one of them would awaken Jennifer so they could eat together before Daddy went to work.

"What's the new situation at work that you were praying about this morning?" Hope inquired as she slid a stuffed ranch omelet in front of her husband, then checked to see if more orange juice needed to be thawed and mixed.

"I'm not sure. When we were out in Vegas, Gene had a meeting with the founder of Featherweight Software. She's rumored to be the newest software billionaire. Anyway, ever since then Gene's been behaving strangely, almost like he's hiding something from us," Mark said. "He's always been so open with us about everything before. Now I've got this gut feeling that something's about to happen, but I have no idea what."

"Definitely sounds like something to hold up to God and seek His guidance," Hope responded as she reached for her coffee mug.

A few minutes later Mark was out the door. Hope settled Jennifer in front of a *VeggieTales* video while she showered and did her hair and makeup. She next had a short Bible study time with Jennifer before strapping her into her car safety seat and delivering her to school (first grade), an eight-minute drive away. Fifteen minutes later she arrived at the TV station.

"Morning, Hope," a video editor greeted as she walked in the door of the newsroom. "You ready for a busy day?"

"What's up?" she answered cheerfully.

"You didn't watch the early news?"

"No. Did I miss something?" Both noticed the news director approaching.

"Brother! Have you got a busy day ahead of you, girl," Bob Knoller announced in his typically gruff manner. "We've got a local angle on a story coming out of Philadelphia. Seems there's some nutso religious cult group up there called, uh"—he looked at the papers in his hands—"Heaven's Portal. Something like that. Yeah, Heaven's Portal. Anyway, their leader thinks he's the modern incarnation of Jesus. Apparently he's been telling his followers that our government is about to start a nuclear war, and if they want to go to heaven, they have to commit suicide."

"Oh, no. Not another one!" Hope exclaimed.

Knoller nodded. "Yup. Another one. Officials up in Philly have already counted more than two dozen bodies. The local angle is that a house over in west Memphis is supposed to be their headquarters for this area. The police there have found eight bodies so far. I'm sending you and a live unit over there to find out anything you can about them. Set it up for a live feed at noon." He started to turn away, then whirled back on his heels. "I almost forgot. New York has told us they're thinking about doing a documentary about this, so they'll be watching what you feed. Do a good piece, and you could be on the network tomorrow night."

Goodness! Hope thought as Bob turned away. "OK, who's my producer? Who's my sound? Who's my camera?" she asked.

Bob answered from halfway across the room. "Cindy is your sound; Murray is your camera; Tony is your linkup technician; and you're the producer. Now get going before the competition beats us to the story! I want a live shot in"—he looked at the clock on the wall—"112 minutes. It'll take you 70 or so minutes to get there, so get moving!"

Hope headed for her desk to pick up her field makeup kit, then by the soda machine for a canned drink to carry along. Murray came up behind her and shoved several pages of wire service copy into her hands. "We'll be waiting in the truck," he said. Sure enough, Hope was the last to climb into the extended cab of the large truck that was really a production studio on wheels. The box behind them was filled with all sorts of production and editing equipment. A pneumatic mast in one corner could be raised to a height of 70 feet to direct a signal at the broadcast tower from a distance of up to 50 miles. Beyond that they'd either have to find a hilltop to transmit from or use one of the satellite antennas on the roof of the box to hit an open channel on one of a half-dozen satellites in geosynchronous orbit 25,000 miles above the equator.

Either way, with all their audio and video channels it was just like being in the studio—except that she could be standing in ankle-deep mud with the wind whipping her hair around and rain stripping her makeup. It had happened, she reminded herself. The only problem she expected today would be melting in the heat of a warm September sun.

With Tony at the wheel, the foursome found their way through city traffic and onto the I-55 bridge across the Mississippi River into west Memphis, Arkansas. They found the address just a few blocks from the Interstate highway off-ramp. Another station was already there, sans live unit. That meant they would have to relay tape back to their station by car. Either they'd already sent tape back or they would be doing a rush edit when they got back to their studios, Hope judged. Either way, Hope and her crew from channel 3 probably would have the only live shot on the noon news.

The coroner's crew was starting to wheel sheet-covered bodies out the front door and into a waiting station wagon. A row of hearses from local mortuaries waited in the street. Murray shouldered his camera and captured the somber scene, setting up angles making plainly obvious the long faces of the police and other workers on the scene. A deputy sheriff directed inquiries to a sheriff's lieutenant who was sitting in a nearby patrol car.

"Can you tell us what happened in the house? How many people are involved?" Hope asked after introducing herself. "Ma'am, we'll have a statement in just a few minutes," he replied in a syrupy Southern drawl.

"We're supposed to go live right on the dot of noon. Can we expect you to make your statement by then?"

"Ma'am, it won't be my statement. It'll be Sheriff Stevens makin' the statement, an' he'll make it if 'n when he gets here, an' it won't do no good to rush 'im."

"Barney Fife meets Heaven's Portal," Hope muttered to no one in particular as they walked away.

"You got that one right," Murray answered. He handed the tape from his camera to Tony in the van, who cued it up in an editing console and did a quick review to pick what section he would roll during the live feed. Murray inserted the replacement tape cartridge in the camera and installed a fresh battery. From an equipment rack inside the van he retrieved a tripod that he set up a few paces outside the gate across the front sidewalk. He and Tony worked together to run a cable from the truck to the camera.

Cindy set up a metal stand with a large screen on it that would moderate the intense sunlight and soften the shadows on Hope's face. On the other side she set up a large white reflector to soften the shadows further. She put a piece of silver "gaffer tape" on the edge of the street to remind Hope where she should stand so the lighting would be perfect.

Hope took advantage of the others being busy to settle herself onto a fold-down seat inside the air-conditioned production van. Using a small pull-out shelf in an equipment rack as a desk, she studied the wire service copy and what notes she had made thus far. Her mind was racing to describe the scene for the viewers when Tony handed her several pages of wire-service story that had just arrived on the fax machine. They could go with what they had, but it would be better if the sheriff would show up in time to give them a statement on camera before the competition arrived in force.

At 10 minutes to 12:00 the control room was demanding final details on how much story would be coming. They had video of the covered bodies being removed. They had Hope doing a stand-up to describe the scene. Then the sheriff arrived. Murray snatched his camera from the tripod and raced toward the sheriff with Hope and Cindy in hot pursuit. The cable was too short. With a quick twist Murray disconnected the cable and let it fall to the pavement. He would roll tape and take it back to the van later. Cindy chased along with a large microphone on the end of a pole. A wireless transmitter would carry the signal to the camera. Somewhere along the way she managed to reach up onto the camera and turn on the receiver unit. She poked the pole past Murray so that it would arrive at the same time he did and pick up whatever was said.

"What can you tell us, Sheriff?" Hope asked as the man pulled himself erect and put on his best for-the-camera smile. The competing station's cameraman took up a position to the side. A third cameraman appeared on the other side. It was their prime news competitor. Then she looked around and saw that neither competitor had a live unit on the scene. channel 3 had the advantage.

"What we have here is a terribly tragic situation, a most re-grettable situation," the sheriff proclaimed. "We were notified this morning by the police department in Philadelphia, Pennsylvania, that this address was linked to the deaths there. A deputy was dis-patched to the scene. There was no answer to his knock at the door, and the door was unlocked, so he went inside and found everyone dead. So far we have eight confirmed deaths. We do not have identities on any of the victims at this time, but we expect to have most of them identified within 24 hours."

"How long have they been dead?" one of the other reporters asked, stealing the words from Hope's lips.

"The medical examiner and investigators on the scene tell us that they've been dead somewhere between 36 and 72 hours. He won't know a more precise time of death until he's had more time to examine the bodies and start doing autopsies."

"Can you describe the scene inside the house? Was there any evidence of foul play or violence?" Hope asked.

"There was no evidence of foul play. Everything was very neat and orderly. All the victims were found lying in bed, so we suspect their deaths were caused by an overdose of some kind of medication."

"Thank you, Sheriff," Hope declared as she turned to go back to her marked position for the stand-up report.

"This is getting too close," Tony protested. "We're only two minutes to air. I'll cue it up the best I can, but we'll have to run that interview raw."

In a moment Murray had the camera reattached and on the tripod. Hope kept the wireless microphone in her hand as she faced the camera. Tony took the newest tape from the camera and cued it to replay the answer to Hope's question. Without time to rewrite her report, she would just have to wing it.

"We're live in 20 seconds!" Murray announced. "Ten seconds."

Hope could hear the anchor back in the studio in her ear-phone, her lone corded connection to the camera. "Let's go live to Hope Lancaster, who is on the scene in west Memphis." Murray gave her the "Go!" signal.

"Eight people are confirmed dead in an apparent group sui-cide motivated by religion," she started. Glancing at the van, she could see a monitor Tony had put in the doorway for her to view. The tape was showing the bodies being carried out. "The sheriff told us moments ago that they were tipped off by the po-lice in Philadelphia, Pennsylvania, who found a connection to the Heaven's Portal mass suicide there. An officer was sent to the scene, and it was he who discovered the bodies in this house." The monitor showed Hope with the house behind her, then switched to the latter part of the interview with the sheriff. She closed out the report with a statement about the identities of the dead being determined within the next 24 hours and a promise to keep viewers informed.

"We're clear!" Murray announced. Hope relaxed and took a sip of her soda, then stepped back in front of the camera to do a variety of stand-ups that could be reedited for the 6:00 news that she would be anchoring. Tony transmitted them to the station, where the news director would pick one to run all afternoon as a promo for the evening newscasts.

Everyone was silent during the first few minutes of the drive east.

"You know, as long as I've been in this business, I'm still not used to seeing bodies," Cindy said softly. "I think that's the most I've seen at any one time."

"Did you catch the odor coming from the house?" Murray asked.

"Didn't you see my nose turning up?" Hope answered. "I hope I didn't look funny on camera."

"No, you looked good," Tony replied.

"You know what that smell was, don't you?" Murray asked. "That was the smell of rotting bodies. There was no air-condi-tioning in that house, or somebody turned it off before they did themselves in. The last time I smelled that was back when I was in Somalia."

"You were in Somalia?" Cindy asked.

"In the Marines. We were protecting the port in Mogadishu

and the armed Somalis—everybody called them Technicals for some reason. They drove these Toyota Land Cruisers with machine guns mounted on the back and carried AK-47s or M-16s. They'd get high on this leafy stuff they chewed all the time. They called it Kat. They'd get high; then their warlords would send them by to shoot at us and try to steal the food we were protecting that was supposed to help feed all the starving people. Only difference was that they were so high that they couldn't shoot straight, and we didn't miss very often. Then the people who came to pick them up would shoot at us and we'd shoot back, and the pile of bodies in the street would just get bigger. Now, add the equatorial sun and those bodies lying out in the sun, and it wasn't long before we were all wearing our gas masks." He paused for a moment. "Yeah, that was the smell of death back there. I'd hoped I'd never smell that again."

Silence filled the truck cab.

"If you don't mind, I'll pass on lunch," Murray offered after a full minute. No one disagreed with him.

CHAPTER Six

The crew returning to the newsroom was in no mood for celebration, yet those receiving them were in high spirits. "Well done!" the untypically upbeat Knoller congratulated them. "You guys gave the best examples of last-minute professional reporting that I've seen in years!"

"Thanks," Hope muttered, sitting down at her desk. The images and stench were still burned into her brain.

"It gets better," Knoller said with an ear-to-ear grin.

"Oh, really?" she looked up.

"New York loved it. They want you to be the local field reporter for a network special airing tomorrow night. They're sending a producer down tonight to work with you tomorrow. They want us to reedit your live piece for tonight's MBS evening news, and they want an extended live report for the special tomorrow. Isn't that great?"

"Yeah, that's great."

Knoller bent down to look Hope in the eye. "Girl, if that's excitement on your face, I'd hate to see you in a bad mood. What's got into you?"

"What we saw. What we taped. Eight innocent people duped and dead. Eight people who would still be alive if they just hadn't blindly followed a false messiah."

"Hey! You're not getting all emotionally involved now, are you? You've got to keep your journalistic edge and try to be objective."

Hope looked up, fighting tears. "I wish I could. It was so . . . so sad. So preventable. And don't go giving me that claptrap about 'journalistic objectivity.' I think I'm a better reporter because I admit to my feelings," she said defensively. "It makes me care about the people I report about, and I think that makes me both a better person and a better reporter."

Knoller studied her gaze for a moment longer. "You keep that fire, girl. Maybe this'll be your ticket to the network."

Working with an editor to prepare the report for 6:00 was emotionally taxing, but gradually Hope regained her professional composure. Yet she walked into the studio at 5:50 with a feeling of sadness beneath her smiling and upbeat camera face.

By the time she got home, Hope was becoming excited at the prospect of working with a network producer the next day. The shock of the scene was fast fading into a memory, and the next morning she bounded out of bed without complaint at having to be to work two hours early.

Peter Leventhal, the MBS news producer from New York, was talking on his cell phone when she walked into the newsroom. "Let's get going," he said, phone still to his ear, as he waved the rest of yesterday's team toward the door. Two more joined the group, a second cameraman and a lighting technician.

"We're starting out today doing family interviews," he announced as they climbed into the truck. "The family of one of the victims in Philadelphia lives down here. That's how the police in Philly figured out to call down here. Plus, we'll try to get interviews with the families of the other victims as soon as we have IDs on them."

It was obvious that not all of them would fit in the truck. "I guess somebody's got the jump seat in back," Tony declared as he slid behind the wheel. "We've got two jump seats back there, with seat belts, if you're game."

"Tony, you ever edited while on the road?" Peter asked.

"No. Why?"

"Can anybody else drive this thing if you have to edit on the road?"

"Uh, I guess Murray or Cindy can drive it."

"Good. Got any strong bungee cords or rope?"

"Are you threatening me?" Tony shot back playfully.

"Sure am," Peter declared. "Got three new rolls of that really sticky gaffer tape, too. Seriously, folk, I've got a feeling time's gonna get really tight later today, and we'll be tying down your chair in back so you can edit tape while we're driving between locations."

Tony cast Peter a disbelieving glance.

"I'm not kidding. I've done it before. And the crew won a Peabody Award for reporting excellence."

"Well, one of the jump seats is in front of the editing console. I'd have to sit sideways, but I guess could do it. We'll just have to keep the generator running while Wild Man Murray over here drives."

The two new members of the team took the jump seats.

The day became a frenetic dash between locations interviewing as many families of the deceased as possible. By 4:00 six of the eight local victims had been identified, and three of the families had granted short interviews. One family refused to go on camera. Most of the victims had lived in the Memphis area, even though they'd died across the river.

Peter punched the "end call" button on his cell phone for the umpteenth time. "We've got an ID on victim seven," he announced. He typed the address into his laptop computer, and a mapping program gave him the location. "Turn right at the next light, go three streets, and turn left."

"You have a name?" Hope inquired, pen poised above the remaining few inches of blank paper in her reporter's notebook.

"Perry Williams. White male. Age 26."

Hope felt her jaw drop. The neighborhood was not far from where she grew up, and the name sounded familiar. If anyone saw her expression, no one said a word. Fear grew with every house they passed, peaking as they parked in front of a simple frame house with a small porch edged with zinnias. Though she recognized the place, she kept her camera face and did the interview. It seemed to her a mechanical exercise void of her usual verve.

Thirty minutes later they were back outside with the others, hauling equipment. "What's wrong, Hope?" Cindy asked. "You're looking really pale."

"I knew him."

"Really! What an insight," Peter exclaimed. "What an angle." He opened the truck door for Hope to climb inside. "Tell me about him."

"I dated him a few times back in high school. He was a clean-cut kid, the kind a preacher didn't mind his daughter dating. A regular at church. Seemed like a really stable kid, not the kind you'd expect to get mixed up in a cult like this."

Peter eyed Hope for a moment. "I get the feeling there's more to this than you're telling. Out with it."

"He took me to the senior prom."

"How soon could you put your hands on a picture of you two?"

"No way!" She shook her head vehemently "I'm not going that far." She looked out the window, unconsciously chewing a fingernail. "OK. I'll say on camera about having known him and that I went to the prom with him—but we dated only a few times. We never were serious, and I'd be very uncomfortable playing up myself to make a better story!" Tears filled her eyes.

Peter nodded. "OK, just voice comments. Do them in your stand-up. I really, really like this angle. Makes it more personal. It gives the story a real gut-tugging connection. You follow?"

"Yeah. Your story, my guts," Hope answered, wondering how in the world she would ever compose the words to express tastefully what she felt, because right now the one thing she wanted most in the world was just to get away to a private place and cry.

Peter looked Hope straight in the eye. "You *can* tell about this in your stand-up?"

Fighting to regain her camera face, Hope nodded.

"OK, folks! Let's do a rough edit right here before we go back over to the house," Peter ordered. "Leave it loose, and we'll shoot it over the bird to New York and let them do the tight edit. They'll fax us back any voice-overs just before we go on the air, and we can do 'em then."

Tony slid into a chair in front of the editing console. He reached up and flipped a switch under the "Generator" sign, and a low rumble shuddered through the van. Once the power meter stabilized he began turning on and warming up the various computers and editing machines. The raw video, recorded digitally by the camera, was loaded into the computer at a speed many times the normal viewing rate. Peter checked his notes to give edit points marking the start and end of what he thought were the most useful parts of the interviews and which of the camera angles to use.

As Peter and Hope reviewed the rough edit, Murray wrapped his right hand around a joystick that aimed the satellite transmission antenna on the roof of the van. First, he pulled it backward to lift it from its facedown position, a posture picked to minimize wind resistance while traveling. Next he consulted a chart giving him the compass bearings for various satellites in geosynchronous orbit above the equator. Following a dial giving him the compass bearing of the antenna, he swung it clockwise to that bearing. Then he pulled back on the joystick, listening on his headphones for the tracking signal that would tell him when the antenna was aiming directly at the invisible bird in space.

Murray keyed a microphone switch. "MBS New York, this is Memphis Belle. How do you read? Over."

Murray repeated his call before receiving an the answer, "Memphis Bell, this is MBS New York. We read you loud and clear. You are free of distortion. We are ready to download whenever you're ready."

"MBS New York, Memphis Belle. We will send on a three-count. Three . . . two . . . one . . ." Murray pushed the "Transmit" button, which turned from green to red and stayed that color as the transmission flew from the antenna.

Four minutes later the button was again green, and Murray waited for the confirmation from New York that they'd received the transmission. "Memphis Bell, this is MBS New York. We have nine minutes and 17 seconds of recording. The system reports no errors or distortion. Do you have anything more to send?"

"That's negative," Murray answered. "Memphis Belle is clear and shutting down for relocation."

Seven minutes later the equipment was shut down and the crew were belting themselves into their seats for the trip back across the river.

Hope looked at her watch. *Normally I'd be going into the studio about now,* she thought as they arrived back in front of the house where members of Heaven's Portal had lived and died. No other media were around, but a steady flow of people were driving slowly by. Others stopped and added to the growing pile of flowers and candles along the fence, turning the place into a shrine.

A deputy sheriff approached them. "We're ready to block off

the street when you need it," he offered. Peter thanked them and said they were ready.

"How'd you arrange that?" Cindy asked.

"That's my job as producer. I'm supposed to make it all happen, right?" he laughed as they began unloading equipment and setting up. A cluster of curious onlookers formed to watch whatever was about to happen.

A moment later the same deputy approached Peter again. "I've got a guy down here with a catering truck. Says he's supposed to be here. Do you know anything about it?"

Peter looked at his watch. "He's right on time. Let him in. Tell him to park right in front of our truck."

"Who's that?" Murray asked as he saw the catering truck approach.

"Supper," Peter replied as he lifted a roll of power cable. "We don't often get this kind of service on location, but I thought I'd better be nice to you if I ever wanted to work with you again."

Peter and Hope worked on her lines as the crew finished their setup. Cindy stood in for Hope as the camera angles were established and the lighting adjusted. The fax machine delivered the script and other details from New York. Suggested corrections were faxed back. Phone calls confirmed the final edits, and it was time for a run-through. The program would be "live to tape," meaning it would be recorded, but there would be only one take. Everything—including tongue tumbles and miscues—would air two hours later.

Hope waited on her starting mark until receiving the signal from Murray. "Good evening, Brandon," she answered the welcoming remark from the anchor in a studio somewhere in New York City. "This is the house where eight people were found dead yesterday, people who died believing their departure from this life would hasten both the end of the world and their arrival in heaven." The picture changed to the scene of the previous day as the bodies were being taken out. Hope's recorded voice described the scene. Several times the report shifted back to Hope speaking live. Then it was all over.

"Great job," Peter exulted. "New York loved it! Now let's get something to eat and get out of here."

Peter approached Hope as she was removing her wireless

microphone and earphone. "First time live on the network?"

Hope nodded. "First time."

"You did good. You're network material," he added. "You hungry?"

"Starving! You know what was the hardest part about that?"

"What?" Peter answered.

"Looking past the camera, seeing that catering truck, smelling that food, and hoping the microphone wouldn't pick up the rumbles from my stomach!"

~ ~ ~

A very tired Hope settled into the living room couch next to her husband to watch herself "live" on network TV for the first time. "Well, how did I do?" she asked after it was over.

"How soon do we sell the house and move to New York?" he teased. "I'm so proud of you. You did super!" He leaned over and gave her a passionate kiss. She didn't kiss him back.

Mark looked at his wife. "What's wrong?"

"It's just such a sad, terrible story. I can't believe so many people would follow a false messiah, somebody who would tell them to kill themselves. I mean, did you see the hurt on the faces of those parents? And that sister in Philadelphia? That was awful! Horrible! I can't imagine how they're feeling right now."

"And that guy you dated back in high school."

"Yeah, him too." Hope sat with the sadness of the moment drowning her attention even for the commercials on the TV. Mark hit the remote control mute button, and now the sounds of raindrops hitting the patio deck were the only sound in the room.

"I was just thinking about something Jesus said," Mark mused. "Where is it? Matthew 24? Anyway, it's where He said that in the last days there would come delusions strong enough that, if possible, even the very elect would be deceived."

"That's supposed to make me feel better? Even the very elect being deceived?"

"Well, he didn't say the elect *would* be deceived. He said the delusion would be so strong that it could deceive them if they allowed it to."

"That's frightening to think about, Mark. I mean, you and I could be deceived and be lost," Hope said quietly. "I wonder what makes the difference. What keeps the saved from being deceived?"

Mark shrugged. "I'm not sure. I guess studying the Bible so we can know when something is right or wrong."

"You know, what I'm wondering about is how the leader of that Heaven's Portal group could deceive those people. You know, what did she do or say that made people want to follow, even follow her to the point of killing themselves."

"I don't know. Maybe they just needed to belong to *something*. Or maybe they didn't spend enough time with their Bibles, and they couldn't recognize the falsehoods their leader was teaching them when it was right in front of them."

"Yeah, but the frightening thing was how she used the Bible to deceive them."

CHAPTER SEVEN

A s was her nightly habit just before retiring, Hope stepped quietly in the dim glow of the night-light spreading gently across Jennifer's bedroom. Bending down, she reached out and lightly touched her daughter's forehead. It was warm.

"If she still has that fever in the morning I think I'd better take her back to Dr. Chapman," Hope told her husband as she settled beside him on the couch. "It seems as though we just get her over one bug and finish the course of medicine and she's right back on it again."

"Do you want to take her, or should I?" Mark asked.

"I'll take her," Hope offered. "They've always got a couple openings first thing in the morning. If I can get her there by 8:30 we shouldn't have a long wait. Maybe I can even be to work on time too." She paused, thinking. "I'd better call Mom and see if she can babysit again."

As her own bedtime arrived Hope again checked on Jennifer, only this time she carried the digital thermometer that she pressed into her daughter's ear. It read 100.7 degrees. "What do you think? Should I wake her up and give her some children's Motrin?"

"If she's asleep, let her sleep," Mark answered. "If you wake her up, no telling when she'll get back to sleep."

Hope resisted the instinct telling her to disagree, then turned and trod quietly across the hall to her own bedroom. "I'm worried about her," she confided to her husband as she slid beneath the covers. He was already asleep.

Twice in the night Hope rose and took the thermometer to

check on Jennifer. Each time the reading was higher, the second time nearing 102 degrees. She was stirring, so Hope got her daughter to swallow a dose of medicine to reduce her fever. But sleep would not return, so Hope cuddled her long-legged daughter in her arms in a rocking chair in the living room.

"Mommy, I gotta—" Jennifer blurted out, then spewed across the carpeting.

"Mark!" The sharp exclamation roused him from slumber and brought him on quick steps. He arrived in time to find Jennifer bent over the toilet with the dry heaves. "I think it's time we took her to the ER," Hope declared. "Do you want to take her? Or should I?"

"How about both of us?"

Hope shook her head. "One of us needs to get some sleep and be ready to go to work tomorrow. Uh, later today. I don't have to be to work until 10:00, and your boss gets upset if you're not there, so why don't I take her?"

Mark yawned widely. "OK, I'll at least help you get into the car." He took Jennifer in his arms so Hope could get dressed.

"What's wrong, Daddy?" Jennifer asked weakly.

"Mommy's going to take you to the emergency room so we can get a doctor to look at you and get you some medicine to help you feel better, OK?"

"I feel bad, Daddy," she said limply.

"I know, and we're going to do something about it. Mommy should be ready in just a minute."

Hope threw on some jeans and a T-shirt before stepping into slip-on shoes and grabbing her purse. In moments she and Mark had Jennifer strapped into her usual position in the back seat and were waving to each other through the darkness as Hope backed the car out of the garage. Mark then went to the bathroom for a wet washrag to clean Jennifer's mess out of the carpet.

Twenty minutes later Hope and Jennifer walked in the door of the pediatric emergency room, a surprisingly busy place for 3:10 in the morning. She strode urgently to the main desk, Jennifer clinging to her hand.

"May I help you?" the weary person dressed in hospital scrubs inquired.

"I have a very sick girl here. She's got a high fever. I tried giving her some children's Motrin about 45 minutes ago"—she looked at her watch—"but she threw it up."

"What's her temperature?"

"Last time I checked it was close to 102. She feels hotter now than when I put her in the car."

"Just a moment," the receptionist ordered as she picked up the phone. She punched four numbers and waited for a moment. "I have a 6-year-old child here with a high fever . . . OK." She hung up. "Go right to the triage nurse." She pointed toward an exam room.

The triage nurse took Jennifer's temperature, asked a few questions, and sent the pair directly into the main emergency room, where a nurse directed them toward a bed. Two minutes later an obviously very tired young physician introduced himself. He asked a few questions and quickly examined her. "I'm not finding any evidence of an ear infection or tonsillitis, or anything like that," he said. "I'm thinking this must be some kind of virus. If that's what it is, there's nothing you can do but take Tylenol or children's Motrin and wait it out."

"But she's throwing up," Hope protested. "How is the medicine going to do any good if she can't keep it down?"

"Let's give her something to help with the nausea," the doctor said. "The nurse will come back in a few minutes with a suppository. That'll control the nausea. It'll help her sleep, too." He wrote on the chart for a minute, stood, and left.

The eastern sky was beginning to lighten as mother and daughter arrived home, the first wishing to do what the other was doing with the help of medication. Mark was still asleep, his alarm not set to go off for another 20 minutes. Still, he arose to greet his family and inquire of the diagnosis. When Hope told him that Jennifer was asleep in the car, he slipped out—in his pajamas—to pick her up and carry her inside.

"We managed to find a 24-hour pharmacy and get her prescription filled. The doctor says it's probably a virus of some kind. There's no visible ear infection or other signs of disease. So she's just supposed to rest and drink plenty of fluids. If she starts vomiting, we'll give her one of these butt bullets," she said with a laugh, holding up a box of Phenergan suppositories.

Mark looked at her quizically.

"Well, *that's* what they called them at the hospital. They inserted one while we were still in the ER. That's why she's sleeping." Hope looked at the little girl, sound asleep on the couch. "Poor baby."

Mark took Jennifer to her room as Hope set about making breakfast. "You going in to work today?" he asked as he eyed her across a steaming mug.

"Up since 3:00. I think I'm gonna call and tell them I'll be late, then try to get a few hours' sleep."

"You'll still look tired."

Hope took a bite of her toaster waffle. "Not much I can do about that now, can I?" she said after chewing. "At least I've already asked Mom to watch her. Even if she could go to school, she can't go to day care with a fever." She reached for the juice. "Anything happening at your work today?"

"More of the same, I guess. Ever since we were in Las Vegas, Gene's been spending a lot of time out in Silicon Valley."

"What's he doing out there?"

"That's what we'd all like to know. We think he's got something big on his mind, but since Vegas he's not said much of anything to anybody. That's what's got us all so puzzled. It's just not like Gene to be that way."

"Something big? How's he been behaving?"

"Well, generally in a good mood. He's just not taking the time to chat with us the way he used to. You know, no water cooler gossip. That sort of thing. Keeps to himself a lot. Plus he keeps making these trips west, and he leaves us totally in the dark about what he's doing."

"Doesn't sound like the Gene I remember meeting. Who'd he meet at the show?"

"Lisa Ferrar."

"Who's that?"

"Founder and CEO of Featherweight Software."

"Uh-huh. Is this personal or business?"

"How am I supposed to know? He's not telling us anything. I mean, one rumor says he's fallen in love. Another says they're negotiating a merger or a buyout. I don't know what to believe," Mark said.

"And what do you think?" Hope queried.

"I have no earthly idea. You know what puzzles me? Wherever he's going, he's not flying on a commercial airline. He won't even let his assistant take him to the airport anymore. So I think he must be traveling on somebody's private jet. The whole thing has me feeling uneasy."

"Why?"

"Oh, it's the stories of what happens when a company gets bought out. Usually it's the better programmers who get raises or relocated, and everybody else gets downsized. Companies aren't bought so much for what they're doing as for the people they have doing it."

"What do you know about this Lisa somebody?"

"Not much. I saw her in passing a couple times at the show. Met her once very briefly. She's probably the most beautiful CEO in corporate history. Got lots of money. I mean, she's on the list of the 500 richest Americans. Seems like a really nice person."

Hope yawned. "I guess you'll find out what Gene's up to when he decides to tell you," she offered as she bent over to give him a kiss on the cheek. "You have a nice day. I'm going to bed."

Thirty minutes later Mark was snaking his car through traffic. Rising early brought him to the office early enough that he parked in the row of spaces closest to the three-story glass-and-steel building. Gene Mitchell, the founder and owner of Mitchell Software Developers, was already there. That he was there before everyone else was no surprise.

Mark took the stairs to the second floor and turned left through the double doors toward his office, one of a series of numbered doors with nameplates along a hallway leading to Gene's suite at the end. Mark's door was the last on the right. As he reached into his pocket for the key he thought he heard two voices, one male and one female, coming from behind Gene's door. The female voice sounded different from Carol's, his executive assistant.

Settling into his ergnomically correct chair, Mark saw that the message waiting light on his phone was blinking. He lifted the receiver and punched in his four-digit retrieval code. A feminized computer voice told him that he had seven messages waiting, one of them tagged high priority. He pressed the number 1 button to get that message.

"This is Gene Mitchell. An all-hands luncheon meeting will be held today at noon in the banquet room of the Holiday Inn down the street. The purpose of this meeting is to announce a new direction that our company will be going in the future, so I hope all of you can attend. It is extremely important that everyone be there. Please remember to set your voice mail to automatically pick up on all calls during this time."

"Is this when we learn what all these trips west are about?" Mark wondered as he scanned his desk to begin organizing his day. He set about returning calls from customers and brainstorming with the programmers under his command about graphic challenges they were facing. It seemed as if the day had just begun when someone reminded him that it was time to head down the street for the lunch meeting Gene had announced.

"I'll bet Gene's landed a major new customer," one coworker suggested.

"Well, the way the economy's been going, I'll bet he's announcing that we're losing a customer," someone else countered.

"He wouldn't treat us to lunch to announce that!" the first argued.

"Betcha we've been sold," a third surmised.

"Don't ask me to move to Silicon Valley," a fourth protested. "No way I'll move there. I hear they've got bad smog, and two-hour commutes on clogged freeways are the norm out there."

Further surmising and polite argument continued as the crowd flowed into the motel's banquet room and found seats around the assorted circular tables. A large banner reading "Mitchell Software Developers, Commitment to Quality Programming" was mounted on the end wall behind a raised podium on a small stage. Mark found his place marked with a name card at a table near the front reserved for the original core group of Mitchell Software employees. Two places at the same table were marked with cards simply reading "reserved."

At five minutes after noon Gene Mitchell strode confidently into the room from a side door. A gasp of surprise filled the room as people realized he was holding hands with a strikingly beautiful woman Mark immediately recognized as Lisa Ferrar.

The couple smiled broadly as they strode to the stage, where Gene stepped to the podium and Lisa stood a pace beside and behind him.

"Hello, Mitchell Software!" Gene proclaimed with enthusiasm, then waited for the murmur of conversations to cease. "Anyone here a software freak?" he asked playfully.

"We're software freaks!" came the shouted reply of the faithful.

"I've called you here to share a couple items of news, at least one of which I think you'll be very happy to hear," Gene continued. "Most of you know that my first wife, Margie, died seven years ago from cancer. Those of you who know me best know how lonely I've been since then." He paused to let the anticipation rise. "But things have changed recently. A few weeks ago a group of us were out at the software show in Las Vegas. It was there that I met this beautiful woman, Lisa Ferrar, who is founder and CEO of Featherweight Software." He turned and extended his hand toward her, which she took and stepped up close beside him. "A lot has happened over these past few weeks, and Lisa and I have called you together today to announce that she has agreed to marry me."

An enthusiastic round of applause mixed with whistles and shouts filled the room. It began to die down; then the couple kissed, and the celebration rejuvenated for nearly a solid minute.

"The wedding's going to be right here in Memphis. I insisted on that because I've come to think of each and every one of you as family, and I want my family to be able to attend the wedding." Another cheer filled the room. "There's more news to share, but it can wait until after we eat," Gene proclaimed. He then called a man to the front whom everyone recognized as an Independent Baptist minister. He pronounced a blessing on the meal that included a special invocation of divine blessing on the engaged couple.

Gene spent the next several minutes introducing Lisa to those at the reserved tables in the front of the room. Then the waiters arrived with plates of baked chicken on wild rice with mixed vegetables, mashed potatoes, and corn bread. Polite conversation during the meal dwelt on a variety of friendly topics while everyone wondered what was coming next.

After seeing that most had finished their dessert, Gene

again stepped to the microphone. "If I could have your attention, please," he asked, then waited for conversations to cease. "Lisa is going to share the second big news item we want to announce today."

A generous round of applause greeted Lisa as she stepped to the podium. "Good afternoon!" she declared in an energy-filled, girlish manner. A smattering of voices around the room responded in kind.

"Gene and I are looking forward to celebrating our wedding with you. This afternoon we'll be circulating your personal invitations. Now, judging by the size of this group and assuming most of you have at least a spouse, if not children, this may turn out to be the biggest wedding celebration Memphis has seen in a long time.

"You know, Gene wasn't the only one who has made a marriage proposal recently. I've made one to him, too. A corporate marriage proposal. And I'm happy to say that Gene has accepted. So I'm really excited to tell you that as of right now, Mitchell Software Developers is being bought by Featherweight Software and from now on will be known as the Memphis Division of Featherweight Software."

Lisa paused as a stunned silence filled the room. Then came a smattering of applause that died quickly.

"I know this comes as a surprise to you. Maybe even a shock. I know news like this brings a lot of uncertainty with it, so I'm going to level with you and give you all the details I can right now, so listen up," she declared firmly as the CEO side of her personality took command.

"The first question on everybody's mind when a merger or buyout is announced is: 'Do I still have a job?' The answer is a resounding yes! You still have a job, and you will have it for the foreseeable future."

A polite round of applause relieved some of the tension.

"You know as well as I do how the software industry works. There are up times and down times, and we have to live with that. Right now the market is down, but I see only up times in Featherweight Software's future. In fact, it's our need for talented people like you that led me to make the buyout offer."

Lisa paused to let the words sink in. "Over time your operations and development groups will be reorganized, and some of you may be transferred to our home office in Palo Alto. That's going to take a few months to work out, and if you're one of the people we invite to move west, I assure you that we'll make it well worth your time.

"No doubt at different times you've seen salary comparisons and wondered if you couldn't use those comparison charts as a tool to help you get a raise. I know you've been doing that, because Gene says over the past couple years you've given him a stack of those charts." Lisa smiled as a chuckle ran through the room. "What's more, before leaving Palo Alto yesterday, I checked with our Human Resources Department and found that about 20 percent of you have at one time or another applied to work at Featherweight. Well, for those of you who got those horrible form letters in reply, I'm here to tell you that as of today, you're hired!"

The next round of applause was a little stronger.

"What is more, also effective today, your salaries are being adjusted to match the Featherweight pay scale. Each of you will receive a letter this afternoon telling you what your new pay rate will be. And let me tell you one thing, I don't think I'll be hearing any jokes about your checks weighing less than a feather!" A cheer mixed with enthusiastic applause.

Lisa continued for several more minutes before Gene returned to the podium and dismissed everyone to go back to work.

Just after 2:00 the company messenger began his rounds delivering business-sized envelopes bearing the Featherweight Software logo and the recipient's name. Inside Mark's envelope was a personalized form letter from Lisa Ferrar welcoming him to the company and announcing that his pay rate was being increased by 35 percent.

"Do you like it?" Gene asked from the open office door.

Mark's head jerked upward in surprise. "I didn't know you were there."

"Is that enough?"

"It's a very unexpected surprise. I think I can get used to it."

"I'm glad," Gene said, pulling up a chair. "You've been one of my right-hand people for a number of years, and I've given Lisa a really positive report about you. I'd even call it glowing, so she's expecting great things out of you." He leaned forward for emphasis. "I can promise you this—if you show her over the next year or so that you're giving 110 percent, you'll be skipping levels on those industry pay scale charts."

For an instant the men looked straight into each other's eyes. "Thank you, Gene. I really appreciate it."

"You deserve it, man. You also deserve this." He handed Mark a second envelope. Inside was a check for $165,000 drawn on Gene's personal account.

Mark's jaw dropped in surprise. "Wha . . . What's this for?" he finally stammered.

"A buyout bonus. It's a personal thank-you for all the hard work you've done over the years when I couldn't pay you what you were worth. You and the other nine original troopers who worked all those extra hours for little pay when we were first starting out are getting this little extra. It makes me happy to do it!"

Mark fought for the right words, then looked into Gene's eyes. "Thank you, Gene. You're a real friend. I guess I shouldn't be surprised, because there've been so many times in the past that you've done special things for us because you cared. Thanks, Gene. I really mean it."

Gene just looked at Mark and grinned.

"Tell me something, Gene. Why'd you do it? Why'd you sell? I thought you wanted to run your own show for the rest of your life."

The boss leaned back in his chair and studied his tented fingertips. "I used to feel that way," he said. "Man, you know how tough it was after Margie died. But time passes, and after I met Lisa I realized how tired and lonely I was. I kept thinking that the company had become my mistress and was consuming my life. Being with Lisa restored my inner being and made me happy in a way I never dreamed would ever happen again after Margie's death." He laughed. "It sounds corny, but it's like I've been reborn, and the thing I want most is just to be with Lisa. So—as the kids would say—I'm just following my heart."

He stood up. "Well, I've taken enough of your time. I will say that I'm awfully glad it's working out well for everyone else, too."

Mark stood up, too, and put out his hand. "Thank you again!"

he said passionately. "And uh, Gene, I hope you don't mind if I take the rest of the afternoon off. There's something I've been wanting to do for a long time, and *this*"—he held up the envelope—"makes it possible."

Gene grinned. "Go right ahead. I don't think anybody's going to be doing any work this afternoon anyway."

CHAPTER **EIGHT**

At precisely 2:01 p.m. the fax machine in the newsroom at channel 3 began to hum and produce a cover sheet bearing the logo of Featherweight Software's Public Relations Department. A statement including quotes from CEO Lisa Ferrar detailed how the company was buying Memphis-based Mitchell Software for $126 million in cash and stock. While the company would be reorganized, all employees would be retained.

The junior news producer assigned to scan stories off the fax machine glanced at the three-page printout and headed for Hope's desk. "Your husband works over at Mitchell Software, doesn't he?" the producer asked.

"Uh-huh," Hope answered, barely looking up from the story she was editing.

"Well, they just got bought out." The producer dropped the story on her desk as Hope whirled around in surprise. "Say what?"

"Yup. One hundred twenty-six million in cash and stock. Company's gonna be reorganized as the Memphis Division of Featherweight Software. Nobody's gonna get fired, and the president of Mitchell Software is marrying the CEO of Featherweight."

Hope felt her heart leap into her throat and a tremor in her hands as she picked up the press release and began reading. Her heartbeat began slowing and the tremor disappeared by the end of the third paragraph. At least Mark still had a job. She reached for the phone and dialed his direct phone number. After three rings his recorded voice mail greeting began playing.

She hung up and dialed the Mitchell Software switchboard.

"Featherweight Software," the smooth female voice answered. "How may I direct your call?"

"This is Hope Lancaster. I'm trying to reach my husband, Mark, and I'm getting his voice mail. Could you please page him?"

The operator laughed. "Yes, ma'am. You know, I think every spouse is wanting their husband or wife paged this afternoon! Just a moment." The line went silent as Hope was put on hold. Two minutes later the operator returned with news that Mark was not answering his page.

It was challenging for Hope to keep her mind on her work the rest of the afternoon and to deliver the 6:00 newscast without appearing distracted. But her mind was racing, seeking confirmation of what impact the news would have on their family.

The first answer sat in the driveway as she came down the street toward home. Mark was wiping the dust off a brand-new metallic-blue Mercedes M-class sport utility vehicle while Jennifer watched from a folding chair on the lawn. "What's going on here?" Hope gasped as she exited her own 5-year-old Honda sedan.

"Well, we got bought out today—" Mark started.

"I saw the press release," Hope cut him off sharply. "I tried all afternoon to call you. And now I see you were out car shopping. Tell me, how in the world are we affording this?"

"A buyout bonus. Plus, I traded in the old Ford. This, my love, is completely paid for. Including the license and insurance for the next year!"

Hope rested her hands on her hips. "And how much money do we have left over after this shopping spree?"

"Just under $130,000," Mark told her as he swung the dust cloth over the back window. "You like it? We'll get you one too, if you want."

When she did not answer, Mark looked around. She was just staring at him, her mouth agape as she tried to form words.

"A hun . . . a hun . . . H-h-h-how much did you say?"

"Well, the bonus was $165,000. Plus I got a 35 percent raise. That puts me on the same level as a senior programmer out at Featherweight's corporate headquarters in California, less the cost-of-living differential they get for having to live in Silicon

Valley. Anyway, I decided to take the afternoon off and do a little shopping."

"I see," Hope answered, then nearly tackled her husband as she raced to embrace him. "Honey! That's wonderful! I just can't believe it!"

"I guess I'm still in shock a little, too."

Hope gently pushed away from her husband. "There was something else in the press release about some people having to move out to Palo Alto. I hope you're not one of them," she said.

Mark shook his head. "We don't know yet. That'll be decided in a couple months after the top managers from Featherweight have done their reorganization here. Hey, you want to take it for a spin?" He held up the keys.

An excited grin spread across Hope's face. "You bet!" she said as she snatched the keys. "Come on, Jennifer!"

"You won't believe how many computers and sensors this thing's got in it," Mark announced as he buckled his seat belt. He pointed to a control on the driver's seat. "This will remember how you want your seat positioned. All you have to do is press one button and it moves to where you want it. There's even a seat warmer to take the chill off the seat when you first get in it on a cold morning."

"Neat-o!" Hope exclaimed.

Mark looked in back to check Jennifer's seat belt. "There's even a sensor in the back that detects if a child is sitting there and in case of a collision keeps the rear-seat air bag from going off. And when have another child, it'll even detect if the safety seat is mounted properly."

Hope turned the key and began backing out of the driveway. A half hour later they pulled back in.

"Well, do you think you'd like one for yourself?" Mark asked.

"Maybe," Hope answered after a thoughtful moment. "I kind of had a minivan in mind. You know, so I can help take groups from Jennifer's school on field trips. That sort of thing."

"You can do that with one of these."

"Yes, but it isn't a minivan. This doesn't say Mom's Taxi all over it. I've seen some Toyota minivans lately that I really like. I want to take a closer look at them before I decide."

"Well, I guess if that's what you really want," Mark said, a hint of disappointment in his voice.

"Oh, Daddy! Quit fighting and just let Mommy have it," Jennifer interjected.

"No, darling. This is my car. You can ride with me whenever you want."

"OK, Daddy. But you have to take me everywhere. And I mean everywhere. Can you take me to the mall?"

"When did she turn into a teenager?" Hope asked with a laugh.

~ ~ ~

The cool winds of autumn stole into the Memphis area, painting the trees with color and changing wardrobes from short sleeves to sweaters and even coats in the morning. Hope found she was using more hair spray to keep her locks in place when doing outside reports. She also was getting spoiled by how much easier it was to drive her new Mercedes SUV through city traffic than the old Honda they'd traded in.

"Come on, honey! We've got to get you to school and me to work," Hope called to Jennifer as she took her coat from its hook on the back of the front hallway closet door. "Let's not make me late to work, OK?"

They headed for the garage. Hope pulled the wireless key chain from her purse and pushed the button that turned on the electronic seat warmer. That was one feature of her new SUV that she really liked. She was just reaching for the door handle to let Jennifer in when the van seemed to jump toward her. Then it felt as if she was losing her balance, as everything began to sway.

But it wasn't her! Indeed, everything around her was moving. From every direction came the sounds of the house creaking. Rakes and shovels hanging on their wall rack danced in sync with each other as the vehicle did a dance of its own on its suspension. Jennifer cried out in fright as she grabbed her mother around the waist. Hope braced herself the best she could against the vehicle.

"Make it go away, Mommy! Make it go away!" Jennifer screamed as first a rake, then a shovel, and all the other tools on the rack fell to the floor.

As suddenly as it had begun it was over. The pair held each

other tightly as the relief sank in. Hope straightened up on wobbly legs and searched her purse for a tissue to wipe her daughter's tears. Jennifer did not want to let go even to take it. For several minutes she held tightly to her mother, her tears wetting her mother's skirt.

"It's OK now, dear," Hope said softly as she peeled her daughter's arms from around her and bent down for a neck hug. "It's OK."

"What was that, Mommy?"

"Another earthquake. Remember that one a few months ago? Only this was a lot stronger. But it's over. C'mon. It's time to go."

Hope opened the car door, and Jennifer seemed all too eager to get her feet off the garage floor. She buckled herself into her seat more quickly than usual.

As Hope walked around to the driver's side her gaze was drawn to a new feature on the outside wall of the garage: a crack that extended upward nearly three feet from the foundation. A narrow ray of sunlight shone through, landing on the glossy surface of the vehicle. "That was a lot worse than the other one," she said to herself.

The earthquake was the main topic of conversation at Jennifer's school. So far no damage had been found at the school, but a detailed search was under way.

The quake had the newsroom abuzz too. Crews were scrambling to get live field reports ready for the noon telecast. Hope soon found herself heading to Beale Street with a basic two-person crew to do live on-the-street interviews with tourists in town for a jazz festival. It was utterly unscripted. She snared three tourists and asked them a few questions to learn where they were from and what they thought about the quake. Then they waited seven minutes until the control room shifted to their location. For one minute she asked the tourists their reactions and observations. Then it was time to pack the gear back into the van and head back to the studio.

Hope's afternoon was filled with gathering local stories for the 6:00 newscast, the local impact of the quake being story one.

The National Earthquake Monitoring Center reported that the temblor had been centered at a point in eastern Missouri along the New Madrid Fault and had registered 4.9 on the

Richter scale. That was powerful enough to do significant local damage and minor damage over an extended area. Given the increasing level of quake activity along the fault system, seismologists predicted that more quakes would follow.

On her midafternoon break Hope phoned their homeowner's insurance agent. "I'm really sorry, Hope, but your policy doesn't cover quake damage. Earthquakes are special coverage that, to be honest, isn't even available in our area because it's been so long since the last damaging quake was recorded."

"It's not so bad, hon," Mark consoled her later. "We've just paid off the house with the remainder of my bonus, so instead of making mortgage payments we'll just have to pay a contractor to come in and repair it. It's just one of those things."

~ ~ ~

One of the oddball features of an ancient and slow-moving river like the Mississippi was that you could be going upstream by heading south on a river that generally flowed from the north toward the south. Such was the case for the *Missy M*, a 65-foot diesel-powered towboat pushing northward a string of 11 barges loaded with coal. Two days before, they'd been tied up at a pier on the Ohio River just west of Paducah, Kentucky, where an overhead conveyor had dropped the combustible cargo into the cavernous holds of the barges. In another two days they would be tied up at an electric generating plant some 70 miles north of St. Louis, doing the reverse process.

Deckhand Boyd Stevens enjoyed the night shifts aboard the *Missy M*. They provided quiet time in the fresh air in which he could smell the scents that wafted off the land. Depending on the time of the year and what was growing nearby, he had learned to identify the distinct smells of ripe cotton being harvested, mature wheat, and several other crops that grew in the fields just the other side of the levees lining the sides of the river.

The night shifts also provided times of quiet and solitude during which he could take his Bible and a deck chair and walk to his lookout position at the front of the barges. His job was to watch for floating obstacles and small boats that might be in the path of the barges and not showing up on radar in the pilot-house. He carried a small two-way radio with which to communicate those reports to whoever was steering at the time. Since they moved at only eight knots against the current, all it really required of him was that he pick up a night-vision device and scan ahead about every 10 or 15 minutes.

Boyd's job as a lookout was mostly a waste of his time, because the most frequent obstacles on the river were fishermen whose boats had running lights and who usually kept out of the shipping channel. As for floating logs, well, they just got run over. Once in a while one of them would hit a propeller, and a few days later they would put into a port where the boat could be lifted out on a dry dock and the propeller bent back into shape and rebalanced. But that had happened only a handful of times in his seven years on the river. Next year he would take the Coast Guard test that, if he passed, would certify him as a towboat skipper. Then he could look for a job commanding one of these rigs instead of just being a deckhand.

Sitting near the front end of a string of barges was the quietest place on earth, Boyd felt. Unless they had a strong trailing wind he couldn't even hear the rumble of the diesel engines at the rear of this assemblage of lashed-together watercraft. It was just him and the breeze. At night he used the quiet and the glow from a running light to study for his upcoming exam or read his Bible. Tonight it was the latter. Out here he could study and pray without fear of being taunted by his rowdy and intemperate crewmates.

Boyd settled into his chair at the left front of the first barge. Just to his right rose the corner of the wall surrounding the cavernous cargo hold stacked high with coal. From this position he could not see the *Missy M* at all. He checked the waterproof radio that was strapped onto his neon-orange life jacket, and keyed the microphone mounted on his left shoulder. "Lookout to *Missy M*. How do you read?"

"Lookout, I read you loud and clear. Hey, stay awake out there, OK?"

"Sure, Jimmy. I'll let you do the yawning, since you're driving," he answered.

Boyd unzipped the waterproof case in which he carried his Bible and extracted the well-thumbed volume. He opened it to the book of Revelation and began reading in chapter 6. A cloud slid in front of the moon, making the darkness around him seem even deeper.

What does all this mean, Lord? Boyd prayed as he read about the four horsemen of the Apocalypse. "And I beheld," he read in verse 12, "when he had opened the sixth seal, and, lo, there was a great earthquake; and the sun became black as sackcloth of hair, and the moon became as blood."

Boyd noticed the river turning westward again and decided it was time for a scan of the water. It was in these turns that they were most likely to come upon a fishing boat strayed into the channel. He turned on the night-vision device and lifted it to where he could view the three-inch screen. Even with the moon behind a cloud, the device turned the scene into daylight. He swept from right to left. No fishing boats. That was good. Then a movement in the darkness caught his eye, and he swung the device around to his left, looking backward almost directly down the side of the string of barges. Off in the distance he could see the lights of the Interstate 57 highway bridge where it crossed the Mississippi River at Cairo, Illinois. While the bridge was a number of miles downstream from the *Missy M,* the twisting of the river now put the bridge just north of due east from their position. The bridge appeared to be moving up and down! That was weird. Then the lights blinked out as the suspension span twisted, broke, and fell into the river.

"Jimmy! Did you see that?" Boyd shouted into his radio microphone.

"No. What?"

"The highway bridge off to the east! It just collapsed into the river!"

"You're seeing things, man. Couldn't happen."

"Jimmy! I know what I saw. It just fell into the river. I'm not kidding! We gotta report it."

"Yeah, right. Like they're going to believe it unless we were under it when it fell!" Jimmy called back. "Forget it. You're seeing things. You've been reading your Bible again, right?"

"Well, yeah. But I'm not imagining things. I really saw it fall."

"Well, it's downstream and there's nothing we can do, so we'll let it go. Just keep watching for fishing boats."

Boyd looked again through the darkness, first with binoculars, then with his night vision device. He could make out the lights on the approaches to both sides of the span, but the center was dark. He watched, transfixed, as one set of westbound headlights dropped off into the abyss, then a second, and a third. A fourth stopped just short of the blackness. Then trees blocked Boyd's view.

Trembling, he sat down in his deck chair. What had he just seen? Did he really see what he thought he had seen? *There were people in those cars! No, it couldn't be.* Suddenly he wasn't so sure.

~ ~ ~

Six miles upstream from the *Missy M*, Missouri County, Missouri, deputy sheriff Alicia Thornton was taking her nightly patrol along the levee that formed the human-made western boundary of the mighty river. It was one of those invigorating autumn evenings, with the temperature in the upper 50s and a light breeze under mostly moonlit skies. Driving the two-lane road atop the levee was a perfect time to get lost in your thoughts and commune with your Creator, she always thought. That's why she enjoyed this shift and this place.

To the untrained eye, the levee was nothing spectacular. If you looked closely as you approached you could see how, many years ago, the U.S. Army Corps of Engineers had labored mightily to contain the mighty river and prevent it from flowing out of its banks. To do so they'd used large cranes pulling digging scoops to lift dirt toward the river and raise the embankment several feet above the water. That created a low spot on the landward side of the levee that had been turned into several small lakes that were kept stocked with prizewinning fish. Tonight she could see the lights of a number of fishing boats shining and winking across the nearest lake.

Every few miles access to the levee was gained by a network of roads. It was mostly men and women going fishing who drove their beat-up pickups along the roads to the ponds or the river itself. Young lovers used the roads too, because they were unlit and provided unlimited access to views of moonlight on the water.

Alicia stopped at a point midway along her patrol route and turned off the ignition. The only radio sounds came from the speaker/microphone attached to the left epaulet of her uniform shirt. She stepped out of the patrol car and inhaled the autumn air deeply into her lungs. It smelled of leaves and water and a hint of bonfire. A few yards downstream she saw a small pier reaching out to an automatic device for measuring the depth and speed of the river. There had been some vandalism in recent months, so it was her duty to check it each night. She took advantage of the night to walk the last hundred yards and give the apparatus a quick once-over with her flashlight. Everything was OK.

"Base, Bravo Twenty-one," she said after keying the microphone on her shoulder.

"Bravo Twenty-one, go ahead," the dispatcher replied.

"Base, Bravo Twenty-one. The monitor is OK. I'm heading back north."

"Roger, Bravo Twenty-one."

Alicia picked up her pace as she strode through the darkness toward her car. The moon was bright enough tonight that she did not need to use her flashlight for walking. In the distance she could see the running lights of towboats and their barges as they plied the waters of the mighty Mississippi. If she stopped and just stood on the levee, she could actually feel the power of all the water flowing past. It was an awesome yet peaceful feeling to be in the presence of such power.

Then she stumbled as if an unseen hand had pushed her. She recovered, then found herself fighting just to stay upright. Thirty yards away her car bobbed up and down as if it were dancing. In about 30 seconds it all ended as suddenly as it had begun. Alicia's legs felt as if they were made of rubber, but adrenaline surged through her veins as she stumbled back to her car and turned the ignition. Already the Sheriff's Department's main radio channel was crowded with reports of an earthquake.

Alicia tried several times to break in and report that everything appeared OK where she was, but she couldn't get a break. Multiple units talking over each other made it hard for anyone to get through. Then she thought to go out and again walk the path she had just taken, this time with her flashlight turned on. Almost immediately she found a six-inch-wide crack in the levee, with a stream of water flowing through four feet below her feet. She found a second crack about 10 yards farther on, and a third an equal distance beyond the second.

Dashing back to her car, Alicia joined the jumble of radio traffic trying to report to the dispatcher. Finally she got a response.

"Bravo Twenty-one, go ahead," the dispatcher replied.

"Base, Bravo Twenty-one. I've found at least three cracks in the levee. Each one is about six inches wide, with visible water flow going through it. I think we need to sound a flood alert, because it looks as though we could have a serious problem here. Please notify the Corps of Engineers."

"Roger, Bravo Twenty-one."

Alicia spun her car around so that she could head back to the road that would return her to the farm fields. Along the way she bumped over two more cracks. At both she stepped out of the car to straddle each one and shine a spotlight down into the abyss. Both times the light caught the reflection of flowing water. From the last one she saw a stream of muddy water spewing out of the landward side of the levee and into the pond below. She was reaching for her radio microphone to deliver a new report when she heard the dispatcher announce for all units to begin sounding a flood warning, because the levee was in danger of breaking.

Once she was off the levee, Alicia touched the switches for the lights and siren and sped toward the nearest farmhouse two miles away. Thankfully, after the floods of years past, the only people allowed to live in these low-lying areas were the farmers themselves, and mostly they'd built their houses on the occasional high spots that sometimes were tall enough to stand above floodwaters. Gravel flew as she braked in the driveway and changed from siren to loudspeaker.

"This is the Sheriff's Department! Flood warning! This is not a drill. Repeat: Flood warning! This is not a drill. The river levee is in danger of breaking. Evacuate to higher ground immediately. Repeat: Evacuate immediately to higher ground."

She waited a moment for a light to appear in an upstairs window. A pajama-clad figure opened a window, leaned out, and waved. The message had been delivered. Alicia spun her car around and raced off toward the next farmhouse a mile and a half down the road. The farmers in this area all knew the evacuation drill. Given enough warning, the farmers, their families, and hired hands would soon be assembling at the designated evacuation center, a high school in the nearby town that had always been above past flood crests.

As she topped one small rise, Alicia saw flashing lights in the distance. The local volunteer fire department had been alerted and was already helping to spread the evacuation warning.

CHAPTER NINE

On the bow of the first barge being pushed by the *Missy M*, Boyd Stephens turned back toward his folding chair and thought about what he had just seen. Maybe he had imagined it, he tried to convince himself. No, it was just too real. Whatever, he would have to wait and find out. So he swept the waters ahead with his night-vision device. No fishermen. No obvious floating logs. No reason to radio the pilothouse. But the water did look a little strange. The wavelets kicked up by the breeze sweeping across the water had an odd appearance. Instead of being regular and moving with ease, it looked as if each was covered with a layer of tiny wavelets. It reminded Boyd of the time in high school physics class that the teacher had put a large, shallow bowl of gelatin dessert on a vibrator and the class had measured the number of waves that formed at different speed settings. The effect on the water lasted for a few seconds, then disappeared. The moon again slid from behind a cloud to set the wave caps aglow, and the breeze remained steady. Together they reassured Boyd that maybe, just maybe, he'd been dreaming. He sat down and tried to resume reading his Bible, but his concentration was gone.

The *Missy M* slowly turned the bend in the river and assumed a northwesterly course. Such twists were common on the Mississippi River. Indeed, until channeled by decades of work by the U.S. Army Corps of Engineers, the river twisted and turned far more along its lengthy trek to the Gulf of Mexico than it did now. Often after eroding the narrow neck of land separating two turns and forming a new channel, it built up a wall of sediment that turned the former channel into a lake now severed from the river. As a kid, Boyd remembered reading a story about boys a hundred years before who had floated several miles downstream from their house on a raft to reach the nearest town. Then, to get back home, they floated downstream again for a short distance before crossing a narrow portion of land where two turns of the river reached their closest point. After hauling their raft across, they would again float downstream for a short way before repeating the process. Two or three crossings would take them downstream to the very house they had floated away from earlier.

Somewhere in the distance to the west over the levee Boyd could see the twinkling lights of a police car. He wondered where the driver was going, driving so fast. Coming around the bend about six miles ahead, he could make out the running lights of a southbound barge tow much like the one he was riding. In 10 minutes or so they would pass almost silently in the darkness. As he prayed, Boyd watched the lights as they slowly grew closer. But after a few seconds they made a turn to the west and disappeared. "Hey, Jimmy!" Boyd keyed his radio microphone to call the skipper on duty in the pilothouse.

"What's up, Boyd?"

"You're going to think I'm seeing things again. Just tell me, that southbound tow a few miles ahead of us—where is it now?"

There was a moment of silence during which Boyd moved to a position where he could see the pilothouse. Silhouetted against the sky above it was the rotating bar of the radar antenna. Underneath in the pilothouse Boyd could see the top of the skipper's head as he bent over the radar screen.

"Uh, Boyd. You're not gonna' believe this, but it was there a minute ago an' it's . . . well, it ain't there now."

"I believe it. It was headed toward us; then it went west."

"You said it went west?"

"That's right, Jimmy. It went west."

"There's nothing west but levee and farmland." Jimmy paused to study his radar scope again. "Boyd! The levee's broken!"

Boyd felt the barge beneath his feet begin to slow before he heard the scream of the *Missy M*'s diesel engines shifting into reverse at full emergency power. Thousands of tons of steel and coal shuddered as the relatively tiny towboat at their rear tried to pull them instead of push. As much as he wanted to run to the rear and jump aboard the towboat, Boyd knew that would be a very dangerous thing to do right now because the cables holding the barges and towboat together were being overstretched by the differences between forward inertia and the backward-straining diesels. If one of those cables broke it would lash about like a mighty knife, killing whatever deckhand was unlucky enough to be close. He'd once seen the results of a cable break. The whipping cable had cut through the steel sidewalls of a deckhouse like a razor through paper. Three crewmen eating their dinner inside had been killed instantly. So Boyd knew that his only safe place was right where he stood at the furthest forward part of the raft of barges. He held his position and watched over the next five minutes as the behemoth slowed to a crawl, then began backing up. Now, as the *Missy M* began to move backward, he thought he could see the levee break in the moonlight.

Though the engines were in full reverse power they had only a temporary effect on the *Missy M*'s relative motion because of the volume of water flowing out through the levee break. The more water that flowed out, the more of the levee that was eaten away and the greater the volume of water escaping onto the low-lying farmland. A monstrous lake was being created, growing a dozen acres each second. As the outflow continued, the water level upstream of the break soon dropped to below the level downstream. Because water flows downhill, the downstream portion of the Mississippi River above the upstream altitude reversed course and began flowing upstream.

As the now-northbound current grew in speed the skipper of the *Missy M* soon realized that all his reverse power was having less and less effect, and after 20 minutes or so it was having no effect at all. With engines roaring in full reverse power it stood still in the river, then slowly began moving upstream. If the crew was going to prevent suffering the same fate as the other barges with their towboat, they had to free themselves of their load and devote all their power to escaping. The same engine power that could move barges at up to 10 knots could move the boat by itself at twice that speed.

"Get back aboard!" the awakened captain of the *Missy M* ordered Boyd over the radio. "We need to cut the barges free!"

Boyd ran with every bit of strength toward the squared-off foredeck of the *Missy M* and dove past the vertical frames that actually pushed against the barges. Somehow he landed on his feet and did not stop until he was almost halfway down the length of the 65-foot-long boat. That was when he ran into a crewmate dashing forward to carry out the skipper's dangerous order. They all felt through the deck as much as heard the change in engine sound as Jimmy brought the throttles to idle to relieve the tension on the cables. Sweating crewmen worked quickly to release the winches and loosen the turnbuckles binding the barges to the *Missy M*. A space began opening between the towboat and barges. Then cable ends slipped into the water, and the towboat was freed from her gargantuan cargo. As quickly as the last cable fell free, the skipper spun the wheel and pushed the throttles. The *Missy M* turned about and began a downstream race for survival. Within moments the *Missy M*'s crew lost sight of their barges, and minutes later they too took an uncharted turn toward the west into what should have been dry farmland. Then they disappeared from the ship's radar.

The *Missy M* made good time turning east around the next bend of the river. One more turn would direct them southward toward Cairo, Illinois, and the I-57 bridge. Jimmy realized that he still had the night vision device hanging around his neck. He switched it on and scanned the riverbank. The water had obviously dropped several feet since they'd passed less than an hour before. Now, instead of being able to see lights over the levee, the only lights visible were stars. "Collision alert! Collision alert!" the captain called over the deck loudspeakers.

No other towboats were visible. "What could we possibly run into out here?" Jimmy called to a crewmate as he wedged himself against the frame of the ladder leading to the pilothouse, a place he thought he might survive a collision. Then Jimmy turned the boat toward the bank, slowed the engines, and let the towboat run softly aground. The roar of the diesel engines slowed to a low rumble as the flat-bottomed boat settled against the river bottom. Within moments it began tilting sternward as the river continued falling away from beneath it.

Jimmy came down the ladder to check on his crew. "Why'd you do that, Jimmy?" one asked. "What's going on?"

"We were running out of river. There's a break in the levee a few miles upstream, and all the water's spilling out onto the farmland instead of helping us float. So I'd rather put it someplace where it wouldn't be damaged than take a greater risk farther out," he said.

Two hours later the first light of dawn crept over the eastern horizon to reveal the *Missy M* resting on the muddy bottom, completely out of the water. As the light grew, the crewmen could see the partly buried accumulation of two centuries of navigation lining what had been the bottom of the river. Here and there fish splashed in the low spots that had not drained, and hundreds of other fish of various description lay dead or dying in the mud. In the center of the river a few hundred yards away a half-mile-wide channel still flowed.

"Prob'ly 'cause that part's too low to flow the other direction," Jimmy surmised to a crewman who had joined him to sit and pass the time as they waited for the Coast Guard to come and pick them up. "We might as well be calm and hunker down for a few days, 'cause we're not goin' nowhere and the Coast Guard's so busy doing rescue work out to the west that they can't get to us for a while."

"Anybody want fried fish for breakfast?" the cook suggested.

"Now, Cookie! All these years you've been aboard 'n you don' know better'n that?" a crewman shot back. "I'll eat fried fish on a Sunday afternoon at a church fish fry, but not fer breakfast."

"Well, I was jus' eyein' that big catfish down there an' thinkin' I could snare it with a boat hook. It's a big 'un, an' I thought it'd make some great fillets."

"If we're gonna have to wait for the Coast Guard to come 'n get us, we might as well have some fun," Jimmy observed. "Get a boat hook, Cookie. If you can get us a fish while it's still fresh, we'll eat it."

~ ~ ~

A few miles away in Cairo, Illinois, Tyrone Adams, manager of the city's water and wastewater system, was just sitting down to breakfast at a local coffee shop as the sun peeked over the eastern horizon. "Mornin', Ellen," he greeted the server, who slid a steaming mug of coffee under his nose. Two cubes of sugar and a drop of cream. It was a morning routine practiced enough times that he didn't even have to give his order. She saw him arrive and knew automatically what to serve.

"What do you think of what's happenin' out on the river?" Ellen inquired.

"I don't know what you're talkin' about," Tyrone answered.

"There was another earthquake last night over on the New Madrid Fault. Registered 6 point something on the Ritter scale, or whatever they call it. Anyway, it broke the levee over by Texas Bend. Tore a giant hole in it. What with the break and the river washing more of it away, there's a break about two or three miles wide. From what I hear, Texas Bend is clear under water this mornin'."

Tyrone normally sat in the booth farthest from the blaring TV mounted up on the wall in one corner of the restaurant. But after hearing Ellen's report, he picked up his coffee mug and moved to the empty table nearest the TV.

"Mornin', Terry," he called to another regular morning customer. Terry returned the greeting and invited him to come to that table where he could hear better. "Sounds really bad over there. Judgin' by where we're located, looks like we'll be in the middle of the rescue effort, don't you think?"

Terry wasn't kidding. Cairo, Illinois, was located on a narrow neck of land bordered on the east by the Ohio River and the Mississippi on the west. Interstate 57 crossed just north of the city, just above the town of Cairo Junction. U.S. Highway 51 ran north-south through Cairo, then turned east on the south side of town, where it crossed the Ohio River into Kentucky. Where Highway 51 turned east, U.S. Highway 60 ran south until it crossed the Mississippi River into Missouri. Any disaster relief effort staged from the east would come through the area because those were the primary river crossings for 50 miles either north or south. Local motels would be packed. Restaurants would be busy around the clock. Sales at area stores would be brisk.

CNN came back from a commercial break, and the anchor in New York began detailing the fragmented reports from the area. Communications to the towns of Texas City and Charleston, located just south of the levee break, had been cut off. Survey aircraft had just been launched to look over the damage, and no reports had been released to the news media.

"On the phone we have, uh, Charles Siefert, a long-haul trucker who's calling us from, uh, Mr. Siefert, just where are you calling us from?" the anchor said.

"I'm on Interstate 57 where it crosses U.S. Highway 60. I'm on my cell phone."

"Mr. Siefert," the anchor continued. "What town is that near? Can you give our viewers some sort of reference?"

"Well, uh, my GPS unit says I'm about two miles east of the town of Charleston, Missouri."

"Can you see the floodwaters from where you are?"

"You bet I can. Can't see nuthin' but floodwaters. I'm parked on an overpass over Highway 60. The highway down below is completely covered by water. I can see just the tops of the sign-posts above the water. There're cars down there completely under water. From where I am there are two, maybe three cars with people sitting or standing on top of them."

"Mr. Siefert, how far does the flooding extend?"

"As far as the eye can see. I can see telephone poles and buildings standing up through the water, but there's water as far as I can see. It's like I'm in the middle of this really big lake."

"Are you in any danger?"

"Uh, no, I'm not in any danger right now. But there's no way I'm driving out of here, because just off this overpass the road's back under water. I mean, coming up here onto the overpass I was driving in water at least a foot deep in places, and it's just gotten worse in the couple hours I've been stopped. It's like I'm on an island in the middle of the ocean, only this is supposed to be the flat farmland of Missouri!"

Tyrone looked at the growing cluster of people around him and realized that this was a totally new situation. Fortunately, the city of Cairo, Illinois, got its water out of the Ohio River on the east side of town. If the Mississippi River went down, they wouldn't be affected. Or would they? Something about the question troubled him as Ellen slid a familiar plate of scrambled eggs, bacon, toast with jam, and orange juice in front of him. Intuition told him that he would be having a much longer and busier day than usual. He ate and departed with such haste that he forgot to leave his usual tip. *He'll get it next time,* Ellen thought to herself. *He always does.*

Nine minutes later Tyrone arrived at the city's water purification plant on the Ohio River side of the city. Instead of entering by the front door and going to his office, he walked around the plant and out onto the pier that reached 200 yards into the river. At the end of the pier a trio of large motors stood on their driveshafts above pipes two feet in diameter that extended 20 feet down into the murky waters to pumps that pulled the precious liquid upward and into the purification plant on shore.

Normally Tyrone required only three or four steps onto the pier before he was above water. This morning he counted 16 steps. The level in the Ohio River was dropping too.

Tyrone walked to the end of the pier and listened to the hum of the motors as they labored. They were operating normally. He looked over the railing at the water below. This close to the shore the current was more gentle than out in the deeper channel, and the water flowing past these pipes made a wake that was barely visible. Normally the gentle current made only a small wake in the water as it flowed past the intake pipes. This morning it was a distinct V shape with a lead wave at least two inches high. The river was running much faster than normal.

What really caught Tyrone's attention was the amount of wet pipe standing above the water. The wetness told him that only a short time before, the water had stood more than four feet above its present level. As he watched, the level dropped another half inch. A depth marker mounted against one of the pier pilings measured the depth of the water to the top of the pump intakes. Normal depth was somewhere around 22 feet, plus or minus one or two, depending on the season and the amount of rainfall upstream. The numeral 18 was now above water with the number 17 just becoming visible through the water. How much lower could the water level drop before the pumps started pulling air, losing their prime, and failing to supply water to the city of Cairo, Illinois? To answer that question, Tyrone would have to figure out how much farther the Ohio River would fall. Hopefully the Army Corps of Engineers would have that answer.

In his office Tyrone spun his old-fashioned Rolodex card file to find the number to dial to reach the Corps of Engineers office in Paducah, Kentucky. It rang and rang and rang. After about 20 rings he hung up, then looked at the clock on the wall: 7:40.

"Bureaucrats!" he muttered. "It must be nice working for the federal government, 'cause they don't start work till 8:00!"

A man wearing a matching uniform shirt with the name Sam embroidered above the left breast pocket stood in Tyrone's doorway. "River's down to the 16-foot marker. It looks like the rate of drop has been slowing a bit. About the only thing going up is the current. One to two is normal. We're at six knots and rising."

"OK, Sam. What's your estimate of what's happening?"

Sam pulled up a chair, turned it around, and straddled it in front of Tyrone's desk so that he could prop his arms on the back. "The way I figure it, it looks like most of the flow in the Mississippi's been cut off by this levee break over in Missouri. We've got all this water backed up in the Ohio River that normally runs real slow because it doesn't have all that far to fall. Now, take away 20, maybe 30 feet of depth in the Mississippi— we've got all this water backed up in the Ohio that's rushing downhill to fill that void. It's just a question of time till the Ohio's a rushing stream. If it hasn't happened already, in a day or two you'll not be able to run anything upstream slower than a speedboat anywhere downstream of, oh, Evansville."

Tyrone let out a whistle. "Evansville? You really mean it?"

Sam nodded. "Question is, how low will it go here?"

"Yeah, that's the question I'm trying to answer, but nobody goes to work at the Corps of Engineers until 8:00," Tyrone retorted. "I'll make you a bet. This has never happened before, and their computer models won't do 'em a bit of good 'cause they're not programmed for an event like this.

"Tell you what I want you to do. Get our engineer on the phone and ask him what we have to do to keep water flowing here in Cairo if the river goes down below the level of our pumps. We could be in a situation in which every hour counts, and we're lookin' at having to do some engineering on the fly to keep the water flowing. So get on it."

"Yes, sir," Sam answered, pushing himself out of the chair.

CHAPTER TEN

Good morning, Hope. I hope I'm not calling too early," the male voice on the phone greeted her cheerfully. The voice sounded familiar, but her early-morning mind couldn't place it.

"Who is this?" Hope demanded.

"Oh. I'm sorry. This is Peter Leventhal, MBS News. I'm the producer from New York you worked with a couple months ago on the Heaven's Portal story. I hope you've got your travel bag packed."

"Why do you ask?"

"Well, the network brass have decided to buy out your contract with channel 3—at a nice premium, I might add—because we need a field reporter on this Mississippi River disaster story that's breaking. My gut feeling is that this story's going to be really, really big, so we're bringing in everybody we can put on it. You're a pro and I've worked with you, so that's why I wanted you. How soon can you be ready to travel?"

"What Mississippi River story?"

"You haven't heard?"

"No, I guess not. I just got my husband and daughter out the door to work and school. Should I turn on my TV?"

Peter laughed. "Like right away. MBS, of course. But any of the news channels will do. It's about the only thing they're talking about. Listen, I want to get people on the ground in the area as soon as we possibly can. You do what you have to do. Just call me back in 30 or 40 minutes and tell me when you can be ready to fly. I'll give you more instructions then. You got that?"

Hope jotted down the number that Peter gave her, and

hung up. The news was stunning. First of all, she'd been promoted to the network. It meant a big pay raise. It also meant a
lot of time on the road away from home. It was the sort of career move she'd dreamed about for years. And Peter wanted an
answer in the next half hour! "Mark, you'll never believe who
just called me," Hope exclaimed. Her husband sat in traffic
speaking into his cell phone. "Peter Leventhal, the MBS News
producer from the network that I worked with on the Heaven's
Portal story. They're picking up my contract, and they want
me to tell them in the next half hour when I can leave to work
on a really big story."

Mark didn't miss a beat. "This is the break you've been dreaming of, sweetheart. Go for it!" He wheeled around a corner a little
too fast, then slowed down. "By the way, what's the story?"

"I don't know. Something about the Mississippi River. He just
said it's really, really big. It's on all the news channels, and they
need everybody they can get to work it."

"Must be the levee break."

"Levee break? Where? How bad?"

"Bad! It's somewhere up around Cairo, Illinois. I just heard
about it on the radio. They're saying it's flooding a huge area in
southern Missouri. How long will they need you?"

"I don't know. Peter didn't say. Maybe I can be home in a
few days."

He pulled into his parking place in the parking garage.
Having had a few moments to digest her news, he didn't feel as
enthusiastic. "Hon, today is Thursday, and Saturday is our wedding anniversary. I was looking forward to taking you out to dinner and a movie."

Even as she talked, Hope pulled open a dresser drawer and
picked up underwear to pack. "This is a career move, Mark. I'm
not excited about leaving you and Jennifer, especially on such
short notice. But if I pass it up, I don't know if I'll ever get the
chance again." She tossed several pair of socks on the bed, then
went to their walk-in closet to choose shoes. "Honey, I tell you
the truth, our anniversary had slipped my mind. I'm sorry. I
don't like missing that. But . . ."

"Who's going to take care of Jennifer?" he asked. He could
visualize her puzzled shrug.

"Well, I guess you'll get to be Mr. Mom for a while. You can cook and take her to school and all that. You'll be fine."

His voice was plaintive. "I'll miss you."

She sank down on the bed. Why were there no clear-cut decisions in life?

"I'll miss you, too. I promise to call every day, OK?"

Hope dialed Peter's number. He answered on the second ring. "Peter, this is Hope. Where am I going?"

"Here's the scoop. We're going to be setting up operations at the airport in Cairo, Illinois. There's good highway and rail connections into the place, and we've chartered three helicopters to ferry our crews around. We've got a field studio going in by road that'll be there in about 10 or 12 hours. Right now I've got a field crew on the ground with a portable satellite system. If you can get to Cramer Aviation out at Memphis Airport, there'll be a plane waiting to take you up there. You'll be the second correspondent there. We're paying a premium price to buy out a block of rooms at the Holiday Inn next to the airport. Now, about what to pack. This is your first time out, isn't it?"

"You're right. What conditions are we going into?"

"Pack for anything and everything. You'll need foul weather gear, mudders, hiking boots. Go comfortable. But remember, you're going to be on camera, so don't forget your makeup and hairbrush. How do you look with your hair down?" He laughed. "I don't think you'll be able to maintain your current hairstyle."

"Should I pack a suitcase or a backpack?" Hope queried next.

"Both. Bring the backpack with a sleeping bag and air mattress if you have them, because we never know when we'll have to camp out someplace in the middle of nowhere."

"OK," she said. "I've called my husband. Give me a couple hours to take care of some things here at home and pack. I'll be at the airport at, oh, say, 11:30."

"Can you make it in 90 minutes?" His fast, clipped words showed his stress. "We really need to get you up here and out in the field right away, so we can make deadline for the 5:00 broadcast. You'll probably be live on that one."

"I'll do the best I can."

Hope moved fast. She threw a half dozen different outfits into a suitcase and shoved a number of items off her makeup table into a carry-on case. In the garage she pulled together a number of camping items that she and Mark hadn't used since before Jennifer was born: A two-person tent. A sleeping bag and air mattress that she hoped did not leak. A small cookstove with a bottle of fuel, matches, small kettles, and utensils. *What a motley assortment of stuff!* she thought. Toiletries and other items. She blew the dust out of her old hiking boots and rubbed leather balm on them before stuffing them in the backpack.

Then, one last thing. Driving as fast as she dared, she went by her daughter's school and asked that she be allowed to tell her goodbye. Her mother heart didn't know if that was a good or a bad idea, but she couldn't stand the thought of Jennifer's discovering she had left—without a word.

Cramer Aviation was on the unfamiliar side of Memphis International Airport, so she carefully followed the signs. She introduced herself at the desk, and a minute later was directed to a pilot who was doing his final weather check. Ten minutes later they were stowing her luggage into a twin-engine turboprop Cessna that soon joined the lineup of mostly commercial airliners waiting for their turn on the main runway. She surveyed the luxurious interior of the plane and wondered if this was a portent of how she'd be traveling in the future. It was pretty nice.

From the air the Mississippi River looked quite normal until reaching Kentucky. It was there the water level began to appear abnormally low. As they approached Cairo, Illinois, the pilot swung westward to fly over the expanding flood zone and the levee break itself. Everywhere below was a scene of either devastation or a peaceful, expansive lake, depending on what was in your view at the time. Lines of utility poles marked the edges of submerged roads. Here and there the roof of a house or barn poked up through the waters. An area of turbulence indicated where the central current was flowing, and the river was cutting a new channel across the farmland.

On approach to the Cairo Airport the impact on the river downstream was dramatic. Several towboats, one with barges still attached, rested either partly or completely aground in what used to be navigable river channel. A stream one fourth the river's previous width twisted along the center of the riverbed.

The impact on the Ohio River was becoming obvious, too, as

those waters rushed downstream to fill the void left by the absence of water in the Mississippi River channel.

Hope's plane banked and turned onto a final approach, then bumped gently against the asphalt runway. The pilot taxied to the front of one of several hangars and shut down. The few people on the ramp seemed intent on going about their own business, so she headed for the flight operations building to inquire where MBS was setting up operations.

"They've taken over the big storage room," the receptionist answered politely, pointing the direction. Hope walked the few paces and saw a scene of utter chaos as a pair of technicians, surrounded by a mountain of travel cases and partly unpacked equipment, were trying to create order from utter confusion.

"You the MBS crew?" Hope inquired.

"What's it to you?" one of the men answered gruffly.

"Don't worry about him. He's grouchy 'cause of bein' up all night," another answered. "I'm Lee Brickman," he said, extending his hand to shake Hope's. "What can I do for you?"

Suddenly Hope had second thoughts about being on this job. The amount of equipment needing to be set up. The gruffness of a crew member. How would she get along? "Uh, I'm Hope Lancaster from channel 3 in Memphis. Peter . . ."

"You're Hope!" Lee exclaimed. "Good to meet you." He pumped her hand with extra vigor. "I'm so glad you're here. Peter's told us about you. Hey, don't worry about Grumpy over there. And if you forget my name, just call me Happy."

"Lee Brickman is Happy?" Hope questioned. "How'd that come about?"

"Oh, a few years ago there were seven of us working a big story, and we worked such long hours that we started calling ourselves the seven dwarfs. It just stuck. I'm Happy. JD is Grumpy. Kevin over there is Sleepy. I think three of the other four are on their way and will be here in the next few hours. Say, has Peter got you doing anything special until he gets here? No? Good, 'cause your wardrobe ain't right for a situation like we're in."

Hope looked down at her dry-clean-only blouse, designer skirt, and pumps with two-inch heels. Then she blushed slightly, realizing that she had neglected to change her clothes before leaving home. "You got any clothes with you that you don't mind getting dirty?" Lee asked.

"In my suitcase outside."

"Go change into some jeans, then come lend us a hand."

"Uh, how far is it over to the Holiday Inn?"

"Couple miles," Happy answered. "They've got a shuttle bus, and a couple of us have rental cars. You want to take mine? But I'll warn you, you won't be spending much time over there. Did you bring a sleeping bag?"

"Sure did."

"Leave it here. You may find it easier just to curl up in a dark corner—that is, if you have any time to sleep."

Hope found the women's restroom and changed into jeans and a cotton blouse. She donned a pair of thick hiking socks before pulling on her waterproof hiking boots. Lee and JD had unpacked two more cases by the time she returned, and a wall of monitors, video recorders, and editing controllers was growing against one end of the room.

"Pick a case and open it," JD growled. "We'll tell you what to do with it. No, not that one. It's just cables. That one." He pointed to one of the larger cases. The two twist-lock latches on each side turned stiffly, almost causing Hope to break a manicured fingernail. The lid of the box inverted and latched together with the lid of a matching case to form a work table. Hope barely had it assembled before JD dropped a notebook computer onto it and began hooking up power cables. "Editing controller," he declared. "Also where you'll get your e-mail, edit your copy, set up your graphics, etc., etc."

JD grumped at her again the next time she tried opening a case. "I hate these bimbo reporters they keep sending me out to work with," he grouched. "They come to us wearing six layers of makeup and their hair lookin' like they're heading for a beauty pageant. Not only that, their purty nails keep them from doing any real work."

"You see why we call him 'Grumpy.' Don't pay him any attention. He's the fastest and best video editor we've got. That's why he's here," Lee confided to her when JD was out of the room. "Just buy him supper tonight, and you'll get along with him OK. Oh, and if you see one of those big chocolate-chip cookies like you buy at the mall—that oughta sweeten him up. He loves 'em."

"Hope! You bring waterproof boots?" Peter Leventhal shouted from the doorway.

"Hey, Peter! Will these boots be enough? 'Cause I get the feeling I'll soon be needing chest waders to get through the bull that's piling up in here," Hope called across the mess that was beginning to resemble a production studio control room.

"Don't know. Just go with these guys. They're your crew right now." Peter smiled and thumbed over his shoulder to the trio behind him. "The network wants a report on the air operations aspect of the disaster effort. The Missouri Air National Guard set up helicopter operations over at Mississippi County Airport near Anniston. But the place is about to be flooded out. So they're picking up and relocating over to Sikeston. We've got a chopper being fueled up, and these guys will be ready to go by then. You had lunch?"

Hope looked at her watch and shook her head as the realization that it was well past her regular lunchtime sank in.

"OK. Grab a couple MREs from the supply kit over there and get out to the bird. Oh, and don't take a hairbrush. I want you to look like you're in the middle of a disaster."

"Is there a rule against looking good when the world's gone bonkers around you?" she shot back. Peter just grinned back and nodded as he walked away.

"OK! Somebody want to tell me what an MRE is and where to find a couple of 'em?" Hope yelled to the room.

"Meals Rejected by Ethiopians!" Grumpy yelled back. He took a few steps to a stack of boxes against one wall, pulled aside the flap of the top one, reached in, and tossed a brown-colored plastic bag her direction. "Catch! There's your lunch," he called to her. A second bag came flying almost before she'd caught the first. "There's your supper! Military Meals Ready to Eat. That's what MRE stands for. They're about as appealing as dirt, but when you're hungry and there's no steakhouse around, you can learn to eat them."

The label on the first said "Chicken Tetrazzini," or something similar. The last part of the print was smudged. The second was mac and cheese. The contents also included such things as a brownie, vegetables, and even instant coffee with a pouch of nondairy creamer. "Just read and follow label directions, and you'll be eating like a soldier," Grumpy said.

On the ramp 100 yards beyond them, the rotor of a six-seat Jet Ranger helicopter began to turn as a fuel truck pulled away. "That's our ride," called one of the crew, whom Hope judged to be the lead producer. "I'm Mike," he said as they boarded and strapped in. They were barely aboard when Mike punched the intercom and told the pilot they were ready to go. The helicopter lifted, skimming low over the ramp, then climbing and turning westward.

"We're going to have to stay low. Can't go any higher than about 5,000 feet today because of these rain clouds we've got moving in," the pilot announced. "I hope that's high enough for your aerial shots."

"Guess we'll just have to make do with what we can do," Mike called over the sound of the engine.

First, the helicopter flew southwest and circled where the two highway bridges leading into Cairo had collapsed into the Mississippi. A National Guard helicopter was loading up the last of the people who'd been stranded between the bridge collapse to the east and the flooding to the west. A roadblock of abandoned vehicles crowded the highway leading up to and onto what remained of the bridge.

The National Guard was gone by the time the crew arrived at Mississippi County Airport. But a quartet of local pilots was working to save what aircraft they could from the rising waters that now encroached the edges of the parking ramp. Planes had to taxi through a growing, deepening puddle to reach the runway. In time the runway would be cut off, so the pilots were racing the floods to get everything out that they could move.

One after another the four pilots would take off and fly 10 minutes northwest to the airport at Sikeston, Missouri. After parking the planes, they climbed aboard a six-seat plane flown by a fifth pilot who ferried them back to Mississippi County Airport to repeat the process. Because of the time it took to prepare each plane for flight, they averaged rescuing about six planes per hour. The pilots barely stopped to talk with Hope and the video crew documenting the scene. Only a handful of small, single-seat or two-seat planes remained. The wide puddle across the ramp to the runway had grown into a running stream dividing the paved areas of the airport. "Not a problem," one of the pilots yelled toward the camera with a wave before starting the engine of the little Piper Super Cub. He glanced toward the wind sock. It showed a stiffening breeze out of the north. Hope pulled her coat tighter as the pilot gunned the engine and aimed into the wind. Forget the runway. He was using the open space of the parking ramp for his takeoff roll. Hope held her breath as the wheels raced toward the encroaching edge of the water, then lifted with plenty of distance to clear.

"Great shot!" the cameraman exclaimed. "Boy! If this doesn't tell the story!"

"OK, all aboard. Let's get over to Sikeston and catch them landing the last few planes," the producer ordered. "Hope, I want you to come up with a description of this scene to record en route." They piled back aboard the helicopter, this time with Hope facing backward so the cameraman, pushed against the back wall and with his lens set as wide as it could go, could record the shot. With a mere two feet of space between them, Hope felt like the lens was right in front of her eyes.

The much faster Jet Ranger soon caught up with the little Super Cub. The cameraman slid open the side door, and the cold November wind, further chilled by their airspeed and the giant rotor spinning above them, swept through the cabin.

"In a desperate race against the rising floodwaters, most rescue workers are concentrating on saving people and, occasionally, livestock. Just as others who are working to protect their livelihoods, this group of dedicated pilots is scrambling to get the last of the airplanes out of Mississippi County Airport and to higher ground at Sikeston Airport some 10 minutes' flying time away." Hope kept her eyes on the lens as the cameraman turned away to zoom in on the little plane as it made its final approach to Sikeston Airport. The cameraman nodded to indicate it was a good take.

Peter looked up from a huddle as the team entered the flight operations building. "How'd it go?"

"It'll work," the producer reported. "Not exactly studio work, but it'll do."

"OK. You've got 20 minutes to wrap it up. Then we've got to cue it up for air. Brandon's here, and in one hour he's flying out to the site where he's doing the evening news live.

Hope looked around to take in the new and unfamiliar faces that had arrived while she was in the field. Among them was Brandon Campbell, the anchor viewers usually saw from a studio in New York City. Brandon was also executive producer, meaning he made the calls about what stories went on the air. It was a role he obviously enjoyed, and the network's ratings said the viewers thought he was doing a good job.

Brandon looked up, smiled when he saw Hope, and excused himself from the huddle. "So we finally get to meet. Say, that was some good work you did on Heaven's Portal. That's why I wanted you for this," he told her.

"Well, thank you, Brandon. It's a pleasure finally getting to meet you," Hope replied. "I'm looking forward to working with you."

Brandon looked at his watch. "Have you checked in over at the motel yet?"

Hope shook her head.

"Better take the chance to get checked in. Can you be back in, oh, 40 minutes for a walk-through? Then we're flying out to the broadcast site. I want you there with me to introduce your report."

"I've got a problem. I don't have a car."

Brandon reached into his pocket and handed her a set of keys. "It's the silver Impala parked out back."

Hope was back in 30 minutes. She barely walked in the door before Peter handed her a script and pointed her toward one of the helicopters 200 yards away on the aircraft parking ramp. "Got your mud shoes or boots? You're gonna need 'em. Take your makeup kit, too," he yelled after her.

She had her makeup bag with her, but looked down to eye her athletic shoes. Come what may, they'd just have to do.

CHAPTER E LEVEN

he helicopter, a civilian version of the U.S. Army's Blackhawk, lifted smoothly into the air and headed swiftly west toward the broadcast site. In eight minutes it was circling a clearing on the southwest side of the river where no trees lined the levee and a smaller helicopter was already parked. A few hundred yards away rested the *Missy M*, aimed shoreward but tilted down by the stern as it rested on the bottom. Already technicians were aboard finishing their setup of the equipment that would transmit directly to the temporary broadcast center a few miles away at the Cairo Airport.

Between the dry land of the levee and the *Missy M* lay the sloped river bottom that had not seen the sun in nearly a century. In places it was covered with pebbles smoothed by the current. In other places the mud was firming up as the water it held trickled downward in little rivulets toward what remained of the river's flow. Judging by the looks of their pants, the technicians who'd carried all their equipment to the towboat had sunk up to their knees more than once.

Hope zipped up her coat and pulled on her gloves, then checked to make sure her shoulder bag was secure before following Brandon and the site producer down the slope. Mud covered her shoes almost to her ankles by the time she reached the extension ladder propped on a large rock that enabled everyone to climb aboard safely.

Brandon and the site producer conferred to be sure all was ready to go on the air in a few minutes. Hope's report would come after the first commercial break. "When I introduce you, I'll turn to you, and you'll take it from there," Brandon instructed.

Now all there was to do was wait for the moment that the broadcast would begin. The butterflies in Hope's belly were threatening to fly down her arms and legs when, at last, a technician switched on the lights set up around the rear deck of the towboat. It was the exact feeling she'd had on her first day as a TV reporter fresh out of college.

"Two minutes to air!" the producer shouted.

Hope found where she had leaned her backpack against a bulkhead on the aft deck. "Where's the restroom?" she asked a crewman who was watching a few feet away.

"You mean the head?"

"The restroom. Whatever you call it on a ship."

The crewman nodded. "The head. Just in that door to your right." He pointed down the side deck.

Hope pulled hard to open the door against the stern-down angle of the ship and then pushed the opposite direction to keep it from slamming against her leg as she stepped over the high threshold. It felt odd standing on the sloping deck surveying her face in the small mirror. A few strokes with a brush did all she could with her hair. "I've got to get an easier style," she said impatiently, shoving the hairbrush back into her makeup kit and pulling out a compact to retouch her makeup.

Back on the aft deck of the *Missy M,* Hope stood to the side as Brandon welcomed their viewers and gave an overview of what had happened just a half day before and the impact of the rerouted Mississippi River on eastern Missouri. Then he introduced two reports detailing the economic and personal impacts of the disaster.

"We're coming to you tonight from the aft deck of the *Missy M,* an 80-foot Mississippi River towboat that—until the levee broke early this morning—was pushing a raft of 11 barges loaded with more than 30,000 tons of coal. They were headed for an electric generating plant north of St. Louis." Brandon spoke to the camera directly in front of him. "The captain and crew of the *Missy M* were able to cut away their barges, leaving them to the mercy of the river, while they used all their power to try to escape." A view from a circling helicopter showed viewers where the *Missy M* rested. "As you can see, they didn't make it very far

before they ran out of water and the captain decided to run it
aground in a controlled manner. His action prevented more serious damage to the boat and kept the crew from being washed out
onto the flooded fields of Missouri with their barges."

During the commercial break Hope did a sound-level check
on her wireless microphone and took her position a step away
from Brandon. Following the cue that he was back on the air, he
introduced her as the new member of the MBS News team.

"Thank you, Brandon. What we found this afternoon in the
flood zone was a heroic effort by a small group of pilots to save
the planes at their airport from the rising floodwaters," she said,
then the taped report began. Sixty-four seconds later her part of
the program was complete. She stepped away from Brandon and
found a place to sit and watch the rest of the broadcast.

A six-minute wrap-up of major news stories from around the
world was slotted in the last part of the program. Included was a
story of the Israeli Army's attack on the Palestinian refugee
camps in the Gaza Strip. Hundreds of Palestinians, both civilians
and militants, had been killed over the past several weeks, and
the surrounding Arab nations were threatening war if Israel
failed to stop the bloodshed and withdraw quickly.

It seemed to Hope that as quickly as it had begun, the broadcast was over and the technicians were packing their gear. In a
few minutes a small crane lowered their equipment cases over
the side of the *Missy M,* then crew members hefted it up the
slope to helicopters waiting atop the levee. Hope picked up two
of the smaller cases, then began looking for solid footing in the
deepening twilight.

Brandon had his cellular phone to his ear, Hope noticed as
she approached the Blackhawk. He continued talking until the
pilot signaled that he was ready to start the engines, a noise that
would surely drown any conversation.

"You did a good job," Brandon said with a brisk nod as he
buckled in beside Hope and pulled on his headphones. "New
York wants you to reedit your report. Do it over, only a bit
longer. Take more time to bring out the human-interest angle.
Oh, and have it ready for tomorrow's early-morning news."

Hope's mouth dropped open, and she shook her head in
disbelief.

"Yeah, your deadline is 5:00 a.m. local. They want you live on the air from our operations center at 6:06 sharp. You'll intro your piece, then do some ad lib Q and A afterward, along with giving any updates from here that have developed overnight."

Hope looked at him in disbelief. "You're saying that I have to reedit my report tonight, get some sleep, and then be on the air at 6:00 a.m.? You've got to be kidding!"

"Welcome to the network, girl," Brandon laughed. "It looks glamorous from the outside, but once you're 'in' you learn to grab sleep when you can, 'cause you're going a lot of places you'd never go on vacation and you're telling people about it at all hours of the day and night. Sometimes, when airtime rolls around, it's daytime where you're reporting from, and sometimes it's night. But wherever you are, you're working on New York deadline time."

Hope just nodded. *OK, kid,* she thought. *Welcome to the world of the big guys. You should have known it'd be tougher than small town stuff.*

When the chopper landed and they were at the OPS center, Hope made the happy discovery that the production crew had already received New York's request for the longer story and had a rough cut ready for her to review. She recorded several voice-overs that would be edited into the proper places. All she'd have to do the next morning was the live introduction and story exit—that is, if her eyes were open.

Tired as she was, she couldn't wait to call Mark and tell him about her day.

"They want you on the air for the early news? The show we sometimes watch while we're eating breakfast?" he asked in disbelief.

"That's right. Brandon tells me that I'll learn to look awake at any hour of the day or night, I'll be able to fall asleep on any airliner in the world, and I'll have my camera face ready whenever it's needed."

Mark had answered the kitchen phone, so now ran a glass of water while he talked. "So, you think you're going to like being a reporter for the network?"

Hope paused. "In truth, sweetheart, I don't know. I'm barely started. I figure I'll begin answering that question in a couple weeks. By then I should have a feel for how things are going to work out." She sighed. "How's Jennifer doing? Is it too late to talk to her?"

Hope couldn't see the worry lines crease his forehead. "She's been feeling a little sick today, so she's already in bed. Actually, after-school day care called, and I had to leave work and go pick her up."

"It was that *bad?*" Hope asked. "What's the problem? That stomach thing again?" The butterflies she'd felt a few hours ago fluttered back with reinforcements.

"Well, I don't know if it was *that* bad. You know how day care is. They don't want any contagious kid lying around there."

"So it *is* that stomach thing that was going around?" Hope suddenly felt sick herself. Not so much worried, as conflicted. Her first night away on her first big break, and her daughter was sick again. She trusted Mark, of course, but that wasn't the issue. Should she even consider expanding her career when she still had a 6-year-old? Tears filled her eyes. She was too tired even to reason it out.

"Hope . . . are you still there? Hope?"

"I'm sorry. I was just thinking. Give Jennifer a hug for me and tell her that I love her, OK?"

"Of course, sweetheart. When do you think you'll be home?"

"I don't know. Let's see, today's Thursday. If I were to guess—well, we could be here a week or more. I guess it all depends on how big this gets. I mean, we've got a couple hundred square miles over in Missouri that are either under water or about to be under water. There are barges filled with coal and grain and whatever else floating around and running into houses and knocking over power lines and all that. It's a really, really big mess."

"What are they going to do about it?" Mark felt glad to hear the reporter side of his wife click into gear. "Do you think they'll rebuild the levee or just let the river go where it's going to go?" He chuckled. "Your dad will be eager to know the inside scoop."

"Last I heard, the Army Corps of Engineers was looking at both options. Problem is, if they don't rebuild the levee—and quick—in a week or so there's going to be a major economic disaster because of all the cargo carried on barges that normally go up and down the Mississippi. But rebuilding that levee's a major project that'll take some time. They've got to find a lot of big construction equipment to do the job. Then they've got to get it there, and that's going to be harder than before because so many highways have been cut off by the flood. Mark, you'd have to see it to believe it. There's just no easy or quick way to get into the site."

Just then Mark heard a whimper from Jennifer's bedroom, then another. "Will I see some of this on the morning news?" he asked his wife.

"Oh, yes. And maybe you'll even see me!"

"Well, I've got to do a few things before going to bed, and you've got to get up early."

"Don't remind me. I'm exhausted. But listen, do keep an eye on Jennifer."

"I will, sweetheart. Of course." Even then his ears were turned to the murmuring coming from her room.

Hope sighed. "Look, I don't know what my morning's going to be like, but I'm going to want to know how Jennifer's doing. If I don't call you, call my cell phone before you go to work. Leave me a message if nothing else. OK?"

"OK. And don't worry about her. She'll be fine. I love you."

"I'll try not to worry. Love you too."

~ ~ ~

Montgomery "Monty" Watts was not prepared for the meeting he was about to walk into. For the past 16 years he and his top management team had kept the River Bend Electric Generating Plant operating at peak capacity. They'd solved a host of operational and maintenance problems. They'd been through shutdowns when equipment was installed to prevent even the smallest amount of coal fly ash or other pollutants from getting into the air. In contrast with his childhood when the smoke plume from plants like this one were visible from many miles downwind, today you might see a little steam.

Watts turned to his office window for one last opportunity to compose his thoughts. From the second floor of the plant's administrative wing he could look up at the high walls of the plant and barely see one of the three smokestacks towering above the back of the main building. To his far right was the railroad receiving center, where railcars loaded with coal were unloaded by uncoupling them from the train and, one at a time, clamping them into a giant vise that rolled them upside down and emptied them in 90 seconds flat. That was necessary for, at full operation, the plant's giant steam boilers burned one railcar load of coal every two and a half minutes. Letting the coal drain through the doors in the bottom of the railcars took upward of eight minutes per car. That was just too slow.

Railcars were lined up as far as he could see before the tracks turned and disappeared behind a line of trees. Still, he knew that the railroad delivered only about 40 percent of the coal his plant consumed. Straight out his windows he saw a line of coal barges being unloaded. The black rocks came spewing off the end of a high-volume conveyor onto ever-growing and ever-moving mountains. Day and night, rain or shine—in the best weather and the worst—at any given moment at least two barges were being unloaded.

The executives at Missouri Electric Cooperative, the company that owned River Bend, required that at any given time Watts keep a minimum of a seven-day supply of coal on hand or en route. Right now, between the two trains being unloaded, the barges at the pier, and the coal on the ground he had 8.2 days' supply. The Missy M was scheduled to arrive in another six to 12 hours with 11 barges of coal, but the towboat had been downriver from the levee break. Amid the flurry of phone calls today with utility managers and the coal companies they bought from, he'd learned that the Missy M was high and dry with her barges floating around somewhere above the fertile farmland of eastern Missouri. Making things even worse, the quake had damaged several rail trestles that crossed the river, so trains delivering coal from the same sources would be delayed up to four days as they were routed onto other tracks.

"Forget using trucks to bring in more coal," Watts muttered to himself. Electric generating plants burned so much coal that supplying them by truck would be like trying to fill a swimming pool by spitting into it. There just weren't enough trucks to do the job for his plant and all the others impacted by the quake.

Watts knew that coal-fired electric generating plants supplied

113

51 percent of the nation's electricity. But for Missouri Electric Cooperative that number was closer to 70 percent. The two nuclear plants the co-op bought from were already running at full capacity, and hydroelectric was at max too. Other power could be brought in on the nationwide electric power grid, but that could supply only so much power before other cities in other states began having their own supply problems. It was only a question of time until the coal ran out and cities such as St. Louis, just a few miles to the south, went dark.

The man took a deep breath and stepped through the conference room door. He scanned the faces of the people around the table. Their eyes revealed that they knew what was happening as well as he did, yet they were hopeful, looking to him for leadership—if not a solution.

Watts straightened his shoulders and gripped the edge of the wide conference room table. "I guess you'd have to be living in a cave not to know what happened last night a way down the river," he began, "or not to know what it's going to do to us and our customers."

The six faces around the table—his top plant managers—nodded silently.

"My biggest concern is for you and your families and how we will all survive if this goes on for an extended period," he said somberly. "Missouri Power is working on a way to stretch the coal supply. The objective is to keep homes lit and warm for as long as we can and to keep essential industries and services functioning. To do that we're asking our larger electric consumers to shut down immediately. That should reduce demand enough to buy us an extra two or three days before we experience any blackouts. If we have to, we'll go to rolling blackouts during the day, but we'll be at full demand at night, because people will be heating their houses."

Everybody knew what would happen when the power went off. Homes would grow cold. Unless they happened to use natural gas, they would be unable to cook. There would be no running water to drink, wash dishes, or flush toilets. Lamps and appliances would not work. Cars would soon stop running because there'd be no electricity to run the gas station pumps. These problems would be repeated all along the Mississippi

River and its tributaries. In short, life in the central part of the world's most industrialized nation would revert to a preindustrial state until the electricity was restored.

"How long will this go on?" someone asked quietly.

"It's a question of when the Army Corps of Engineers can plug the levee and get the water level back up. Their best guess right now is at least a month on the levee and another week after that before they can inspect the river and declare it safe for navigation." Watts took a deep breath. "So until then, the governor has declared a state of emergency and has asked the president to declare the eastern part of the state that'll be impacted by the power outages a disaster area."

Mark yawned and stretched before reaching over to turn off the clock radio beside the bed. As was his habit, he rolled back onto the bed to give his wife a hug and kiss—only she was not there. Her absence snapped him awake. Yes, for now he was "Mr. Mom," and needed to get Jennifer up and ready to go to day care. In that same moment he remembered that she'd been sick. *Well, at least she's slept through the night,* he thought. *She'll probably be fine this morning.*

He trod softly across the hallway to rouse her.

"Up and at 'em, Sunshine!" he called cheerily as he turned on the light.

Jennifer rolled over. Her fair face was flushed. "I don't feel good, Daddy. Where's Mommy?"

"You know where Mommy is, precious. Do you want to get up and watch her on the morning news?"

Mark reached down to help his sleepy daughter get out from under the bedcovers, and his arm brushed against hers. She felt abnormally warm. Immediately he placed a hand on her forehead. She was burning up. "You stay here, honey," he instructed before dashing to the bathroom for the digital thermometer. She sank back onto her pillow.

He returned and rested the probe inside her ear canal, pressing the button to take a reading. In a few seconds the display showed 104.2 degrees.

"Do you think you could swallow some medicine?" he asked.

"I feel like I gotta throw up," she groaned, then leaned over the side of her bed and began a series of dry heaves.

"So much for that idea," Mark said to himself. His mind was running in several different directions, but mostly he felt panic. "You stay here in bed. I'm going to pull on some clothes and take you to the emergency room."

Jumping into jeans and a T-shirt, Mark checked his wallet to be sure he had some cash and his medical insurance card. A short time later he was back in Jennifer's room scooping her from her bed, pulling the blanket along to wrap her against the cold outside. Walking only by the morning light coming through the windows, he fairly dashed to the garage where his Mercedes SUV stood waiting. Though traffic was light at this hour, it still seemed to take forever to arrive at the pediatric ER.

"I've got a 6-year-old here with a temperature above 104, and she can't hold down any medicine," he said urgently as he reached the reception desk.

"Just a moment." The receptionist picked up the telephone to relay his news to the triage nurse. A minute later father and daughter were escorted into an exam room where the nurse confirmed the fever. She punched a button on an intercom. "I'm bringing back a 6-year-old with a temp of 104.6," she declared, then paused. "Bed 16? We'll be right there."

She turned. "Follow me," she ordered. She led father carrying daughter through a set of double doors and down a hallway to another room. Almost immediately a pair of nurses appeared and with little small talk began taking vital signs. Alarmed, Jennifer started crying.

"It's OK, honey," Mark comforted. "Could you wait just an instant till I get her more comfortable?" he asked the nurse. He settled his daughter on his lap, gently holding her so the nurses could listen to her heart and lungs, get a blood pressure cuff on her arm, and in general do what they needed to do. The little girl lay with her head against her father's chest.

One of the nurses lay a gentle hand on Jennifer's head. "A doctor will be in here as soon as possible," she told Mark.

Jennifer gasped. "Daddy, I feel like I gotta throw up again."

The nurse took a kidney-shaped basin from a cabinet and held it under Jennifer's mouth as she dry-heaved. Tears ran down her cheeks, and she buried her face in Mark's chest.

"I need to start an IV," the nurse who seemed in charge told

Mark quietly. "We need to get a line open anyway, but she seems dehydrated. I want to get some fluid in her."

Mark nodded, stroking Jennifer's hair, then stood up to place her on the bed.

First the nurse placed a small anesthetic patch on Jennifer's arm on the spot where the needle would be inserted. "We'll put this on for a couple minutes, and that way you won't feel a thing," she said soothingly.

Three minutes later the patch came off, and Jennifer went into alarm mode as her arm was swabbed, then into panic at the first sight of the needle. Mark and one nurse held her firmly, trying to keep her arm from wiggling until the IV needle was inserted, the tube attached, and the drip started.

"See, that wasn't so bad, now was it?" the first nurse comforted.

"Take it out! Take it out!" Jennifer screamed as her arm was taped to a board to prevent her from moving too much.

The second nurse adjusted the speed of the drip coming from the IV bag. Both Mark's and Jennifer's eyes watched as it moved down the tube and disappeared into her arm. "That should help you feel better real soon," the nurse declared before turning and leaving.

"You just rest here for a little while, OK?" the other nurse said kindly. "The doctor will be here in a few minutes. Now you show Daddy what a big girl you are. Would you like a Popsicle?"

Jennifer nodded as tears streaked her cheeks.

"What flavor? Cherry? Grape? Orange?"

"Cherry," Jennifer said weakly.

The hustle of the past few minutes was replaced by the muted sounds of cushioned shoes passing beyond the curtained room. Mark felt his daughter's forehead. Was it already slightly cooler? Or was he imagining things? He couldn't tell.

"Do you know how much I love you?" he murmured.

"Lots and lots and lots," Jennifer answered weakly.

"And lots more than that," he emphasized as he bent over and gave her a hug. "We're gonna make you all better. I promise." He lifted his head from the embrace and studied his daughter's face. There was something about her expression, the sunken look of her shadowed eyes, and the paleness of her cheeks that frightened him.

A clerk arrived a few minutes later to get his insurance information and multiple signatures on the obligatory forms. A glance at Jennifer showed that she had fallen asleep. Mark unfolded the blanket lying at the foot of the bed and placed it over her. Curled up as she was, she looked so small. He sat down in the chair against the wall and closed his eyes. What time was it, anyway? He opened his eyes, studied the walls, and tried to figure out what was in the different boxes in the cupboard in the corner. He was restless. Where was the doctor? Was this place *that* busy?

He saw a TV remote lying on the floor, picked it up, and pushed "power." The TV was mounted high in one corner of the room, and an early-morning news program was giving details about world and national events, including the disaster on the Mississippi River. The program on which Hope would be reporting would not begin for another 45 minutes.

He'd just gotten involved in a report on the Middle East when a young physician clad in blue hospital scrubs hustled into the room, a medical chart in hand. "How are we feeling this morning, Jennifer?" she asked, awakening her.

She moaned. "Awful."

The doctor did a quick, efficient physical exam. Mark saw Jennifer wince as her fingers pressed against the area of her liver. She turned to Mark. "I'm going to order some blood tests. We'll see what they show and take it from there."

"What do you think's wrong with her?" Mark implored.

"I'm really not sure. That's why I'm ordering the tests. Hopefully they'll tell us what's going on. I'll come back when we have the results."

"Are you going to keep her here in the ER?" Mark asked to her retreating figure. But she had disappeared as quickly as she had come.

Looking at Jennifer's pale face made the apprehensive knot in Mark's stomach draw tighter. The arrival of a lab technician with a tray of needles and tubes didn't help him relax either, though the man worked as quickly as he could and managed to get blood on the first poke. Four vials of blood later he exited the room.

"How much more are they going to do to me?" Jennifer cried.

"That's all," Mark said hopefully, though without conviction. But in moments she was asleep again, and he settled back into the chair to face the indefinite wait ahead.

He adjusted the TV volume, loud enough to hear but not so loud that it would awaken Jennifer. The early show had a story about some fashion designer's new winter lineup. Then they interviewed a wide-eyed starlet about her new movie. The report included interviews with the producer and lead actors.

Thirty minutes passed. Forty-five. Mark's heart seemed lodged in his throat. He wished Hope were here with him. No. He was glad she was being spared the fear that seemed to cut off his breath. His mind wandered. He stood up, walked the three steps to the bed, and placed his hand on his daughter. He was still standing there when the doctor reappeared.

She too stood by the bed, her eyes on her new patient. With a worried look, Mark sat back down in the corner. Then the doctor pulled a rolling stool to where Mark sat so she could talk with him at close range. "Mr. Lancaster, I'm sorry for this wait. The word from the lab is that they're running another round of tests on the blood samples we sent up."

She took a breath, watching his face. "It appears from the first round that your daughter is suffering from a type of leukemia. The reason they're running further tests is to determine exactly what type of leukemia it is. But while we're waiting for those test results I want to go ahead and admit Jennifer so that we can start treatment right away."

The doctor's words were like an icy fist grabbing Mark's heart as it skipped a beat and leaped into his throat. "Leukemia?" he choked out. "That's deadly, isn't it?"

"Oh, no. Not always." Her voice was crisp and professional. Reassuring. We'll be able to answer that question better when this next round of test results are back from the lab. I've asked Dr. McCormick to take over Jennifer's care. Dr. McCormick is a pediatric oncologist—one of the best doctors in his field. He'll come see you after we've got Jennifer settled up on the unit."

It was too much to comprehend. Too much to remember. He had a hundred questions—but his mind was blank. Mark felt the strength drain from his legs as he sank back against the wall. The doctor stood, gave Jennifer's foot a little squeeze, and told her goodbye. Then, as quickly as she had arrived, she was gone to her next patient.

"What's loo . . . kee . . . ? What's that the doctor says I have?" Jennifer asked.

"Leukemia," Mark answered involuntarily. He felt as though another person was inhabiting his body and moving his vocal cords. His breath came in short, shallow gasps. "It's going to be OK, sweetheart," he told her. "Close your eyes and sleep again. I'll be here."

He watched as her eyes fluttered shut, opened, then shut again.

Head leaning against the wall, he felt the overpowering need to talk to Hope. His right hand reached to his belt, where he found the cell phone. He had no memory of clipping it there as he dressed, but thanked God that it was. He punched the speed dial for Hope's cell phone. Two rings later he got a recorded message saying the cellular customer he had dialed was not available. Did he want to leave a message? No. He punched the end call button.

Mark looked up at the TV. Hope was delivering her live report from the disaster scene, her voice narrating the pictures of devastation and the efforts of assembling relief workers confronting the situation. "This may not be the largest natural disaster in our country's history, but its economic impacts could turn it into the largest financial disaster in modern history," he heard her say. The picture changed to the anchor in New York.

New York. Yes! MBS News headquarters! If only he had the phone number!

What to do next? His mind felt muddled. Get the news headquarters. Just then a nurse stepped in to check the flow of the IV. She made a small adjustment, turned to say something to Mark, and opened her eyes wide.

"Sir! You cannot use that cell phone in here."

"I can't?" He was puzzled. "I just did."

"There's a sign on the wall. Right there," she said impatiently. "A cell phone interferes with our cardiac monitors. You'll have to go outside of the building."

Mark felt like a scolded child. "But I can't. I can't leave my daughter. And I need to get hold of my wife."

For the first time the woman seemed to actually look at him. "Where *is* your wife?"

He pointed to the TV. "Up there. Right before you came in, she was up there." With a shake of her head, the nurse left the room.

Now he didn't know what to do. He stood up, paced back and forth alongside the bed. Jennifer slept soundly. Maybe they'd put something in the IV to relax her. He didn't know. He didn't know much about hospitals, about being sick. And he didn't know what to do. He needed his wife.

He stopped pacing, burying his head in his hands. "Lord, God," he prayed, "I've got to reach Hope. Please keep Jennifer asleep till I get back. Don't let her wake up and be afraid." Eyes shut, he swayed slightly and caught himself with one hand on the edge of the narrow bed. Jennifer didn't stir. So he tiptoed from the room, stopping by the nurses' station to tell someone he was going outside. The man in charge promised to keep his ear turned to Jennifer's room.

At a trot Mark hurried through the ER waiting room and out into the morning. He sank down on a bench and called directory assistance. In less than a minute he was connected with the MBS headquarters.

"This is Mark Lancaster, husband of Hope Lancaster. Can you get a message to her for me? I've got a family emergency and need to talk to her right away." His heart pounded in his temples. The urgency he heard in his own voice told Mark just how close he was to absolute panic.

A moment later a second voice came on the line, and Mark repeated his request, adding that he was calling from the ER. "I'll relay it to the production center immediately, but I'm not sure how fast they can get it to Hope," the man answered sympathetically, giving Mark a direct-dial number to call the next time.

"Bless you! Thank you!" Mark punched off the phone and hurried back inside. The whole exchange had taken less than two minutes.

Back in the hospital Mark stopped by the men's room. He splashed cold water on his face, then scrubbed it dry with a paper towel. His mouth felt so dry he could hardly swallow, so he ran water into his cupped hands, bent down, and drank it. He had to get back to his daughter. The ER receptionist buzzed open the door to the examining area, and Mark walked through.

Jennifer was still asleep. He stood beside her a moment to make certain she was actually breathing, then drew a deep breath himself. He had to think. Exhaustion ran through him from head to foot. After another lingering look at his daughter, he touched her hand with one finger and again quietly eased out of the room.

Again in the ER lobby, he asked directions to the coffee shop. There he bought a large soft drink and a package of peanuts. He pulled up a long swallow of the cold, tingling soda, then refilled the paper cup. A minute later he sank down in the chair by his daughter's bed.

~ ~ ~

Though Hope was standing on the eastern bank of the Mississippi River while delivering her report, she and the crew were in communication with the production center at Cairo Airport, which, in turn, communicated with the New York office via satellite. A producer caught her attention through her earphone and delivered the relayed message. "Your husband called New York and asked us to tell you that your daughter's sick and in the hospital. He wants you to get home as soon as possible."

Hope's camera face crumbled. Her first instinct was to rip the earpiece from her ear, toss off the microphone, and run. But a look around delayed acting on the impulse. Her feet stood on a piece of plywood placed on the ground under a tent. The tent was on the eastern levee of the Mississippi River near Cairo, Illinois. They'd used four-wheel-drive SUVs to reach this spot, and there was no quick escape. At least a half hour would pass before she could get back to the production center. Plus, she was scheduled to do three more live reports over the next 90 minutes. Panic shivered through her body. *What to do next? What to do? What was it, anyway? What was wrong with Jennifer?*

"Uh, Hope," the producer back at the airport called over the intercom channel. "I'm sending Andy out to cover for you. He'll be there in about, oh, 40, maybe 45 minutes." She nodded, too numb to reply. "If you can do the next standup, we'll have you out of there right after that. OK?"

"I guess," she answered without conviction. She searched in her purse for her cell phone. It wasn't there. She must've left it on the charger back at the Holiday Inn. She had no way to call Mark and find out what was going on. All she could do was try to put her camera face back on, give the report just after the bottom of the hour, and wait for her replacement. She felt as though she were marooned at the end of the earth. The minutes seemed to stretch on forever. She didn't know how she'd live through it.

But time passed. At last she gave the second report, and Andy arrived. Hope fairly flew into the vehicle and found her way back to the production center at the airport. Brandon Campbell met her at the door. "Go ahead and get your things at the motel while we work out your transportation," he said. "We'll get you to your daughter as quick as we can."

Hope's hands threw things into her suitcase and backpack, but she hardly even noticed. In the flurry her cell phone ended up in her purse. In less than 30 minutes she was back at the airport. Running through the doorway of the converted storage room, she found Brandon sitting at one of the makeshift desks. He hung up the phone as she approached. "Your chariot awaits," he said, pointing toward the door. "Listen, I hope your daughter gets well right away. Just let us know when you'll be back."

At his kind words and tone, the tears she'd been fighting filled her eyes. "Thank you," she whispered, then turned toward the aircraft parking ramp. A man she recognized as one of the helicopter pilots took her suitcase and led her to the Blackhawk. He slid the side door closed as she buckled her seat belt, then walked around to the pilot's door and lifted himself inside. A few seconds later the whine of the turbine starter filtered down into the cabin and through Hope's thoughts. Then came the gentle vibration of the rotor spinning. Long minutes passed as the pilot did his pretakeoff checklist. Then he pulled back on the collective, and they began climbing southward into the growing overcast sky. "We're on an instrument flight plan for Memphis," he told her over the intercom. "We should be there in about 90 minutes. If you want, when we get close to Memphis, I'll see if we can land on the hospital's helipad. That way you'll be right there."

"Well, my van's at the airport," Hope said slowly. She felt weighted. Talking seemed as difficult as swimming through sand. "But if . . . if you can take me . . . right to the hospital . . . "

The Blackhawk's straight-line course for Memphis intersected several times with the Mississippi's meandering, first taking them over the flood zone in eastern Missouri, then over parts of Kentucky.

"That's the city of New Madrid, the city that the earthquake fault is named for, over there to our right," the pilot spoke through the intercom.

Hope looked, but had to wait for a low cloud to pass before she could see the town. At this distance she could see that the rerouted Mississippi River was trying to cut a new channel and direct its flow through the town itself. *How much of the town will be left next week?* she wondered, biting her lower lip. Her hands clasped and unclasped. "Please, God . . . please, God . . . please," she whispered. "Please take care of her. Please."

The river's course meandered westward. The helicopter crossed into Tennessee, first above the sprawling Reelfoot Lake dotted with the boats of fishermen getting an early start on their weekend. Now, when it was not obscured by clouds, the Mississippi River was just a dark line on the western horizon.

"You still want to land at the hospital or go to the airport where your car is?" the pilot asked as familiar landmarks began identifying their approach to Memphis.

"The hospital . . . if you can."

A minute later the pilot was back on the intercom saying that the air traffic controllers at Memphis International Airport had cleared them to land on the hospital's roof. "They want me to leave as quickly as I can because a medevac chopper is coming in right behind us," he said. "When you get out, just close the door firmly and keep your head down until you're inside the building. I'll lift off as soon as you're inside the door."

Tears filled Hope's eyes. "I really appreciate this," she told him.

~ ~ ~

Mark's phone buzzed against his waist. He jerked toward his daughter. She'd been stirring in her sleep ever since they'd moved her out of the ER to a hospital room. He gripped the phone but didn't turn it on. He was a man who respected rules. He'd wait until he could slip away and pick up the message that was bound to be waiting for him. Surely it was from Hope.

Eventually a nurse came in, and Mark hurried out to a lobby. The call had been from the MBS technician who'd taken his message. He said that Hope was en route, but he didn't have an arrival time. Back in Jennifer's room Mark watched the hands of the clock creep around its white face. Then, somewhere off in the distance, he heard the drumming whine of a helicopter's approach. Another medevac, he guessed, but he strained to hear it land. In less than two minutes he heard it rev power and lift off. Six minutes later Hope burst through the doorway, dropped her luggage, and fell into her husband's arms.

CHAPTER THIRTEEN

W hat's wrong with her?" Hope implored as she leaned over the bed guardrail to embrace her sleeping daughter and stroked a lock of dark hair from across her face.

"The ER doctor ordered blood tests, then told me it's some kind of leukemia." Mark's voice broke on the last word and could barely pronounce it. "That's about all she said. Oh, and that another doctor would be coming to see Jennifer soon."

Hope stroked her daughter's hair and arm, taking care not to touch the IV tube or the heart monitor wires connected to her chest. "My poor baby. Mommy's here, and we're going to do everything we can to help you get better. I promise."

The sick child awakened enough to realize her mother had come. "I love you, Mommy," she said weakly. "Do you have to go away anymore?"

At that the flood of emotions kept back by the dam of self-control broke, and Hope began to weep. "No. No. Mommy doesn't have to go away for a long time. I'm home now to take care of my precious girl."

Mark set a chair by the bed so Hope could sit close to their daughter, then filled Hope in on what they'd been through since early morning. She stood up to place her hand against Jennifer's forehead. Still feverish, though perhaps not as hot as before. "Are you hungry?" she asked her.

Jennifer shook her head.

"She had a Popsicle in the emergency room and lost it a couple minutes later. One of the meds they've put in the IV is to control nausea. It's also what's making her sleepy."

Some time later Hope stood up and walked to the window. It wasn't much of a view—another wing of the hospital and the roofs of nearby buildings drawn in shades of gray under an overcast winter sky. "When's that doctor going to be here?" she asked impatiently. "Who is he, anyway? Do they just assign someone to Jennifer that we don't even know?"

"No matter who it is, we wouldn't know them," Mark said logically. "This is a pediatric oncologist. A specialist in children's cancer." Again, he almost choked on the fearful words.

"Did they say when he'd come?"

"Maybe they'll know down at the nurses' station." Mark seemed glad to leave the room. Hope paced from window to bed, then back to the window. *This is a nightmare. This isn't real.* She didn't hear Mark open the door and slip in.

"They've paged him," he said. "Maybe we'll have an answer in a little bit."

Hope spun around. "In a little bit!" The words jumped angrily off her tongue. "That's got to be the universal medical excuse. They don't know now, but they'll know in *a little bit.*"

"Shush," Mark whispered. "She's sleeping."

His long legs took him to his wife's side even as he spoke, and he drew her close. Hope pulled away.

"My child is sick. No! My baby is dying . . ." It was all she could do not to gag on the words as a new wave of emotion flooded through her. "My child is dying, and this unknown doctor—this specialist—can't bother himself to come see her and to tell us what's going on!" Again Mark drew her close. She collapsed against him, sobs shaking her frame. Burying her face in his sweater, she sobbed out the guilt and fear that she'd kept in during the hours since she'd gotten the message that her daughter was seriously ill. Jennifer slept through her tears. From the hallway the quiet footsteps, cries, and muted voices of the routine hospital activities continued.

Mark and Hope were still at the window, arms around each other, lost in their own frightened thoughts when brisk footsteps approached, then stopped outside the door. Hearing a knock, they turned to see the door open and a tall, middle-aged Black gentleman wearing the ubiquitous knee-length white doctor's lab coat step into the room. A stethoscope looped out of an overstuffed pocket, and the embroidered name above a breast pocket confirmed his status.

"Hello. I'm Dr. McCormick," he declared softly, extending his hand to shake with the parents. "I'm a pediatric oncologist and have been asked to check on your daughter." He walked to the bed and spent a full minute looking at Jennifer, noting her color, watching her breathing. He placed a hand on her forehead, then put his stethoscope to her chest. Only then did he turn back to her parents. "Let me get another chair so we can all sit down and talk. Or would you prefer to go to the conference room down the hall?"

The panicked look on the parents' faces answered his question. "I'll be right back," he said. A moment later he returned with another chair. He pulled all three chairs into a close circle, and sat with his knees only inches from theirs. Mark reached over and rested his hand on Hope's. She wrapped her fingers tightly around his.

"I know this is a terrible shock to you," Dr. McCormick began. "In all my years of medical practice I've never found a polite or easy way to tell parents that their child has a life-threatening illness." He paused to take a deep breath and let his words sink in. "The blood tests show that Jennifer has what is called acute myelocytic leukemia. It's a type of cancer affecting the white blood cells, which are called leukocytes. Hence its name. It's a very serious illness, and it's only fair for me to tell you that the recovery rate is around 50 percent."

Mark and Hope looked at each other in shock, then turned their gazes back to Dr. McCormick.

"Mr. and Mrs. Lancaster, I want you to know that we're ready and able to do everything we know how to do to save your daughter's life. I am the specialist here in this hospital, but you are free to call in another specialist for a second opinion. I realize that this has hit you out of nowhere, and you have a lot of decisions to make."

Again he paused. Hope shrugged. *How could anyone make a reasoned decision under such circumstances? And another specialist? They didn't know any other . . .* Yet she appreciated his candor and openness. Instinctively she trusted him.

"The treatment of this disease is not pretty," he continued.

"Jennifer is seriously ill, and the treatment will make her even worse before she gets better. Still, the sooner we begin treatment, the better. Every day the cancer is allowed to run unchecked through her body is one more day closer to letting it kill her."

"How do we know the diagnosis is correct?" Mark asked.

"The lab work. By scanning the blood samples we took and counting the type of cells we see. Leukemias are cancers of the blood, and acute myelocytic leukemia is characterized by the presence of certain deformities in the leukocytes, which are a kind of white blood cell. All blood cells have a normal life span. They're born, they work, and after a time they die. But when the leukocytes become cancerous, either they don't die or they live a lot longer than they're supposed to, and they multiply more rapidly than normal leukocytes," Dr. McCormick explained.

He paused a moment and studied Mark's and Hope's faces to see if his words were sinking in. What he saw was shock. He could repeat himself later if he had to, so he continued.

"Each day we'll do another blood test and give you a number. That number is how many of the cancerous cells we find in a milliliter of blood. Her count this morning was 147. That's serious. It's when her count gets to zero and stays that way for 10 days that we'll be able to say she's in remission."

Hope bit her lip. Her knuckles were white against Mark's hand. He took a deep breath. "Dr. McCormick, we have to trust you. We don't know where to turn. How do you plan to treat Jennifer?" he asked.

"We'll start with two very potent anticancer drugs. To borrow a military term, they're the 'heavy artillery' in our arsenal of medicines. These are newer-generation drugs, so they don't have as much of the terrible side effects of the older drugs, especially the nausea. The first course of treatment is for 10 days. In the beginning Jennifer probably won't feel much like eating, so we'll feed her through the IV. Most patients lose some weight during this time, but the most noticeable thing is that in about a month your daughter will lose her hair."

Hope gasped. Things were happening too fast. "Her hair?"

The doctor shook his head in empathy. "I know, Mrs. Lancaster. She's a beautiful child, and no parent wants their

130

daughter to lose all her hair. But it's important to remember that we're working to save her life. Her hair will start growing back in a few weeks, which—I have to tell you—will be just about the time the second round of chemotherapy will begin.

"There'll be two rounds of chemo. While she's in the hospital we'll do daily blood tests. After she's released I'll want blood tests three times a week. I want her to stay in the hospital through at least the first round of chemo. If she's feeling well, come the second round we'll let her come to the clinic."

The three—the parents and the doctor—looked at the slight form outlined under a blanket just a few feet away. For the first time since she'd gotten the message, something like peace crossed Hope's face. Maybe there was a small light at the end of this very dark tunnel.

"Are you people of faith?" Dr. McCormick asked.

"Yes," Mark answered.

"Then may I pray with you?" Both nodded, and the doctor held out his hands to hold theirs. Sitting in a prayer circle, he asked God to give Hope and Mark strength in the trial they were facing. He prayed that God would guide both him and the medical staff as they made decisions about Jennifer's care, and that His healing power would be evident in her recovery."

"Amen," he said.

"Amen," Hope and Mark echoed.

The doctor reached into a pocket of his lab coat, extracted two business cards, and handed one to each. "Call me anytime you have a question. I am serious about that. Now, here is something else. Here at the hospital we have a support group of parents of children with cancer. If it's OK with you, I'll send someone from the group by to see you a little later today."

"OK." Mark nodded, unsure of what he was agreeing to.

Dr. McCormick rose to leave. "In a little while a nurse will be here with the first dose of the chemotherapy. I'll be back to check on Jennifer this evening."

The door closed, and Mark and Hope clung to each other as if alone in a raging storm. Again sobs racked Hope's body. Mark's tears wet her hair. Only their daughter was at peace, thanks to the medicine making her sleep.

An eternity later Hope pulled a pack of tissues from her

purse, stepped to the window, and blew her nose and mopped her eyes. She stared out at the gray cityscape. Below, small cars pulled up to red lights, then sped on when the lights turned green. Tiny people walked through the doors of McDonald's and Taco Bell. Life was going on as usual. The plain, ordinary lives of people who knew nothing of insidious diseases that could kill small children. That *did* kill small children. These fathers and mothers were innocent of such things—just as she'd been a mere 24 hours before.

Several minutes passed. Hope turned away from the window to study the face of her sleeping child. She walked over and caressed her arm. A tear traced down her cheek and dripped onto the bedsheet. She hardly noticed as others followed.

Mark stood on the opposite side of the bed, his face creased with concern though his eyes were dry. Hope looked up. "What are you thinking?" she whispered.

His face hardened. "I'm just wondering why God would let this happen. Why He would do this to an innocent child like Jennifer."

From the hallway came the sound of a squeaky cart with a bad wheel being pushed beyond their door. The indistinct words of two nurses rose and faded.

Hope shook her head. Opened her mouth to speak. Closed it.

"That's a tough question, but I don't believe God did this to her," she said at last.

"I'm going to get some air," Mark told her.

She nodded. "You OK?"

"Yeah, just antsy. You know me. I'm a pacer. I need to get out and walk." He paused at the door. "You want any coffee or anything?"

"No. Well, a bottle of water would be good. Mark, I love you," she whispered.

A long, deep sigh. "I love you, too."

~ ~ ~

The door opened, and a nurse entered, carrying two small IV bags filled with colored solutions. Laying them on the bedside table, she left the room, returning with a second IV stand to which a pair of electronic pumps were attached. It took her several minutes to hang the bags, run their tubes through the pumps, and connect the lines into the IV tube leading to Jennifer's arm. She kept up a line of cheerful talk as she worked.

"That looks more like plumbing than nursing," Mark quipped. His words brought a short smile to Hope's face.

The nurse laughed. "Just don't ask me to unclog your toilet," she shot back. It was enough to make Mark crack a small smile too. She finished the setup and left, saying that she'd be back periodically to make certain everything was going as it should.

Mark and Hope sat in silence. Neither felt as if they had anymore tears.

Silence again reigned in the room as each was lost in their own thoughts. Time began passing in cycles of crying followed by prayerful protest to God, then just sinking into the pain of realizing that their only child might not live.

"There's no pain in the world like it," a voice calmly announced from the doorway. Hope and Mark turned in surprise. Deeply lost in their own thoughts, they'd not heard the door pushed open or the couple step inside.

"I'm Kevin Berringer, and this is my wife, Sheila," the man said with an outstretched hand and a warm smile. "Dr. McCormick called us. We're from the leukemia support group."

In the instant before he spoke, Mark took their measure. *A little older than we are. Honest, open faces.* "It's nice to meet you," he said as he shook their hands. "I'm Mark Lancaster and—he motioned toward the bed—this is my wife, Hope." Sheila slipped to Hope's side to embrace her as Kevin wrapped Mark in his arms.

"When did you find out?" Sheila asked them.

Mark looked at his watch. "A few hours ago. The doctor in the ER told me it was some kind of leukemia but didn't know what kind. Dr. McCormick gave us the lowdown, oh, a couple hours ago. What did he call it, Hope? Acute myelo-something or other."

"Acute myelocytic leukemia?" Sheila said knowingly.

"Yeah, that's it," Mark replied. "Dr. McCormick must've just called you."

"Well, actually, he called us before he came to see you," Kevin told them. "That's the way he is. He wanted to be sure somebody could be with you as soon as possible after you got the news."

Sheila stepped to the head of the bed to look at Jennifer before turning back to Hope. "One thing we really appreciate about Dr. McCormick is how much he cares for both his patients and their families," she told Hope. "He's a great doctor. We love him."

"That's good to hear," Hope said, unconvinced. *Why are these people really here? What do they want with us?*

Sheila looked intently at Hope. "Have we met before?" she asked. "There's something familiar about you."

Hope shook her head. "I'm not sure. In my business I meet a lot of people who remember me, but later I have no idea where we've met."

"Oh! I know. Hope Lancaster! I should have recognized your name. You're the evening newscaster on channel 3!"

Kevin looked puzzled. "But weren't you on the MBS Morning News this morning? Weren't you someplace in Illinois talking about that disaster on the Mississippi?"

"They moved me up to the network just yesterday, in fact," Hope said, her eyes on her daughter. "I'd hardly arrived when Mark called me about Jennifer."

Sheila lightly touched Hope's arm. "I know you're scared to death and have a million questions, but probably can't think of a one. Would you like to go with us to supper, and we could talk there?"

Mark and Hope looked at each other, their stomachs suddenly rousing to declare their emptiness. "Supper? That would be great," Mark told them. But Hope shook her head. She didn't want to leave her daughter's side.

"She's fine. She's sleeping. She won't even notice that you're gone," Sheila urged. "You do need to eat. The hospital cafeteria isn't that great, but there's a good Italian restaurant across the street. Our treat."

"That's very generous of you," Hope said, glancing at Mark. She knew what she was going to do, but he didn't have to join her.

Mark's eyes darted toward their daughter, then to the Berringers. He was empty. "You go on, hon," Hope told him. "I'm not going to leave Jennifer."

Sheila frowned. "One of the first things you've got to learn when you have a child with cancer is that if you don't take care of yourself you can't take care of your child."

This is all I need! Hope thought irritably. *As worried as I am, some woman I've met five minutes ago telling me what to do with my child.* She forced herself to assume her camera face. "I know you mean well, but if there is one chance in a hundred that Jennifer will wake up and find herself alone, I'm not taking it."

"Mark," she said, taking charge of the conversation, "you go. Please. And bring me some carryout. I don't care what it is, and I don't want much. Maybe bread and a small salad." She managed a smile. "I'm not hungry, but it won't hurt me to eat a little."

Sheila shrugged. "OK. Whatever you say. We can talk later if you like."

Once they were gone Hope sank gratefully into the recliner that sat between the bed and the wall, fumbling with the lever until she raised the footrest. *Thank You, Jesus, for this time alone,* she prayed. *Give me courage. Make me strong for Mark and Jennifer.* Tears filled her eyes, and she wiped them away with the back of her hand. Hope. A woman who'd always known what she wanted and worked her tail off to get it. A woman of confidence who felt comfortable being in charge. She'd been thrust into a whole new game, and she didn't even know the rules. She closed her eyes. *Dear Lord in heaven, are You there? Tell me, Lord, what am I going to do?*

~ ~ ~

"Do you have a child with cancer?" Mark asked cautiously as the three waited for the elevator.

The caution wasn't needed, for Kevin's whole face lit up at the question. "Yes, we do. Our 14-year-old son. He's in remission right now, and healthy as a horse. He missed a lot of school, but now his grades are great, and he even competes on the swim team." Kevin was one proud dad. "I'll show you his picture when we get to the restaurant."

The elevator door opened, and they stepped inside. Sheila pushed the button. "Jason had the same form of leukemia your daughter has," she told Mark. "That's why Dr. McCormick asked us to see you. We've been through it, so we can help answer some of your questions."

~ ~ ~

News of Jennifer's illness spread quickly through their family and their church. By evening Mark and Hope were recounting the day's events to a stream of well-wishers while Jennifer slept restlessly a few feet away.

"You're looking tired," one observed to Mark.

Somehow the comment made Mark yawn widely. "It's been a long day," he replied. "I've been at the hospital since before dawn."

"Let me drive you home," the man offered. "You look as though you need to get some sleep."

He shook his head. "I don't want to leave. If I get tired, I'll just curl up in that chair over there." Mark gestured toward the recliner. "It seems to be for tired parents."

"Honey, you go on home. I'll stay with her tonight," Hope told him. "After all, you had her on your mind all night. You can relieve me in the morning. I'll sleep on the recliner."

Mark studied his wife's gaze. It was tempting. He hadn't realized how exhausted he was until he'd sat down in the booth at the restaurant. In that comfortable place—away from the frightening, unfamiliar din of the hospital—he'd felt his whole body sort of sink in on itself. He'd had a hard time keeping his mind on his hosts, though he appreciated their encouragement and definitely wanted to talk with them again. After all, they'd been through the wild ocean that he and Hope had just been thrown into. And they'd survived! Yeah, he definitely wanted to see them again, and to meet their son.

"Mark?" Hope's voice brought him back to the hospital room. "Let the Berringers take you home."

"I don't think so." He was forgetting something important. What? Raising both hands in a gesture of *Wait a minute,* he tried to remember. At last! "My car's in the hospital parking lot. I don't need a ride."

"OK, I'll at least walk down with you," Kevin told him. The other visitors soon departed as well.

Hope sat delicately on the side of Jennifer's bed, stroking her daughter's arm, and singing softly "Jesus Loves Me." Tears choked the words in her throat, but she struggled through the verse to the chorus: "'Yes, Jesus loves me . . .'" Wiping her eyes with a tissue from the bedside tray, she rose and moved to the window where she stared out at the darkness cloaking the city.

Someone knocked gently on the partially open door. "Mrs.

Lancaster," an aide called softly, "there's a call for you at the nurses' station."

"OK." It must be Mark.

"Since it's after visiting hours all calls get routed to there," the woman continued. "Shall we put it through to you here? Or do you want to come down there?"

"Uh, I guess here's all right. You don't think it'll wake her?" Hope asked.

The aide shook her head. "I'll forward it to you in just a moment."

Hope held her hand on the phone on the bedside stand so she could answer on the first ring. "Hello," she said softly.

"Hope? This is Peter Leventhal. How's your daughter?"

"She's sick, Peter. Thanks so much for calling. This has been a terrible day. She's really, really sick. The doctor says she's got acute mye . . . Oh, I can't even say it. It's some kind of really bad leukemia."

"I'm very sorry. That's frightening."

Hope collapsed into a chair. "It is. I'm scared. Really, really scared, Pete. They've already started her on two different chemo drugs. The doctor says if they're real aggressive in attacking this then she has a better chance of surviving."

There was a short silence; then Peter said, "Are you saying this could be . . . fatal?"

"Yes." Her voice broke. "Kids . . . kids *die* from this."

Peter got control of his voice. "Well, Hope, I want you to know that everybody on the team is pulling for Jennifer—and for you, too. A group of us here got together and had a special prayer meeting to lift all of you up before the Lord."

"Thank you, Peter. That means a lot." Hot tears stung her eyes. "Tell everyone thank you. And tell Andy that I appreciate him covering for me today. I don't know when I'll be back. I hope it will be soon."

"Listen, Hope, you're part of the MBS family. But we want you to take care of priority one—and right now that's your daughter. If there's anything we can do, don't hesitate to let us know. Is that clear? I mean anything, 'cause we watch out for each other."

"OK." He had to strain his ear to hear her.

"I do appreciate your calling. I'm sorry I'm not in better shape," Hope struggled to say.

With repeated assurances that the team was thinking of her, Peter hung up, and Hope sat back down by her daughter. "'Jesus loves me, this I know . . .'"

FOURTEEN

Friday drifted into Saturday as the hours alternated between catnaps, the visits of caring friends and family members, and the tedium of waiting for time to pass. Mark and Hope took turns going home to shower and change clothes, returning to again wait out the hours by their daughter's bed. Somewhere along the way a cousin took Hope to the airport, where she retrieved her van.

Early Sunday morning Jennifer stirred, opened her eyes, and saw her mother sleeping in the recliner. "I'm hungry," she said quietly. Hope did not respond.

"Mommy, I'm hungry," she repeated, this time a little louder. Still Hope remained in exhausted slumber.

"Mommy!" Jennifer called loudly.

Hope jerked awake. "What? What's wrong?" she asked, panicked. In that moment she saw Jennifer looking at her. "Well, lookee who's awake. I'm so glad to see your eyes open." She smiled, then looked at her watch. It was just after 5:00 a.m. "What are you doing?"

"I'm hungry."

"Do you feel like you can keep some food in your stomach?"

Jennifer nodded.

"Let me go down to the nurses' station and see if I can get something for you." Hope returned a minute later with a single-serving carton of fruit-flavored gelatin. Jennifer devoured it speedily.

"Think you can hold some more?"

Jennifer shook her head. "My arm hurts," she whined.

139

"Where, darling?"

Jennifer pointed to where the intravenous tube fed into her arm. "Tell them to take it out."

The stress knot in Hope's stomach grew tighter. "They can't take it out, honey. That's how they give you the medicine to fight what's making you sick." She patted her daughter's arm to comfort her. "Hey, your hair's an absolute mess," she teased to distract her. "Let me brush out the tangles. OK?"

Searching through the various personal items they'd brought to the hospital, Hope soon found a hairbrush and, sitting on the edge of the bed, gently worked it through her daughter's long tresses. It wasn't long before the bed head was gone, and if you didn't look too hard at her dark, hollow eyes, Jennifer seemed almost like her old self. "You look lovely, sweetheart. You're probably going to have some visitors later. Do you think you'll feel up to it?"

Jennifer considered the question. "I guess so." She shrugged. "I don't feel good. But I'm starting to feel a little better. Maybe for a little while, I guess."

The answer spread a smile across Hope's face. With a little jump she realized it was the first time she'd actually smiled since getting the emergency call three days before. Maybe, just maybe, there was hope that her daughter would get well. She leaned over and gave her a kiss. Jennifer, tired out from eating and talking, settled herself back down in bed and closed her eyes.

~ ~ ~

"Good morning!"

Dr. McCormick's cheerful greeting shocked Hope back to reality. She'd been so absorbed just looking at Jennifer that she'd shut out the rest of the world. Now she jumped in startled surprise. "How is everyone this morning?" he asked.

Hope looked up with a cautious smile. "I think she's getting better. She woke up around 5:00 and said she was hungry! She sat up on the bed and ate a small fruit gelatin. Then I brushed the tangles from her hair, and she lay back down and went to sleep. But—she told me that she's feeling a little better."

The doctor stepped to the opposite side of the bed and took Jennifer's hand between his two larger ones. Their voices had awakened her again.

140

"So you're feeling better this morning, are you? You wouldn't be wanting to get out of this place early, would you?" he teased.

Jennifer pulled back, a little afraid. Awake and feeling better, this was the first time she'd actually noticed her doctor. "I want to go home," she pouted. She pointed at the IV tube. "I want you to take this thing out of my arm right now!"

Hope felt embarrassed at her daughter's sassy tone, but Dr. McCormick shot her a look that said it was OK as his brow wrinkled in thought. "I don't think we can take that out quite yet. But the medicine in that bag up there also comes in pill form. You're a big girl, Jennifer. If you can start taking pills—and if you can keep them down—I'll be happy to have the nurse take the needle out of your arm. Do you feel as though you can keep from throwing up?"

Jennifer nodded soberly. "I'll do my best."

"Now, I've got to warn you. They're really, really big pills and might be hard to swallow."

Jennifer nodded soberly.

A teasing smile spread across Dr. McCormick's face. "I'm joking. The pills aren't *that* big, and I don't think you'll have any trouble swallowing them." He leaned down to whisper in her ear. "I've got some good news. You want to hear it?"

Jennifer nodded.

"I think you're starting to get better. There aren't as many of the bad cells running around in your blood this morning as there were yesterday. This is the first time your blood count has gone down, so I think it's the first sign that you're starting to get well. Now, do you want me to tell your mom, or do you want to tell her?"

Jennifer smiled. "I'll tell her."

"What secret are you two keeping from me?" Hope asked, her eyes sparkling at the grins on their faces.

"I'm starting to get better!" Jennifer announced with almost her normal energy.

"Oh, sweetheart. That's wonderful!" *Thank You, God.* She felt herself tearing up again. "So when can you let her go home?" Hope asked the doctor.

"Not so fast. We've got a long way to go." He chuckled. "I'm rejoicing with you, but she's just starting to get better. This morning, for the first time, her count was down. Just slightly, but down. That's the first sign of progress. Plus, look at her. Doesn't she look a lot better than she did on Thursday?"

Jennifer held her arms open wide for a celebratory hug from her mother.

"If it's OK with you, Jennifer, I need to talk to your mother outside for a minute," the doctor explained as he backed away from her bedside.

He followed Hope into the hallway and down to a small lounge. "Is she really getting better?" she implored.

"Yes. Yes, she is, but how long she will stay that way is another question. You must remember that acute myelocytic leukemia is a very tenacious disease. We attack it, and it retreats. Then it comes back. We attack it again, and it goes away for a while. Then it comes back, and we attack it again. It is very important that we keep monitoring her closely so we can attack it vigorously just as soon as it appears," the oncologist emphasized. "I'm hoping she can go home once she completes this first 10-day round of chemotherapy. Once we let her go home, I want blood tests on her every other day for the next couple weeks. After that we'll back off to twice a week for a month or so, then once a week. After that, we'll just have to play it by feel and see how it goes."

Hope let his words sink in before answering. "What if it comes back?"

"It's not a question of *if* it comes back. The question is *when,* and when that happens we'll just have to attack it again and see how she responds. Sometimes we have to do two, three, maybe even four rounds of the chemo before a patient goes into long-term remission. Sometimes the chemo works only once or twice, and the next treatment round is a bone marrow transplant. We just don't know until we get there." He sighed. "God gives us only one day at a time, and all we can do is take one day at a time."

The news gave Hope a small measure of courage. Still, the thought of repeated rounds of chemo and maybe even more severe treatment broke through what courage she was summoning. Dr. McCormick saw the tremble as she lifted her hands to her face, and placed his hand on her shoulder. "May I pray with you?"

She didn't look at him. "Please do."

Wrapping Hope's hands in his, Dr. McCormick closed his eyes and prayed. "Heavenly Father," he began, "please give Hope and Mark courage as they face this trial and strengthen Jennifer as she battles this disease. Lord, I ask You to fill the Lancaster home with the peace of Your presence. Please give me a special measure of wisdom as I treat this special little girl. We have strong medicines that work well, but we know that only You are the true and master physician, so I ask that You rest Your healing hand on Jennifer to heal her. But most of all, Lord, work through each of us to bring glory to Your name. Amen."

"Amen," Hope murmured, comforted. "Amen."

Dr. McCormick gave her hand a squeeze. "Hang in there," he said. "We're with you all the way." Then he was gone, hurrying off to see more sick children and their parents.

Mark arrived just after 8:00 to find his wife and daughter both asleep, an empty breakfast tray sitting on the table over the bed. Only crumbs were left. He smiled at the sight, then placed a hand on Hope's shoulder and gently shook her awake. "Good morning, beautiful," he said sweetly. "I think you ought to go home and get some real sleep. You stay here much longer, and visitors will wonder who's the sick one."

"That sounds like"—Hope yawned—"a good idea. I think I'm ready to do that." Then she shared the news from Dr. McCormick.

"That's terrific!" Mark grinned from ear to ear. "That's almost too good to be true."

~ ~ ~

The string of visitors from church began shortly after Sunday dinner. Already friends in Mark's and Hope's Sunday school classes had signed up to bring food to their house on a regular basis so there would be food waiting for them the odd times they were home. Children in Jennifer's class had carefully printed and drawn pictures on a giant get-well card. Other friends had volunteered to stay overnight at the hospital with Jennifer so the parents could sleep at home.

Then the well-intentioned but verbally inept began arriving.

"Mark! Mark!" a familiar voice called from down the hallway. He turned from his conversation with Hope's parents to see

143

Tina coming their direction, a toddler on one arm and an infant in a stroller. She embraced Mark and Hope's parents warmly. "I came as soon as I heard. How's she doin'?"

"She's starting to do better. Hope's with her. She's sleeping right now. That's why we're here in the lounge. The doctor says she'll likely go home after this first round of chemo." Mark's voice was light and happy.

"Wow! I'm sure glad she's getting better, but with cancer you never know, ya know," Tina declared with self-important confidence. When my father got cancer they said he was getting better and they sent him home; then he got worse and died in a few days."

The weight that had lifted from Mark's chest at the morning's good news settled back down again. Tina continued saying something about cancer and how leukemias—especially childhood leukemias—were always fatal, but his mind just wasn't absorbing it. His gaze wandered past Tina's face and down the hall toward the elevator, where he saw Kevin Berringer step off it. His eyes stayed locked on Kevin as he approached.

Kevin understood the situation in a heartbeat. "You had lunch yet, Mark?" he interrupted the woman.

"Uh, I've already eaten," Mark answered.

"Well, what do you say we go get a cup of coffee or something? I'm buying."

What a relief. Thank You, Lord, for Kevin, he thought. "Uh, sure. I'll see you later, Tina. Thanks for coming by."

"You ever read the book of Job?" Kevin asked as the elevator doors closed and they were alone.

"I guess I probably have. I mean, we've probably discussed it in Sunday school."

"Job was this really rich guy, the richest in the whole area. He had a big family, a passel of adult kids. One day Satan challenges God to a contest. Satan is sure that he can make Job curse God, and God lets him try. So Satan destroys everything Job owns—all his livestock, all his servants, his children. Everything.

"You can imagine! No, I guess no one can. Well, of course, Job is devastated. He goes into mourning and sits in an ash pit for several days. Then, to make matters worse, he gets terribly painful boils all over his body. Some of his friends come by, and

144

they're so shocked by what they see that they just sit with him for a number of days without saying a word."

The elevator door opened, and they stepped out on first floor. "A nonstop," Mark laughed.

"Let's go in the snack shop here," Kevin directed. They both picked up bottles of juice from the beverage cooler, and Kevin picked up a couple of fresh pastries for his friend. After paying, Kevin continued the story.

"OK, so these so-called friends came a long distance to comfort Job. But when they start talking, things go from bad to worse. They're trying to comfort this guy who's just lost everything in the world and is suffering indescribable pain. Even his wife had told him to curse God and give up and die. And these guys? They're in the category of, well, if they were Job's friends, then Job didn't need enemies! They told him he must've done something wrong to deserve all the disasters that he had suffered. But Job knew he was honest and true to God. He just knew God wasn't punishing him."

The static-filled noise of a page over the public-address system jolted into the story. Kevin waited until static and voice had stopped. "The point I'm drawing from this is that you're on the right track," he said, pushing a fruit-filled roll to Mark. "You're doing everything you know to do right. You're a good father. As soon as your daughter was sick you got her the best medical care available. You haven't done anything wrong. But still you have people like that woman up there filled with good intentions but saying all sorts of hurtful things. Sheila and I had the same thing. They don't mean anything bad by it. They just don't know how or when to keep their mouths shut. Putting up with people like her was the toughest part of our Jason's illness." Kevin closed his eyes, for a moment reliving it all over again. "Once when he'd had a bad reaction to some meds, some well-meaning person from church started a rumor that turned into a report that he had died. Friends sent us sympathy cards. Imagine how we felt to open *those*. We actually received a funeral bouquet—on the day he finally started getting better!"

"Unbelievable," Mark said with a shake of his head. "That's unbelievable."

"But true. You laugh, because you fear that if you let yourself cry you'll cry forever. Putting up with people like that woman who just nailed you has got to be the toughest part of what you're going through." He tipped up his juice and drained the last swallow. "What they say can be really painful. Maybe not when they say it, because you reject it then. But later—when you remember what's been said—that's when it weakens you. You know, what used to make me the angriest was knowing that they didn't know what they were talking about, but I had no way to shut them up. And you know what?"

"What?" Mark asked, wearily pressing his fingers against his forehead.

"The most important thing of all. The Lord is working. Your daughter is getting better. This is round one. We don't know how many rounds you'll face in the future, but each one will make you stronger for the next, and God will work through this experience to increase your faith." He dropped his clasped hands on the table, as if in prayer. "You've got to hold on to Him, Mark. Tight. I mean death-grip tight. Otherwise Satan will use this trial to ruin your faith."

CHAPTER

A wedge of light sliced through the darkness of Jennifer's room as nurse Marsha Gentle pushed open the door oh-so-quietly and slipped into the room. She hated to awaken the child just to take her vital signs, but she dared not simply let her sleep. As she looked down, her gaze was met by open eyes.

"What are you doing awake at this hour?" Marsha asked just above a whisper.

"I can't sleep."

"Well, how are you feeling?"

"Better since they took out the IV. My arm doesn't hurt except for just a little spot."

"So what's keeping you awake? Would you like for me to read you a story or sing you a song to help you go to sleep?" Marsha looked closer at the little girl. "Something's bothering you, right?"

Jennifer hesitated. "I guess . . ."

Marsha leaned over the bed rail and took Jennifer's hand. "Do you want to talk about it?"

Silence.

"If you want, you can tell me what's bothering you."

Silence, but Marsha saw her face relax a bit.

"Did someone hurt your feelings?"

"No," Jennifer whispered. "It's something this lady from church said."

"What was that?"

The little girl's face crumpled as if she were in pain. Tears welled up in her eyes. "She said . . . she said . . ." The tears grew

147

larger and began tracing down both cheeks as she choked on her words. "Dr. McCormick told me I'm getting better, but she said I'm going to die!" She began to sob.

Marsha let down the railing and took Jennifer in her arms. For several minutes she just held the sobbing child.

"Am I going to die?" Jennifer implored.

Marsha stroked her hair and rocked her from side to side. "If Dr. McCormick says you're getting better, then you are, I can tell you that. He's a smart doctor, and he doesn't lie!"

That soothed Jennifer's spirit for a moment, and the sobbing subsided. She took the tissue Marsha gave her to wipe away her tears, while the nurse prayed silently for wisdom to comfort and answer this seriously ill child.

"But . . . but what if it's true?" Jennifer continued. "This lady said that leukemia always comes back, and a lot of kids die from it."

Marsha studied Jennifer's face before answering. She did not want to confuse her or to give her more information than she could understand. She wanted to comfort her, not give her more to worry about. She sighed. *Give me the right words, Father in heaven.* She reached up and switched the light over the bed to its lowest setting so they could see each other better, then pulled up a chair next to the bed. "Dear heart, I think you and I need to have a real heart-to-heart talk," she said softly. "Do you want to sit on my lap?"

"OK."

When they were settled, a blanket around the little girl, Marsha began. "You're a big girl, 6 years old, and you're asking a straight question, so I think you deserve a straight answer. Are you ready?"

Jennifer nodded hesitantly. "I guess so. What do you mean?"

"What I mean is that I'm going to tell you exactly what I know and hope that helps you understand what's happening. Is that OK?"

Jennifer nodded, this time with more confidence.

"OK. Here are the facts. You have a cancer of the blood cells. It's a really mean sickness, and it's true that some kids who get it die. Right now you're getting better. What will happen next week or next month, we don't know. We have great doctors and nurses here to take care of you if you get sick again. But you know what's most important of all?"

Jennifer shook her head. "What?"

"Do you love Jesus?"

"Of course I do!" Jennifer declared. "I go to Sunday school."

Marsha smiled. "That's great, because Jesus is our Savior. That means He loves us so much that He's promised to come back and take everybody who loves Him to heaven to live with Him for ever and ever." She paused, waiting to give Jennifer time to grasp her words. *Perhaps it's providential,* she thought, *that neither of her parents are here tonight.* For the past couple days Hope had been fighting a bad cold, so today she'd popped in for only a few minutes morning and afternoon, wearing a mask as a precaution for Jennifer. Mark had been on full-time hospital duty—every bit as attentive as Hope—but had slipped out around 1:00 a.m., to get a few hours' sleep in his own bed, he'd told the head nurse. *Maybe she's lying here thinking because both parents are gone . . . or maybe it's something that's been on her mind a long time.*

Marsha's right hand stroked Jennifer's back as she continued. "Best of all, there won't be any sickness or dying after Jesus takes us to heaven. But Jesus hasn't come yet, so people do get sick and die. Even children. So you know what?"

"What?"

"Jesus knew that before He came back a whole lot of people who love Him were going to die." She paused, searching for the right words. "You know, sweetheart, some people live to be 100, but finally even they die. Well, Jesus promised that those of us who love Him but who die before He returns—when He comes back to this earth He's going to wake us all up. And He'll give us brand-new bodies that will never die. Our new bodies won't even get sick! Isn't that wonderful?"

Jennifer looked doubtful. "I guess so. But I'm afraid." Her lips trembled as though she would begin crying again.

"What are you afraid of?"

"I'm afraid of dying. I don't want to die."

"Oh, Jennifer," Marsha answered. "Do you remember a story in the Bible about a man named Lazarus?"

She nodded. "He was Jesus' friend. We learned about him in Sunday school a few weeks ago."

"That's right. He was one of Jesus' best friends. But he got sick and died. Do you remember what Jesus did when He got there where Lazarus was buried?"

Jennifer smiled. "Yeah. Jesus brought him back to life."

"That's right. Jesus called to Lazarus and told him to wake up. Now, *that's* a very important part of the story." Marsha waited, praying to choose the right words. "You know that a lot of people think that when you die you go straight to heaven or to the bad place," she stated gently.

"Yeah, that's what happens. My grampa's a preacher," Jennifer said proudly, "and he told me."

"But that's not what Jesus said," Marsha said softly. "Maybe no one's told your grampa what really happens when people die."

Now Jennifer was really puzzled. "What happens?" she asked suspiciously.

"Do you remember that in the story of Lazarus, Jesus told His disciples that Lazarus was asleep and He was going to go wake him up? The disciples said not to wake him up because if Lazarus was sleeping, then he was getting well. Then Jesus told them that Lazarus was dead." Marsha waited a moment to make certain Jennifer was following the story. "You see, Jesus compared death to sleeping."

Jennifer shuddered. "Does that mean that when I'm sleeping I'm *dead?*"

"Oh, no," Marsha laughed. "But that's a good question. Jesus said that death is like sleep, because when you're asleep you don't know what's going on around you. And when you die, you don't know what's going on around you then, either.

"The resurrection morning is going to be like waking up. Only the best part is that it will be Jesus waking you up—instead of your mommy or daddy. Jesus will wake you up to take you to heaven."

Jennifer looked up at her with wide eyes. "Jesus will wake people up and take them to heaven?"

"That's right."

"Will my mommy and daddy be there?"

"They love Jesus, don't they?"

"Yes. They take me to church and tell me Bible stories."

Marsha smiled. "Well, OK," she said simply. "They love

Jesus, and you love Jesus, and God promises that you'll be in heaven together."

Jennifer sat silently, nestled against the nurses' chest, soaking up what she'd just learned. "I like that Jesus will wake us up and take us to heaven," she said with a big yawn. "I think I'm ready to go to sleep now."

With a little boost from Marsha, Jennifer scrambled up onto the bed. Marsha took her vital signs, turned off the light, and reset the side rail. "Good night, sweetheart," she said in the darkness.

"Thank you," Jennifer said sleepily.

"Whatever for?"

"For telling me about Jesus and what it's like to die. I love Jesus, so I'm not afraid anymore."

"Sweet dreams," Marsha bade softly before closing the door.

~ ~ ~

"Do you have a dog or cat at home?" Dr. McCormick inquired.

"No. I'm allergic to animals, so I can't have any pets," Jennifer answered.

"Do you have a favorite teddy bear?"

Jennifer nodded vigorously. "I have a bunch of them. I like to line them up across the top of the head of my bed where I can see them. My favorite's a red one named Max."

Dr. McCormick smiled. "Well, I imagine Max has been pretty lonely without you this past week or so, don't you think?"

Jennifer giggled and nodded.

"Well, my little friend, how would you like to go back home and give Max a big hug?"

"Go home? When?" Jennifer asked, excited.

"Today! Just as soon as we can get you checked out of here."

"Mommy! Did you hear that? I'm going home!" Jennifer exclaimed, bouncing up and down on the bed in her excitement.

"Praise the Lord!" Hope cried. "Dr. McCormick, we've been praying for that news!"

He grinned. "Well, *I'm* thrilled to be able to deliver the news." He turned to Hope. "Mrs. Lancaster, I've written out some instructions and have already made appointments for her to come to the clinic for follow-up testing. The clinic is in the building next door to the hospital. There are no restrictions on her activities. Let her do whatever she feels like doing."

Just then Jennifer yelped as she bounced a couple of inches above the mattress. The doctor laughed. "Whatever she wants—within reason." He pointed a teasing finger at his patient. "Girl, I think you're feeling better!"

Turning back to Hope, his voice was all business. "Keep pushing the liquids and the exercise, because the more she does, the better she's going to feel. The medication will make her feel a bit run-down and will probably cause some sores in her mouth. The nurse will give you a supply of the mouthwash we use to treat that, too. I've also made an appointment for her to come see me at the office next Thursday. And, of course, call me if there are any problems."

Dr. McCormick excused himself as mother and daughter hugged in celebration of the long-anticipated news.

Twenty minutes later Mark walked through the door to find his daughter fully dressed and sitting impatiently on the bed. "What are you doing dressed?" he asked.

"I'm going home! Dr. McCormick says I can go home!" she exclaimed.

A disbelieving look crossed Mark's face, then was just as quickly replaced by a broad smile. "That's wonderful news. Uh, where's your mother?"

"I don't know." She'd been in the hospital long enough to confidently know the ropes. "Maybe talking to a nurse. Or maybe in the bathroom."

"Well, then I'll just sit down right here beside you, and we'll wait for your mama, and then we'll get you outta here!"

Ten minutes later Hope returned from the nurses' station where she'd been going over details of her daughter's dismissal. "Mark! How did you know that we're going home?" She frowned, puzzled. "You couldn't have known. What are you doing here? Why aren't you at work?"

"The company sent everybody home. It seems that this thing with the Mississippi River has cut off coal supplies to the electric generating plants. The announcement was that we're shutting down the office to help conserve electricity." He shook his head. "At any rate, we all get to go home and work there and coordinate using the Internet."

152

A surprised look crossed Hope's face. "Wow. This situation's getting really bad, isn't it? I guess that I haven't been paying much attention to the news. Funny, isn't it?"

"Yeah." He laughed. "The newswoman's forgotten the news. But you're right. The situation is getting pretty dicey."

"I'm surprised. I've been so focused on Jennifer that I've paid no attention to what's been happening in the rest of the world."

"Yeah, me too. But on the way over I heard a radio report that a large section of the country within 75 to 100 miles of the Mississippi is going to be without electricity for several hours a day."

"But why would it affect us here?" Hope asked.

Mark shrugged. "I'm not sure. But if you look out the window at the end of the hall you can see the river, so I guess we're in an area that'll be affected at least a little bit."

Just then an aide arrived with a wheelchair. "You ready to bust out of this place?" she asked with a grin.

"You bet. But I'll walk, thank you," Jennifer answered politely.

The woman laughed. "I know how you feel, but hospital rules say you ride until you get to the door. Once you're out the door you can walk wherever you want."

Hope bundled Jennifer into her coat and pulled a bright-blue knitted hat down on her long dark hair. "*Now* you're ready," she laughed. "It's cold out there."

Jennifer eyed the wheelchair. "OK, I'll ride," she said. "But as soon as we get to the door I'm getting up and running away, because you have too many needles and other things that make me go 'Ouch!'"

~ ~ ~ *

En route to the door, Jennifer decided she'd rather ride home with her father. The aide remained with her—she stood next to the wheelchair, a wide smile on her face—while her parents diverted to the parking garage. Hope paid her parking fee and headed straight home, while Mark threaded his way around the block toward where his daughter was waiting.

"Her mom and I have been praying for this day," Mark told the aide as Jennifer got into the car. He checked to make certain she'd buckled her seat belt, and they pulled away. "Want to stop and get a goodie on the way home?" he asked as they neared a convenience store.

"Yeah! I want a candy bar! They wouldn't let me have any in the hospital."

"All right. One candy bar and a tank of gas coming up."

All pumps were busy, so Mark gave Jennifer a dollar bill and told her that she could go into the store and buy the candy. Oblivious to the cold wind, she bounced out of the car, eyes shining, and ran the few yards into the store. His eyes on her, Mark waited for a pump to become available. A moment later the car ahead pulled out, so he eased forward. He inserted his ATM card in the reader slot, punched in his personal identification number, inserted the nozzle into the filler tube, and began pumping the gas.

"Hi, Mark!" a familiar voice called from the other side of the pump. "How's Jennifer doing?"

Mark looked up to see a longtime friend from church. Around the same age as Mark, his main job was welding, but—as he'd tell you—his real job was spreading the gospel. Mark's eyes lighted up to see him.

"Oh, hi, Jerry. Jennifer's doing great! In fact, we're taking her home from the hospital right now and"—he pointed toward the store—"she's in there picking out a candy bar."

Jerry leaned across the concrete island and slapped Mark on the back. "Man, that's wonderful news. We've been praying for her to recover. Patti will surely be happy to hear this."

"I tell you, Jer, we've appreciated everybody's prayers and cards and visits." He shook his head as emotion washed over him. "This has been a rough time for us, and all your prayers have been a real support."

"Glad to do it, man." Jerry hung up the fuel pump, picked up the squeegee, and began cleaning his windshield. "Say, what do you make of what's happening because of that problem up on the Mississippi? Isn't that something?"

"I can't say I've paid much attention to it," Mark confessed.

Jerry smiled. "Oh, of course. I understand." His face was a study of concern. "But what I've been reading about the events that'll happen just before the Rapture, man, we could be just days away from being snatched away from this old sin-filled planet." He grew more animated and excited as he spoke. "Hey! Are you coming to that seminar this weekend on last-day events and the rebuilding of the Temple in Jerusalem?"

"I don't know if I can come," Mark countered.

"Well, you ought to try. Maybe Patti can watch Jennifer. I mean, you've really got to come, Mark. Brother Robertson—you know who he is, don't you—is offering us a chance to literally participate in making Bible prophecy come true so that the Rapture can happen. We're not far from being in heaven with Jesus! It's gonna happen in our lifetimes. Are you—?"

His question died on his lips as the over-pump lights went out, the fuel pump display went blank, and the pump stopped. Mark looked around. The store interior was dark, as were all the area buildings. The overhead traffic lights were out at the intersection, too.

"This must be a power failure. Now how am I to know how much I owe for this gas?" Mark puzzled aloud.

"Their computer has a backup power system, so it'll remember and recover when the power comes back on. Just check your bank statement online the next time you get a chance," Jerry told him.

"Good idea. Thanks," Mark said. "I'll see you. I'd better go check on Jennifer." He hung the nozzle back in its cradle and twisted the gas cap into place. Inside the store he found his daughter at the checkout window begging the clerk to take her money.

"I can't take your money, dear, because without electricity the cash register doesn't work, and I can't give you correct change," the clerk explained. "But if you want it, just go ahead and take it."

Jennifer placed the candy bar on the counter. "I can't. My daddy says I can't take something if I haven't paid for it, and you won't take my money, so I can't have it."

Mark took her hand and escorted her back to their SUV. "I'm sorry about the candy bar, honey, but I'm proud of you for not taking it without paying," he said as they drove away. "Listen, I'm sure we have a goodie at home you can have. Besides that, we want to celebrate your coming home, so I'm sure Mom's going to fix you something special for your first night back at home."

They found Hope setting up the old two-burner camp stove atop the kitchen range. "I heard on the radio on the way home that the electricity's going to be off at least four hours. They say the power plant is low on coal, and the nuclear plant is down for a 60-day maintenance cycle that started before the levee broke." She finished pumping pressure into the fuel tank, turned one of the adjustment knobs until she heard the hiss of fuel moving toward the burner, and struck a match. It went out. Another match. No fire. Another match.

"So we have a choice, either a cold lunch or one cooked on this old camping stove—if I can ever get this thing lit."

As Dr. McCormick had predicted, with the continuing chemotherapy ulcers erupted in Jennifer's mouth and throat, and her typically bouncy energy faded into listlessness. The mouthwash helped relieve her discomfort, but new sores replaced older ones as soon as they healed. She started taking a nap each morning and afternoon. Though her blood counts showed that she was getting better, it was painfully obvious that she was not well.

Over the next few days Mark learned to plan his working at home around the scheduled daily power outages. Anticipating how the house would cool during those periods, in the last hour before the power went off the Lancasters and their neighbors set their thermostats in the upper 70s. Of course, that caused an even larger overall drain on the power supply.

By the time electrons again flowed to their hungry appliances, most people were wearing several layers of clothes and perhaps even a coat inside their homes. Prices on kerosene heaters soon reached premium levels—when they were available. The price of kerosene, too, was out of sight.

Mark ordered two long-life batteries for his notebook computer so that he could work through the power outages. Somehow Federal Express managed to get them delivered exactly as promised by the manufacturer. When the power was on, Mark would insert one into his computer until the power meter showed it was fully charged, then exchange it for an uncharged battery. Typically he was draining the second battery or starting on the third when the power returned.

To Hope's distress, MBS News starting calling, asking when she could return to work. At first Brandon Campbell and Peter Leventhal were cooperative. Then they became more insistent. Her daughter was out of the hospital and recovering. Mark was at home, and relatives could watch Jennifer when needed. Hope had a contract with them. Why couldn't she return to work?

It got so that Hope dreaded the ring of the telephone. These men had no idea—no idea—what it was like to have a small child crying from the pain of the mouth sores, a child who fell asleep on the couch after being up only an hour, a little girl who was still on chemo and who needed her mother, not a babysitter. Yes, she understood a contract. She understood their point of view. Still, all that faded into irrelevance when she saw her daughter's pale face and shadowed eyes.

"Hope, I need you for three days. Just three days," Peter pleaded. "Three nights running we're doing a one-hour special about the disaster, and we want you to do the report this next Thursday night. Since channel 3 is owned by the network, we can let you do your part of it from there. But you've got to be here first. What do you think?"

Normally Hope would have been torn between her maternal instinct and her professional drive. She'd loved her work, and she expected to love it again. Yes, it would feel great to get out of the house and back in front of the camera. But what was that Peter had said when he'd first called the hospital? Her daughter was priority one! That was exactly it! Her daughter was mending, but still gravely ill. She was 6 years old. She needed her mother. It seemed that none of the big guns at MBS could comprehend that simple fact.

"Let me think about it," she told him at last. Anything to buy some time. "If I do this, I have to work out a number of things. I'll give you an answer tomorrow."

"OK." He sounded irritable. "Call me by 10:00 a.m." It was not a request; it was a command.

"I'm just not sure what to do," Hope explained to her mother. "It's gotten to the point that if I don't go back to work I'm afraid I'll be fired, and with so many people losing their jobs as a result of that miserable earthquake, I don't know if I could get another job."

Her mom listened sympathetically. "You know, sometimes you have to make hard choices, and there's no easy answer, but God gets you through. Mark's working at home, and you know that I'll help. I can come on over and stay days with Jennifer while you're gone. In fact, I could spend the nights there too, if Mark needs to be out late."

Hope opened her mouth to protest, but Susan put out a hand to hush her. "Are you kidding? I'll love doing it!" Her voice grew soft and tender. "She's my granddaughter. I'd die for her if it would make her well."

Hope and Susan spent the next half hour going over all the possible problems and potential solutions. "I have to feel OK about leaving her," Hope kept saying. "I know you'll take good care of her, Mom, but I have to feel OK about going back to work."

Hope phoned Brandon Campbell the next morning. "I have it worked out—for this one job," she told him. "We'll see how it goes, and I'll tell you up front that I can't promise anything after this." As she spoke, the image of her daughter's pale face and listlessness filled her mind. She took a deep breath and straightened her spine. "But if I'm going to be a member of the team," she went on, "I want to carry my full weight. I want to be in the middle of it like everyone else."

She hardly slept that night, second-guessing her decision. She'd thought that once she'd made the decision, it would be easy, but it wasn't. Mark encouraged her to go. He awoke as she tossed, unsleeping, held her in his arms and promised with a chuckle that between her daddy and her grandma, Jennifer would be spoiled rotten by the time her mom returned.

That Jennifer seemed too weary to care that she was leaving hurt Hope more than anything. *Give it to God,* she told herself as Mark took her to the airport. *You made your decision. Jennifer's in God's hands whether you're there or not.* Praying helped, but her eyes stung just the same.

MBS had sent a chartered twin-engine plane to pick Hope up at the private aviation terminal at Memphis International Airport. Jennifer rode along with them. Her thin body chilled easily, so Hope had dressed her in layers and instructed Mark three times on how to do the same. Mark barely concealed his impatience at the repeated instruction. The thought of separation was hard on both of them.

"Are you sure it's over this way?" Mark asked as they drove past the expansive Federal Express facility with its dozens of aircraft parked on the ramp.

Hope nodded. "I'm sure, hon. Remember when I first went up to Cairo? Same place I had to park for that trip. Only you and Jennifer will be picking me up when I get back." She looked over her shoulder to the back seat. "Right, sweetheart?"

"Right, Mommy."

In only a few minutes it was time for goodbye hugs and kisses all around as the ground crewman delivered Hope's two suitcases to the plane. Minutes later father and daughter were waving to a plane ascending into the clear, cold, windy winter afternoon.

~ ~ ~

"Welcome back!" Peter greeted Hope loudly from across the operations center.

"What's changed? What's the story?" Hope shouted back.

"We're sending you and a crew about 90 minutes north of here to the little town of Millersville, Illinois. The town's been completely without electricity for three—no, four—days, and even in the daytime the temps have been below freezing. So people are resorting to whatever means they have to keep warm—and they're not all good. They've had such a rash of house fires that the local volunteer fire department's been run ragged trying to fight 'em all. Anyway, this morning when they went to a fire, one of their two pumpers ran out of gas before they could get there. The second pumper—because there wasn't any heat in the fire hall—had frozen, and the pump had cracked open and wouldn't work. The tragedy is that four people died in that fire." He shook his head in disbelief.

Peter handed Hope a summary sheet. "The local fire chief will meet you out there. Tigger will be your cameraman. Sleepy will be your sound person, and Grumpy your light man."

Hope's eyebrows went up. "Did you say Tigger, Sleepy, and Grumpy?"

"That's who I said," Peter grunted as he searched for something in the growing pile of paper on his makeshift desk.

"But I thought Grumpy and Sleepy were editors."

"Yeah, but I'm putting them out in the field today. They've

160

been holed up here since the start, so I'm giving them some real-world time.

"Oh, and another thing. I don't know if you noticed, but the local power is out, so we're operating on generators. Everybody—even you—gets to take a turn on the pump watch. That means hauling gas cans, cranking the hand pump, whatever it takes to keep our generators and aircraft refueled. And let me tell you, that can be a real bear, because the pump moves only a pint of fuel every rotation, and one of those smaller helicopters out there carries 160 gallons. That's more than 1,200 turns, and by the end you'll be feeling every one of 'em. As for the Blackhawk, well, you can imagine."

"I guess I should be glad we're driving."

"Yeah," Peter grunted. "Only 60 or so turns. Now get moving."

Hope looked at her suitcases beside the door as she and the crew hurried out to their assignment. *Guess I'll get them over to the motel tonight,* she thought, resigned to the fact that in these trying conditions it was everyone for themselves. She went through her mental checklist to make sure she had everything she needed: a fresh notebook, just wide enough to hold comfortably in her hand; two inexpensive black ballpoint pens; a couple granola bars to nosh on.

Tigger pulled a pair of batteries off the charger and dropped them into his equipment bag, then shouldered his camera on the right and pulled the bag's shoulder strap over his left shoulder. He looked an inch shorter under the weight as he headed for the door. Sleepy and Grumpy each grabbed large equipment cases and carried them out to the SUV they'd be driving on this assignment. Last to go in the vehicle were two cases of MREs, each holding an assorted dozen of the barely palatable meals.

"You expecting to get stuck somewhere?" Hope asked Grumpy in passing as she headed for the front passenger seat. All she got in reply was an indecipherable grunt and shrug of the shoulders.

~ ~ ~

Carter Robinson, owner of Village Center Hardware Store in Millersville, also served as chief of the Millersville Volunteer Fire Department. The crew met him in front of the darkened and silent store and followed his directions to the scene.

Throughout their history the Millersville Volunteer Fire Department had functioned using hand-me-down equipment surplussed by larger cities. The pumper truck dispatched to the fire had been carefully maintained, and the sun reflected in bright rays from every polished surface. Stacks of hose were carefully laid in their trays with nozzles attached. Spare air bottles awaited use by firemen wearing breathing apparatus. But under the circumstances these items were useless, for the fire truck was stranded on the roadside after running out of fuel. Barely visible in the distance lay the still-smoldering ruins of the house where the Armstrong family had perished in their beds.

Chief Robinson put on his firefighting coat, boots, and helmet for the interview. "So I look like a fireman and not like I run a hardware store," he explained as the crew readied their equipment. Grumpy hid a microphone inside the chief's coat to pick up his voice instead of the wind whipping across the flat Illinois farmland.

"We just ran plumb out of fuel," Chief Robinson explained. "Without electricity we can't pump no gas, so we just can't answer fire calls anymore. If it burns, I'm real sorry. There's nuthin' we can do."

"Besides you and the man driving the other truck, how many of your volunteers were able to respond to this alarm?" Hope asked him.

"Only three had enough gas to get here. Then, well, it's pretty obvious there wasn't much they could do once they got here but wait till the fire burned out and look for what was left of the bodies."

"How did the Armstrong family die? What caused the fire?" Hope asked.

"The neighbors said they'd hooked up an old wood-burning heater that hadn't been used for several years. The state fire marshall says the chimney probably set the attic on fire, and the family all died from smoke inhalation."

Chief Carter paused. "Fortunately—if there's a fortunately in dyin' in a house fire—they were sure to've been unconscious—or even gone—before the flames got to them. Once the fire was out, we found their bodies in what was left of their beds." He blinked rapidly. "I mean, nobody wants anybody to die in a fire, but if I *had* to die in a fire, that's the way I'd want to go."

Four oblong objects rested on the ground beside the house. "What are those?" Hope asked.

"Body bags."

Hope could not believe her ears.

"Can we turn off the camera?" Chief Carter requested.

"We're clear," Tigger reported, taking a half step back from the camera.

Carter stared at the ground and kicked at a frozen dirt clod, then answered without looking up. "The county coroner's office and the local funeral home couldn't come. They didn't have the gas to come out and get the bodies. Since the weather's below freezing, we just slid 'em into body bags and left 'em there for pickup later when one of 'em has the gas to come out here and get 'em." Carter toed another dirt clod.

"I think we're through here," Hope murmured after several seconds of silence.

Tigger unclipped the camera from the tripod. "We need to get some footage of the house and a different angle on the truck." He and Grumpy walked off toward the charred remnants of the house. Sleepy began taking down the lights and packing them in their case.

"I was wondering if I could ask you something," Carter said. His eyes barely rose to meet Hope's for the shortest of glances before returning to the ground.

"What's on your mind?" she answered softly.

"Do you have any food you could share? We're out."

For a moment Hope had no idea what to say.

"How many in your family?" she asked.

"Four. Me, the wife, and two kids—they're 14 and 17. We're clean outta food and no way to get to anybody that's got any. Least that we know about."

"Let me talk to my crew when they get back," she told him.

Chief Carter stayed behind as Hope walked toward the rubble. She walked half the distance until she could see the body bags more clearly. The north wind tugged at the heavy black plastic and pressed it over the forms inside. The sight stopped her in her tracks. Her eyes followed her crew whenever they moved to a new position, but as soon as they stopped and began recording, her gaze went back to the silent black row.

~ ~ ~

"My house is right over there," Chief Carter pointed to a house just outside the small cluster of stores that marked the center of Millersville. "You want to come in and meet the family?"

Hope looked at Grumpy, who answered, "That'd be nice, sir, but we've got a deadline to meet, so we've really got to be getting back to Cairo." He signaled to Carter to follow him as he opened the driver's door. Going around to the rear, he opened the back door and passed him the two boxes of MREs.

The look of puzzlement on Carter's face quickly turned to gratitude. "Thank you! Thank you!" he repeated as Grumpy closed the door.

"You handled that well," Hope said as Grumpy slid back in the driver's seat.

"Why do you think we have so many of 'em back in Cairo?" he replied.

Hope smiled. "I think we need to find you a new nickname."

~ ~ ~

Hope began working out mentally how to tell the story as they headed toward the main highway leading south toward Cairo. "Could somebody pass me the player and the tapes?" she asked.

Sleepy turned around, managed to open one of the equipment cases behind the back seat, and passed the equipment up to Hope. She plugged the power adapter into the computer power outlet and dropped the digital cassette into the player. Its four-inch screen flickered to life. She fast-forwarded through parts, then backed up the tape to review the better visuals. From time to time she paused the tape and copied the timing numbers from an LCD readout into her notepad so that the film editor could find the place again when he began assembling the actual report.

The different views of the burned house and the stalled fire engine filled one tape. The interview with Chief Carter was on the second. She reviewed parts of it several times and noted a number of places with good sound bites. Then she just let it run.

"Hey, Tigger! I thought you turned off the camera!"

"Did I do something wrong?"

"Uh, well, he did ask us to turn it off," she answered.

"Well, Leventhal's number one rule is never turn off the camera. It's better to have it and cut it than wish you'd recorded it."

"I guess you're right, but I'm not going to use it. I mean, he *did* ask us to turn it off."

"Yeah, but that's the punchiest part of the story!"

"I guess so." Hope bit her lower lip and looked out the window at the farmland. "I want Peter to look at it and decide. I just don't feel right about using it."

"I'm still in shock," Hope told Peter as they returned to the Ops Center.

"Good! Can you package it in, oh, 75 seconds?"

She nodded. "Sure. Then I'd better get cracking. Who's my editor?"

"You. We're running a skeleton crew here now. I'd give you Grumpy or Sleepy, but I'm sending them out to set up for tonight's broadcast. You've got one hour till we need it for the East Coast newscast."

At her request, Peter viewed the recording made after Chief Carter had asked that the camera be turned off. "Use it as a voice-over with the chief talking while you show the bodies," he ordered.

Fifty-five minutes later Hope handed the chief broadcast technician a DVD with her edited report recorded on it. He watched it, proclaimed it good, and began typing commands on his control computer to sequence it into the broadcast.

"Where's Brandon?" Hope asked. "I heard he was still here."

"He was," the technician replied. "Left about an hour ago to set up for his live shots out at the levee break. The Corps of Engineers is getting close to closing it up. Could happen as soon as tomorrow—if the weather holds. There's a big storm system just to our north that's dumped a load of snow over the past couple days, and now a warm front's moved across the area. So all that snow's melting and turning into water that's going to flow downstream and try to wash out the levee just as they're trying to close it up. Should be fun to watch."

"Who's covering that?" Hope asked.

"You." He turned away to decide another item for the evening's broadcasts.

"Four minutes to air," someone called from the control desk in front of the wall of monitors showing all the various video inputs—from a live camera, videotape, computer memory, and DVD. "Brandon's on his mark and ready. We're ready. Now, folks, let's all put our thumbs together and start twiddling to make the clock move faster," the technician declared with mock seriousness. All the response he got was a smile crossing the faces of the other broadcast technicians as they stayed focused on their tasks.

"Two minutes."

"One minute. Everybody stand by!"

On one of the screens Hope saw Brandon Campbell spit out a candy of unknown description, take a sip of water, and hand the bottle to someone just off camera. He then put on his camera face and positioned himself to look the world in the eye. The prerecorded introduction played, and an announcer's voice from New York declared, "This is the *MBS Evening News.* Coming to you tonight from the scene of America's greatest natural disaster."

The picture on the on-air monitor showed construction equipment at work, then pulled back to show Brandon Campbell in the foreground. "Tonight the round-the-clock effort to force the mighty Mississippi River back into its banks is hours away from success. Sometime tomorrow the Army Corps of Engineers and its contractors hope to push the last truckload of dirt and rock into that narrowing channel behind us. Filling that hole will put the mighty Mississippi River back into its banks and allow thousands of acres of Missouri farmland to drain. Considering how many cities are without electricity tonight and how many people are without jobs—or even food—as a result of this earthquake and the breaking of the levee, the cost of rebuilding will likely be the smallest of expenses resulting from this disaster."

Hope turned away. There was something about being in the middle of such a story that gripped her and made her adrenaline pump. At the same time the personal, individual enormity of suffering almost overwhelmed her.

The first field report focused on a Missouri town that had

been wiped out by the flooding. One after another of the residents voiced conflicting decisions on how they'd get on with their lives. Some wanted to return and rebuild as soon as the waters subsided. Others had already decided to abandon whatever property they owned and begin their lives wherever and however they could.

For a time Brandon Campbell turned to world events and the increasing tension in the Middle East. Another Palestinian suicide bomber had blown himself up, this time at a fast-food restaurant in a pedestrian mall in the Israeli port city of Haifa, killing seven. The Israeli cabinet was meeting to discuss how best to respond to the ongoing terrorism.

Returning to the domestic news, there was a story about Wall Street's negative reaction as companies in almost every sector of the economy were reporting reduced earnings and even losses as a result of the disaster. The stocks of many companies were dropping: electric utilities with shut-down power plants, department stores with falling sales, even supermarket and drugstore chains. The nation's economy was not just staggering, but racing toward upheaval. Leading economists were starting to use the word "depression."

Then with two minutes left to go, Brandon began the lead-in to Hope's report. "We wanted to leave you tonight with a story that captures the enormity of what has happened here in human terms. We sent our reporter Hope Lancaster to Millersville, Illinois, where the fire department can't answer emergency calls because the lack of electricity prevents them from fueling their fire trucks. We close our broadcast tonight with her report."

The picture changed to that of a shiny pumper truck reflecting the sun, a burned-out house in the distance. Hope began painting the verbal picture. Then came clips of Chief Carter's remarks mixed with Hope's voice-overs helping to tell the story. But the final scene had no human voice, only the moan of the wind blowing across the frozen earth as it rattled a loose piece of charred roofing tin and rumpled the stiff plastic of the body bags in the foreground. The haunting sounds continued as the closing credits rolled.

Then the on-air picture changed abruptly to a lively promo for a comedy airing later that night.

"That's a wrap. Let's get picked up and organized for tomorrow," Peter commanded as soon as the closing credits aired and programming shifted back to the New York City's MBS broadcast control center. "Are there any stories that we need to shoot or edit tonight for the morning news?" A producer handed Peter two DVDs with a printout detailing how they were being scheduled in the morning program. A second producer delivered details about who would be reporting live and from where.

"Hope, the closure ceremony at the levee is scheduled for sometime after 10:00 a.m. tomorrow. Be here by 9:00," Peter commanded, "and we'll put you on the bird over there. We've managed to get a crane in for a bird's-eye view of the actual closing. There should be some good video that'll need a live voice-over. I want you there."

Hope stared off into space, only vaguely aware that Peter was talking to her.

"You OK, Hope?" Peter asked.

Startled, she looked his direction.

"How early do I need to be here to help with fueling the helicopter?" Hope asked.

A teasing smile crossed his face. "Gotcha!" He threw back his head and roared. "Listen, the fuel truck's got a power takeoff driving the pump, so nobody has to crank anything. I was just kidding you."

"I need to get out of here for a while," Hope said, turning to the door. "Anyplace open where I can go eat and be alone for a while?"

"Only place I know of that's open is Café MRE," Peter answered. "Now if you just want to be alone, there's lots of space outside to take a walk."

"You know, you're a real gourmet," Hope said sarcastically as her eyes wandered to the stack of boxes against the wall labeled Meals. Ready-to-eat.

"Well, at least they won't give you the trots like the food I've eaten in a few places around the world," he answered.

Hope picked a box without reading the contents and extracted a chicken-something-or-other meal. She looked at the brown wrapper and turned up her nose.

"It beats going hungry," Tigger sing-songed as he walked past.
"Yeah, but not by much," she shot back.

~ ~ ~

When it had become apparent that the MBS crew would be in Cairo for an extended time, someone had located some two-by-fours and paneling and divided a storage room on one side of the small aircraft hangar into a bunk room for the different genders. Military-style stacking bunk beds filled each room. When you wanted to sleep, you took whatever bed was available or unoccupied.

"Shades of summer camp without the waterskiing," Hope said to no one in particular as she surveyed the room and picked a top bunk that was empty. She unrolled her sleeping bag and slid her suitcase under the lower bed.

Fortunately the water in the building was heated with natural gas, so there was no restriction on how much hot water a person could use. Hope took the time to wash her hair well, then combed it out before setting it with old-fashioned curlers. Then she smeared a good layer of night moisturizing cream over her face

"I'm glad you're on *that* side of the wall," a male coworker exclaimed as she made her way to the bunk room.

"Yeah, but in the morning you'll still be ugly," she teased playfully. It felt good to be working again, Hope realized as she settled onto her bunk. Even so, her heart was back in Memphis with Mark and Jennifer, and she couldn't wait to return to them.

~ ~ ~

Sliding off her bunk, Hope wrapped her coat around her body, picked up her cell phone, and tiptoed into the now-quiet production room. She felt her way through the darkness to a corner as far from the "dorm" as possible.

"Hello?"

"Mark! Wow, it's good to hear your voice!"

"Hi, sweetheart," he said. "I just saw you on TV. That was a real tear-jerk story. You were very professional, but I could tell it really got to you."

Hope took a ragged breath and let it out. "Yeah, you know me. It was a tough story. Those . . ." Her voice dropped to a whisper. "Those body bags. Mom and Dad and two kids."

"It's hard to comprehend, isn't it?" Mark commented.

"It is. But you know—" She sank down against the wall and pulled her coat even tighter. "Mark, do you remember my friend Karen, who spent a couple of years teaching in a developing country?" Even as she spoke she visualized the young woman. Fresh out of graduate school with a passion to give something back to the world that had treated her so well.

Mark chuckled. "Of course, I know Karen."

"Well, I remember her telling me that in the winter the classrooms were so cold that both she and the students dressed in layers of shirts and sweaters. They even wore knitted mufflers and caps in the classroom. Some of the kids wore old gloves with the fingers cut out of the right-hand one so they could take notes easier." She laughed. "Mark, Karen *taught* in that get-up. She said it was bone-chilling cold, but that's how it was, and she got so she didn't think much about it."

Both were silent for long seconds, then Mark asked, "So what are you saying?"

Hope shrugged as though he could see her. "I don't know. I suppose . . . I guess . . . well, we Americans have had so *much* for so *long* that we're like infants unable to handle anything uncomfortable." She coughed a couple of times. It was cold where she was too. "Mark!" she said, passion filling her voice. "Mark, four people *died* in that fire because . . . well, I don't know *why*. Maybe they were afraid of being cold, or they didn't know how to fix whatever it was that malfunctioned and caused the fire. We're just used to having so much!"

Mark sighed. He'd had a long day. Jennifer had thrown up twice. It broke his heart to see her so sick. Thank the Lord for a few hours of electricity to run the washer and drier, and thank Him for Susan, who washed the sheets and blanket while he worked at his computer. He had more than he could handle in his own small world. He couldn't stretch his mind to include the charred bodies of a family that only wanted to stay warm.

"How's Jennifer?" Hope broke into his thoughts.

"Well, you know."

"I don't know!" she countered, irritable. "How *is* she?"

"Oh, sweetheart, she's OK. She had a rough day. Threw up

twice, but your mother is terrific with her. And I'm here too. She's OK. Really."

Hope hadn't realized that tears were so close to the surface. "I shouldn't be here," she moaned.

"Seriously, it's fine. Mom lay down with her until she went to sleep tonight. Oh," he brightened. "I dug out the intercom we used when Jennifer was a baby and set it up in her room and my office and our bedroom. I can hear every move she makes."

"That's good. That's a good idea." They talked a while longer, simply taking comfort in hearing each other's voice. Then Hope started thinking aloud about what she'd seen all day.

"Mark, it's like life's been reduced to an almost-preindustrial state. You can't drive your car because there's no electricity to pump the gas. You can't cook on an electric stove because there's no electricity. In a lot of places you can't call on the telephone because it uses electricity and the phone company's backup batteries have all died. You can't get money at the ATM—assuming you have any left—because they aren't working." Her voice had risen, her tone shrill. "You can't shop at the grocery store because you don't have gas to get there, but say you've managed to carpool—when you do get to the store you can't pay because all the cash registers are computerized. The stores are in chaos. If it requires electricity, you can't do it."

"It's amazing how much we rely on electricity," Mark mused, mentally calculating everything in their home that required the invisible power.

"Even so, we're lucky," his wife said. "I mean, we're hearing stories of people on the verge of starvation."

"Oh, Hope, I find that hard to believe," Mark told her. "It takes a good while to actually starve to death."

"Well, someone's going to check into it. However, we're running a story on the morning news about a mother whose baby died from an ear infection because she couldn't get him to the doctor or get the antibiotic he needed. An ear infection! How many ear infections did Jennifer have when she was a baby?"

"Several," Mark answered thoughtfully.

"Can you imagine that mother's anguish? I mean, your child's running this high fever, and you know all you need is an antibiotic to help him get well, but you can't get it because you can't get to the doctor." Hope choked on her words.

"This happens every day in many countries around the world," Mark mused. "We've been so fortunate for so long . . ."

"Well, anyway, because of that situation this afternoon the Illinois governor ordered the National Guard to set up generators to keep the phone system operating. They're also setting up medical aid stations that people can come to."

"Without transportation, how will anyone get to the aid stations?"

"The National Guard is to go around and check on everybody they can reach and transport them to medical aid stations if they need it."

Silence filled the connection for a few seconds as both pondered the problems and implications of that.

"So what are you and Jennifer going to do this weekend?"

"We really haven't decided. There's a new VeggieTales movie opening this weekend that I was thinking about taking her to see if she's feeling up to it. Plus, your dad sent over a copy of that book by that fellow Robertson. The one about the Rapture and the rebuilding of the Temple in Jerusalem. I'm reading it when Jennifer's in bed."

"Is it good?"

"Yeah, matter of fact, it is," Mark answered. "He presents a pretty convincing case that we're about to witness the final events in this planet's history before the Rapture. It sort of puts everything else in perspective, Hope. To tell you the truth, I'm getting excited."

Silence filled the connection again.

"Something wrong, hon?" Mark asked. He'd picked up the book again and was studying the back cover.

"I guess I'm still pretty absorbed in that story I did today. It's one of those that grabs you by the gut and is hard to put behind you."

"Yeah." He didn't remind her that they'd just discussed it.

"I guess, well, the fact that four people died, and the neighbors who were supposed to save them couldn't because the fire department didn't have enough gas in their trucks to get the last few yards to the fire, much less enough water to fight it."

It was Mark's turn to be silent. "That's pretty dramatic, all right."

"But I don't think that's what's disturbing me," Hope said slowly.

"Well, what is?"

"Millersville wasn't the first place this has happened. This kind of tragedy is being repeated all over the blackout zone. This is just the first time we've reported it—and things like this aren't supposed to be happening until during the Tribulation." She paused. Her voice dropped even lower. "I'm wondering if things are really going to happen the way I've been taught, or if somehow the Rapture's already happened, and we've been left behind."

"I don't know, sweetheart. I just don't know."

CHAPTER SEVENTEEN

The pilot circled several hundred feet above the work area on the river levee, then gently set the helicopter down on the temporary helipad marked by spray paint on the hard-packed dirt. Two hundred yards to the south stood a cluster of construction trailers with a U.S. Army Corps of Engineers project sign in front. The pilot took off as soon as his passengers were away from the heaviest rotor downwash.

"You must be Hope Lancaster from MBS," the only man in sight wearing a suit and tie said as he put out his hand to greet her. "I'm Oliver Nelson, public affairs. It's a pleasure to meet you." He beckoned her through a door he held open just as the rotor downwash from an arriving helicopter began blowing their hair and clothes. Hope swept a bundle of hair back off her face and noted that Mr. Nelson was doing the same, the difference being that his covered only partly a mostly bald pate.

"Your remote truck and crew got here a couple hours ago. They're set up in a good vantage point to see everything. Say, you're based over at Cairo, aren't you? How long did it take you to get over here?"

"Fifteen minutes."

Mr. Nelson laughed. "What a contrast. You know how long it took your remote truck to get over here?"

Hope nodded. "They left last night."

"Traffic's been really jammed up since the earthquake took down the I-57 bridge. We're two, maybe three hours' drive from St. Louis, and it's taking us a minimum of five hours to get there," Mr. Nelson observed. "It's ridiculous. I sure hope they

174

can get that bridge rebuilt in a lot less time than the two years somebody estimated."

Inside the building Hope found a beehive of activity as engineers bent over tables studying drawings and progress reports. Satellite weather maps were pinned on the walls along with dozens of miscellaneous items. "This is where all the work's been coordinated from for the last three weeks or so," Oliver Nelson explained. "In there is the project superintendent's office. You'll meet him in an hour or so at the press conference before the last loads of rock are dumped into the gap. We just need to get you signed in here and issue you a hard hat before we go out to the work area."

Hope signed in on the visitor log and was given a hard hat emblazoned across the front with *Hope Lancaster, MBS News* in tape printed on a lettering machine. "Maybe you can give me some detail on what's happening with the river in the area that's been flooded," she said. "Down at Memphis, where I live, the water dropped a couple feet for about a week, then went back to normal. Where's this new channel the river's been cutting? And where's it dumping back into the old channel?"

Mr. Nelson thought about the question. "We've got an entire team at our regional office up in St. Louis working to answer that, but I can give you a five-cent answer." He led her over to a wall where a large printout of a satellite photo was pinned.

"We're up here." He pointed to where the photo showed the water spilling through the broken levee. "This photo is about three days old. See how the river has formed these meandering channels? That's the way the river flowed some 150 years ago, before it was dammed and the levees built. Near as we can tell, the river's making at least three channels between here and where it flows back into the old channel down here"—he pointed to a spot on the lower part of the photo—"at the town of New Madrid. Does that name sound familiar?"

Hope nodded. "Of course. The New Madrid Fault. You know, I flew over that area a few days ago. It looked like the river was about to take out the town of New Madrid."

"Well, almost. The river is using old drainage channels such as creeks and small rivers, so they're swollen and flooding and dumping a lot of water back into the main channel at New

175

Madrid. And just a couple miles north of town one of these twists in the new channel is eating its way west within a half mile of Interstate 55. We've got a crew down there building up a dike to try to stop it. You can imagine what would happen if the river cut that highway, too! But our real solution is cutting off the water up here where we are so it doesn't get down there."

"Assuming that the levee repair works, how long until the river can be back open to barge traffic?" Hope asked.

"Now, that's the $64,000 question. Or, in our case, the $64 billion," Mr. Nelson laughed. "We estimate three to four weeks to survey the river bottom and mark the channel before the river will be open for navigation. Now, that's the Coast Guard's job. They set and maintain the navigation buoys. The Corps of Engineers maintains the levees and dredges where the Coast Guard says the river bottom needs to be dredged."

"Three to four weeks before the barges can start moving?"

Mr. Nelson nodded. "Officially. But the scuttlebutt says we'll see our first raft of barges pass here this afternoon or tonight—once the water level's back up to where the Ohio River comes in. You know, as the work's been going along, the river's been coming up a bit at a time. It's down only a foot or so right now. So it's more of an insurance question than any-thing else."

Hope looked up from her notepad. "Insurance? Explain."

"They get charged higher insurance premiums if they go through an area where the Coast Guard's not marked the chan-nel. Maybe they can't get insurance at all. So what happens if they run aground on a sandbar that's built up because of the changed river current? From what we've been hearing, most of the towboat skippers think they'll be safe if they just stick to the middle of the river."

"When will the river be back to full depth?" Hope asked.

"It's almost there right now. We've been closing the levee break bit by bit, so the water level's been coming up slowly all the time. Right now we're only about a foot or so below where it should be. The only thing keeping them from running right now is that the river is officially closed above the Ohio River, until the levee break is filled."

The MBS production truck was a five-minute walk down the

176

levee from the job site trailers. Walking into a chill wind along the way made Hope thankful that she'd worn wool pants and her long coat, in contrast with a reporter from a competing network who was wearing a knee-length skirt and tightly clutching her coat around her shivering frame.

The MBS truck stood in the middle of a row of nearly two dozen local and network satellite broadcast trucks of various description clustered behind a viewing stand hurriedly constructed for the occasion. Two levels of risers at the back let the TV cameras and still photographers see over each other, and the heads of the reporters congregated at the front to hear the dignitaries make their pronouncements about the significance of the event. A few yards beyond the speaker's stand, a small torrent of water rushed through the remaining 30-foot-wide gap in the levee. A row of oversized dump trucks bearing large rocks stood ready for the signal to empty their loads into the gap.

Waiting for the ceremony to begin, Hope's mind wandered to Jennifer and Mark. She'd managed to talk to Mark before she'd begun her day. She'd awakened him, but she didn't care and thought he was actually glad. Jennifer had slept well all night, he'd told her. In fact, was still asleep. Now, standing here in the biting wind, she laughed at her mother-foolishness. She'd made Mark get up and go check on Jennifer in her bed—just to be certain. He'd done so cheerfully. *He's a good guy,* she thought, *and a great dad. No wonder I love him so much.*

Precisely at 10:00 a.m. a cluster of dignitaries strode to the speaker's stand to be introduced. The district and national commanders of the Army Corps of Engineers were there as well as the governor of Missouri and the construction superintendents.

"Today we're witnessing the climax in one of the great contests between man and nature that the Corps of Engineers has a long history of winning," the Corps' national commander proclaimed. "Few people understand the awesome power of this river. We've witnessed what can happen when disaster strikes and a levee is broken. Thousands of truckloads of rock and dirt have been dumped into the gap, and hundreds of pilings driven down to bedrock, to get us to the point you see today." The wind whistled through the microphone, catching his words and flinging them back toward him. He raised his voice a notch and spoke distinctly to make certain he was heard and understood. Hope noticed, and admired his ability.

"This final act you are about to witness is small compared to the challenge we have seen in recent days. There were times when the flow of water through the gap was so strong that huge rocks were swept away seconds after being dumped. But over the past few days the torrent has been slowed. In minutes you will see it stopped.

"Our society depends on this river being contained and re-strained to support commerce. The mighty Mississippi is a water highway supporting commerce up the center of our great country. In recent weeks we've witnessed the terrible, even tragic, results of this river highway being interrupted. But today we are returning the river to its previous boundaries so that it can begin serving us again."

Each of the other officials made a few brief remarks, then the signal was given for the work to resume. Alternating truck-loads of large and small rock were dumped into the gap, then smoothed by large bulldozers as the gap narrowed. In about 20 minutes the flow was reduced to a trickle, then halted. The river rose visibly. More truckloads of dirt and smaller rock were dumped and pushed into what remained of the gap as the levee once again rose above the flow.

"Ladies and gentlemen, the Mississippi River is back within its normal banks," the national commander proclaimed.

~ ~ ~

Eighteen miles up the Ohio River, the *Missy M* sat tied to a coal loading pier on the Kentucky side of the river. Secured to the front of the powerful towboat was a raft of 12 coal barges. The overhead conveyor had stopped filling the last barge some 90 minutes before. Normally the crew would have cast off their mooring lines and headed downstream within minutes after the loading was completed. But this morning the six-man crew sat in the compact dining room watching the levee completion story on the TV mounted inside an overhead cupboard.

"Well, gentlemen, it's time to go back to work," the skipper declared as he rose from his seat and stretched. "Stand by to cast off all lines and head north. Kyle, you start at the bow. Greg, you start at the stern. You guys work toward each other."

Kyle and Greg pulled on their coats, gloves, and hats and then fastened their mandatory bright-orange self-inflating life vests around the outside of their insulation before heading out. They made their way out the door, forward along the narrow side deck, and up the ladder onto the barges, which were roped together into a raft four long and three wide. One line on the port side of each barge held them against the loading pier.

"Forward lines are free," Kyle radioed to the skipper in the pilothouse.

"Aft lines are free," Greg reported. A burst of static followed his report.

"Gentlemen, we are under way," Jimmy radioed back as the diesel engines roared to life, first pulling the *Missy M* and her cargo back into the slack water at the side of the river, then pushing out toward the current. Fifteen minutes after the first line was cast off 48,000 tons of coal were being borne easily down the Ohio River toward the mighty Mississippi. Two hours later, just past Cairo and the buoy that marked the start of the Mississippi River channel, the skipper turned the wheel hard to the right, added power on the left propeller, and shifted the right into full reverse power. Water roiled and boiled from under the right side of the *Missy M* as it fought to change the course of the barges. Completing the turn took nearly 10 minutes, and for a moment the lashed load stood still as the skipper adjusted the throttles to measure the speed of the current. "Two and a half knots," he declared aloud to himself before pushing the throttles forward to begin making eight knots upstream.

~ ~ ~

Inside of an hour Hope had completed her stand-ups for her evening news report and transmitted the whole package to Peter in Cairo. "What've we got to eat?" she asked as she looked around the inside of the production truck.

Someone pointed to a cardboard box. "More MREs. Take your pick. We've got two or three different kinds of chicken, pork and beans, a couple beefs, and even a vegetarian."

Hope groaned. "What time's the chopper getting here to pick me up?"

"'Bout 20 minutes," the lead video technician piped up. "They'll be leaving Cairo in about five minutes or so. They'll have you back in Cairo and on your plane home in about an hour."

~ ~ ~

Jennifer flew into her mother's arms just a few steps away from the plane that returned her to Memphis International Airport. "Mommy! I'm so glad to see you!" she cried as she threw both arms around Hope's waist and held on.

Hope returned the embrace, thinking that she could hold her tight for a week, then reached out to include Mark in the hug. "I'm so glad to be home. What's for lunch?" she asked. "You would not believe what I've been eating!"

"Well, they say the electricity will be back on in time for us to cook something, so what do you want?" Mark asked.

"Anything that doesn't taste like an MRE."

"Why not?" Jennifer asked. "I kind of like 'em."

Hope shot Mark a demanding glance. He shrugged. "Hey, when you told us you were eating MREs, well, she wanted to know what they were. So I went to the camping supply store and bought several. I mean, they weren't great, but they weren't all that bad," he said. "Worst part is the price. I mean, they've more than doubled in price above where they were a couple months ago. We could all eat at Wendy's or McDonald's for the price of one MRE."

"Well, I guess they're not all that bad, but just imagine having only MREs to eat for four days. The first one was OK, but after that it was all downhill," Hope declared. "Know what else I want besides a home-cooked meal?"

"What?" father and daughter chorused together.

"A bubble bath. I want to soak in a hot bubble bath until my skin gets all wrinkled up. Then I want to go out and get my hair done."

Everyone laughed as they hurried into the SUV. The weather hadn't gotten any warmer while she was gone, Hope noticed. "The power must be back on," Mark observed as they pulled through an intersection. "That traffic light wasn't working when we came the other way."

Hope turned around to look at her daughter. A red-and-blue

knit cap covered her dark hair. Hope wondered if Susan had bought it. It was pretty, but dark shadows circled the child's eyes. Even so, she flashed her mother a bright smile.

"Ah! It's good to be home!" Hope exclaimed as she walked through the garage door into the kitchen. She turned to embrace her husband once again, raising her face for another kiss. He kissed her, but something felt wrong. She pulled back and looked at him. "What's wrong?"

"Nothing we need to talk about now. Let's see what Jennifer and I can pull together for supper while you enjoy that bubble bath." Mark looked her direction but not *at* her, and her heart jumped into her throat.

"No, Mark. Something's wrong. I can see it in your face. Tell me about it," she hissed. "Is it Jennifer?"

"No! No, nothing's changed there. Her blood counts are still getting better." He drew her into his arms. How he hated the fear that filled her eyes. He kissed the top of her head. "I never could hide anything for very long, could I?" he exclaimed.

"Mommy. Come here," a little voice called. "There's a surprise."

"All right, I'm coming." Hope tossed Mark a wink. "I'll be back. You stay put!" She squeezed his hand and followed the voice to Jennifer's pink-and-white room. The little girl had a tea party set up around a small table. Dolls sat in two of the small chairs. The other two chairs were empty.

"You sit here, Mommy," she directed. "I'll sit here. And Madeleine and Isabella will sit there!" Loving the lilt in her voice, Hope eased herself onto the small wooden chair. It was only then that she saw that juice filled the tiny cups and raisin cookies covered the small flowered plate in the center of the table. *This* was going to take a while.

"Grammie helped me," she said proudly. "I told her what I wanted, and she made the cookies. I helped her stir in the raisins."

"This looks beautiful," Hope told her. And it was. She recognized one of her mom's embroidered tea towels serving as a tablecloth. "Am I hungry!"

~ ~ ~

"OK, I got an e-mail from Gene yesterday," Mark began

hours later after Jennifer had gone to bed. "It's not good news. Everybody's being laid off indefinitely. Sales are down as a result of this river disaster and all the power outages, so everybody's being laid off until it gets better."

"Laid off?" Hope asked with alarm in her voice. "Can you get unemployment compensation, or something like it? What does that do to our health insurance? Will we be able to keep Jennifer in treatment? How will we pay our bills?"

Mark waved his hands for her to sit down. "Relax, honey. Yes, I'll have unemployment compensation for a while. And remember that buyout bonus I got? We paid off both cars and put enough on the principal of the house loan that it'll be paid off in only two years. It'll be tight, but we can make it that long." He countered her worried look with a confident smile. "We've still got your paycheck. That'll cover the mortgage and utilities and things like that. If we have to, we'll just dip into our savings."

Lips tightly pursed, Hope just stared at Mark.

"You don't believe me, do you?"

"No! No, I don't." She shook her head. "I wish I had your level of confidence that things are going to get better. I don't think you realize just how bad things are, and what an impact this river disaster is having on the nation's economy."

"Hope! It'll all be over soon," Mark countered.

"Oh?" She stood up and strode to the window. "Mark, I've been out there—where it's all happening. I think it's a lot more grim than anyone in power is letting on."

"Really, sweetheart? You're missing one key thing."

She didn't turn. "And that is—?"

"The Rapture," he declared. "It won't be long until we're in heaven and looking back on this world while everybody who's left behind has to go through the Tribulation."

"You sound so confident." She almost kept the sarcasm out of her voice. "Until we're snatched away, I think I'll save on the electric bill by taking a quick shower. I'll see you in a few minutes." The last words were flung over her shoulder as she headed up the stairs.

"You don't sound very happy about it," Mark shot back.

She stopped on the fourth step and turned around. "Right now I'm just thankful to be home. I want to enjoy a hot shower in my own bathroom. I want to eat a home-cooked meal instead of MREs for breakfast, lunch, and supper. I want to sleep in my own bed. Do you mind if I enjoy those things for a little while?"

Mark just stared.

"What's got you so all fired up about the Rapture, anyway?" Hope demanded.

"Because I've spent this weekend reading Reverend Robertson's book on last-day events. And you know what's got me really excited?"

"What?"

"The idea that—in the next year or two—people could actually be rebuilding the Temple in Jerusalem and causing the fulfillment of Bible prophecy."

Hope sighed. "Tell you what. You read some more while I go take a shower. Then I'm going to bed early, because I want to enjoy sleeping in *my* bed with *my* husband instead of in a sleeping bag on an Army-style bunk bed in a room with 10 other people. Tomorrow morning I'm going out to get my hair done so I'll look good when I host tomorrow night's edition of Disaster in the Heartland. After that, Peter's given me two days off, so maybe we can attend that seminar together. But until then I'm focused on the here and now!"

~ ~ ~

The next night at five minutes to 8:00, Mark and Jennifer sat down in front of their large-screen TV with apple juice and a big bowl of popcorn to watch Hope's edition of the nightly disaster documentary. Jennifer snuggled against her daddy with a happy sigh.

"And now, reporting from Memphis, Hope Lancaster," the announcer intoned as the opening graphics dissolved into the screen.

"Good evening. Tonight we have good news and bad news. The good news is that the Mississippi River is again within its banks, and barges loaded with coal are already moving up the river toward electric power plants."

"I like seeing Mommy!" Jennifer giggled.

"Me too," Mark agreed.

"In another week or so barge traffic on the river will be back to normal. That means darkened cities up and down the center of America's industrial and farming heartland will soon have their electricity restored, and disrupted lives can begin returning to normal. Products from factories along the Ohio, Mississippi, Missouri, and other rivers will again move freely to their destinations. As that starts happening, millions of laid-off workers are hoping they'll soon be called back to their jobs and—as a result—will be able to feed their families once again."

The picture changed to a split screen with Hope on the left and a field reporter on the right. "Correspondent Rhea Thomas in St. Louis tells us more about that," Hope said crisply. The image of the reporter zoomed out to fill the screen.

"That's right, Hope. Just a month ago it was normal to flip a light switch and expect a room to light up. But these past few weeks have changed people's perspective," he intoned.

The picture changed to the mayor of St. Louis. "I always took having electricity for granted. I'm hopeful we can get our electricity restored in the next week or so. If that happens, come Thanksgiving we'll truly be giving thanks to God—and the Army Corps of Engineers," he declared.

The reporter continued with a capsule version of the economic disaster in the St. Louis area.

"That's just a sampling of the impact," Hope picked up the narration. "This crisis is having such a large impact on our nation's economy that one observer has compared it to the estimates made by war planners back during the cold war of what might result if our nation suffered a limited nuclear attack. We turn now to Wall Street correspondent Martin Baker, who gives us a closer look at the true costs of this calamity."

Mark listened to the report with decreasing attention until Hope reappeared on the screen. He smiled. Truly he was blessed to have a loving, loyal wife who was also talented and beautiful! He slipped his arm around his daughter and held her close. He might not have a job, but he still had the two most precious people in his life. Yes, he was blessed.

"I love you, Daddy," Jennifer said.

"I love you too, sweetie."

By 8:30 two things were clear: the nation was in deep trouble and Jennifer, curled against her father's side and wrapped in his arm, was sound asleep. Tenderly he picked her up and carried her up the stairs to her bed. "Nite-nite," he bade as he closed her bedroom door. The only answer was the light whisper of her slumbering.

As Mark settled back into the leather-covered couch, Hope was moderating a discussion between a prominent minister, who was also a university president, and a politician—they disagreed about the significance of the disaster. The first declared that it was a wake-up call, one of God's warnings to the nation and the world that the Rapture was about to occur. "Any day now you could be going down the freeway when suddenly the car in front of you swerves off the road because its driver has been snatched away," he warned.

The politician disagreed. "Natural disasters happen. That's why they're called 'natural' disasters, and the American economy has an amazing ability to recover from disasters. It may take us a year or two, but we'll bounce back and once again be on the road to prosperity. I recall when—"

"Uh, gentlemen," Hope's voice was composed but urgent. "I hate to interrupt you, but I'm getting word of a breaking story. There's been another suicide bombing in Israel. We're going to break away and go to Frank Burton, our correspondent in Jerusalem." The screen split again, showing Hope on one side and the reporter on the other. "Frank, what can you tell us?"

"Hope, less than an hour ago a Palestinian suicide bomber detonated an explosive device attached to his body at a bus stop in Tel Aviv. Early reports say the bomber was trying to board a bus when the driver realized what he was trying to do, began shouting a warning to everybody around, and closed the door in front of him. It was at that moment that the man set off his device. The word we have from Israeli officials is that at least four people were killed and at least another dozen have been injured. Again, at least four people have been killed and a dozen wounded when a bus driver closed the door in the face of a suicide bomber, and that bomber set off his device in the crowd outside the bus. There is no word yet what the Israeli government's response will be. Hope, back to you."

The camera shifted back to Hope. "Thank you, Frank. We'll await further developments as they happen." She paused for an instant to collect her thoughts and listen to instructions from the director talking in her hidden earpiece. "It would seem that this is a night filled with disaster, first a natural one here in the United States and then a human-made one in Israel reminds us that the world is still turning, and things still happen in other places even though our attention is focused here. Folks, we're going to conclude tonight by listening to people who have been touched by the Mississippi River disaster. Here's their story in their own words."

First up was a Red Cross worker at an emergency shelter in Missouri who told of the spirit of cooperation among the displaced people she'd encountered. Mark picked up the remote control and turned off the TV. His wife would be home in less than an hour, probably wanting a little something to eat, then to relax for a few minutes and then go to bed. He, however, had another idea. First, he checked the kitchen to be sure all food had been put away and the dirty dishes put into the dishwasher. Next, he went around the house attending to all the little things Hope typically checked before retiring for the night: that the back door was locked, that the lights above the patio had been turned off, and so forth.

Then going to a cupboard, he picked up a number of candle bases, inserted long, scented tapers into them, and placed them strategically around the kitchen, living room, stairway, and upstairs bedroom. When he ran out of the candle bases, he took saucers from the cupboard and placed small votive candles on them. After several minutes he paused to survey the placements and smiled at the thought of his plan.

When Hope was an anchor at the station, it typically took her 35 minutes after she went off the air until she was home. So 32 minutes after she went off air he picked up a lighter and, starting in the bedroom, began setting the wicks aflame and turning off the lights as he went through the house. Finally, he lit a cluster of scented candles arranged about the living room and kitchen. An instant after flipping off the kitchen light he heard the grumble of the automatic garage door opener beginning its task.

Two minutes later Hope came through the door. "Hi, hon! I'm home," she called out. "What's up?" Her husband stood at the end of the kitchen, a lighter still in his hand. "The lights go out again?"

"No, I turned them off. I thought it might be nice to have a little candlelight and togetherness, you know, just you and me," Mark said with a smile. He slipped the lighter into a drawer and, arms open, walked toward his wife. She raised her face for his kiss. His arms went around her . . . he'd not realized how lonely he'd been for her. He poured his soul into a passionate kiss and she responded as if she'd missed him even more than he'd missed her.

At last they drew slightly apart. "Umm . . . you mind . . . if I take off my coat?" she murmured. He assisted, barely letting her out of his reach, then wrapped her in his arms again.

"What got this started?" she asked.

"Watching you on TV tonight . . . made me think . . . how lucky . . . I am . . . to have you . . . how much I've missed you . . . these past few days . . . how beautiful you are . . . how much I desire you . . ." he said between kisses.

"Do I have time . . . to go slip into . . . something . . . more comfortable?"

Mark let her slip from his grasp, their eyes keeping contact until she reached the foot of the steps. "Aren't you coming?" she asked over her shoulder.

"Just let me blow out these candles."

CHAPTER

Mark rolled over in bed to enjoy the now-uncommon pleasure of cuddling up to his wife, only to find that he was
alone. Lifting himself up on one elbow, he looked across the
bed to the clock radio. The large numerals glowed 6:10. More
than that, it was Sunday. No light came from the bathroom.
Where was Hope?

He sat up and dropped his feet into the thick carpeting as
he searched for his slippers. Stepping into the hall, he glanced
into Jennifer's room, where his daughter lay sound asleep,
bathed by the gentle glow of her night-light. Her shoulder-
length brown hair appeared in greater disarray than usual. Ever
the organized computer programmer, he catalogued the observation for later attention.

At the top of the stairs was where Mark first noticed the
glow coming from the living room. Peering from halfway down
the stairs, he saw Hope wrapped in a fluffy bathrobe, with
matching slippers on her feet, sitting on the couch, with one
book open in her lap and another to one side. "What are you
reading?" he asked softly.

Hope jerked in surprise. "Oh! You startled me." She placed a
hand over her heart. "I didn't hear you come."

"Must be pretty interesting to have you that engrossed," he
said as he sat down opposite the second book and wrapped an
arm around her shoulders. "What are you reading?"

"Well, I've been thinking about what one of the guests we
had on the program last night was saying."

"Who was that?"

"Reverend Fallbrook. You know, the president of that university in Virginia who's so active in political issues. He was saying that this disaster on the Mississippi River and all the economic disruption it has caused is a warning from God that the Rapture is near, perhaps just days away. So I thought I'd read my Bible and see what it says so I'd know for myself."

"What answers are you finding?" he asked.

"Well, the first thing that I've realized is how little time I've been spending studying my Bible. Do you know how long it took me to find my Bible and concordance?"

Mark shrugged.

"About 10 minutes. Ten minutes, Mark," she emphasized.

"What's so significant about that?"

"Mark! We're talking about the end of the world. We're talking about the events we hear Daddy preach about at church, warnings that Jesus is about to take His people away and that the rest of the world is going to be plunged into great tribulation like has never been seen in history. And it took me 10 minutes to find my Bible!"

Mark thought several seconds before answering. "I guess you've got a point. I mean, I always figured that what I heard at church was all I really needed to know, and since God was taking care of the important stuff, why should I worry?"

Hope turned to face him. "Well, just reading this morning I've gotten worried, because Jesus warns us that before the end there'll be a delusion so strong it will almost deceive the very elect, Mark! I don't want to be lost, and I sure don't want to be one of those left behind to have to go through the tribulation that's coming after the Rapture."

Mark gazed into his wife's eyes and measured the intensity of her focus. "Know what I love about you?" he asked.

"What?"

"How you know just the right things to be serious about and what not to worry about," he said with a teasing twinkle in his eyes. "I mean, I don't know what kind of trouble I'd be in if you weren't keeping me on the straight and narrow."

"This is serious, Mark. Really, really serious."

Mark gazed into his wife's eyes a moment longer, then stood up. "My tummy's rumbling. What do you want for breakfast?"

"I hadn't thought about it. Whatever you're fixing." She turned back to her reading.

Mark opened several cupboards and soon had two place settings on the table along with toaster pastries, cold cereal, milk, and juice. Aroma from the coffeemaker filled the rooms with eye-opening scent.

"You've never been much of a cook, have you?" Hope teased as she pulled a chair back from the table.

"I can burn toast with the best of 'em. Now, tell me, what have you learned in your reading?"

Hope dropped a pastry into the toaster and pushed down on the slide on the end. Next she reached for the juice pitcher and began filling the glass in front of her. "Well, I was reading in Matthew 24. You remember it?"

Mark poured cereal into his bowl. "Can't say that I do."

"In it Jesus is talking about the signs of the end of the world. You know, warnings . . . such as, if people say He's in a secret place, don't go there. That sort of thing."

"Isn't that the chapter your dad's always quoting from about two people doing something and one gets taken, and the other left?" Mark asked her.

"That's the one." Hope took the hot pastry from the toaster and dropped it onto the saucer next to her cereal bowl. "Let me read you something . . . starting in verse 37. This is from the NIV. 'As it was in the days of Noah, so it will be at the coming of the Son of Man. For in the days before the flood, people were eating and drinking, marrying and giving in marriage, up to the day Noah entered the ark; and they knew nothing about what would happen until the flood came and took them all away. That is how it will be at the coming of the Son of Man. Two men will be in the field; one will be taken and the other left. Two women will be grinding with a hand mill; one will be taken and the other left' [verses 37-41]."

Mark stirred milk into his cereal and took a bite. "I remember that part. Let's see if I've got this straight: when Jesus comes, He takes His people away in the Rapture. That's the part about one being taken and the other left, right?"

Hope nodded.

"Then everybody else has to try to survive the seven years of

190

tribulation before they can be saved. Right?"

"That's supposed to be what happens," Hope answered.

Mark reached across the table and slid the Bible around where he could read it. "You know what puzzles me?" he asked a moment later. "Verses 27 and 28. 'For as the lightning comes from the east and flashes to the west, so will be the coming of the Son of Man. Wherever there is a carcass, there the vultures will gather.'" He shook his head. "What puzzles me is that if the Rapture is supposed to be secret, and we'll see only the results, why does Jesus say right here that His coming will be like lightning? I mean, the only way you can avoid seeing lightning is to be in a windowless room with your eyes closed. And what does He mean about a carcass and vultures?"

Hope finished her mouthful of cereal and took a drink of juice. "I don't know about the carcass and vultures, but I do know that the Rapture is going to be a secret event. Jesus won't come visibly until after the seven years of tribulation."

Mark scanned the chapter as he ate more cereal. "Uh, dear. I hate to disagree with you, but this chapter doesn't say anything about seven years of tribulation. It talks about a lot of things that—as I somehow recall—happened around the fall of Jerusalem in A.D. 70. Then it warns against false prophets and false Christs. *Then* it says His coming will be as visible as lightning, and—"

"Let me see the Bible again—"

"—it talks about signs in the heavens. Then it says all the nations will mourn when the Son of Man comes." Mark bent over the page, one finger tracing the words. "Look Hope, Matthew 24:30 says, 'All the nations of the earth will mourn. They will see the Son of Man coming on the clouds of the sky, with power and great glory" [NIV]. His voice rose with surprise. "Excuse me, dear, but *that's* not a secret event. Lightning's pretty hard to hide."

"Yeah, but the Rapture is going to be secret," Hope countered. She slapped the now-cold pastry back on the saucer. "Why do I buy these things? They taste like cardboard!"

"Just a sec," Mark said. He went to the living room and retrieved the concordance Hope had been using earlier. He turned a few pages forward, looked for something, then turned back two pages. "You know what?"

"What?"

"This is weird. I can't find 'rapture' in here anywhere. This concordance is supposed to have every single word in it that's in the Bible, and 'rapture' isn't among them. So that must mean that the word 'rapture' isn't in the Bible."

"But what about the verses I read a few minutes ago about that time being like the time of Noah? Or what about the two people being in the field or at the mill, where one is taken and the other left behind?"

Mark shook his head. "I don't know. I'm just trying to figure this out." He raised a hand to stop Hope's next question and flipped the pages of her Bible. "Look here," he said a moment later. "This is puzzling. Think. What happened to Noah?"

"What do you mean?"

"Verse 37 says, 'As it was in the days of Noah, so it will be at the coming of the Son of Man.' Now listen, Hope. Noah and his family were inside the ark, and they were saved. It was the people *outside,* the wicked, who were swept away and lost. Something isn't adding up here."

"What's not adding up?" Hope asked. She leaned over to read Matthew 24:37 for herself.

"OK, follow me on this." Mark stood up, pacing as he talked. "When we talk about the Rapture we talk about the people who get taken away being saved and everybody that's left behind having to go through the Tribulation so they can have another chance to be saved. But that isn't what happened when Noah went into the ark. It was the other way around." Mark unconsciously clasped his hands together and flipped them over for emphasis. "We've got it backward, Hope! In the time of Noah, it was the people who were *in* the ark who were 'left behind'—and they were saved. And it was the people *outside* who got taken away—and they were lost. They didn't get a second chance to be saved."

Hope shook her head. "I don't follow. Are you telling me that the Bible is saying something different than what we believe?" she asked defensively. "That what I've grown up believing—and that my father has taught all his life—is wrong? After all, he *is* a minister."

"I'm not arguing with you or your father. I'm just reading what's here. And I don't see anything here that says Jesus will return secretly." He shook his head, almost in disbelief. "However, I do see several warnings about being ready when Jesus comes."

Hope looked at the clock on the wall. "This is too much to think of early in the morning. I'm sorry I ever started the subject." She stacked their few dishes and carried them to the sink, then turned to Mark with a determined smile. "Thanks for fixing breakfast."

"Yeah. Such as it was. You're welcome."

"And for—being so good with Jennifer . . . and for loving me."

He put his arm around her, and they stood at the sink window, looking at the cold, gray morning. "You know, I spent the weekend reading Reverend Robertson, and now a few minutes with Matthew 24 has turned me on my head."

"Oh, Mark!" She pulled away. "We've got enough trouble without worrying about this."

He drew her back against him and kissed her forehead. "You're probably right, but I have a little time on my hands. I'm going to look into it some more."

"OK." She didn't sound convinced. "And I'm going to go get our daughter up."

"It's Saturday," Mark countered. "Let her sleep."

"Well, I'd like for her to be on a regular schedule," Hope said. "I think it's better for her to have a routine." She left the kitchen and turned toward the stairs. A minute later her shriek echoed through the house.

Mark flew up the stairs toward the sound. "What's wrong?"

Hope stood in the middle of the room, her gaze fixed on their daughter, one hand clasped over her face below saucer-wide eyes. Her other hand gestured toward their daughter, just awakening and sitting up in bed.

"What's wrong?" father and daughter asked in chorus.

"Look! Look!" was all Hope could say. Clumps of Jennifer's brown hair lay on her pillow. A bare patch of scalp reflected the overhead light as she sat up. "Her hair is falling out," Hope moaned. "My baby's hair is falling out."

The sight took even Mark's breath away. All the parents could do for a few seconds was stare.

Jennifer stretched and yawned. "What's wrong?"

"Your hair, sweetheart. Your hair is falling out." Hope rushed to take the child in her arms as if rescuing her from some monster.

Jennifer looked at the pillow, a look of surprise across her face. Then she slid off the bed and stood before the mirror her mom had hung at eye level the year before. "Ooooo. Pretty yucky, don't you think?" She ran her hands over her head. Clumps of hair festooned her fingers.

"Yucky isn't the half of it, sweetheart. It's awful!" Hope declared.

"Don't have a cow, Mom," Jennifer said with a shrug. "We knew this was going to happen. At Dr. McCormick's office they gave me a video about what to expect. It said that about four weeks after I started taking the medicine all my hair would start falling out. It's OK. It's happened to other kids." Hand over her mouth again, Hope listened with disbelief at her self-composed little 6-year-old. "The video said that girls usually wear a scarf or a wig for a few weeks. When I'm through taking the medicine my hair will grow back."

Mom and dad stared at their daughter in surprise. Where did she get this maturity? They'd had no idea she was so aware of what was happening.

"I guess someone told us this would happen, but I let it get buried under all the other things we were told," Mark said quietly.

"Oh, Jennifer!" Hope exclaimed with a bit less panic in her voice. "I just can't believe it . . . I mean . . . that it's . . . I just can't believe it."

"Sweetheart, I guess the next question is What are we going to do about it?" Mark asked both his girls. "Do we just let her wrap her head in a scarf? Does she wear a baseball cap? Do we buy her a wig? What?"

Hope picked up the clumps of hair from the pillow. "I want to collect these so we can have a wig made for her. That way at least she'll look natural because it'll be her hair."

"Do you have any idea how much it'll cost to have a wig made?" Mark asked.

Hope shrugged her shoulders. "It doesn't matter. I want my daughter to look normal. I don't want . . . " She bit her lip and did not finish the sentence.

Jennifer pulled a hairbrush through what remained of her long hair. Each stroke picked up long, loose strands, spreading the baldness farther across her head. Soon half her hair remained anchored in random spots across her scalp.

Hope sighed deeply and wiped away a tear. "What do you think, sweetheart? Should we cut off what's left?"

Jennifer studied herself in the mirror. "Yeah, I guess so. I look pretty weird like this, don't you think?" Giggling, she stuck her thumbs in the corners of her mouth, pulled it wide, and stuck out her tongue.

"Jennifer!" both parents gasped, then Mark laughed. "Way to go, girlie," he said, putting his head next to her and trying to cross his eyes.

Hope left the silly twosome to rummage through her bathroom cabinet, returning with a set of electric hair clippers. "Remember these?" she asked Mark.

"Yeah, I remember we bought them when we had Wiggles."

"Who's Wiggles?" Jennifer asked.

"A little dog of your mother's we had when we first got married. We thought we'd save money by clipping her ourselves."

Both parents smiled at the memory, their first smile in several minutes, then burst out laughing. "What a mess! I'm glad she didn't care how she looked." Hope laughed. "I guess these'll do what we need to do with Jennifer, don't you think?"

Mark nodded. "Just try not to bark or wag your tail too much while Mom's doing it, OK, Jennifer?"

Several minutes later and the deed was done. Hope eyed the tangled pile of hairs. "Guess there's no easy way to turn this into a wig, is there?"

Mark shrugged his shoulders.

The phone rang. Hope went to their bedroom to answer it and returned several minutes later. Mark eyed his wife. "Let me guess. They've called you in to work today."

She nodded. Her eyes were bright. "It's just local. They want me to go over to the station and reedit some stuff from last night. I should be back after lunch." Suddenly she remembered. "But Mark! My daughter's hair just fell out. I can't go to work!"

"Why not? I'm here. I'll take care of Jennifer."

"But I don't want to go."

Mark put his hands on her shoulder, gently guiding her toward the door. "You go on to work. I'll take care of things here."

Hope turned. Husband and wife eyed each other in silence. "Jennifer . . ." she began.

"It's OK, Mommy. I like being with Daddy."

"I'll hurry. I'll be back by noon." Her office efficiency took over, and she went to her daughter's chest of drawers. "It's chilly inside and out," she told the girl. "Do you want to wear your new sweatshirt?"

"Sure. I guess so."

"I'll tell you goodbye before I leave," she said, resigned, then walked out of the room.

"You go ahead and get dressed. I'll have breakfast ready," Mark told Jennifer as he followed Hope out the door.

She hurried into her bedroom, pulled on a pair of dark wool slacks, then an olive-green shirt and matching sweater. Recently Mark had started teasing her about wearing dark colors all the time. Somehow, dark colors felt comforting. She didn't know why.

She winced—seeing a mental image of her brave daughter—as she pulled a hairbrush through her new short cut. *What can't be cured must be endured.* The tried and true saying surfaced from somewhere deep in her mind. *Lord, God, please help me. Help us. Help Jennifer* . . . Her eyes and forehead wrinkled in a frown. *And Mark. Keep him in Your care. Don't let him go off on some wild religious tangent* . . .

A little face cream. No makeup. It didn't matter just there in the office. A little lipstick to offset the drabness of her outfit. She was ready to leave.

Jennifer was pouring a bowl of colorful cereal circles when Hope departed. "Don't worry about me, Mom. Dad and I will be OK," she tried to reassure her mother.

"Does this mean I can have a wig?" Jennifer asked Mark as soon as they heard the garage door closing.

"Let's say grace first, before we talk about that," Mark told her. He poured a cup of coffee and sat across from her.

"I'll say it," she said cheerfully. They bowed their heads, and Jennifer quoted: "God is great, God is good, and we thank Him for our food. Amen." She giggled. "Only there's just *me* eating. I don't think you can thank God for coffee. It's not good for you."

"You got me there!" He took a sip. "This is decaf. Now then, do you really want a wig? It'll be only a few weeks before your hair starts growing back."

"Yeah, but it'll be really, really short, and it'll take like forever to grow out. The kids on that video were wearing wigs, and they looked normal. So, can I have a wig? Please, Daddy?"

He smiled. "I guess so. But you know, I'd feel a lot more comfortable if your mother took you to look for it. I mean, I don't know the first place to look for something like that."

Jennifer looked him up and down, her face knowing. "You know how it is with Mom. She goes to the station for a 'couple hours' and comes home in five or six. So I think it's up to you and me. Grandma always looks in the yellow pages. Find an address, and let's go," she instructed.

"I guess we could do that." A moment later both heads were bent over the "wigs" listings in the phone book. Jennifer couldn't read all the words, but she wriggled in her chair at the drawings of wigs promoting different shops. "This one looks like it's the closest," he declared, his finger on some black lettering. "Plus, it says they have chemotherapy wigs. I wonder what that means."

An hour later father and daughter walked into the shopping center and loosened their coats. Jennifer pulled on her father's arm. "Daddy!" He leaned closer. "Those people are staring at me!" she hiss-whispered. "They must think I look weird. Let's hurry up and find the place."

"Well, sweetheart, put your knit cap back on."

A big sigh. "OK. I just didn't expect people to be staring at me."

Several minutes later they entered the shop and were greeted by a woman who took in the situation with a knowing glance. She guided them to a corner, explaining that these wigs were designed especially for chemotherapy patients. "Just look around and tell me what color and style you want, and we can start trying them on," she offered. "Take your time." She winked at the little girl. "Try them all on if you like. I'll be back right after I take care of this other customer."

Mark began looking for something similar to Jennifer's previous hair style: long and straight, below the shoulders in a dark brown, but Jennifer had other ideas. "I like that one," she declared, pointing to a long blond curly wig.

"I don't know," Mark stalled. "I just don't think that shade is you. Let's try one of these," he urged, pointing toward the brown shades.

Ignoring him, Jennifer lifted the curls from their stand and pulled the wig over her head. She ran to the nearby mirror, tugging on the hair until it set evenly. Then she shook her head, laughing as the curls bounced.

"Mommy would kill us!" he protested. "Here, try on this short dark-brown one."

Reluctantly she pulled off the golden curls and fitted the wavy brown wig on her head. Her eyes lighted up when she looked in the mirror. "Give me another one, Daddy," she called. "This is fun."

Jennifer tried on every single wig in the chemo section while her dad assumed the role of "her lady's helper," fetching and returning the wigs at her command. When he realized that the clerk took it in stride—even entering into the game—he relaxed and enjoyed it too.

In the end, nothing could change Jennifer's mind. "The blond one, Daddy. The curly one!" she begged. He noticed the ever-present shadows under her eyes and how tired she was from the few minutes of fun. *What does it matter?* he finally thought. *A wig is not a life-or-death matter . . .*

"You'll get used to it, Daddy," she urged, eyes twinkling at her reflection.

He gave it one last shot.

"But Mommy—"

"It's just a few weeks until my hair starts growing back, so what's the problem?"

He laughed and turned to the clerk. "We'll take it! I'd tell you to wrap it up, but Jennifer may want to wear it right now."

~ ~ ~

"Who's that in the den?" Hope asked as she walked into the kitchen from the garage. All she could see were blond curls over the back of the sofa.

"Jennifer," Mark answered.

Jennifer turned away from the TV cartoons. "Hi, Mom," she called.

Hope's jaw went slack. "Jennifer?"

Jennifer jumped down and did a pirouette for her mother to see her hair from all sides. "What do you think, Mommy?"

Hope just stared. Finally she found her voice. "Nice, honey."

"Mark!" She stalked toward the stairs. "Mark!"

He looked at Jennifer. She'd turned back to the cartoons. He knew what he had to do. He followed his wife.

He followed her into the bedroom. She closed the door. "OK, what's happened? When I left this morning our daughter was bald. Now she's a blond. She looks weird. Did you do what I think you did?"

"Don't you like it? I think she's cute as a blond," he answered.

"No, to tell you the truth I don't like it. It doesn't go with her skin color at all." Her words were sharp and clipped. "You went out and bought her a wig. You didn't even have the courtesy to wait for me to do it with her or at least for us to go as a family."

"I'm sorry." His shoulders slumped. "She begged to go. I thought it was the right thing to do."

"But you didn't wait for me. I was gone only a few hours. I was just down to the station. I was gone only a few hours. Why didn't you wait?"

Mark waited a moment before answering. "I guess we got used to doing things without you," he said softly. "I'm sorry."

He waited. She didn't reply. She pulled off her blouse and sweater, then stepped out of her slacks. She jerked open the closet door, stepped inside, and rummaged for a sweatshirt. She rejected the white shirt for a navy blue, then opened a drawer and pulled out some jeans. Still in the walk-in closet she yanked the shirt over her head, then stepped into the jeans.

Mark waited, remorseful.

Hope sighed. "I'm sorry I got angry. It's just that . . . well . . . All morning I thought about taking her to get a wig this afternoon. I really hurried. I didn't say an extra word to anyone." She glanced at her watch. "I got home with time to spare, and was looking forward to doing it." A half smile curved her mouth. "A mother-daughter thing, you know."

Mark gathered his wife in his arms as she fought the tears welling up in her eyes.

"I just can't believe this is happening," she cried, her head against his chest. "I leave in the morning and my daughter is bald. I come home and she's a blond. I'm sorry. I guess I'm having a hard time getting used to your taking care of her when I'm away, and your deciding things different than maybe I would've."

W ell, I think Jennifer looks cute as a blond," Susan Morris declared to her daughters and daughter-in-law as they prepared December's first Sunday meal. "Let her have a little fun."

"Let me tell you, it was a big shock yesterday getting up and discovering that my daughter's hair was all falling out, then coming home and finding out that she'd gone from brown to bald to blond in one day," Hope responded. "I don't know which was the bigger shock, her losing her hair or Mark going out and buying her a blond wig. I almost strangled him for letting her pick that shade."

"But she looks so cute!" sister-in-law Carla countered. "I like it."

Hope looked at the other women. "Looks like I'm outvoted," she declared. "She stays a blond." She laughed, shaking her finger at Jennifer, who'd crept up behind her grandmother. "But only until your hair grows back!"

Susan sighed. The weight of Jennifer's illness lay heavy on her heart. "I'm so glad the river's back up to normal levels," she said cheerfully, changing the topic. "I guess the coal barges are getting through down here, because we've still got power, and I hear that even some factories up north are starting back to work."

"We've had it easy down here," Hope told her, her mind filled with the figures, facts, and faces she'd experienced in the past weeks. "Most of our coal comes in by train, so we've had only a few power interruptions. But up north it's a lot different. In some areas up there 80 percent of their electricity comes from coal. It'll be another three or four weeks before their power is back full-time."

"Hey, Hope! What's the chance of the network sending you overseas sometime?" Allison queried from the dining room, where she was placing cutlery on the table.

"Don't know until they call me. I mean, I never know where I'm going next. I just get a phone call, and they tell me to get on a plane. It's a day-to-day thing, depending on what happens."

"That would be fun," Allison said, just a little envious of Hope's glamorous life.

"I hope they don't send you over to the Middle East," Susan told her firmly. "Judging from what I've been hearing, things could get really hot over there in a big hurry. Plus, they've got those Palestinians and Israelis doing those suicide bombings."

"Well, as a matter of fact, I had a call on Friday asking if I'd be interested in going to Jerusalem," Hope replied. She didn't look at her mother.

"Jerusalem!" Allison exclaimed. "Can I come along?"

"Well, I don't even know if I'm going. It's all very preliminary. What's happening is that the wife of the Jerusalem Bureau reporter is pregnant. She's here in the U.S., and she's having some complications. They plan to rotate him home in the next week or so, and they're deciding who to send over to replace him. Could be me, or it could be somebody else."

Susan Morris became uncharacteristically quiet, a mood Hope long ago learned to recognize as her being upset about something but not wanting to show it. For the next several minutes she spoke only to give instructions, but her words were short and to the point, and she avoided other conversation. Finally, when the meal was on the table, she called the expanded family to the dining room for the blessing. Aubrey Morris invoked God's favor upon everyone, then parents set about filling plates for the children who were seated at a smaller table nearby.

"Dad, what do you think about the points Reverend Robertson was making this morning about all these things such as the threat of war in the Middle East being signs of the end?" David asked.

"Well, I think he's right on track. If the Antichrist is going to broker peace in the Middle East, then the people of the area have to be so tired of war that they're willing to risk peace. And that's what's going to open the way for the rebuilding of the

Temple in Jerusalem." Aubrey placed the serving spoon back into a casserole dish and passed the dish on to his right. "Like he said, the Temple's going to get rebuilt, the Rapture is going to happen, and we're going to be enjoying being in heaven while this world is suffering the Tribulation."

General conversation continued on a variety of topics for several minutes until Susan noticed that Hope was eating very little and sometimes just pecking at her food with her fork. "Hope, honey, are you OK?" she asked.

"Oh, I'm fine," she smiled back. She forked a candied sweet potato to prove it. "I'm just puzzled about something."

"What's that?" David asked from across the table.

"About these things Reverend Robertson's been talking about. I mean, we believe the Rapture is going to be secret, right? The redeemed are just going to disappear. Poof! They're gone."

"That's right. You've known that since you were a child, so what's puzzling you?" her father answered.

"Well, a couple things. First, I've been reading my Bible a lot lately, and I'm wondering why I can't find the Rapture in the Bible. I mean, the word 'rapture' isn't in the concordance, and everything I've found about the end talks about Jesus' coming's being visible."

"Well, now, that can be explained—" Aubrey began.

H'mm, that's a switch, Mark thought. *I wonder when she came to that conclusion.* He cut his eyes toward his wife, but if she saw him, she didn't acknowledge it.

Hope didn't stop for a breath. "But Daddy, in the second place, Jesus compared His return to being like lightning that can be seen from the east to the west; the elements melt with great heat, there are earthquakes, mountains fall, and great big events like that. What's confusing me is that if Jesus talks about His coming's being visible and destructive, how can it be secret? Daddy, how is it you and Reverend Robertson can talk about its being secret?"

Aubrey stared at his daughter with a stunned look that turned to anger. One by one the adults stopped talking and eating as everyone realized the glare he was flashing at his daughter. "What heretic has gotten a-holt of *you?*" he finally barked. "You sound like you've been studying the Bible with some cult."

"No. I've just been reading my Bible," she answered calmly.

"Well, haven't you read where Jesus said His coming would be like a thief in the night?"

"Yes. But don't you remember that a few verses before that Jesus said His coming would be as visible as the lightning? The only reason I can find for His comparing His return to being like a thief was a warning for people to be watching and ready all the time."

"What about Jesus' statement about His coming's being like what happened in the time of Noah?" Aubrey countered.

"I'm not sure what to make of that one yet," Hope admitted. A red flush warmed her face. Even the children's table had grown quiet.

"Mark made an interesting observation about that the other day," she went on.

Aubrey's gaze moved to the next chair, where Mark sat. "Mark!" he said. His commanding tone held both a question and a challenge. "Don't tell me you're the one leading my daughter astray."

"Uh, I was hoping to stay out of this," Mark answered awkwardly.

"Well, I'd like to hear what 'interesting observation' you made the other day." Aubrey dipped his fork into the well of gravy over his mashed potatoes.

Mark nodded, his fork in midair. "It was really pretty simple. At least I think it is. Jesus compares the time of His return to the time of Noah. Now, as I recall, Noah preached for 120 years. Then he and his family went into the ark, and God closed the door a week before the Flood came. The people outside were partying and mocking the people who were locked in the ark . . . that is, until the rains came and swept them away." Now Mark's face was flushed. Few people challenged his father-in-law. He took a sip of tea.

"So your point is?" Aubrey pressed.

"My point is that the people who were taken away were lost, but the people left behind—the ones inside the ark—were saved. Now, that's just the opposite of how we use the story to teach about the Rapture. We teach that the people who are taken away in the Rapture get saved, but the people who are left behind are lost—unless they accept a second chance to be saved." Mark's eyes darted from his father-in-law to David to Hope. He took another sip of tea, then continued, looking at Hope's father. "The way I read it, Dad, we've got the whole story turned around backward, and we're trying to make Jesus say something He didn't."

Fire flashed in Aubrey's eyes. Susan placed a warning, calming hand on her husband's arm. Sensing his wife's signal, he drew a deep breath before speaking.

"Young man," he declared in measured tone, "I've studied the Bible for a lot of years, and I've always believed that Jesus was teaching that the people who are taken away are the first ones saved. Now, son, are you telling me that I've been wrong all these years?"

"No, sir," Mark replied. "No, sir, I'm not saying that. I'm just pointing out the way it seems to me that Jesus used the model. As I read it, it seems plain that the ones the Bible says were 'taken away' were forever lost—and *that* raises another point." He leaned toward Aubrey. "Where do we get the idea that the people Jesus doesn't take away with Him will have another chance to be saved?"

"The seven years of tribulation begin with the Rapture," Aubrey declared. He had studied this all his life. Why were Hope and her husband coming at him with this *now?* "You'll find it in the book of Daniel, chapter 9. The one-week prophecy."

"I think we ought to find something else to talk about," Susan interrupted them both. "Carla, how's your pregnancy coming along?" she asked across the table.

"The pregnancy's fine, but I'm not. I can't wait for it to be over. You know what the third trimester is like, Mom."

"I *do* know that," Susan laughed, picking up the jelled salad that sat in front of her. "Here, David," she said, "have some more. I made this with you in mind."

With his eyes on Aubrey, David took the bowl. "Do you know what Reverend Robertson shared last night that got me really excited?" he asked.

"What?" two voices answered.

"Mommy!" a high, loud voice called.

"What?" Susan automatically answered.

"I'm through eating!"

"Me too."

"Me too, Mom," Jennifer said.

Susan got up to help the toddlers, and Jennifer, ever the little mother, picked up the youngest and wiped his face with her napkin. Hope noticed that her daughter had eaten very little, but even as she thought it, decided not to mention it. She pulled her attention away from the children's table back to her father and Mark. After the interruption, David was talking again.

"I was thinking about people preparing to rebuild the Temple in Jerusalem," he told the table. His eyes shone. "I mean, the idea that we can actually have a hand in fulfilling prophecy—now, that gets me excited."

Allison spoke up. "I wonder how long it will take them to raise the money for the project? You know, with all the gold that's needed for the Temple, that's going to be a lot of money."

"Yes, it will," Aubrey agreed, "but that'll be just another of the miracles God will perform as a demonstration of His power to save. When people see how God works to make it happen, they won't be able to deny His power any longer, and many will be converted."

"What I'm wondering about is what it'll take to get that Muslim mosque—you know, the Dome of the Rock—removed from the Temple Mount without inciting all the Arabs into a holy war." Mark wondered aloud.

"That's what we have to wait on the Antichrist to do first," Aubrey observed. He turned to his wife. "Remember when we bought the land for the church, the fight we had with the city over that old house on the corner that we wanted to tear down? But the city wouldn't let us because it was on the roster of historic buildings. Just getting permission to remove the house to a new site was almost a miracle in itself. After that, the construction project was simple."

Susan laughed. "And then the house collapsed and fell apart while it was being moved!"

Aubrey smiled broadly and gently shook his head at the memory. "Then the buyer sued us for breach of contract because the house fell apart. Well, we may have ended up losing the money from the sale, but we were rid of the house and got to turn the lot into parking area for the church."

Conversation meandered onto several topics as the family went back to their unfinished meal. Hope was glad. Family controversy made her uncomfortable, and she hated to challenge her dad. With one ear listening to the children, she finished her roast and vegetables and asked for another of Susan's famous popovers. She didn't notice Susan rise to bring in the dessert from the kitchen.

"Dad, are you OK?" Carla asked. The tension in her voice caught everyone's attention. "Are you OK?"

Aubrey Morris sat silently, staring straight ahead. His face was pale, and a sheen of sweat moistened his brow. "I don't know," he answered softly, adding almost with surprise, "I don't think so."

Susan dropped the dessert tray noisily on the counter and flew to her husband's side. "What's wrong?"

"I can hardly breathe, and I've got a pain shooting down my left arm," he said in a raspy whisper. He sucked in a whistle of air. "I feel like there's . . . an elephant . . . on my . . . chest."

For a moment everyone sat in stunned silence, then someone uttered the words "heart attack." Three people rocketed from their chairs to assist him into the living room and onto the couch, where they tried to make him more comfortable.

"Someone call 911," a voice shouted.

Seven pair of eyes turned toward the telephone table in the corner of the room. Jennifer held the receiver to her ear. "My grampa's having a heart attack," they heard her say.

"Jennifer! Get off the phone right now!" Mark ordered in a panic.

Jennifer calmly held up her hand. "I'm talking to the 911 operator," she said. "I'll let you talk to my daddy." She handed the phone to Mark.

Following the directions from the 911 operator, the family did what they could to help Aubrey be comfortable as they waited in growing tension for the ambulance to arrive. Jennifer was sent to the street to wave down the ambulance and lead the paramedics into the house. The men and women worked quickly and efficiently, attaching electrodes to Aubrey's chest and connecting him to a heart monitor. They inserted an IV into one arm and, after receiving instructions from the hospital emergency room, injected a medication into the IV. His chest pain began easing, and in minutes he was en route to the hospital. The entire extended family followed close behind in a short caravan of vehicles.

At the hospital all but Susan were left waiting in the emergency room. Time crept by as they fought their fears, held little ones as they napped, or chased them as they burned off energy. Generally everyone wondered what the holdup was, why Susan didn't come out with new bulletins, and all watched the double doors for a doctor to come out with some news. Twice they joined hands in a prayer circle, asking God to spare the life of their precious father and grandfather.

Waiting was difficult—for every friend and family member sitting on the plastic-covered chairs. An overhead TV filled the room with its murmur, but few even tried to listen. Every head in the waiting room rose in an instinctive inquiry at the whisper of the pneumatically operated double doors that led where they could not go—into the ER rooms. Who was exiting? What news did they bring? An hour and more passed before Susan appeared, looking terribly drawn. In an instant the family gathered to hear her every word.

"The doctors said it was a mild heart attack, but it was caught in time and he'll be OK." She sank gratefully into the one padded chair that David stood up and offered. "They gave him something to break up the clots that were blocking his arteries, and the pain in his chest went away in just a few minutes." She sighed. "For the most part his heartbeat's back to normal. They'll be taking him upstairs in a few minutes for an angiogram to see exactly what's happened."

"That's wonderful," Allison whispered.

"Praise the Lord!" exclaimed another, and another, and another.

The family picked up the toddlers and pressed together around Susan's chair, praying with weak-kneed thankfulness to celebrate their father's survival. Then they followed directions up the elevator and down a hallway, at last to the waiting room outside the cardiac catheterization lab where they paced nervously or chased bored children who decided to amuse themselves by running up and down the halls and seeing what was hidden behind closed doors.

If they'd thought that time passed slowly while they waited outside the ER, it stopped altogether here. Hope watched the large wall clock for several minutes to see if its hands were actually moving. An older man sat in a corner, a magazine in his lap. David and Mark struck up a conversation with him. Carla walked to the end of the hallway, trying to ease her aching back. Jennifer toyed with a jigsaw puzzle, then gave up and made a game of it for the younger kids. Someone went for soft drinks and orange juice. Jennifer made up games for the toddlers. Susan sat quietly, endlessly rubbing one hand over the other. Allison fixed a cup of tea for her from the hot pot and tea bags in the waiting room. Susan thanked her, cupping her cold hands around its warmth.

"Mrs. Morris?" A man wearing a paper hat and booties and green hospital scrubs stood in the doorway. He held a large manila envelope typical of those used to file X-ray films.

"That's me," Susan answered, wearily pushing herself up from a chair. Her face and tone held raw fear.

"I'm Dr. Hoffman," he said as he shook her hand. His eyes scanned the assembled group. "Are these members of your family?"

Susan nodded. "They're my children and . . . my family. We were just finishing our Sunday dinner when this happened."

"All right. Mrs. Morris, first things first. Your husband came through the cardiac catheterization with no problems. He'll be in the recovery room for a while, and after we talk you can go in and see him if you like."

Hope slipped an arm around her shoulders. The doctor stepped over to a light box mounted on the wall, pulled a sheet of film from the envelope, and clipped it onto the box. The family crowded around.

"This is your husband's heart, and these are the coronary arteries," Dr. Hoffman said, tracing along dark lines with a pen. "In this procedure we inject a dye into the bloodstream and follow it as it moves through the heart. As you can see here . . . and here, two of your husband's coronary arteries were at least 70 percent blocked. This one over here"—he held the pen steady—"was more than 80 percent blocked. This is the one"—his pen stopped on it—"that was giving him the heart attack and the one we think was completely blocked when he came in, before we gave him the clot-busting drugs.

"These shadows that you see here, here, and here are the stents we put in to open up these narrowed areas. What we want to do now is give him a day or two to rest while we keep an eye on him. Then if everything's OK on Tuesday or Wednesday we'll let him go home."

Dr. Hoffman unclipped the X-ray, slipped it back in the envelope, and turned to leave. He paused, and turned back. "Oh, just one request. He's a little sore right now from the procedure we just did, and a little groggy, so don't give him too much attention, OK? We wouldn't want him to get too spoiled now, would we?"

"No. Don't go yet!" Hope, ever the reporter, touched his sleeve. "We have some questions."

He tapped his foot. Clearly he had other things to do.

"Dr. Hoffman, just what is a stent?" she asked. "How does it work? Will it stay there forever, or will it have to be removed?"

"Does this mean he won't have to have open-heart surgery?" Susan asked.

"Is there any further treatment?" Carla wanted to know.

Quickly, efficiently, Dr. Hoffman answered their questions. He was reassuring but gave no long-term promises. "We don't foresee any immediate problems," he concluded. "We'll be talking about diet and exercise later. Right now, we just want him to rest and concentrate on getting better."

Dr. Hoffman turned and was gone. For a moment everyone just stood in silence.

"Praise the Lord!" Stephanie exclaimed as a round of celebratory hugs began. Tears flowed down Susan's face. "Praise the Lord," she whispered.

~ ~ ~

Two mornings later Susan Morris delivered her husband back to the house. Then, after checking to be sure he was comfortable, she excused herself to go grocery shopping. "I've got to get a few things for this diet your doctor's put you on," she explained.

"Yeah, yeah. That diet. I think I'd rather die," Aubrey groused. "I can't eat this. I can't eat that. I have to eat like a rabbit. When I was younger I used to hunt rabbits and eat 'em. Now my doctor wants me to eat like 'em."

210

Susan smiled. "It's all to keep you from having another heart attack," she soothed, as she eyed the list of foods he could eat. "What do you want for lunch?"

"A juicy T-bone steak with fried potatoes and creamy cole slaw. And for dessert I'll have apple pie with a hefty scoop of the highest-fat ice cream you can buy right on top of the pie!"

"What's put you in the mood for all that?" Susan asked.

"Doing without it, that's what," he grumped.

"Now, you just sit there and read or watch TV until I get back," Susan instructed as she edged toward the door. "If it's any consolation, we're both going to be on this diet so we can get used to it together."

"Doctors! Diets! I just want to live, you know?" he complained.

"That's the point," Susan shot back. "Keeping you alive so we can listen to your complaining."

CHAPTER TWENTY

D o you have a valid passport?" Brandon Campbell inquired.

"Oh, yes."

"Good. You'll need a visa, of course, and I want you in Jerusalem as soon as you can get it. I need an A-team reporter, and your name's at the top of the list."

Jerusalem! The city where Jesus walked, where He died and was resurrected! The thought of going there sent a shiver of excitement running down Hope's spine. Did she want to go? Yes! But her daughter was in the middle of chemo . . . She couldn't just up and leave. Thoughts collided in her head as she tried to reason through the opportunity. Jennifer was doing OK. Good, actually. The sight of the blond curly wig still distressed Hope, and the fact she'd lost her hair, but otherwise . . . And she'd drawn so close to her daddy through the experience. Mark. She didn't know what her husband would think about her going overseas and to one of the world's potential hot spots at that.

"Listen," she heard Brandon say, "you can probably think of a hundred excuses not to go. But I can give you a hundred reasons to go. It'll be a terrific career move—and in case of a family emergency, you can be home in 24 hours."

He'd read her mind, and it *was* the professional opportunity of a lifetime. She grimaced. Bit her lower lip. "Look, I have to discuss this with Mark first."

"We don't have time for that." Brandon's voice had a hard edge to it that Hope hadn't heard before. "This is your big chance. Believe me, this opportunity may not come again, and

I've got at least two other reporters who'll jump at the chance. You're my first choice."

"OK. I'll go." She nodded, half to convince herself she was doing the right thing. "I'll get the visa, and I'll go." Mark and Jennifer wouldn't like it, she knew. They'd just have to get used to it. After all, she was a network news reporter, and that meant running off to all sorts of places on short notice and being away for days at a time.

"Good!" Brandon responded, then went on to give her instructions. She was to fly to Washington, D.C., that evening. At 8:00 the next morning she'd go to the Israel consulate and get a news media visa. After getting that, she was to go to Dulles International Airport and get the next available flight with connections to Ben Gurion Airport outside Tel Aviv. She could fly first class only if all coach class seats were taken. A producer from the Jerusalem Bureau would meet her at the airport.

"Don't worry about the cost. Use your company credit card. Just get on the next available flight after you get that visa stamped in your passport and get over there," Brandon instructed.

The thought of going made her a little weak in the knees, both from excitement and from fear. After all, in addition to being the land where Christ had walked and died, Israel was also the land of suicide bombers. The severe way the Israeli military responded to them had caused the country's neighbors, Egypt and Syria, in particular, to threaten war. "Listen, I'm going to be with a professional crew, people who've been there and know their way around," she defended against Mark's protests. "Besides that, if I get in danger I'll go on camera looking like those reporters you see wearing combat armor and a helmet with the letters 'TV' on them in white tape so nobody thinks they're soldiers."

It still didn't ease the concerned look on Mark's face.

"You're not going to get shot at, are you?" Jennifer weighed in. "Or be close to one of those suicide bombers?"

Hope shook her head. "I surely hope not. I don't want to be in the middle of it, just show up afterward and tell everybody back home what happened." She looked down her written checklist of items to pack and saw that somehow everything had fit inside her two suitcases. Last, she turned to the bedside stand, picked up the Bible she had been reading so much lately, and slid it into the large outer pocket of her purse. "I guess I'm ready to go."

Mark gave her another look of protest, then decided it would be fruitless. He zipped one suitcase closed as she labored with the other. "I'm glad these have good towing handles and wheels," he said in a resigned tone.

"Hey, overseas duty pays an extra $100 a day. Plus, if I get shot at, that amount doubles for hazardous duty pay," she teased.

"We can use the extra pay, but we'd rather have you here," Mark countered. He refused to join her teasing tone. "If you have to collect any hazardous duty pay, we'll just have to pray they have poor aim."

"Or I'm behind the ones doing all the shooting," she answered.

~ ~ ~

The flight from Dulles International Airport departed at 8:47 p.m. and touched down at London's Heathrow Airport eight hours later, which with the time difference worked out to mid-morning. She managed to sleep enough en route to be some-what alert as she walked through the international terminal to catch her connecting flight to Rome, yet tired enough to know her body was totally out of sync with the sun. Her flight to Tel Aviv landed just before dark, and by the time she transited cus-toms and reached the street a rainy night sky presented a drab scene. By now her body was telling her it was time to be awake and active even though she felt utterly drained of energy.

According to the instructions she'd been given, Hope scanned up and down the sidewalk in front of the terminal for a dark-complected man carrying a sign with "MBS-Lancaster" writ-ten in large letters. Well, there were plenty of swarthy men, some of them waving signs, but none with her name. So she waited. Individuals and groups moved through, some boarding buses to hotels. Still, she waited. Then, at the far end of the taxi line, she saw a man leaning against his car holding a small sign that looked like it was made from a folded sheet of notebook paper. She stepped closer and thought she could make out the first three letters: MBS. She blinked and looked again to be sure her tired mind was not deceiving her. She was right. The first three letters were MBS. That must be the man waiting for her, so she pulled her piggy-backed suitcases that direction. As she drew closer she looked again. Well, the first part was right, but the remainder read "Lawnchester."

"Excuse me, by any chance are you waiting for Hope Lancaster?" she inquired.

"Yes. Yes," he replied in heavily accented English with a vigorous nodding of his head. "Hope Lawnchester. Is that you?"

She extended her hand. "I'm Hope Lancaster, MBS News. You must be Ehud."

The man shook his head. "I'm Ishmael," he said in passable Arabic-accented English. "I work for Ehud. I take you to him."

In seconds the suitcases were in the trunk, and Ishmael was sliding behind the wheel. They soon pulled onto a broad highway, following an exit labeled "Jerusalem" in both English and Hebrew. Thirty-five minutes later they turned off a main thoroughfare onto a side street, then into a short driveway crossing the sidewalk. The smells of Middle Eastern cooking tweaked Hope's nostrils as Ishmael nosed the car between pedestrians and down the alley to the parking lot behind the building. "We're here," he announced as he shut off the ignition.

Hope stepped out and looked around. The building facing the street was four stories high, and the one against which they were parked appeared to be two stories. Cinder block walls the same height stood to either side on what must have been the property lines. Two doors opened into the taller building. Ishmael grabbed Hope's suitcases, expertly pulling them along the uneven pavement. "This way," he said as he unlocked the door closest to the alley. Through the other doorway Hope could see people scurrying around in a kitchen. The pungent scents of what they were cooking stirred her stomach.

Inside, Ishmael opened the doors to a small anteroom with stairways leading both up and down, and an elevator. "We take the elevator. That is, unless you want to carry your suitcases up four stories."

The elevator opened into another anteroom, this one with a single glass door on which the words "MBS News Jerusalem Bureau" were professionally painted. Pushing the door open, she found an empty reception desk and a network of modern offices outfitted for video production and office work. Seeing the famil-

iar confusion of people darting from one office to another, Hope
let herself relax. She'd arrived.

"We haven't had a receptionist since the *Intafadah* began,"
Ishmael explained as he placed Hope's suitcases on the floor. "The
receptionist lives on the West Bank, and the Israelis won't let her
get through checkpoints. We've applied for a permit for her to live
on this side of the line, but the government keeps turning it down.
They say she's related to someone who might be a terrorist."

"That sounds bad," Hope observed.

Ishmael shrugged. "If you are Israeli, everybody who lives
on the West Bank is related to somebody whom the Israelis
think is a terrorist. That's just life in the Middle East."

A large man with a two-day beard and a bed-head haircut
turned the corner. "You must be Hope," he declared gruffly as
he held out a bear-sized paw to shake her hand. "I'm Ehud Stein,
the bureau chief. Glad you're here. Ishmael will show you to
your room over in the dorm and get you oriented over there.
See you in a couple minutes." As quickly as he'd arrived, he
turned on his heel and was gone.

The "dorm" was a network of bedrooms on one side of the
bureau where several of the staff lived full-time, or bedded
down to catch naps at odd hours between live broadcasts to New
York. There were two bathrooms that looked like they needed a
good scrubbing. Hope selected one of the dorm rooms, tested
the mattress, and decided it was acceptable.

"We generally eat one or two meals a day at one of the
restaurants down on the street," Ishmael explained, though most
of the staff bought food at a grocery store a block away and kept
it in the kitchen. "I'll show you around later. But now I think
Ehud wants to put you to work."

Hope groaned. The first thing she wanted to do was call
home and reassure herself that nothing had changed, that
Jennifer and Mark were doing fine. But the thing her body
wanted most was sleep. Jet lag was hitting hard. The very last
thing she wanted to do was work.

"I hope you're a night owl and know how to get combat
naps, 'cause we're eight hours ahead of New York," Ehud said,
his voice a low growl. She wondered if he was a heavy smoker.
"We time our live reports for the early morning, evening, and

late night newscasts coming out of New York. Six a.m. in New York is 2:00 p.m. here. Five p.m. there is 1:00 a.m. here, and 10:00 p.m. there means we're bright-eyed and bushy-tailed at 6:00 a.m. That is, *you* have to look bright-eyed and bushy-tailed because you're on camera. The rest of us don't care what we look like."

Where did he get that expression? Hope thought, almost laughing out loud, but all she asked was "So, when do you sleep?"

"Sleep? What's that?" Ehud snorted. "Catch it when you can."

Looking around, Hope saw stage lights mounted on small trusses running along the ceiling near a large picture window. "Must be where I do my stand-ups," she said to herself, not intending for anyone else to hear.

"That's right," Ehud answered. "We can go out on the balcony if we want, but it's more comfortable in here. Gives us the same skyline backdrop. If we want, we can use the green screen over there," he pointed to a side wall, "and insert a picture from a camera we've set up somewhere. I'd like to put one of the remote-controlled cameras on a tower up on the roof where we could pan across the whole Jerusalem skyline. But the government won't let us do it. National security."

"What do you think I'll be reporting about?" Hope asked.

"War. The whole place is about to explode in full-blown war one of these days. It's a slow ratchet-up, but that's the way it's headed," Ehud declared. "We've got the Israelis cracking down on the Palestinians for terrorist attacks. The whole Arab world has gotten behind the Palestinians as their way of leveraging power against the United States. We've got Syria on the north building up their Army to invade through Lebanon. We've got Egypt to the south and west building up their forces in the Sinai Peninsula. My guess is they're just waiting for the right moment to attack Israel. And when they do, we'll be here to report on it in living color." He spread his hands like a peacock spreading its tail.

Hope's heart skipped a beat. Would her first overseas assignment be covering combat? That wasn't what she'd had in mind. The look on her face said so too.

Ishmael read her expression. "Listen, if you came here to do touchy-feely stuff such as midnight Mass Christmas Eve at the Church of the Nativity in Bethlehem, well, we might be able to work it in. But most of what we report about here is the growing tension between the Jews and the Arabs. Take my word, they're the ultimate dysfunctional codependent couple. They can't live with each other, and they can't live without each other. So that means people like you and me get to sit here and draw overseas and hazardous duty pay reporting about it."

Hope struggled to swallow past the lump in her throat. What scared her was the smile on Ehud's face. He actually enjoyed the prospect of covering a war. "When do we go out?" she asked.

"Whenever anything looks like it might happen." Ehud looked her up and down, almost as if seeing her for the first time. "Hey, you look thoroughly jet-lagged," he told her. "Go grab some shut-eye and come see me in the morning."

~ ~ ~

There were six other members of the Jerusalem Bureau team: photographers Ben and Joshua, soundmen Karl and Yuri, and editors Shoshana and Misha. The first two were born-and-raised Israelis. The third was a German, the fourth a Rumanian, and the last a Russian immigrant. Ehud, an American raised in New York City, had emigrated to Israel to discover his ancestral roots. By Ehud's accent you'd think he was a native Israeli. "I guess that's what being raised in Brooklyn does to you," he explained with a shrug. Shoshana was another American expatriate, and she spoke without an accent.

Ishmael was the lone Arab employee, a Palestinian by birth and a continual source of insights and connections within the alleyways and twisting streets of Jerusalem and the refugee camps of the West Bank.

~ ~ ~

"The first piece of video you're going to record is your will," Ehud instructed the next morning.

The look of astonishment on Hope's face betrayed her thoughts.

"I'm not kidding. This may not be an official war zone, but before we take you anywhere on the West Bank or anywhere else that might be dangerous, we've got to have a will on file. I want you to write it, and we'll tape it when you're ready." The tone in Ehud's voice told her he would accept no excuses.

Writing what she would say was troubling. Of course, she and Mark had a will and life insurance, but Hope had never before considered her mortality or how her husband and daughter might continue without her. At Karl's suggestion she made personal statements to Mark and Jennifer, telling them how much she loved them, how much she wanted them to keep believing in Jesus, and that she was giving everything she owned to them. The whole tape lasted all of three minutes, but Hope felt emotionally wrung out when she finished.

"You're gonna make me cry," Misha mocked as he copied the tape onto a minicassette for shipment to New York and storage in a vault where it would be accessed only if needed.

The sun was setting as Joshua and Yuri came through the door, weary from lugging their equipment and literally chasing a story on the West Bank. "I'm getting too old for this stuff," Joshua complained as he placed his camera on a bench, extracted a cassette, and handed it to Svetlana for editing. "There's some good footage there—a soldier shooting a kid at a roadblock. The Arabs will love it."

Ehud strode into the room with his sleepy eyes and overall perennial appearance of having just awakened. He watched a few seconds of the video as Svetlana transferred it into the editing computer. "Ben and Karl already brought in the official reaction," Svetlana answered. "Funny how we can have the official reaction before we get the first report about what happened."

"Yeah. You know how long it takes to get through those roadblocks," Joshua complained.

"Hope, since you're new, let Joshua write your copy, and you do a stand-up over there," Ehud growled. "Let him know when you're ready."

One hour later with the illuminated skyline of Jerusalem glowing through the window behind her, Hope put on her best camera face and hoped she didn't look too tired. On cue she began. "As if passions were not already inflamed enough, today more fuel was splashed on the emotional fire that is the West Bank when an Israeli defense force soldier shot and killed a 12-year-old Palestinian boy in the West Bank town of Nablus. An IDF spokesman said the boy was armed with a weapon, but as this video clearly shows, he was armed with only a rock."

The report went on to detail other points of tension and to show pictures of the funeral for a Palestinian gunman shot and killed by Israeli soldiers the day before. She concluded the report with the crisply spoken words, "Hope Lancaster. Jerusalem." Just saying it—Jerusalem—sent a shiver up and down her spine.

"Good. Get it on the bird to New York, and then let's all go out to supper," Ehud commanded.

"Supper?" Hope questioned. "It seems like I just had breakfast, and you're talking about dinner."

"That's jet lag for you, hon," Yuri observed. "You'll get over it in a couple days. You'll know you're over it when the rest of the world is out of sync with wherever you are."

~ ~ ~

A small degree of awareness crept into Hope's consciousness somewhere in the dark hours of the night. It was expanded by the unfamiliar odor of the bed, the strange pattern of light and shadow cast by the glow around the door to her room, and muffled sounds from elsewhere in the building. She tried just lying still in the hope that immobility would help her relax and fall back asleep, but it only made things worse. Finally she decided to get up. Feeling through the darkness for the lamp on the bedside table, she bumped the telephone, and then found the switch.

For a few seconds she was blinded by the low-watt bulb, then blinked as her eyes adjusted to the light. *Where am I?* she thought in a panic, then remembered. She was in a run-down dorm room at the MBS Bureau in Jerusalem. The alarm clock showed that it was a little after 1:00 a.m. She stretched, then rose from the bed and picked up the sweater and pants she'd worn the day before. In one motion she pulled her soft comfortable T-shirt over her head, stepped into the pants and slippers, then slid her arms into the sweater. Opening the door, enough light streamed from around the corner to illuminate her way in the darkened hall. She heard rough snoring from behind one closed door.

Hope's slippers scuffed lightly on the tile floor as she trod down the hall to the restroom. Exiting, she heard voices through the production room door and decided to investigate. Around the corner she found reporter Terry Ross being interviewed by

Brandon Campbell from New York City.

"Terry, our sources at the Israeli Ministry of Defense tell us that the Syrians in the north and Egyptians in the south and west are massing forces in such large numbers that there can be no question their intent is to invade Israel. What their precise objectives are, only the Syrians and Egyptians know. The Israelis have begun a call-up of their reserve forces and are strengthening their defensive positions to try and fend off the attack when it comes.

"What does seem certain is that we are only days away from a major attack. Starting tonight, we'll be keeping a 24-hour watch here, and we'll let you know the moment anything happens." Terry's last words were as strong as his first, and he kept his eyes on the camera for several seconds until the broadcast technician seated at a console with his back to him announced that they were clear.

"You must be Hope Lancaster," Terry said with an extended hand as he stepped out from under the illuminated stage lights. "When did you arrive?"

"Yesterday. At least I think it was yesterday." They both smiled.

"I know the feeling. Only I'm about to get it going the other direction for the umpteenth time. I don't know which direction makes the jet lag worse."

"So when do you go home?" Hope asked.

"Now that you're here, as soon as I can get on a plane," Ross told her with a smile. "My wife's pretty anxious to have me home, and I have to admit that I'm eager to get there. This is our first child, and she's having some complications."

"Serious?" Hope asked.

"Serious enough," he said. "Listen, I've put together a briefing book for you. It's in your in-box over on the wall. It'll give you the names and phone numbers of a lot of sources and a lot of background info on them. Some of 'em will take a while warming up to you, but for the most part they'll be cooperative. Just tell them you're replacing me," Ross instructed. "Now, if you'll excuse me, I'm going to start packing. There's a 4:30 flight to Rome that I'd like to try to be on."

"Then why are you in such a hurry?" Hope questioned, puzzled.

"Because it's just a little more than three hours from now."

"Oh." The thought penetrated Hope's not-quite-alert consciousness. "You think you'll make it through airport security in that short of a time?"

"Yeah, they're thorough. But when you've been through Ben Gurion Airport as often as I have, they know you pretty well. They know who they can trust and who they can't." He flashed a tired smile. "It's no problem anymore. A quick baggage search, a few questions, and I'm out to the gate."

"Well, good luck," Hope said. "Have a beautiful baby."

"Yeah! That's the key," he laughed. "And to keep my beautiful wife." He turned, then stopped at the doorway. "Hey, it was nice meeting you. Maybe we'll meet up again on a story somewhere." Then he was gone.

In her semiawake state, Hope surveyed the broadcast room. It really was a model of compactness and simplicity. There was the window wall against which the on-air reporters stood to give a background of the ancient city. Standing in the center of the room was a bank of editing equipment, a camera switcher, and the satellite broadcast controls. Behind it stood a row of desks where bureau staffers worked.

"Hi, Hope. I'm Shoshana. Shoshana Stein." The broadcast technician held out her hand to shake Hope's. "But most people call me by my middle name, Ruth. I'm *really* glad they finally sent a woman reporter. It's been hard putting up with all these guys."

Hope smiled, enjoying Ruth's teasing. "Looks like I'm going to be of service in unexpected ways!"

Ruth's eyes shone. "You know, I'm truly glad to meet you. That was some great reporting you and the others did on the Mississippi River disaster. Some of that looked pretty dramatic."

"I guess it was." Hope's last syllable merged into a yawn. "I'm sorry. I've got a good case of jet lag. That's the only reason I'm awake at this hour. Where are you from, Ruth?"

"St. Louis. About four years ago my parents decided it was time I got in touch with my Jewish roots, so they sent me to live on a kibbutz up near the Golan, up in the north."

"So. Did you get in touch with your Jewish roots?"

Ruth smiled, leaned back in her swivel chair, and looked at the ceiling. "Yeah, I guess I did."

"Maybe you can help me understand something then," Hope told her. She sat down in an empty chair and spun to face her new friend. "Why is it that the Arabs and the Palestinians are so angry with Israel? It seems to me—though I admit I know very little compared to someone who lives here—that Israel's just trying to exist, right?"

Ruth nodded. "The Muslims hate us just because we're Jewish. Being here just makes us a concentrated target to shoot at. They've declared war on anything and everything Jewish around the world. Here just happens to be the focal point of the conflict and where they've suffered their worst defeats."

"So . . . what's the solution?"

"I don't know. Somehow, some way, we've got to find a way to coexist. I mean, this is our land over here, and the West Bank—that's their land. We need them as workers to keep Israel strong and to survive; they need the jobs we offer. We can't live without each other, and we can't seem to live with each other. So you tell me, what's the solution?"

Hope pondered the situation for a long moment, and when she spoke it was without thought that the person she addressed was Jewish. "I guess the only solution is for Jesus to come. You look at all the things happening—not only here, but around the world—and the threat of war here, too. The Rapture can't be far away."

Ruth shook her head, disgusted. "You're just like all the rest."

"What do you mean?" Hope asked. She had a chill feeling that she'd said something wrong.

"You're like all the other Christians who come over here thinking they're going to convert all the Jews, or that Israel's survival is important to the fulfillment of Bible prophecy. How do you think that makes the Israelis feel?"

Hope looked at her hands. With her lack of sleep, it seemed that they swam above her knees. She'd been challenged and, she reasoned, perhaps rightly so. "Well, I'm not a serious student of prophecy, but that's what I've grown up believing," she said.

Ruth leaned forward and looked Hope in the eye. "Take a lesson: whatever you see in the Middle East, there's a motive behind it, a reason it's being promoted. But you may have to look twice or even three times to understand the motivation."

Suddenly Hope felt wide awake. "Illustrate," she commanded.

"OK. Christians around the world are sending millions of dollars a month to help ensure that Israel survives, right? Why are they doing it?" Ruth stood up and began pacing. "They're doing it because they believe the nation of Israel is the fulfillment of prophecy. OK, who do you think benefits from promoting that idea?"

Hope closed her eyes, thinking. "Israel?"

"Bingo, girl! You're pretty smart for a sleepyhead. If the government of Israel isn't promoting the idea of our country's being the fulfillment of prophecy, they're at least benefitting from it, right?"

"Are you saying that Christians misunderstand the prophecy?" Hope asked. Now she, too, pushed herself up from the chair and began pacing around the room. It was incredible. Hardly 24 hours in this country, and her Christian beliefs were being challenged. Even so, she felt energized by the conversation.

Ruth nodded, laughing. "You're getting smarter by the minute. If you study Scripture—what you call the Old Testament—you'll find that God talks about the people of Israel but never the land of Israel. The land is Canaan. Israel are the people."

"What's the significance of that?"

"The God of Abraham—we consider His name too holy to speak, so Jews call Him *Ha Shim.* It means 'the name.' It was He who gave the land of Canaan to the children of Israel. There's a difference between the people and the land. The name 'Israel' refers to the people of *Ha Shim,* wherever they are: here or somewhere else."

"Even in St. Louis?" Hope asked.

"Yup. Even in St. Louis."

'm glad you decided to join us," Ehud announced as Hope found her way back into the production room. She didn't know if it was a welcome or a rebuke.

Early-afternoon sun bathed the balcony with brightness and filled the production room with light. The entire staff of the MBS Jerusalem Bureau was present. Chairs retrieved from all parts of the office were scattered around a large table placed in the center of the room.

"Beginning today at 9:00 a.m. the Israeli military went on wartime alert. Mobilization orders are going out to reserve units as we speak," Ehud barked. "In short, Israel is readying for war. In an hour we're scheduled to go to the Ministry of Defense and get processed so we can have military IDs and passes to get through checkpoints and up to the front, wherever that happens to be.

"With the threat of war imminent, I want to make sure everybody knows how to operate the equipment we'll be taking into the field. It's brand-new, lightweight, and smaller than anything we've used before." He held up a compact Canon model and almost smiled. "This is our new camera." Hope leaned forward, concentrating, as he listed some of its features and demonstrated how to connect it to the portable satellite phone. The combination of camera and phone would allow them to broadcast live from almost any point on the face of the earth. It would also allow one person to do the job where the older equipment required three. That enabled them to file more reports from more places with the same number of people.

"From this moment on, everybody, and I mean *everybody*— reporter, camera operator, sound editor—carries one of these with them at all times."

Involuntarily, Hope shivered at the though of going into combat. *Maybe recording a will wasn't such a bad idea after all.*

Ehud cleared his throat to quiet comments from the crew. "A couple more things I want to go over. One, the bomb shelter down in the basement has been cleaned and restocked. Ishmael's been working on it the past couple days, and it looks as though he's done a great job. I want everybody to go down there and look around so you can find your way there in the dark. When the air raid siren goes off, the entire country will go black in less time than it'll take you to get down there. That means you'll be finding your way down the stairs by feel, or with a red lens on your flashlight.

"Two, we're setting up a rotating list of people who will stay up here during the air raids. I'll need a reporter or a producer who can go on camera, and a camera operator who's been trained in how to use the night vision system and can run the satellite controls. I think that's just about everybody but Hope. If you're on duty during an air raid, your job is to go live and tell the world what's happening. Don't confirm if New York is running you or not. Be on the air in case they're using you." He paused, looking from one to another around the room. "By all means, don't let them catch you looking stupid."

Even in her sleep-deprived state, Hope remembered a scene from one of those "funniest videos" shows in which a news anchor was caught on the air unprepared and looking profoundly stupid. The memory brought a smile even as Ehud continued. Then her mind wandered again. She compared the readout on her digital watch to the clock on an editing console and reset her timepiece to the local hour. She studied the patterns in the floor tiles and the plastered ceiling, then features on the faces and the haircuts of her coworkers. She was too tired to keep her mind on what Ehud was saying. She gazed out the window at the skyline. Finally the meeting ended.

"You vant to ride wif oos to the Ministry of Defense?" Karl asked.

"Uh. Yeah. I guess," she answered. "When are we going?"

"'Bout 20 minutes."

"Does that give me enough time to call home?"

"Yeah. Yust be soon to collect your new gear, or Ehud's be all over your case. Dis is vun time ee's not going to geef anybody a centimeter," Karl answered in his German-accented English.

~ ~ ~

"How's my precious girl?" Hope asked once Jennifer realized who was calling.

"I'm fine. Dr. McCormick says if I stay in remission another week he'll cut back on my blood tests to once a week." Hope could hear her happy sigh across the thousands of miles. "He says I can go back to school when I feel like it, and I already feel like it, so me and Daddy are getting ready."

"Praise the Lord, sweetheart. I've been praying to hear news like that. Oh, honey! That makes me so happy. Are you excited about going back to school?"

Silence.

More silence. Had they lost the connection?

"Jennifer . . . ? Are you there?"

"I'm here." Suddenly her voice sounded small.

Hope's heart leaped to her throat. "What's wrong, sweetheart? Are you OK?"

More silence. Her mother waited. At last the little girl spoke her fear. "I want to go back to school, but my friends haven't seen me with blond hair. I'm afraid they'll laugh at me."

Hope's heart yearned to be there, to comfort her daughter with hugs and cookies and affirming words. *This is why moms shouldn't leave their kids,* she thought. *Especially a sick 6-year-old.*

"Sweetheart, they'll think you're beautiful," she said. "They'll be jealous!"

"Oh, Mommy," came the exasperated sigh.

"Well, I guess that's just something you'll have to face," Hope gently told her.

A giggled filled her voice. "I could go with my bald head."

"Now, that'd be a sight for sure!" Hope laughed.

They spent the next few minutes talking about other things. Hope used all her reporter's skills to create the experience of Middle Eastern sights and smells and sounds for Jennifer, and promised to look for some very special gifts to bring home. By the time Jennifer gave the phone to her dad, her eyes shone with excitement.

"I miss you" were Mark's first words. "When can you come home?"

"Oh, Mark! I miss you too. But I've just gotten here, silly! I'm afraid they're going to keep me for a while—at least til I get over jet lag," she teased.

Thanking God and technology with every breath, Hope brought Mark up-to-date on what was happening, including the war alert and Ehud's instructions. Then she asked him if there was any news about his job. "Will Featherweight call you back any time soon?"

She heard her husband hesitate and inhale deeply. "No news yet. Gene says they're waiting to see if customer orders start picking up any time soon. But I don't think that's going to happen."

"Why not?"

"You mean you haven't heard?"

"Heard what?"

"There's been another big quake on the New Madrid Fault, and yesterday the levee broke again. The break is about a mile downstream from where they just finished repairing it. Apparently it had been weakened by the first quake, and they didn't spot it."

"Man!" she whispered, visualizing the chaos of the first quake. "So, what's the impact?"

"Well, most people were just getting their electricity back without interruption, and now this next quake hits. It's almost as if God doesn't want them to have electricity," Mark observed.

"That's weird, Mark," she told him.

She couldn't see the shrug of his shoulders but somehow sensed it. "I see what you mean," she added quietly. "I'm sorry. About the people without electricity and . . . everything."

"Well, I'm trying to keep my chin up. I've started putting out my résumé other places, but I'm not real hopeful. I mean, the classified ads in the Sunday paper used to be full of ads for programmers. Even big display ads. Now there's nothing. Zippo. Nada."

"The Lord will provide," Hope said softly, hoping that the disappointment in her voice didn't overpower the truth of her words. "Well, I'm keeping busy."

"Tell me about it." Now, this he was interested in. He wanted to know what she'd heard of the Syrians and Egyptians building up for war.

"They're true," she said, drawing a deep breath. "It looks as though it's going to happen. Probably soon, too." Through Mark's phone she could hear Jennifer's sweet voice alternately singing and talking to her dolls. That world seemed a million miles away, and again her mother heart wondered if she'd made the right decision in coming here. She stood up, stretching, and rubbed the back of her neck with her free hand before telling Mark all she knew.

"Yesterday one of our producers interviewed a deputy defense minister. He said that together the Syrians and Egyptians have more than a million soldiers massing to attack. They think it'll happen within the next week—if the United Nations doesn't make them back down."

"How do the Israelis feel about it? Do they think they can defeat an attack like that?"

"You've got to understand the Israelis," Hope answered from her crash course in their thought and culture. "Their backs are against the wall, and the Syrians and Egyptians are threatening to drive them into the sea. That's why they're such tenacious fighters. They know it'll be a tough fight, but they point to the times they've done it before. Like the Six-Day War when they quickly and badly beat both the Syrians and the Egyptians. Or the '73 War when they beat 'em both a second time. They believe they can do it again."

"You've got to get out of there, Hope." Panic made him sound angry. "Please come home. Now."

"You know that I can't, honey. I have a contract. I just got here." She hated it when her work made him angry. "I miss you, and I never stop thinking about Jennifer. But even if I could just pack up and leave, the airlines have cut back on flights in and out of the country. They've got a new priority system for reservations, and reporters like me aren't very high on the list."

She thought she heard Mark say a quick, harsh bad word. Then silence.

"I wish you weren't there. We miss you," he said at last. "We're praying you get to come home safely and soon."

"I miss you, too. We'll just have to wait this out and see what happens." Hope hoped her voice did not reveal the tears tracing down her cheeks.

Silence again, from both of them.

"Mark, do me a favor, will you? Before Jennifer goes back to school, call her teacher and tell her that she's a little afraid of returning wearing a wig—and a blond one at that. Help her teacher understand. Will you?"

That was easy. Of course he'd do it. He asked for some details and promised he'd do it immediately. Hope's mind was eased on that point. It was the next-best thing to being there herself.

"How's Dad doing?" she asked him.

"Hey, he's fine. He's back to working in the yard and preaching on Sunday and doing everything he's done since who knows when."

"That's great to hear. I'll try to call him when I get a chance later."

"Uh, Hope?"

"Yeah?"

"The other day your dad asked a question about something. He thought that maybe you being in Jerusalem could give us some insights about it. Dad was talking about the conversion of the Jews during the seven-year tribulation period and he was wondering if you've seen anything that could provide an insight into how difficult that conversion will be," Mark said.

"That's a tough question to answer," Hope declared. "On Saturday, the Jewish Sabbath, in parts of Jerusalem and the surrounding towns everything is closed. I was told that they even turn off the elevators over at the King David Hotel."

"So you'd say that conversion process would be pretty difficult?"

"For the observant Jews, for sure. Of course, even here there are a lot of cultural Jews." She paused, thinking. "I'm surely no authority on Scripture. I can't really answer that. Besides, Mark," she continued carefully, "I'm starting to question this whole Rapture and Tribulation theory."

"What have you learned now that I need to know about?"

"Well, I read my Bible a bit on the planes coming over, then I've been thinking about something one of the staffers told me. She's an Orthodox Jew, from St. Louis. She said that in the Old

Testament whenever God talks about Israel, He's talking about the people—not the land. I remember a New Testament passage—in Galatians, I'm just about positive—in which it says that if anyone is 'in Christ,' they are a child of Abraham and an heir to the same promise given to Abraham."

"OK . . ." Mark was thinking, trying to follow her thought.

"I don't think that the Israel spoken of in the New Testament is the nation of Israel at all. I think it's God's people—wherever they are. As Ruth told me, Jews are Jews and belong to God wherever they are."

"H'mm. That's something to think about," Mark said.

"Besides that, there's a big problem with the idea of rebuilding the Temple here in Jerusalem."

"Uh-huh. What's that?" Mark murmured, continuing with "I'm looking up something here in my Bible."

"Mark, it's so interesting. And beautiful. From our window I can look out and see the Temple Mount. The answer's as obvious as the nose on your face: there's a big, beautiful Muslim mosque on the Temple Mount. If you really want to upset the Muslims and start a war, just suggest tearing down the Dome of the Rock mosque and building a Jewish temple there."

"Ah, I found it!" Mark cried, ignoring her words. 'If you belong to Christ, then you are Abraham's seed, and heirs according to the promise.' That's Galatians 3:29. I think that makes the point about Israel's being those who believe in Christ instead of being Jewish by birth."

In that moment Hope looked at her watch. "Ooops, Mark. I've got to go. I love you!" she called across the miles.

"I love you, too."

"Are you going to be watching for my reports?"

"Of course," Mark said. "We're taping every one."

"Quick, put Jennifer back on the phone."

He did. Again mother and daughter said goodbyes. Mark took the phone a last time.

" 'Bye, sweetheart."

"Give my girl an extra hug for me, won't you? And give yourself one, too. I miss you two so much."

"We miss you, too," Mark said, softly repeating as he replaced the phone in its holder, "We miss you, too."

231

~ ~ ~

Hope picked up the compact digital video camera she'd been issued, slid her right hand inside the strap, and fingered the controls to get the feel of them. With her left hand she folded out the LCD display, then with her right thumb pushed the power switch. Good! The batteries were fully charged. An image appeared on the screen, and she began toggling the zoom trigger wide and narrow to test the range.

"Think you can handle that thing?" Karl asked from the back seat of the car.

Hope smiled. "I think so. I had an editor on the student newspaper back at Vanderbilt who kept telling us, "If you can't bring back an interview, at least bring back a picture.""

"Ya," Karl answered in his German accent. "I hod a teacher juss like dat back in Stuttgart. Das vhy I become a soundman."

"Traffic seems lighter than normal today. Plus, I'm seeing a lot more people on the streets in uniform and carrying weapons," Joshua observed.

"How many Israelis are in the reserves?" Hope asked.

"A lot. That's why there's less traffic and more people in uniform waiting to get on buses to their assembly points. When Israel goes to war, the nation goes to war, and commerce almost shuts down. That's why the Palestinians want war: so that they can have jobs running the country while everybody else is fighting!"

Joshua turned right onto a main thoroughfare. While other traffic moved into the left lanes and got ahead, he stayed in the right, content to move at the pace of the buses winding their way in and out of traffic at their various stops every few blocks.

"What's up?" Karl asked.

"I'm not sure. There's something odd about that car ahead of us. That blue Toyota," Joshua said. "Hope, keep your camera on that car. I've got a feeling that something's about to happen."

"What?" she asked.

"I don't know. Just get it on tape," Joshua commanded. Karl leaned forward so he could see too.

"What's he doing?" she asked, lifting the camera in front of her face to get a good view.

"It's what he's *not* doing. He's not going around that bus, as everybody else is. It's as though he's following it."

Hope zoomed in on the Toyota to record the license number, then widened her view to take in both the car and bus. The bus halted two lengths before it reached the shelter at the next bus stop. The passenger in the car got out. Then the driver jerked the Toyota sharply to the left and into traffic, pulling quickly ahead.

She touched the zoom control and widened the picture on the LCD screen. She touched it again and zoomed in on the blue Toyota. Nothing seemed obviously amiss. "What are you talking about?" she asked Joshua. Then the bus angled out of the traffic lanes toward a bus stop shelter in the middle of the block, where two other buses sat.

"Suicide bomber?" Karl asked from the back seat.

At first a man walked calmly between parked cars and onto the sidewalk. Then he began running toward the crowd of uniformed reservists and civilians clustered around the shelter. He shouted something, then thrust his right hand to his chest and disappeared in a blinding flash.

In all happened in an instant, but so much happened in that instant.

As it ripped outward, the explosion blew through the windows, turning the glass into shards that ripped through the flesh of the nearest passengers. The force buckled sheet metal and lifted the bus over a half lane to the left, even as the extreme heat from the detonation charred paint and set fuel forced out of the collapsing fuel tank ablaze. What was left of the bus quickly turned into a smoldering, flaming mass.

The force of the blast—expanding in other directions—carried with it the deadliest part of the device, the hundreds of small nails positioned carefully around the outside of the explosive. These spears first tore through the body of the bomber, ripping the middle two thirds of his body into tiny pieces before continuing their flight to other targets: the bodies of bystanders and whatever structure happened to be in the course of their ballistic trajectory. So in a blinding, blazing heartbeat, four dozen bodies were riddled with these darts, while store windows 200 feet away were shattered, injuring shoppers inside.

Several of those nails also flew toward the car in which Hope and her partners were riding. Their impacts pebbled the car's windshield and side windows into collapsing shards of glass, and flattened the right front tire.

Joshua slammed on the brakes and threw the car into park. "You OK?" he gasped.

"Ya, I'm OK," Karl answered.

"You OK, Hope?" Joshua demanded.

His desperate question didn't penetrate her fright. She just couldn't stop screaming.

"Calm down!" Joshua commanded, grabbing her arm. "Are you injured?"

Hope's scream turned to a whimper as she looked down to survey the damages. She saw a few small rips in the front and right side of her jacket where it had been cut by shards of glass. Broken glass lay across her lap. A scratch on the back of her right hand oozed blood. She reached up to feel her face and removed a shard of glass from her right cheek. "Am I bleeding?" she whispered.

"Not bad. Let's get to work," Joshua commanded as he opened his door. Yuri was already out of the car and opening the trunk to pick up their larger camera gear.

For a moment Hope sat without moving, consciously trying to regain her composure. Then she tried opening her door. It wouldn't move. She checked the lock. It was unlocked. Another try. It wouldn't budge. She awkwardly climbed over the floor-mounted gearshift to exit by the driver's door.

Outside, the first two things Hope noticed were the smells coming from the bus as flames licked it both inside and out—the acrid, nose-burning odor of combusting plastic, diesel fuel, paint, rubber, and flesh. She doubled over, gagging, as the odor hit her in the face. Then she heard the moans and terror-filled screams of the wounded and merely frightened, followed by the two-tone wail of approaching sirens. A police officer on foot patrol came running up, shouting in Hebrew. By his gestures Hope perceived that he was telling bystanders either to begin helping or to get out of the way. Perhaps both.

The trio formed up into a team: Joshua shouldering the standard camera, Karl with his microphone on a long pole that he tried to keep aimed the same direction as the camera, and Hope with her handheld microphone for interviews when she wasn't scribbling in her reporter's notebook or shooting with her hand-held camera. The problem was that her hands trembled so badly that she could hardly hold anything, much less write anything or shoot video steadily.

Chaos. Sheer, raw chaos surrounded them everywhere they turned. There were the walking wounded, those merely struck by flying glass. They had an advantage over many—they were still alive. Blood streamed down their faces or soaked through shirts and trousers from cuts beneath the clothing. The panic and pain on their faces screamed as loudly as their voices, desperate for the help that was now beginning to arrive. Police officers shouted orders to set up a perimeter to keep out the curious and to let the paramedics in to do their jobs.

Then there were the seriously wounded, who lay in pools of blood as the life drained from their bodies. Paramedics clustered around them, deciding whom they could save and who—beyond help—must be left to die.

A final group—those already dead—lay in twisted and torn postures where the force of the explosion had deposited them like limp rag dolls. Others, burned beyond recognition, re-mained in the still-smoldering metal carcass of the bus.

What struck Hope the hardest was the smells: blood mixed with the international mix of foods cooking in nearby restaurants; burning diesel fuel, scorched paint, and charred flesh.

The hiss of a fire extinguisher caught Hope's attention, and she whirled toward the sound to see someone spraying down a human form stumbling out the bus's blackened open door. Several more hisses from the extinguisher followed before the smoke stopped rising from the twitching form.

It was more than Hope could take. Clutching the tools of her trade to her chest, she ducked her head and ran toward some open space. She'd gone only a few yards when what breakfast she had eaten an hour before joined the detritus on the pavement. She spit, trying to rid her mouth of the bitter, nauseating taste, then wiped her mouth on her sleeve. *It's amazing how quickly we lose all dignity,* she thought even as her partners lifted her arms over their shoulders and carried her back to their car, where they opened the door and aimed her collapse toward the seat.

"I'm sorry, guys," she panted. "I'm sorry."

"Das OK," Karl comforted. "Jus take some slow, deep breaths. C'mon. Slow and deep. You're OK." He rested a hand on her shoulder.

A paramedic stopped to inquire of them in Hebrew, and Joshua dismissed him.

"Look at how I'm shaking," Hope said, holding up her trembling hands. "I'm shaking all over. I don't think I've ever been so scared in all my life!"

"That's the closest I've ever been to one of them," Joshua told her. He reached into the front seat, picked up Hope's camera, and began reviewing the images she'd captured. "Look at this!" he exclaimed as he rewound it, then held it toward Karl. "This is amazing! I don't think anybody's caught an actual suicide bomber on tape like this before!"

Karl looked at it and shook his head. Without a word he held it toward Hope.

"We've got to get back to the bureau and get this on the bird, but first we've got to change that front tire," Joshua told them. He looked at Karl, then at the flat tire. "Come on, we might as well get started."

By this time the police had stretched their yellow tape around the area, including their car. Hope judged that the printing probably said "Crime Scene—Do Not Enter," just as yellow tape did back home, only this was printed in Hebrew. And just as back home, it seemed to draw the ubiquitous crowd of onlookers who gawked at every item.

Hope took some more deep breaths and felt a little strength returning to her legs, so she slipped out of the car to see what progress the guys were making with the front tire. That was when she first saw the nails sticking in the outside of the car door. One was completely buried—except for its head—in the door lock mechanism. So that's why the door would not open! Another nail was almost completely exposed at the base of the window about where Hope's shoulder had been. A shudder ran through her body as she touched the nail with a fingertip, then tugged on it to pull it free and examine. It was a common eight-penny builder's nail, but oh, the damage it could do!

~ ~ ~

Hope's strength had returned by the time they arrived at the bureau, but her composure was breaking down. "You got the bomber on tape?" Ehud exclaimed in disbelief. "Amazing! Nobody's *ever* done that before. Never!" He looked at Hope's pale face. "A little too close to the action, huh?"

Hope nodded. "Yeah, I guess so." She'd sunk into a chair and let it roll lazily toward the window. Tears filled her eyes, and she sensed that her mind would replay the sight and sounds and scents for weeks to come. "I've never seen anything like it. There's no words . . . I can't . . . " A sob tore her throat. "There were human beings . . . on fire!" she cried. "It was horrible."

"Anyone find out what kind of bomb it was?" Ehud asked.

It was only then that Hope realized she still had a nail clenched tightly in her left hand, so she held it up for Ehud to see. "A nail bomb," she declared weakly.

"Where'd you get that?" he barked.

"From the car door. It was maybe an inch or two away from where my arm was. If you want to look at the car, I think you'll find some more embedded in the passenger side."

Ehud squatted down in front of Hope to look her in the eye. "Are you OK?" he questioned without his usual gruffness.

She nodded, biting her lower lip. "Sure, I'm OK."

Ehud stood and looked at his watch. "Listen, I want you to get your thoughts together, because in about 30 minutes we're going to do a feed to New York for the early-morning news. I want you to do a first-person report. Just tell what it was like to witness a suicide bombing and how it's affected you. Can you do it?"

"You want me to go on camera like this?" she answered weakly.

He studied her untidy hair, the tears in her jacket, and the trickle of blood dried on her cheek. "Yes! You're perfect. The way you are right now is what gives the story its power. Just tell it the way you saw it. Say how it made you feel."

Hope nodded. *This is why I came, I guess. This is why I left Mark and Jennifer and . . .* Suddenly she was slammed by the realization that she could have been seriously injured. *Is this why I came to the other side of the world? Did I do it for myself, for the*

prestige and excitement, or did I come here to bring my unique per-
spective to the unspeakable horror of hatred on both sides?

Ehud was looking at her, puzzled. "Hope? Will you do it?"

His voice brought her back, and she nodded. "I'll try."

Thirty minutes later Hope sat on the sunlit balcony, wishing for a hairbrush and thorough makeover but obeying Ehud's orders. "Good morning, Susan," she greeted the anchor in New York. The usual cheer was missing from her voice.

"Hope, you look absolutely terrible! What's happened to you?" the New York anchor exclaimed.

"Two hours ago my camera crew and I were en route to a press conference at the Israeli Defense Ministry building when we witnessed a suicide bombing. We were close enough that we caught the actual bombing on tape and to a small degree became victims of the attack. We debated about showing it, because it's so graphic. Then we decided that the first part, in which the bomber actually set off the bomb, wasn't any worse than what most people have seen in the movies. What we won't show you is the 31 people who were badly wounded or the 11 killed. The blood and gore was real, too real and far too graphic to show on television."

The picture changed from Hope to the few seconds of tape leading up to the explosion. "We became suspicious of the men in this blue Toyota when they ignored chances to pass the bus just ahead of them and continued following it," she narrated. "Then this happened." The videotape showed the bomber getting out of the vehicle, running toward the crowd at the bus stop, and disappearing in the explosion.

Then the picture changed to the blown-out store windows, the damaged bus, paramedics carrying out the wounded, and the blanket-covered bodies.

"What I really want to show you is this," Hope said as she held up the nail for the viewers to see. "The bomb was loaded with hundreds, maybe even thousands, of nails just like this one. This nail was part of the bomb, the most destructive part actually. When the bomb went off, this nail—and hundreds, maybe thousands more like it—became darts piercing bodies and anything else they struck. Walking around the scene, we saw bodies riddled by them and found them embedded in the front walls of stores. They flattened our front tire and shattered two of our car's windows. This nail struck the door just inches from my arm. That's how close I came to being either the thirty-second person wounded this morning, or the twelfth person killed."

"Hope, how has this experience made you feel?" the anchor inquired.

"That's a hard question to answer. I still haven't put it into perspective. I mean, my hands are still trembling. But I'll tell you this, if I ever doubt God's power to protect, all I'll have to do is look at this nail and be reminded of what happened today here in Jerusalem."

TWENTY-TWO

The visitor at the front desk seemed polite enough, but something about him turned Ehud from a mere grouch into a tiger on the defensive. Rather than getting up and going to the front desk to greet the man, who asked for him by name, Ehud eyed the visitor on the security camera monitor and communicated through messengers.

"He wants a copy of the video of the suicide bomber and his accomplice," the technician relayed.

"Tell him it's already gone by courier to New York," Ehud snapped.

"I know you haven't sent it out, because your courier leaves in the morning. I would like to speak with your bureau manager. Please get him now." The man spoke clearly with an increased measure of firmness in his voice.

"OK," Ehud told the technician reluctantly. From his tone, the word tasted sour on his tongue. "Run a copy and give it to him. Then get him out of here as fast as you can." Hope walked into the room to hear the last sentence. Seeing her, he pointed to the security camera monitor and hissed. "Don't say a word to that man. Not one. Don't tell him a single thing."

Teeth clenched, Ehud stood up and strode into his office. Hope heard the click of the lock on his door.

"What's going on?" she whispered to the technician.

"That man is Mossad—the Israeli Intelligence Service. You can't trust them."

Hope opened her mouth to ask another question, but stopped when the technician shook his head.

Minutes later the official departed with his copy of the tape, and Ehud came out of hiding. "Why don't you trust the Mossad? I thought they were the good guys," Hope asked.

"Let me tell you a little story. One day a flea and a frog were wanting to cross a stream. The flea could not find a bird to carry him, so he asked the frog for a ride. 'Get on my back,' the frog instructed, and the flea did. The frog could easily have hopped across by going from one rock to another and neither would have gotten wet. But halfway across he decided to swim. As the flea was drowning, he cried out to the frog, 'You knew I couldn't swim, so why did you do it?' To which the frog replied, 'This is the Middle East.'

"The moral of the story," he continued emphatically, "is that in this part of the world you don't trust people, *you use them*— and the Mossad is the master of using people. There are no good guys and bad guys, there's us and them, me and you." He spit into the wastebasket, wiping his mouth with the back of his hands. His eyes were dark and cold. "The Mossad? They're not on 'our' side; they're on the Mossad's side. That's why they betrayed my brother and got him killed. No, they murdered him."

Hope gasped. What was he saying? Could it be true? Involuntarily she took a step backward from the hatred in his tone. He didn't notice. For the moment Ehud was in a different world.

"My brother and I moved here from New York 14 years ago. It's a long story, but he started a business with a Palestinian as his partner. It didn't matter to either of them that the man was a Christian and my brother a Jew. But the Mossad accused his partner of being an agent for a militant group and him—my *brother*—of being an Arab sympathizer. They wanted him to betray his partner." He paced from desk to window, from window to desk, not noticing that his voice and the *click, click* of the wall clock were the only sounds in the room.

"My brother wouldn't do it, he wouldn't betray his friend, so they started rumors among the Palestinians that my brother was an Israeli informant. *Ha!* The Mossad didn't have to kill him. All they had to do was make *that* known, and the Palestinians did the job for them."

"That's horrible," Hope whispered, lamenting even as she spoke the feebleness of mere words. "I'm sorry."

Ehud let out a long sigh. "That's why I've kept my American citizenship even though I consider myself an Israeli." He paused, looked around the room, and shook his head. "Well, let's get back to work. As for you, Hope, you outta get some supper and some rest, because New York wants you to tell your story live for their 6:00 broadcast. That's 2:00 a.m. our time."

As the elevator lowered her toward street level, Hope felt a strange tension rising through her body. It continued as she walked down the alley toward the street. At the sidewalk she found herself looking around, studying all the vehicles to see if a suicide bomber was about to leap out at her. In the restaurant she could not keep her eyes off the people—those who entered, those who got up to leave—asking herself where she would or could dive for cover if a bomber walked through the door. She had little appetite so took most of her meal back to her room in a covered Styrofoam container.

In the bleak dorm room Hope picked up her Bible and thumbed the pages, unsure where to begin reading. She stopped in Psalms and in Psalm 23 her eyes fell on verse 4: "Even though I walk through the valley of the shadow of death, I will fear no evil, for you are with me" (NIV).

Turning more pages, she saw an old favorite in Psalm 91: "He will cover you with his feathers, and under his wings you will find refuge. . . . You will not fear the terror of night, nor the arrow that flies by day. . . . A thousand may fall at your side, ten thousand at your right hand, but it will not come near you. You will only observe with your eyes and see the punishment of the wicked" (verses 4-8, NIV).

"God," she prayed aloud, "I'm afraid. More afraid than I ever have been in my whole life. I came close to being killed today, and I was only doing my job. I don't want to die over here, Lord. I want to go home to my family so I can hold my husband and daughter." Tears filled her eyes and trickled down her cheeks, alongside her nose. "No, Lord, I haven't seen a thousand fall, but today I saw 42 people fall, and I almost became number 43. Please, Lord, keep me safe while I am here—and get me out of here soon!"

Lying across the bed, she let herself cry for several minutes. She wondered if it had been wrong of her to come to Jerusalem in the first place. She wondered if it was wrong to ask God to get her out of there when thousands upon thousands of people had no choice about staying because it was their home. She allowed herself some self-pity before sitting up, wiping her eyes on the bedspread, then making herself presentable for giving the 6:00 news.

~ ~ ~

With Hope away, Mark found himself awakening momentarily each time he rolled over and discovered anew that she was not in bed. Was it the third time tonight? Or the fourth? He wasn't sure. But something awoke him further, a sense that something was not as it should be.

Mark pushed off the covers, sat up, and slipped his feet into the shower clogs beside the bed. A glance at the clock radio showed 3:15. He padded to the kitchen for a drink of water, stopped by the bathroom, then headed back toward bed. But something caught his attention, and he turned toward Jennifer's room. In the semidarkness he listened and looked around. Her wig sat slightly askew on its Styrofoam head, and the glow from the night-light gave it an other-worldly appearance. No, that wasn't it. Then it struck him: Jennifer's breathing was labored, her sleep restless. While he stood there she coughed several times and flopped from one side to the other.

That's when it struck Mark that it hadn't been Hope's absence at all that had awakened him, but Jennifer's coughing. He reached down and felt her forehead. She felt as if she were afire.

Hurrying back to his bedroom, Mark quickly dressed in a pair of jeans and a T-shirt he'd tossed across a chair the night before. Stretch socks and athletic shoes completed the exercise. Only a moment later he was back across the hall, scooping his ill daughter out of her bed. "Jennifer! Jennifer! Wake up, honey," he urged. "You're sick! I'm going to take you to the hospital." Not even attempting to dress her, he grabbed the bedspread with his other hand so that he could wrap it around her. "Stand up, sweetheart. Let's get you in the car!"

Jennifer began another round of coughing. "I'm dizzy, Daddy. I don't think I can stand up," she declared weakly. He lifted her to a sitting position just as she moaned, "I gotta throw up," and pushed herself from the bed toward the door. She sank to the floor, heaving. Mark carried her the rest of the way, leaving a sour trail on the carpet.

Oh, no. No! He checked his thoughts. He would not swear about his sick child. He felt helpless, though, deserted by his wife.

A minute later Jennifer was on her feet but holding both sides of the bathroom door frame. "I'm too dizzy to walk, Daddy. Can you carry me?"

Mark looked at her upturned face in the harsh bathroom light. Its paleness struck a cold fear into his heart and pushed thoughts of driving her to the hospital himself out of his mind. "You stay right there," he commanded. "I'm calling for help." He didn't have the presence of mind to ease her to the floor or wrap the bedspread around her again.

Dashing to his room, he dialed 911 and managed to tell the operator that he had a vomiting child with a sky-high temperature, who also happened to be on chemo. And he, alone, was caring for her at this time.

After a three-minute eternity he heard the whine of a siren in the distance. It grew closer, louder, then stopped as it came up their street. A moment later he jerked open the door for the paramedics. Their breath was visible in the wintry night air. He took them to his shivering, whimpering daughter, stood by helplessly as they gently strapped her on the gurney, piling on blankets against the cold.

Two red lights along the way separated Mark from the ambulance. He mentally kicked himself for not riding in the ambulance with her, for deciding to drive himself, for not noticing that she was sick before she went to bed. He jerked his car toward the red illuminated ER above double doors, shot into a parking space, and slammed on the brakes. "My daughter! Jennifer Lancaster. Which way is she?" he anxiously questioned the woman at the reception desk.

She tapped a computer keyboard, then without looking up said, "She's in triage. They must evaluate her first."

"OK, OK. . . ." He was standing up. "Where is—"

"No, Mr. Lancaster. Wait." She stood now, pointing at a desk along the adjacent wall. "If you'll go on over to the insurance desk you can be with your daughter in a minute or two."

His frustration rising, Mark walked over to the window

under the sign marked "Insurance" and took a seat. In a moment a too-pleasant-for-the-hour clerk greeted him and began asking questions. She typed his replies on her keyboard, then paused to read something.

"Uh, Mr. Lancaster, this says that your medical insurance under Featherweight Software has expired. Do you have any other medical insurance?"

A pounding began at the base of his skull. He could feel it, and shut his eyes against the sensation. No medical insurance? How would he pay for Jennifer's care? Frantically he looked at the clerk for the first time.

It was as if she'd read his mind. "By law we have to take care of your daughter, Mr. Lancaster. It's just a question of who will pay the bill. Since you don't have any insurance, we'll have to ask you to sign a form guaranteeing that you will pay the bill." She tapped a few more keystrokes, and a form clicked out of the laser printer at her elbow. She took the form and pushed it under the glass security window toward Mark. He read it, then scribbled his signature beside the large X she had inscribed.

"Thank you, Mr. Lancaster," the clerk said with a nod. She arranged some papers and tapped the keyboard a few more times. "Your daughter is in the Pediatrics area, bed 3. If you go to that door right over there I'll buzz you through. Turn right, and she will be just a little way down on your right."

Mark muttered a polite thank-you as he arose and turned to locate the indicated door. The clerk was wrong: Jennifer's bed was to the left. She wore a flowered hospital gown. A doctor sat on a wheeled stool, listening to her chest while a nurse stood on the other side of the bed trying to comfort her.

"Can you cough for us again, sweetie?" the nurse asked as the doctor tucked the stethoscope into a pocket. "Only this time, instead of swallowing what comes up I need for you to spit it in here." The nurse held up a small plastic basin.

The next round of coughing began almost spontaneously, and Jennifer managed to comply, dropping back on her pillow, exhausted from the exertion. The medical pair eyed the color of the sputum. "Let's get that to the lab," the doctor instructed.

"How long has she been this way?" he asked Mark.

"She was healthy last night when I put her to bed. No fever

or coughing then, at least not that I recall," Mark answered. He tried to think. No, he was certain. "I didn't notice a fever either. Of course, I wasn't checking for one."

The doctor scribbled some notes on the chart, then motioned for Mark to follow him out into a general area. "I'll be very direct with you, uh, Mr. Lancaster," he began. "I think we're dealing with a pneumocytic pneumonia. That's a serious form of pneumonia that develops fast, and she's got it in both lungs."

The words came too fast for Mark's comprehension. *How could this happen? Why was he here alone to deal with it?* "Wait!" he sputtered. "I don't understand."

The doctor stopped, looked at him kindly, and spoke slowly, as if talking to a child. "Your daughter is seriously ill. If we don't treat her aggressively and immediately, there's a high probability that the pneumonia will kill her. We have a few antibiotics that will attack it—but I don't need the fingers of one hand on which to count them. I'm sorry."

He touched Mark's hand. His fingers were warm. "Right now I want to get an IV started, then a chest X-ray. After that we'll admit her to the pediatric ICU."

Leaning against the wall, the strength drained out of his legs, Mark asked, "What about the leukemia? Has it come back?"

The doctor shook his head. "I don't know, but I've ordered a blood test to check that. Considering how sick she is, I would expect it to appear very soon. I see on her chart that Dr. McCormick is her oncologist. I'll go ahead and notify him and see what he wants to do." He shook Mark's hand, gave him a pat on the shoulder, and left him to return to his daughter.

A few minutes later a young technician entered the room with a tray of needles and tubes to draw a blood sample. She made cheerful small talk with Jennifer, teasing her a bit, and telling a short knock-knock joke. Jennifer actually smiled, then bit her lip, and tried to cooperate. "That wasn't so bad," she said when it was over.

Next the nurse returned with an IV kit, and soon clear liquid flowed into the vein in Jennifer's left arm. Within minutes the contents of a syringe were pushed into the IV port. "That's to help bring down her fever and help her sleep," the nurse explained to Mark. Last, an antibiotic added its faint yellow contents to the calibrated flow.

"I want Mommy," Jennifer whimpered.

"I do too, honey," Mark sighed, stroking his daughter's fevered face. "I'll call her as soon as I can. Maybe she can come home."

Forty minutes later Jennifer was settled into the pediatric intensive care unit, asleep with the aid of the medication and her fever starting to drop. Mark picked up the bedside phone and punched the number for the MBS New York control room. He was told that the phone circuit to Jerusalem was busy with an audio feed, but they'd relay his request to have Hope call as soon as possible.

Now all he could do was wait for the sun to rise and family members to arrive. He made himself somewhat comfortable in the lounge chair placed conveniently by the bed, and tried to sleep.

Dr. McCormick came just after 7:00, greeted Mark, took a quick look at Jennifer, then turned to Mark. "I'm afraid I have bad news. The leukemia has come back. We've got a difficult situation here, for I believe it's the leukemia that weakened her immune system and allowed the pneumonia to form." He paused, giving Mark time to comprehend. "The problem is that another round of chemo will weaken her immune system even further. So what we've got to do is try to knock down the pneumonia and get her strength up, then attack the leukemia."

Mark shook his head. "But that doesn't make any sense."

"No, it doesn't, until you take into account that we can probably knock down the pneumonia a lot faster than the leukemia will develop, but if we don't start knocking down the pneumonia, then the leukemia will advance with even greater speed. All we can do is wait for the Vancomycin to work."

"Vanco . . . what?"

"Vancomycin. That's the antibiotic in the little bag on the IV pole. It's about the only antibiotic we currently have that's effective against the type of pneumonia Jennifer has. We'll keep that going at the rate of one bag every four hours for the next 24 hours, then see how she's doing."

~ ~ ~

"I wish I could come home," Hope cried when she finally

247

raised Mark on his cellular phone. "But as I told you, the airlines have cut back on flights. They say there's a two-week wait to get a seat on a plane." A sob tore at her words. "Mark, pray!" she cried desperately. "Pray that the threat of war eases here or that God will work a miracle anyway and let me come home sooner."

"I will, sweetheart," he told her. "I'll ask our friends at church to pray too."

"Mark." Her voice was small. "I feel so . . . guilty."

"Don't."

The word was lost in a crackle that filled Hope's line.

"What?" she cried. "What did you say?"

"I said 'Don't.' Don't feel guilty."

"Oh." More crackle, this time on both lines.

"I love you, Hope," he called across the distance. "Jennifer and I miss you like everything."

~ ~ ~

Sunset brought a second visit from Dr. McCormick, who took Mark aside for a private chat. Even before he spoke, a knot formed in Mark's stomach at his sober face. "What is it?" Mark questioned, steeling himself for bad news.

"Well, I have some good news and some bad news," Dr. McCormick began. "First, the good news is that we seem to be gaining some ground with the pneumonia. The second good news is that I've found an experimental treatment for the leukemia that so far, in other cases, has worked very well. We can begin it while her immune system is still weak. But because of her weakened immune system, we're moving her into an isolation unit."

"What does that mean?" Mark asked. "Does that mean she's worse?"

"No, no. We're isolating her because her weakened immune system makes her susceptible to all kinds of germs that wouldn't otherwise be a problem. It's a protection for her. But . . . you'll have to scrub in and put on a sterile gown and mask and gloves every time you go to visit your daughter. Also, access to the isolation unit is limited strictly to not more than three people in the immediate family."

Dr. McCormick paused.

Mark nodded, thinking, *OK. This is something we can handle.*
"But you said there was bad news. What is it?"

"The Vancomycin. It's working, but we've run out of it."

Mark's jaw dropped in surprise and shock. "You're *out* of it?"

Dr. McCormick nodded. "I just found out. The pharmaceutical plant where it's made was shut down by the Mississippi River disaster. They've been shut down for more than a month. The other plants that make it, well, they can't produce enough to make up for the loss of that plant. So as far as this hospital is concerned, there's just no more of it available."

"So . . . what can we do?" Mark asked, desperation creeping into his voice.

"We can try to treat the pneumonia with other antibiotics, but I don't think they'll be as effective. Also, moving her into isolation will prevent her from catching another infection on top of the pneumonia. Once she's in isolation, we'll start her on the Leukovidrine—the medication for the leukemia. This is how it all works."

"Wait." Mark stood up, turning his back on the physician. His breath came in sharp, harsh gasps. *This is too much. How does a parent live through this! I can't deal with this alone. I just can't.* His right fist hit his thigh repeatedly. *Dear God,* he prayed, *Dear God . . .* His mind was blank. This was the only prayer he could manage.

Looking out the narrow window, he watched the naked arms of a poplar tree shifting in the wind. He hated poplar trees. They reminded him of cemeteries. *What idiot planted them on the hospital grounds, anyway?*

"Mr. Lancaster? Mr. Lancaster!"

Ah, yes. The doctor. The man who holds all the secrets, who . . .

Mark turned, drew a deep breath. "I'm sorry. Please. It's . . . a little too much."

"I know. You can ask questions when I finish. This is rather high-tech stuff." He took out an index card and jotted some notes for Mark as he talked. "First, we draw a fair amount of blood and isolate out the leukemia cells. Second, the laboratory develops an antibody and starts cloning it. Third, we add the Leukovidrine, mix it up, and let the combination multiply in an incubator for a couple of days. The Leukovidrine is attached to the antibody that attacks the leukemia, so it goes straight to the leukemia and works there, leaving everything else alone."

Dr. McCormick paused to let his words sink in. "As I said before, this is experimental, but it's also cutting edge. It takes four days to grow enough of the antibodies to begin giving them to Jennifer, and I need your written permission before we can begin treatment."

Mark was nodding, thinking, grasping at this chance as if it were gold. "Of course, yes, I'll sign," he agreed. "I'll sign."

"You have to understand that this might not work," the doctor continued, "but I think it's the only chance we have right now."

Mark thought for a moment. "Are there side effects?"

"Yes, few things don't have side effects. However, we'll be monitoring her 24-7, and in truth the known side effects are not extreme."

"OK, yes. I'll sign."

Dr. McCormick slid a clipboard toward Mark for his signature. "We'll get her moved to the isolation unit in the next few minutes and start work with the Leukovidrine right away. We're keeping her slightly sedated to keep her comfortable. The move won't bother her at all."

Mark nodded, numb.

"Oh, and let's not forget something else," Dr. McCormick added. "We need to pray."

Taking Mark's hands in his, Dr. McCormick asked God to give him and Hope strength to bear the trial of Jennifer's illness and for God to preserve Jennifer's life.

"I've taken the liberty of calling the Berringers," Dr. McCormick said as he stepped toward the door. "I expect they'll be out in the waiting room soon."

CHAPTER TWENTY-THREE

Mark paced the hallway outside the isolation unit as the staff got Jennifer situated. The hospital running out of Vancomycin had grabbed the knot in his stomach and tied it even tighter. He felt frantic to do *something.* But what could he do? He had no medical background. He had no idea how the medical supply system worked. He felt helpless and alone.

The Berringers had come. They prayed with him, feeling helpless also, but hoping that their presence would be a comfort. Family members arrived with worried faces and questions. He appreciated their hugs and prayers. Still, he felt powerless. Then a nurse came to tell them that Jennifer was now settled in the isolation unit on a different floor. She told the group how to get there.

Mark was the only person allowed inside the unit. An energetic nurse with a wide smile instructed him on how to scrub his hands and arms and then dress in a sterile gown, booties, and face mask before entering Jennifer's room. It took several minutes, for he did not want to be the one to introduce germs into her environment! Once properly attired, he opened the door. In general the room was similar to the cubicle in the pediatric ICU from which she'd been moved. Then he swallowed to correct a difference in air pressure: the incoming air was sterilized and the room was pressurized so that any leaks would flow outward instead of admitting germs.

He reached out and took the hand of his sedated daughter. Touching her with a layer of latex between them felt odd.

Mark bent down to kiss her on the forehead through the paper mask between his lips and her skin. Even through the paper he could tell that her fever had returned. "I love you," he whispered in her ear as tears welled up in his eyes.

"I think you need to go out," the nurse said softly. "We can't let even your tears touch her."

Mark nodded and turned to leave. It was OK. She didn't know he was there. Outside the door he pulled off the gloves and tossed them into a large trash can. The sterile gown, mask, and cap went next. His vision blurred with tears as he turned toward the waiting room and the comforting arms of family and friends.

"I just feel so . . . helpless," he wept. "I wish I could do something. I mean, they've run out of the medicine she needs, so she's just lying there . . . dying." Hearing himself say that last word triggered a new flow of tears.

Mark got control of himself and sat down, his eyes on the TV on the wall in one corner. The others gathered in small groups, talking quietly. Someone asked if he wanted coffee. He didn't. He did want water, however, and feeling himself dangerously close to breaking down again, he got up and walked down the hall, where he bent over the drinking fountain, then went to look out a narrow window. It was a cloudless, windy winter day. After a moment he sensed Kevin Berringer's presence next to him.

"You know what?" Mark asked without turning around or waiting for an answer. "Christmas is only a few weeks away. You know what I want for Christmas?"

"What do you want?" Kevin asked gently.

"All I want is for my daughter to be healthy. I just want God to heal her. Why doesn't He just heal her?"

"I can't answer that question," Kevin replied softly. "No one can. All we can do is depend on God for strength to get through trials as they come."

Mark turned to face him. "I feel as though I've got to *do* something. I just don't know what." Mark wiped away more tears with a tissue from a box on a nearby table.

"I wish I knew what to tell you, buddy. It's a terrible feeling, being helpless."

The two men stood together in silence, bound by the unspoken knowledge that each understood what the other had gone through, were going through. Suddenly Mark's expression

252

changed from desperation to inspiration. "I know! I'll call Gene," he declared.

"Who's Gene?"

"My old boss. He owned the company until he got married and sold it. He's an amazing guy, the kind who can come up with the most amazing resources just when you need them. You name it, he can find it." Mark was almost dancing. "I'm going to call him."

"You have his number?"

"I think so. I think—" Mark began keying through the phone list stored in his cell phone then pushed the dial button. "Gene!" he shouted a moment later. "This is Mark Lancaster. How are you?"

Mark's eyes caught Kevin's, and he gave a thumbs-up. "Hey, Gene, I really, really need your help." He went on to describe Jennifer's illness and the lack of medication.

Kevin's eyes were riveted on his friend. Mark was nodding, nodding. "Yes. Oh, yes. Oh, Gene . . . I can't tell you . . . Yes! OK. Thank you, Gene. I really mean it. I know medicine's a bit out of your usual area, so thanks for at least trying." Mark clicked off his phone and gave Kevin a hug.

"He's going to try."

"That's marvelous. Could be your answer to prayer."

"Yeah." He shook his head, his lips moving. "Yeah, it could be."

~ ~ ~

The Egyptians delayed their attack for two days, hoping that the Israelis would shift defensive forces from the south to the northern front. Instead, three hours before dawn the Israelis launched an attack on the still-sleeping Egyptian armored units, inflicting heavy casualties and blunting much of the force of the coming attack.

The military action left the MBS bureau scrambling. Every time they turned around, New York wanted them to confirm or deny a report carried by one of the wire services or aired by a competing broadcast outlet. They used video shot by Israeli TV crews as well as their own. With the camera and sound personnel in the field with the army, Hope often found herself working solo, lugging her own equipment to briefings at the Israeli Defense Ministry headquarters. Fortunately Ruth and Misha were still in the office to edit her tape and help her prepare live reports for broadcast in the United States. Literally working day and night, she often caught no more than two or three hours of sleep at a time. That made conversations with Mark difficult.

Had she called Mark? Or had Mark called her and been patched through from New York? Hope was too tired to remember, but at least—at the moment—she was talking to her husband, and he had good news. Jennifer's fever was down, and the Leukovidrine treatment would begin tomorrow.

"How did that happen?" Hope asked. "Did the other antibiotics work?"

"No!" Excitement filled Mark's voice. "We got her some more Vancomycin."

"You did? How on earth?"

"It happened so fast, I can't believe I haven't told you. Gene pulled it off. I called him, and he started calling people, and a couple hours later he called me back and told me it was on its way to Memphis on the company plane. His people out there in California put him in touch with a hospital pharmacy in Tijuana, Mexico. The Mexican pharmacist carried an entire carton of the medicine to the border, where he gave it to a courier from the San Diego office. The courier got it through customs and took it to Lindbergh Field, where he met the company plane. Then the plane came straight here.

"It was around 1:00 a.m. when I drove to the airport, but we got it! Hope, you should have been here. It was an entire case of the medicine with her name on it!"

"Praise the Lord!" Hope could think of nothing else to say, and those three words felt woefully inadequate. How do you thank someone for giving your daughter a chance of life? She squealed, jumping up and down. "Praise the Lord! Oh, Mark, I've been so scared. I can't sleep, I can't eat, I—"

"Well, hon, she's not out of the woods yet," Mark cautioned, "but she's not as sick as she was. We still have to wait for the Leukovidrine to work."

Mark felt more than heard his wife's sigh. *How,* she wondered for the hundredth time, *did I think I could be on the other side of the world with Jennifer so ill? Why did I think it was so important to go? Sure, we needed the money, but . . .*

"I just wish I was there with you." Mark's words interrupted her thoughts. "Oh, that doesn't sound right. I wish we were together. And I wish"—his voice dropped—"you were home."

"Me too." Neither spoke for several seconds, each lost in their own loneliness. Then Hope voiced the concern that buying the medicine and getting it to Memphis must have cost Gene a bundle. "Do we—?" she began.

"No, no. When I offered to pay he told me not to worry about it. That it was a gift. He wouldn't even discuss it."

"That's a real friend," Hope mused. "Thank him, and thank God . . ." Over her words an air-raid siren began its wail over the ancient city. "Oops," she said. "I'd better get off the line."

"What's going on?" Mark could hear the piercing sound.

"Air raid. It's probably the Syrians sneaking through the Israeli air defenses, but you never know. I'd head for the air-raid shelter, but New York wants us live on the air whenever anything like this happens."

"Listen, Hope. I don't care what New York wants. I want you in your air-raid shelter. It's crazy for you to be on air during a raid."

"It's OK. Seriously, Mark, it's OK." *If only you knew how much more I worry about Jennifer than about getting hurt.* "They've not gotten through this far yet. Well, only a couple times. The planes have to get past the Patriot missile batteries, and you wouldn't believe how good they are. Not much gets past them. Besides that, we're in a residential and commercial area—a long way from any military targets they'd be attacking."

"That doesn't make me feel any better."

"Trust me. I'm not scared. It looks like fireworks—and it's far away." Hope laughed. "If you can forget that they're deadly, the sight is almost pretty."

"I'm not laughing," Mark told her, irritated. "Just take care of yourself."

"I'll call you when I can." The sound of the siren had swelled until Hope was shouting. "Don't worry, they don't often get this far. They're usually intercepted up over the northern part of the country. The air-raid sirens go off because they don't know where the planes are going, just what direction they're going. It's not dangerous, not where we are."

~ ~ ~

The Syrian Army attacked first by moving into southern Lebanon and easily sweeping aside the Christian militias supported by Israel. Alerted to the attack by their network of spies in the area, Israel immediately began a strong counterattack by crossing the border into south Lebanon. Helicopters and other attack aircraft pursued their targets wherever they could be found as the ground forces established a defensive line some nine miles inside Lebanon. That line held for the better part of the first day, but by the time the sun was low in the sky the Israelis were retreating back to their border and an even better prepared defense line. Lacking experience in night maneuvers, the Syrians halted their attack for the night but resumed with a vengeance as the rising sun temporarily blinded the Israelis. Within three hours the first Syrian tanks were rumbling across Israeli fields and through fortified villages. Israeli commanders worked quickly to regroup their armor and infantry units in ways to begin their own counterattacks and delaying actions. The Israelis turned each valley into a killing zone in which increasing numbers of Syrian tanks and armored personnel carriers became burning coffins for their crews.

~ ~ ~

Colonel Muhammad Abdullah squared his shoulders and strode confidently toward the podium on the back of a truck parked at the rear of the large hangar. A guard at the bottom step snapped stiffly to attention and saluted as he approached.

"Vermin," Col. Abdullah muttered under his breath as he passed the guard and ignored his salute. He fairly flew up the steps and turned to face the assembled troops standing below.

"Parade rest!" an officer standing in front of the truck ordered, then turned in a practiced about-face as his men relaxed, spread their feet apart, and clasped hands behind their belts.

"Men, in minutes we will do what we have trained and dreamed for years of doing. We will launch our missiles and help our Arab neighbors drive the filthy Jews out of Palestine and into the sea!" Col. Abdullah announced. "By doing this you will bring glory on Syria and you will be honored by our great president!" The two dozen men assembled before him erupted in a loud cheer.

For a moment Col. Abdullah let himself revel in the cheering of his men, then held his gloved right hand aloft to signal for them to be silent. "I have even more good news," he proclaimed. "In just a few minutes—as we are driving our missiles outside to their launch sites—we will be joined by our great leader, who will witness our heroism!"

An even louder cheer echoed between the walls of the hangar.

Col. Abdullah looked around the large hangar where they stood surrounded by the equipment used to maintain and service the missile. Fashioned after the old Soviet-made SCUD missiles launched against the Israelis and the infidels who drove the Iraqi Army out of Kuwait in 1991, the Al Hussein was somewhat larger and longer with a greater range. Though made by the Iraqi regime of Saddam Hussein, these missiles had been smuggled across the border into Syria just days ahead of the American invasion that had unseated the dictator. The president of Syria, the son of a similar dictator and not a man known for his kindness toward his people, had at first ordered that the missiles just be stored in this remote location. Why had these missiles been brought across the border for safekeeping in Syria? The answer became obvious when the nature of the warheads had been discovered.

It seemed the missiles might be left here and forgotten by commanders in Damascus. But as the Palestinian situation continued on the West Bank and pressure from the United States demanding that he change his regime grew, the president gave the order to put the missiles into flight-ready condition. Doing that was no small task considering their scientists had only limited knowledge of the missiles. So Col. Abdullah had found the best engineers he could get and put them on the task.

Considering how many forays the American special forces had made into his country identifying possible targets for a future invasion, Col. Abdullah was amazed that this facility had survived undetected. Or had it? For many months he had maintained an increased security patrol around the base to keep prying eyes away. Regardless, after tonight there would be no doubt about what had been here. Maybe those prying eyes would return to see if anything more was stored here.

The pair of missiles resting horizontally on their launch trailers were painted brown but glowed a sickly shade of yellow in the brightness of the sodium vapor lights mounted overhead. Col. Abdullah was proud of his men for what they were about to accomplish. He smiled broadly as he commanded the men to turn off the yellow lights, turn on red ones, then open the large bomb-proof doors at the end of the building. Electric motors began pulling on cables to draw the giant doors open. Minutes later the engines on the launch vehicles cranked to life and the slender missiles began the journey to their designated launch points.

Col. Abdullah followed the first missile out the door in his command car and bumped along the unpaved dirt track as it wound its way two miles to the end of a pocket canyon. This was the designated launch position because the high rock walls on three sides of where they stood would protect the missile from being seen by observers on the ground until it was several hundred feet in the air. Likewise, the ignition flash from their engines would not be seen by any American observations satellite unless it was directly overhead. The Syrians did not know when those eyes in the high sky would be looking, but knew that if the path of the missile was directed at Israel, the Americans would instantly notify the hated Jews of the danger.

A satisfied smile crossed Col. Abdullah's face as he watched his well-trained crew go about their tasks. In minutes the missile stood erect, bathed in the moonlight and looking like a brown finger silhouetted and reflecting against the moonlit mountainsides. An aide approached with news that the other missile team had reached their launch position and would soon be ready to fire.

"Tell them to wait until our president has arrived and given the order to launch," he commanded. The aide saluted and returned to the communications truck.

Turning around to survey the scene, Col. Abdullah picked out a row of headlights in the distance slowly winding along the same path his crew had taken a half hour before. *Ah, that must be the president!* he thought, pulling himself more erect and squaring his shoulders. The lights drew slowly closer until he he could make out the forms of several sport-utility vehicles both in front of and behind a limousine. Four heavily armed security guards exited each and formed a cordon around the president, who stepped out through a rear door of the limousine.

Col. Abdullah snapped to attention as the president approached. "Welcome, Mr. President. We are honored by your visit," he declared.

One of the security men eyed Col. Abdullah with a cold stare that sent a shiver down his spine as if he was being examined by a doctor using an icicle instead of a finger.

Slender of build and tall like his father before him, the president surveyed the scene with eyes that took in everything while ignoring the person in front of him. "Are you ready to fire?" he asked.

"Yes, sir!" Col. Abdullah answered. "My troops are ready to launch at your command, Mr. President."

"I am glad to see this. You are ready, so you will do well," the president said formally. He gazed up with a satisfied smile at the missile shining in reflected moonlight. "For many years we have waited patiently for this opportunity to help our Palestinian brothers by striking a blow against the filthy Jews who occupy Palestine. But tonight! We have a weapon that we have kept hidden from the world. Tonight the world will see how powerful we are when it is the Jews who are burning!"

The president eyed Col. Abdullah. "You should feel proud knowing that you are making history tonight," he declared, and the colonel saw pure evil in the coldness of his eyes and the smile twisting his lips.

Suddenly he understood how this man could kill someone who had been a trusted friend for more than 20 years just on the suspicion that he was being disloyal—and do it without remorse.

"Yes, sir! I am proud to serve you, sir," Col. Abdullah said mechanically.

"Tell me, what are your targets?"

Col. Abdullah invited the president to enter the cramped confines of the command trailer, where he indicated the targets on a map. "Ben Gurion Airport at Tel Aviv and the large Israeli Army base just outside of Jerusalem. We're using the global positioning satellite signal to guide them to precise coordinates.

This guidance system is greatly improved over what it was when the missiles were first delivered to us."

"Very well. You may launch when ready. I will go outside to witness this glorious moment."

"Sir, for your safety I would prefer that you watch through the window from the safety of our command trailer. But if you insist on being outside, please wear these." Col. Abdullah reached into a pocket of his coat, extracted a pair of safety goggles and a container of earplugs and held them out toward the president. At the unexpected move, the nearest security guard flinched visibly, raised his weapon slightly, then lowered it.

The president took the goggles and pulled the elastic band around his head. He was fiddling with the earplugs as he turned away and went outside.

Col. Abdullah looked through the window and watched until the president stopped and leaned against his limousine on the side toward the missile. Judging by where he stood, he estimated that if the missile exploded on launch the president and his entire security team would be incinerated. The "Destruct" switch that would fire such an explosion was only inches from his finger under a safety cover that prevented anyone from touching it accidentally.

He reached for the radio microphone. "This is Col. Abdullah. For the glory of Islam and the glory of Syria, on the authority and command of our honored president, launch!" At his command two technicians at opposite ends of the trailer inserted launch keys into launch locks and turned them to enable the launch sequence to begin. For an instant, Col. Abdullah felt his hand reaching downward toward the "Destruct" button. He touched the cover and started to lift it, then thought of what he knew would happen to his family if he did. He'd seen other officers and their entire families suddenly disappear. Stories of what happened to the disloyal and their families had circulated in whispers over cups of tea with fellow officers as they relaxed in the evenings.

He reached upward and felt the ribbed surface of the "Launch" button for a second, then pressed it firmly. Two seconds later the night sky lit up like daylight, and an ear-splitting roar shook the launch trailer. The missile moved slowly at first, then faster and faster until 20 seconds later silence again settled over the moonlit scene.

The president pointed into the night sky as the second missile began its arc toward the southwest. Then he got back into the car and the entire motorcade disappeared ahead of a dust cloud.

Orbiting more than 200 miles overhead, a satellite originally launched to detect nuclear emissions and missile launches from the former Soviet Union picked up the faint reading given off by a concentration of fissionable nuclear material. The coordinates were in the desert of northeastern Syria. Already it had signaled this curious observation to U.S. military observers located at an Air Force command center. The news was working its way up the chain of command when the satellite signaled first one launch, then two. Confirmation of the visible rocket plumes and their direction of travel was made by an officer watching the live video feed from the satellite. A computer scanning the same picture in the infrared band confirmed the temperature as matching a rocket engine. The officer picked up a phone and punched a button immediately connecting him to NORAD, the Air Force's missile and space monitoring command center located deep under Cheyenne Mountain in Colorado. Next, the message went to the National Military Command Center at the Pentagon, where the two-star general standing watch ordered that the information be relayed immediately to the Israeli Ministry of Defense. The message was delivered in less than three minutes.

Crews operating Patriot antiaircraft missile batteries in northern Israel picked up the missile tracks as they crossed central Syria and relayed the air-raid warning to their commanders. The fire-control radars computed intercept courses and waited for the right time to send the missiles screaming northeast and upward out of their launch tubes.

"Incoming missiles! Incoming missiles! Coming from the north!" Hope heard the announcer on Radio Jerusalem warn. She bent over the camera mounted on a tripod next to the large windows of the production room and pressed her right eye against the viewfinder. Swinging the camera left and up, she zoomed so the lens would take in a hill from which she'd seen Patriot missiles race into the sky on previous nights. She reminded herself of how quickly the missiles would be moving and widened the view so she'd have a better chance of capturing the streak of light made by the rocket engine as it raced into the sky.

Ready as she was, the suddenness of the launches still took her by surprise. There was one missile, then a second. They took divergent paths in the same general direction as they pursued something high up in the darkness. Then she saw the glow of the incoming warheads racing along the edge of the atmosphere and heated by friction with the air. The two pairs of light paths began converging.

There was a bright flash as the first Patriot detonated. "Yes!" Hope hissed and shook her left fist. It had worked! The remains of the explosion began falling earthward in burning arcs. She guessed that the parts would fall somewhere on the distant side of the West Bank or Jordan.

Hope tilted her camera up slightly to keep the second missile in view, then zoomed in to follow it more closely, though at maximum zoom they were just dots of light. The Patriot flashed in the distant sky, but the incoming streak kept moving. A third Patriot streaked out of its launch tube. This one detonated much closer to the incoming warhead. It did not break apart, as the first one had. Though its course had been altered somewhat by the intercept it obviously was still headed for Jerusalem.

Two distant claps of thunder reached the ground, the detonations of the first and second Patriots, followed seconds later by the third, which was much louder. Hope kept the camera trained on the falling dot of light as it came ever closer. She panned right as it grew larger and began moving across her field of view directly toward the Temple Mount. It continued until it was several hundred feet above the ground and directly over the Dome of the Rock mosque, one of Islam's holiest sites, atop the Temple Mount.

Then everything went an unbelievably brilliant white.

Instinctively Hope closed her eyes tightly, but it was too late. The brightness had already blinded her. She tightened her grip on the camera as over the next seconds the blast rolled across the city and the brilliance gathered itself into a flaming center that erupted upward into a raging mushroom cloud. Sight was just returning to Hope's right eye—the one behind the viewfinder—when the blast hit the MBS bureau and shattered the windows inward forcefully. The blast slammed her and the camera against the far wall. Svetlana, the technician at the control console, was thrown hard against the equipment.

"Help! Somebody! Help me!" The screams seemed forced without consciousness out of Hope's throat. Then she stopped to begin taking stock of the situation. By feel she could tell that she was bleeding from numerous cuts. Shards of glass were embedded in some of them. The pillar of fire over the Temple Mount gave more than enough light to survey the situation, but the spots in her left eye made it hard to see. She closed the left eye and tried to survey herself. She pulled out what shards she could find, then carefully picked herself up and staggered toward the large first-aid box mounted on the wall. Well, it *had* been mounted there. Now its contents lay strewn across the floor, so she pulled off her shredded blouse and began using pieces of it to dress her wounds.

Ehud burst breathlessly through the production room door. "What hap—" His words were cut off by the sight of Svetlana slumped against the control console and by the chaos. His jaw went slack at the sight of the pillar of fire and the now-half-mile-wide area that was aflame. The radiant heat from the flames made the room feel like a hot summer day.

Just behind Ehud came Ruth, who'd been slower climbing the stairs. Her breath came in harsh puffs, but she immediately helped Ehud lower Svetlana to the floor and started dressing the wounds on her back. "What happened?" Svetlana asked, dazed.

Once it was clear that all major bleeding had been stopped, Ehud began checking the broadcast equipment and declared that he was heading for the roof to realign the antenna and start the generator. Two minutes later at the muffled sound of the diesel generator starting, the women were glad to see the lights come back on.

Trembling from head to foot, Hope went back to her room long enough to slip on a long-sleeved pullover sweater. On her way back to the production room she picked up a broom lying in her path. Back in the room, she worked at pushing broken window glass into a jagged pile.

"We've got to get back on the air," Ehud commanded breathlessly as he came down the ladder from the roof. After several minutes' work enough functioning equipment was patched together to send a signal skyward. But the path to the bird they normally used was disrupted by the intense electromagnetic activity still going on inside the pillar of flame and smoke. Ehud hauled himself back up the ladder and aimed the antenna at a different satellite.

"What *was* that?" Hope asked no one in particular as she stared at the flaming city.

"Nuclear," Svetlana groaned. "That's the only weapon capable of doing what it did."

Ehud came back down the ladder and worked feverishly at the control console. "Yes!" he shouted. "We've got a bird!" He picked up the phone. "MBS Jerusalem calling MBS New York. Do you read?"

"You went off the air. What happened?" They clearly heard fear in the voice.

"As soon as we can get a camera back up we'll let you see for yourselves," he answered, motioning for Hope to get the camera back up on a tripod. She got it up, but the large camera did not work, so she dashed to her room for the smaller one she had been issued only days before. They had to patch two cables together to connect to the control console, but at least they had a signal going up to the satellite.

Hope took her position in front of the now missing window, clipped a microphone onto a pucker in her sweater, and pushed an earphone into her ear. "We're not sure what kind of warhead was on that missile, but we think it was nuclear," she told the New York anchor.

~ ~ ~

Mark's attention was riveted to the TV in the waiting room outside the isolation unit where Jennifer slept. He watched the split screen—his wife on one side and the New York anchor on the other. "We've just received word from the Pentagon. It has been confirmed that it was a nuclear detonation that exploded over Jerusalem about 20 minutes ago," Hope said solemnly.

"Oh, dear God, she wasn't in the bomb shelter!" Mark cried as he saw the bandaged and bleeding cuts on her face.

CHAPTER **TWENTY-FOUR**

Drained of manpower to fight the war with Syria and Egypt, Israel's fire brigades required four days to extinguish the fires around the Temple Mount. Mostly what they did was let the fires burn themselves out and try to keep them from spreading to the rest of the city. Realizing that it had been a nuclear weapon, emergency workers carried radiation monitors into the area and soon found such high levels of radiation that fire crews were ordered to withdraw from the area.

News of the nuclear attack gave Israel's beleaguered troops new energy, and they began taking the fight to their enemies with increased vengeance. Syrian forces that had penetrated up to 20 miles at some places were soon prevented from retreating and were destroyed where they stood. Breakthroughs in Sinai left Egyptian forces divided and falling back toward the Suez Canal until Israeli warplanes bombed the bridges over the canal, cutting off their escape. Egypt was the first to ask the United Nations to order a cease-fire. Other nations joined the cry for an end to hostilities, but the United States kept using parliamentary procedures to delay the vote in the Security Council calling for a cease-fire until it was obvious to the world that the Israelis had won a clear victory.

The Arab world, upset that their backing of the attack on Israel had been for nought, cried loudly that the nuclear attack had been staged by Israel and the United States instead of having been launched by Syria. After all, one of Islam's holiest sites had been destroyed, and no Muslim would do that. So it had to be the act of an infidel, or so their reasoning went. So as the Israeli

Army began resting after days of furious combat, units received orders to withdraw from the fronts they had just conquered and join the house-to-house fighting breaking out in all the refugee camps scattered across the West Bank and Gaza Strip.

A press conference at the Israeli Defense Ministry featured an expert from the country's own nuclear weapons program.

"Can the radiation be cleaned up and the area made safe again?" Hope asked.

"No," the expert replied flatly in words translated from Hebrew into English. "The reason the damage area was so limited is because the weapon only partly detonated. That is good. Very good. Because if it had fully detonated this building would not be here. But it is also very bad because it left behind a huge amount of high-level radiation.

"When the weapon detonated it did two things," the expert continued. "First, it released so much thermal energy that it melted the rocks and stone buildings on the top of the mount. They were not evaporated so much as they were liquefied. Second, the bomb disintegrated the undetonated nuclear material and distributed it across the blast area, and as the liquefied rocks cooled this highly radioactive material was captured in the molten material and became part of the rocks. That's why the top of the mountain looks like it has a coating of glass and why that coating is so radioactive."

"How long will it take to clean it up?" a reporter shouted.

The expert shook his head. "No. You do not understand. We can clean up a lot of the area around the edge of the blast area because the radioactive material is on the surface. But on the Temple Mount the radiation is *in* the rocks. We would have to remove the rocks. We would have to remove the mountain itself. The removal would be very dangerous to the people doing the work. Plus where would Israel put that much highly radioactive material? In the ocean? In the Dead Sea? Where? We have nowhere to put it."

"How large of an area are we talking about?" another reporter asked.

"About 60, maybe 80 acres on the top of the mountain. That's the whole top of the mountain."

"How long will it stay radioactive and too dangerous for

human habitation?" was shouted next.

The official shook his head. "We can clean up the edge and restore it in a reasonable period of time. A few years. But that top part of the Temple Mount, uh, I'd say it will be dangerous for at least 2,000, maybe 2,500 years."

"Is it possible to build anything over that rock to protect people from radiation?" another reporter asked.

"Not unless you want to put about a two-foot thick layer of lead over the whole area. Do that, and we'll have to start calling it Mount Plumbus instead of the Temple Mount," the official joked.

~ ~ ~

"You've got to get out of there," Mark implored. "I don't care if you have to quit your job. It's too dangerous, and besides, you have a child to think of."

"As if I could ever stop thinking of her, Mark." Hope's voice was tired. "I think this was a mistake. If I'd known that Jennifer was going to get worse . . ." Her voice shook. "I wasn't prepared for this, though I don't think anyone could actually be prepared." Mark tried to say something, but she told him to wait. "I was reading Psalm 91 the other day," she said, "and it struck me that *I* have seen a thousand fall at *my* side and 10,000 at my right hand, but God has protected me. It's humbling, that's all I can say. I really do feel protected."

"The Bible also tells us not to be presumptuous," he shot back. "I fear for your safety, Hope. Don't you even care?"

She laughed. "If you only knew! Listen, Mark. Brandon Campbell called this morning and said a new reporter will arrive in a few days. I fly out next Wednesday, only six days away." Her voice softened. "Can you live until then?" she teased.

Weariness and concern were heavy on his shoulders. "I guess I'll have to."

"Listen. I'll be in New York early Thursday morning, and I have meetings at the network that afternoon. I'm scheduled to leave New York Friday morning, but once I'm in the States I'll see if I can't get that changed to Thursday night. I'm not going to spend a minute more there than I have to. Now, tell me about Jennifer again."

He laughed. "Didn't we cover that already?"

"Tell me again how she's getting better."

"OK." He settled in to repeat the good news. "She looks pretty small lying there in that big bed, but the Vancomycin worked on the pneumonia, and the Leukovidrine appears to be working on the leukemia. She's not in remission yet and her cell counts aren't down much yet, but at least they're not going up. Dr. McCormick says her immune system is really weak, so he wants to leave her in isolation until her counts are down significantly. Everyone who goes in has to scrub up and gown up."

"Is she lonely?"

"She really wants to get out of there. And since she's starting to feel better I can actually sit and have a conversation with her without her falling asleep."

"Give her a hug from her mama."

"I will."

Placing the phone back in its stand, Hope returned to her dorm, lay on the bed with her hands under her head, and looked at the water-stained ceiling for a long, long time.

~ ~ ~

Hope's flight to London was uneventful except for a little turbulence around some thunderstorms forming over the Mediterranean. It was snowing in London, obscuring all views of the city and delaying both incoming and departing flights. Hope decided the sandwich on the flight in hadn't been enough and found a cafeteria in another part of the international terminal. She entered the serving line behind an American family with two children. The older child, a boy she estimated to be about Jennifer's age, stood staring at her.

"Hi," she mouthed at him and waved back.

The boy stood tall and took a step toward her, extending his right hand to shake hers. "I'm Tyler Sorenson," he said in quite an adult manner. "It's a pleasure meeting you."

"Well, Tyler, it's nice meeting you, too. My name is Hope. Where are you from?"

"Cleveland. My dad's been working here for two weeks, and we came along to go sightseeing while he's been working," Tyler answered.

Just then the boy's mother stepped up to them. "Tyler! What have I told you about talking to strangers?" his mother admonished. Then turning to Hope, "Please forgive him, ma'am. I hope he hasn't offended you."

"Oh, no. Not at all. Your son has been very gentlemanly," Hope said, extending her hand to the woman. "I'm Hope Lancaster, and I'm heading home to Memphis."

The two women shook hands. "I'm Julie Sorenson. This is my husband, Tim, and our daughter, Jennifer. We're on our way home, too. Arlington, Virginia."

Hope smiled. "Well, good. You know, *my* daughter's name is Jennifer, too."

Tyler was studying her carefully. "You look familiar," he interjected. "Have we met before?"

"Tyler!" his dad admonished.

"Don't worry," Hope laughed. "I'm getting used to it. I'm a reporter for MBS news, so you might have seen me on TV." She picked up a chef salad and placed it onto her tray.

Now it was Tim who stared at her. "Weren't you in Jerusalem?" he asked.

Hope nodded. "Left there this morning."

"Were you there during the war?" Tyler continued.

"Uh-huh."

"Wow!" Tyler said, impressed as only a child can be. "Did you see any combat?"

"I don't know if you'd call it combat, but I witnessed a suicide bombing, and I saw the nuclear bomb go off over the Temple Mount. Do you think that counts as combat?"

"Dad, do you think that counts as combat?" Tyler asked, turning back to Hope. "Dad works for the Department of Defense."

Tim looked serious. "I think that qualifies as combat."

"I remember watching your live report right after the bomb went off," Julie said. "That must have been frightening."

Hope shook her head at the sights and sounds flooding her mind. "It was terrifying. It wasn't so scary when it happened, but looking back on it later—that's when I got a good case of the shakes from thinking about what could have happened."

They'd reached the cashier and waited as she calculated exchange rates for different currencies offered by the people ahead of them.

"That was some amazing video you shot of the bomb over the Temple Mount," Tim commented.

"Thanks. You saw it?"

Tim nodded, motioning to encourage his family along. "Actually, I spent a lot of yesterday studying it. I was at some NATO meetings in which we were discussing how large a weapon it really was and what damage it might have caused if it had detonated fully."

"Off the record, how big was it?" Hope queried.

"Very unofficially and very off the record?"

Hope nodded. "Very."

"It fizzled. The total output was maybe two kilotons at most. A full detonation would have been more likely in the area of 50 or 60 kilotons—two or three times bigger than the bomb that destroyed Hiroshima in World War II."

Suddenly Hope felt faint. She actually reached out to grasp the serving line guide bar. "If it had gone off, I mean, if it hadn't fizzled, how much damage would it have done?"

Tim took out his wallet. "Let's just say that if it hadn't fizzled you wouldn't be here talking to us."

Hope leaned against the cashier's railing as the color drained from her face. *You just never know! You never know. I go blindly along as if I had good sense, and God still protects me.* She came back to reality the third time the cashier voiced the charges for her food.

"Have a nice trip," Tyler called to her as they parted.

"Nice meeting you." Julie waved as she located her children around the table they had selected.

Hope found a chair of her own, sat down, and bowed her head. Her lips moved, though the words were inaudible: "Lord, I thank You both for this food and for the new insight You've just given me about how You have protected me over these past few weeks," she prayed. "Forgive me for ever taking You or my life for granted. And, dear Lord, keep Your hand over Mark and Jennifer, too. Amen."

The weather delays pushed Hope's departure from London well into the night. Then came an announcement that the flight was canceled. Another airline had an opening in their first-class cabin, so she exercised the option of using her MBS credit card to make the upgrade. After confirming that her luggage was being transferred, she retired to the departure lounge. Settling into a comfortable chair, she opened her laptop computer and started to work on e-mail to friends, but found drowsiness overtaking her. Once her plane lifted into the starlit sky above the snow clouds she asked the flight attendant for a blanket and pillows, and in minutes she was fast asleep. She slept soundly—through the meal and announcements and a snack—until the flight attendant awakened her to say she must place her seat in the upright position for landing at Kennedy Airport in New York City.

Dawn was still three hours away as she cleared customs and hailed a cab. "MBS headquarters," she instructed. Forty-five minutes later she stepped into the winter wind that was whistling between skyscrapers, and pulled her long coat tightly around herself. The security guard at the front desk asked her to sign in, and soon an escort from the news department arrived to lead her upstairs, where she was greeted warmly by the crew of the morning news and variety program.

"You want to be on this morning and talk about your experiences in Jerusalem?" a producer asked playfully as he sauntered past.

"Might as well. I'm not scheduled for anything until late morning," she tossed back. "Just let me put on my glamour paint, and I'll be ready."

"I'm serious," he answered. "Will you do it?"

Now Hope stopped to listen. "Do I look as if I'm ready to go on the air?" she questioned. "I left Jerusalem I don't know how many hours ago and just got off a red-eye from London. My makeup is old, and my clothes are wrinkled. Right! I'll be ready to go on camera in five minutes."

The producer laughed, but looked her in the eye. "I'm serious. I want to put you on. Just go over to wardrobe and pick out something fresh, or let them iron what you've got on. Your pick. Makeup will take care of the rest. I'm going to shuffle something to make you the lead interview in, oh, the second half hour. That gives you 90 minutes to get ready. You might even get a 15-minute snooze. OK?"

Why not? she thought. *This whole experience has been crazy anyway.* "OK. I'll do it."

"Terrific! I'll come see you in makeup and get a few leading questions for the anchor to ask you."

~ ~ ~

Seated in the comfortable interviewee's chair in studio 1, Hope briefly recounted some highlights from her time in Jerusalem.

"We're going to show the footage you shot when you almost became a victim of a suicide bomber," the anchor said. "We want to warn our viewers that this is extremely graphic and that if they have young children it would be wise to turn off their TV for the next 45 seconds or so."

Watching it again on the monitor made Hope shudder and feel sick to her stomach.

"How has all this affected you?" the anchor asked.

"You know, Alan, I really can't completely measure it yet. You see, in the past month I've cheated death at least twice." She held up the nail from the bomb, and the camera zoomed in for a close-up. "This nail is one of hundreds that came from the bomb in the tape you just saw. I pulled it out of the car door just an inch or two from where my arm was. If it hadn't been for the car door I would have been the thirty-second person wounded by that suicide bomber or—if our car had been a few yards closer—maybe the twelfth person killed."

She picked up a glass of water that sat by her side and took a swallow, waiting a few seconds to compose her thoughts. "Then I witnessed the detonation of a nuclear bomb over the Temple Mount. That's how I got this scar on my cheek—from flying broken glass, even though I was four miles from the explosion.

"But I'll tell you one change it's made in my life," she continued. "This is quite personal, but it's a significant part of what happened to me while I was in Jerusalem. I'm reading my Bible in a way I never have before, because I believe Jesus is coming soon and I want to be ready."

This was a new wrinkle, but the anchor took it in stride. "Hope, yesterday we had Rev. Fallbrook as a guest sitting right where you are now. He also expressed belief that these events—the Madrid Fault earthquakes, the bombing of the

Temple Mount—are signs that something cataclysmic is about to happen. Do you agree that what students of the Bible call 'the rapture' is about to occur?"

Hope smiled and shook her head "Well, I'm no theologian. I'm just a Bible student and a journalist who has witnessed some dramatic events. And when I read my Bible, I find Jesus saying that He's coming back to earth to take away the people who love Him. I know that this discussion has political overtones," she went on. "But all the descriptions I read in my Bible describe His coming to be as visible as the lightning that flashes from the east to the west, and that everything left behind here on earth will be destroyed." A camera close-up of her face caught the intensity of her expression.

"I've searched all through my Bible and don't find anywhere that says that Jesus will return secretly and that the people who love Him will just disappear. Neither do I find a word or phrase in the Bible saying that the Temple will be rebuilt in Jerusalem or that people will have a second chance to be saved. I've been looking for all those things, and I can't find them."

"You speak with great confidence, Hope Lancaster. Is this a challenge to Rev. Fallbrook?"

She looked shocked. "Oh, no. Not in the slightest. What I am saying is that I'm a student of the Bible, just as millions of other sincere people in the world are. And though I have studied it from cover to cover, I don't find a single reference to a secret rapture or 'seven years of tribulation' or any of the other related beliefs in the Bible that I've been reading."

"H'mm," the anchor laughed. "We should have our religion editor conducting this interview. But since you started this, did anything happen while you were in Jerusalem that influenced your thinking?"

"Oh, yes," Hope said, nodding. "Since the nuclear bomb attack, the Temple Mount is so radioactive it'll be dangerous to human life for more than 2,000 years. Once I discovered that, I realized that the theory of the Rapture and Tribulation is impossible."

"Because . . . ?" the host queried, with raised eyebrows.

"Well, the Rapturist theory teaches that the Jewish Temple will be rebuilt in Jerusalem just before the Tribulation. Two weeks ago the Temple Mount became so radioactive that it won't be safe for human habitation for at least 20 centuries. There's no way anything could be built there—unless you want it to glow at night."

The anchor looked puzzled. "Your father is a Baptist preacher and theologian, correct?" he asked. "Could *this* cause a little family crisis?" he asked lightly.

His words hit Hope in the pit of her stomach. With her mind on Jennifer and on the minute-by-minute stress of her job, she'd put any potential family conflict out of her mind. "You know, I'm not a prophet," she began. "I'm not making any political predictions. Yes, belief in God and in the Rapture were a significant part of the person I was a few weeks ago," Hope admitted. "But now—I can't believe in a secret rapture anymore."

She leaned toward the interviewer, her face intense. "Do I believe Jesus is coming soon? Absolutely! Do I believe He will come in secret? Absolutely not! The Bible describes His coming as a visible, cataclysmic event that will destroy this planet."

"Then how do you respond to all the millions who—from their study of the Bible—expect the literal restoration of Israel?" the host asked. "After all, this does have political implications for, perhaps, the entire world."

She shook her head, wondering at the wisdom of being in what had become a hot seat. She hadn't realized the extent to which she'd be questioned nor the religious turn it was going to take. She paused, composing a reply.

"As I said, I have no theological training. But I have learned how to study the Word. I read in my Bible that when a person believes in Christ, they become an heir to the same promise of salvation that God gave to Abraham. That makes them a spiritual Jew and a member of spiritual Israel." As she spoke, she felt energized. Maybe God's hand was in her being in the hot seat right now. "I believe that the Bible is referring to those who are reborn in Christ, not those born as natural Jews," she declared, "although Jewish people can be saved. But the kingdom we should all be looking for is the one Jesus will establish after He comes to take away the people He has redeemed."

"So you don't look for a literal restoration of Israel. Either

274

way, there are significant political ramifications . . ." The host left the sentence unfinished.

Hope shook her head. "No. I believe that the 'Israel' Jesus died to save refers to all who believe in Him—from every nation, tongue, and people—not a nation in the Middle East."

CHAPTER TWENTY-FIVE

Hope's flight to Memphis landed two minutes early with a double-thump onto the runway. She and Mark spotted each other from distant sides of the security checkpoint and flew into each other's arms. "Oh, I'm happy to have you home!" Mark exclaimed, holding her as though he'd never let her go. "I'm so glad!"

"Me too. Me too. How's Jennifer?"

"She's improving." Hope's stride matched her husband's, walking to the baggage claim. "Do you want to go straight to the hospital?"

"Of course! I bought Jennifer a gift at the duty-free shop in London. It's a stuffed lion. You know how she enjoys stuffed animals."

Mark shook his head. "We'll have to leave it at home. She's in isolation, remember, for a few more days, anyway. Dr. McCormick says her blood counts are getting better, and it looks like she's headed for remission. The day she has a zero count of leukemia cells is the day she gets out of isolation."

"Let that day be soon!"

The couple eyed the overhead directory sign, surveyed the flow of the crowd, and decided they were on the right path to baggage claim. Moments later they stood with their arms tightly around each other, waiting for the luggage carousel to start moving. "You're not going to glow in the dark now, are you?" Mark teased.

"You'll tell me if I do, won't you?" Hope teased back.

"We need to put a new night light in Jennifer's room. Maybe you should start sleeping in there," Mark quipped, and got a pinch in return.

"The news shows back here have been full of all kinds of talk about how much radiation was released," he told his wife. "Listen to them, and you'd think everybody within 20 miles of the blast was going to die from radiation-related illnesses."

Hope shook her head. "The Israeli Ministry of Defense was pretty concerned about that, too. The surprising thing about the blast was how the fallout got concentrated in the glassified rocks. Where I was, they estimated all the radiation I got was the equivalent of a half-dozen chest X-rays, but that's about it. There shouldn't be any long-term problems."

The luggage carousel started with a jerk, and 200 heads turned its direction. A full minute passed before the first pieces of luggage appeared. "Which ones are yours?"

"I put MBS stickers on them. You can't miss 'em."

In minutes the two familiar black cases arrived. Mark strapped them together for piggybacking and headed for the exit. "They didn't issue you any body armor or other protective gear while you were over there, did they?"

Hope shook her head. "It was available, but I never needed it."

"Well, you may wish you'd brought it home when you meet your father. He's pretty upset at you after what you said on the morning show about not believing in the Rapture anymore."

~ ~ ~

At the hospital Mark led Hope through the maze of corridors to a nurses' station. "Good morning, Kathy," he greeted one of the staff. "This is my wife, Hope."

A look of pleased surprise came over Kathy's face as she stepped away from her computer terminal and extended a hand to greet Hope. "I'm so glad to finally get to meet you. I've been watching your reports on the news. Man! You've been through a lot lately."

Hope smiled. "You can see why I'm glad to be home. It's a bit safer here."

"She's going to need a quick orientation about the isolation rules and how to dress," Mark interjected.

"Sure. Right this way." Over the next 15 minutes the woman

instructed Hope on where to go to change into a hospital scrub suit, where to wash her hands and arms, and how to put on a sterile gown, mask, cap, booties, and gloves before entering Jennifer's room.

"Which room is she in?" Hope asked Mark as they scrubbed their hands and arms with disinfecting soap and disposable brushes.

"Room 3. Over there," Mark pointed. Through the window they could see her sitting up in her bed and watching TV. She did not see them.

Hope's heart leaped with anticipation of seeing and holding her daughter after more than a month away. She dried her arms with extra speed and drove them into the sleeves of the sterile gown the nurse held up for her. Kathy pulled the tie ends around where Hope could knot them at her side.

"Are you allergic to latex?" Kathy asked.

"Uh, not that I know about," Hope answered.

"Good," the nurse answered. "We're out of the regular gloves. One of those impacts from the flood on the Mississippi River, you know. They tell us that the factory that makes our regular gloves is still closed down, so we have to use these surgical gloves that have talcum powder on them."

She looked at Hope's hands. "I'm guessing you're about a size 6." Kathy reached up onto a shelf over the wash sink and re-moved a packet of gloves, pulled the end tabs apart, and dumped the gloves onto a sterile paper-covered tray. She then picked up the gloves by their cuffs and held them for Hope to insert her hands.

"Do you remember your glove size?" she asked Mark.

"Seven and a half."

Another pair of gloves was opened onto the paper and held up for hands to be inserted. "I feel like a surgeon," Mark joked. "Scalpel! Clamp!" The crinkling of his eyes above the top of his mask were the only hint of his smile.

"You're ready to go in," Kathy told them. "Party time!"

Suddenly something about Mark caught her expert eye. "Mark?" she questioned. "Are you OK?"

His brow was gray and covered with beads of sweat. "I feel funny. I think I need to sit down for a minute."

"I'll be right back," Kathy called over her shoulder. She hurried a few paces down the hall, grabbed a chair, and raced back just in time to slide it under Mark's collapsing form. She jerked the mask from his face as he reached up to wipe a gloved hand across his forehead.

"I can hardly breathe," he gasped before rolling sideways off the chair and onto the floor.

Hope's eyes flared wide as she saw Kathy roll Mark onto his back, fingers of her right hand pressing deftly onto his neck. "He's got a heartbeat," she muttered. In a flash she unwrapped the stethoscope hanging around her neck and put it to his chest. This time she said nothing but sprang to her feet and dashed the few steps to a nearby wall phone. Lifting the receiver, she punched in a five-digit code, listened for a moment, then hung up the phone. She was back at Mark's side when an unemotional female voice came over the public-address system: "Code Blue, Pediatric Isolation Unit. Code Blue, Pediatric Isolation Unit."

In the same moment Kathy ripped the latex gloves off his hands. His hands were bright-red.

Time seemed to stretch into infinity before a trio of scrub-suited staff raced their direction pushing a cart of medical equipment. "I think it's a latex allergy," she heard Kathy say.

Two of the staff quickly removed Mark's sterile gown and the green shirt of his scrub suit. "I'll get an IV started," someone volunteered. Another person arrived with a gurney. Mark was rolled to one side and a sheet slid under him. On a count of three the group lifted him up and onto the gurney.

A physician bent over Mark's inert form and listened to his chest. "He's not getting good air exchange much of anywhere. Let's get some epinephrine in him. Stat!"

He looked around. The IV was not yet flowing. "Do we have an Epi Pen?"

A nurse yanked open a drawer on the cart and pulled out a six-inch brown tube a half inch in diameter. She uncovered the ends and pressed it against Mark's leg. A thumb pressed against the exposed end triggered an audible snap. When it was withdrawn a few seconds later Hope saw that a needle extended from the end that had gone through the cloth of his pants and into his leg.

At that, Hope screamed. It sounded to her as if someone nearby let out a long, high-pitched wail. She could hear it, a shrill sound full of fear and despair coming from the depths of the soul.

"Somebody get her out of here!" the doctor ordered. Hands grabbed Hope by the shoulder and steered her toward the nurses' station. She resisted.

"At least stand over here and try not to scream," a male voice commanded. "You've got to let us do our job."

Mark groaned and moved slightly. "I can't breathe," he said hoarsely.

"Get some oxygen going. Eight liters," the physician ordered. One of the staff uncurled an oxygen tube and looped the end around Mark's face under his nose. Connecting the other end to a green cylinder, he opened the valve.

"Are you his wife?"

Hope looked toward the voice and nodded. It was the doctor who moments before had been bending over Mark. "Yes. I'm his wife."

"How did this happen?"

"We were getting ready to go in and see our daughter in isolation when . . . when . . . Mark said he felt funny. Then he couldn't breathe, and he fell over."

"Has anything like this ever happened before?"

Hope shook her head.

"Was anything different this time?"

"I don't know. This is my first time here."

"Different gloves," Kathy stepped up to explain. "We're out of the usual gloves, so we've gone to using the powdered latex surgical gloves. His symptoms started almost immediately after he put on his gloves."

The doctor looked at Kathy. "OK. Let's get him admitted and sent to ICU." He looked back at Hope. "I think he's probably allergic to latex, and the different gloves triggered a severe asthma attack."

"But he's scrubbed up and put on gloves a lot of times before," Hope protested.

"What's different about the powdered gloves is that the talcum powder that lets them slide on easily and keeps your

hands dry inside also has little flecks of latex on it. Those parti-
cles get tossed up in the air when you open the sterile pack
and put them on. People with latex allergies are 10,000 times
more likely to react when using the powdered gloves than the
nonpowdered ones."

"So . . . is he going to live?" Hope stuttered.

"I think so. I'm just glad we caught it in time. Another couple minutes could have been fatal. But we *did* catch it. Right
now he's still in a severe asthma attack, and the question is
what it's going to take to stop it and for him to recover. It may
be a couple days before we can be sure he's out of the woods."

As quickly as he had appeared the physician was gone.

The medical intensive-care unit was somewhere on the
other side of the hospital. The gurney holding Mark had disappeared in the few moments the doctor was speaking with Hope,
so she had to follow directions she only vaguely remembered.
She asked a couple of times, and finally arrived there. Signs on
the closed double doors boldly declared that the next 10-minute
visiting period was nearly two hours away.

This was almost too much. Hope wanted to sink to the floor
and cry. Her daughter awaited her in a far wing of the hospital.
Her husband had almost died and . . .

Then to one side she found a phone with a small sign giving
the number that rang at the ICU nurses' station. She punched
the number and pleaded for an exception. Soon a male nurse
opened the door and guided her to the cubicle where Mark lay.
Another nurse was finishing hooking up a cardiac monitor while
a respiratory technician adjusted a nebulizer that fed a plume of
medicine-laden steam in a tube to Mark's mouth.

"I'm sorry . . . to ruin . . . your . . . homecoming," Mark said
on shortened breaths.

Hope leaned against him and gave him a hug, then moved
down and placed an ear on his chest. He wheezed loudly with
each breath, and she could hear rattling noises from his lungs.

"You'll have to leave now and let him rest. I promise we'll
take good care of him," the nurse told her politely.

"I'll see you in a couple of hours. You get well," she instructed her husband through her tears. She walked through the
double doors as if fighting her way up a hill deep in fog. Only

two hours ago she'd been on her last flight home after living through destruction and death. For weeks her upmost thought had been to return to her husband and be with her hospitalized daughter. Now her husband's life hung in the balance, and she was powerless to do anything about it. All she could do was wait.

Almost aimlessly, Hope turned away from the ICU and began retracing her route to the isolation ward. She'd have to scrub up again, and dress . . . it almost seemed too much. Each step was an effort. Even the goal of finally seeing Jennifer did not help. Then, as she passed a row of elevators, a voice called her name. Sheila Berringer was coming toward her.

"Oh, Hope! You poor dear!" The woman enfolded her in a hug. "Mark told us you were coming home, and I came to see you. Then they told me what happened. How is he?"

At the sight of the familiar, caring face Hope broke down in tears. "I'm not sure. He's really sick. He's wheezing with every breath, and just by holding my ear close to him I can hear all kinds of rattling and whistling sounds from his chest. It was . . . so . . . sudden. I mean, one second he's standing there, and the next he's on the floor."

Sheila embraced her again. "I'm so sorry, Hope. I guess we've got an extra reason for me to stick around. Have you called your family yet?"

Hope shook her head. "Mark met me at the airport just two hours ago, and we came straight here. We were suited up to go in and see Jennifer when Mark collapsed."

"How about if we go see Jennifer together?" Sheila suggested. "I think you're in for a pleasant surprise."

It's amazing what a loving, comforting friend can do for the morale, Hope realized. Just being with Sheila brought a spring back in her step.

The women scrubbed in together. This time Jennifer caught sight of her mother through the window and almost jumped out of the bed in anticipation. Hope couldn't get gowned and masked fast enough. Once ready, she fairly flew through the door. Jennifer held on to her as though she'd never let her go.

It was painfully obvious to Hope that Jennifer had been very ill. It was a shock to see her shiny scalp, and her slender frame had grown so thin. "I can't eat very much," she explained seriously, "but everybody says I'm getting better, and my bad cell counts are going down."

"Bad cell counts?"

"Her leukemia cell counts," Sheila explained. "The other day when she started feeling better she was having trouble saying 'leukemia,' so we just started calling 'em bad cell counts."

"Dr. McCormick says he'll let me out of here as soon as I have my first zero count day." Jennifer pointed to a chart on the wall tracking each day's count. "The way that line's going down, I think I'll be out of here in four or five more days. What do you think, Mommy?"

"What I think," Hope said as she bent over to give her daughter another hug, "is that I like that idea very, very much."

"Hey, where's Daddy?" Jennifer asked. She studied her mother's masked face. "Have you been crying?"

Hope shook her head, unable to reply.

"I heard them call 'Code Blue' over the speakers, and I saw a lot of people in the hall. I thought maybe someone had died."

"All of a sudden your daddy couldn't breathe," Hope told her. "The people you saw were here to help him. He's better, but now *he's* in the hospital, too."

Jennifer gasped. "Daddy's *sick?*"

"See these gloves?" Hope held up her hands. "The hospital ran out of the regular kind, so they gave us a different kind today. Daddy was allergic to them and had trouble breathing." Her eyes crinkled above the mask. "Right now we really, really need to pray for Jesus to help him recover."

"I want to pray," Jennifer offered. Hope nodded her approval and took her daughter's bare hands in her gloved ones.

"Dear Jesus. My daddy's real sick, and I want You to help my daddy to get well real soon, because I love him and Mommy and I need him," Jennifer prayed while her mother's tears moistened her mask.

CHAPTER

TWENTY-SIX

Do you mind if I walk to ICU with you?" Sheila asked as the pair took off their sterile gowns and dressed again in their street clothes.

"Thanks. Right now I need all the courage and strength I can get." Hope tucked her blouse into the top of her pants, looked at Sheila, and began to cry again. "I'm more scared than I've ever been in my whole life."

Sheila wrapped her arms around Hope as the last of her strength melted into tears. "I just don't know how I'm going to make it if I lose him."

For several minutes Sheila embraced her friend. "I'm here for you," she whispered as her sobs subsided. She handed Hope a handful of tissues. "Mark *is* going to make it. You just hang on to that. The crash team were there immediately, and he revived. It was a freak accident, but he's going to be OK."

Hope blew her nose, then smiled through her tears. "Look at me! I'm the woman who witnessed a nuclear bomb go off and 20 minutes later was live on the air telling the world about it, and now I'm turning into a weeping wimp."

"Did you know it was a nuclear bomb?" Sheila asked.

Hope shook her head.

"So maybe you didn't have time to be scared."

"You've got a point." Hope sank into a chair. "You know, back when I was in college, one night a girl who lived just down the hall in the dorm had an asthma attack." She paused, swallowed, then whispered, "She died from it. And now my husband nearly died from the same thing. He's in ICU, and I've got a daughter with leukemia here in isolation. Maybe it's no surprise that I feel as though I'm going to collapse."

"I'm not one bit surprised," Sheila sympathized. She placed a hand over Hope's clenched fist. "But, hey, you'll make it. Right now you may not feel like you can take another step, but trust me, God will help you get through this."

Hope looked at the clock on the wall. "The next visiting period in ICU starts in about 10 minutes. Think we can get there in time?"

~ ~ ~

Aubrey and Susan Morris spotted their daughter some distance down the hall and hurried to greet her. Susan held her close for a long minute as her tears dropped into Hope's hair.

Her father looked at her with narrowed eyes. "Hello, heretic," he said. His words hit her like a slap in the face. A slap would have been easier to take! She took a step backward, and the two eyed each other warily—he with disgust and she with pain.

"Mark was right," she said without thinking.

"Right about what?" Aubrey snapped.

"That I should've been wearing a flak jacket when I met you. Why in the world are you so angry?"

"Because you've gone off your rocker," he shot back. "You've turned against the truth, and *that* makes you a heretic. Then you had to go blab on national TV about no longer believing in the Rapture. Well, if you don't believe in the Rapture, what hope do you have?"

The two faced off in the hospital hallway—father and daughter, old-time preacher and modern young woman. "I asked, what hope do you have!" he demanded.

Hope felt the little energy she'd regained drain from her body, but she straightened her back and looked him in the eye.

"Daddy, I have the promise of Jesus that when He comes every person on earth is going to see Him. More than that, when He comes this world is going to end, and all the problems caused by sin will be over.

"Now"—her voice rose—"if you don't mind, I'd like to go spend some time with my husband. I'd suggest that if you want to make good use of your time while I'm in there, you go back and study your Bible and see what it *really* says—not what some-body tells you it says."

Standing off to the side, Sheila's eyes opened in shock.

"Hope! I'll not have you talking to your father that way!" Susan admonished, fire in her eyes. "Aubrey! This is not the place for a family squabble. Now you two just turn it off, and let's focus on why we're here—Mark."

Parents and daughter eyed each other for a moment, then without a word Hope turned and entered the ICU. Mark's breathing remained labored and the rattles in his chest were still easily audible, even without a stethoscope.

"He's stabilizing, but he's still likely to be having trouble breathing for a day or two," the attending nurse advised. "We'll know more this evening about how quickly he will recover."

The 10 minutes passed in a heartbeat. Hope noted that the next visiting time was four hours away.

Sheila was still waiting when Hope returned. She'd engaged Hope's parents in small talk. "Want to go see Jennifer?" Hope asked them.

"Sure!" Susan answered, and turned to leave. Aubrey followed in silence. Sheila gave Hope a little squeeze and a promise to see her again.

Jennifer's grandparents spoke with her from the phone outside her room while the three waved at each other through the window.

"What's eating Daddy so badly?" Hope asked her mother as Aubrey chatted with his granddaughter.

"Oh, dear, if you only knew. After your interview on the morning show, the head elder called a meeting of the board of elders to discuss if they should keep him as pastor of the church."

"What!"

Susan nodded. "They figure if he can't keep his daughter 'in line' and believing what the church teaches, then maybe he's not doing his job right."

"That's not fair. I came to my belief based on my own Bible study. If anything, he's tried to persuade me to keep believing in the rapture. But I reject it because the Bible just doesn't teach it. Besides that, I'm an adult. If the elders want to contend with me, then let them contend with me. Daddy isn't responsible for my beliefs."

"They don't see it that way."

The women listened as Aubrey chatted with Jennifer about what she wanted to do when she got out of isolation. "So when are they meeting?" Hope asked.

"No date yet. Sometime next week. Maybe the week after. Until then they've asked him not to preach anymore."

Hope sighed. No wonder he was dead on her case. "That's just not fair," she declared.

~ ~ ~

Late that night a bone-weary Hope found her way through traffic to the house she'd not seen in more than a month and dragged her suitcases inside. "Looks like a bachelor lives here," she muttered as she walked through the living room. A layer of dust decorated almost everything except where Mark had sat or walked. Searching the refrigerator, she found the remnants of a pizza delivery dated the day before and popped two slices into the microwave. Then she poured what was left in a gallon milk jug into a glass. All the orange juice was still frozen.

It felt good to be home even if the place needed a top-to-bottom cleaning. At least tonight she could sleep in her own bed without worrying about waking up to do early-morning feeds to New York or wondering when the air-raid sirens would sound. She wolfed down the pizza and milk while she stood, loading the dishwasher. The washing machine got loaded next.

She dragged her suitcases up the stairs, began unpacking, then decided she was too weary to finish the job. She searched one suitcase, then another, before pulling out a pair of satin pajamas that had somehow gotten twisted around her makeup kit. She shook the bottoms loose and let the case fall to the carpet. She dug in a drawer for a T-shirt to wear with them.

Turning toward her dressing table to brush her hair, Hope saw the pile of mail stacked to one side. There were numerous cards from friends and strangers. Too tired to open them, she scanned the return addresses, thankful for the concern of caring friends.

Her computer sat nearby, dust-coated as everything else. On impulse she turned it on. Its busy hum comforted her somehow. She sat down and placed her hand on the mouse, clicking her way into e-mail. "I should have known better than that!" she said aloud, as the screen rolled on and on and on with new messages. Hope leaned forward to see the dozen or so messages at the top of the screen. The most recent ones—"Heretic," "You're crazy," "Praying for your soul," she read aloud. *What's going on?* She clicked on one at random. It was a tirade against her position questioning the Rapture that she'd given on the morning news show. Another click; another objection to her viewpoint. More than 200 had been forwarded to her by MBS.

Quickly she clicked from one to another, reading the first line or phrase. She didn't go through them all. Her hands were trembling, her heart pounding. She jumped up and yanked the plug out of the wall. Enough was enough. She was beyond exhaustion. The bed—that was another bachelor picture. But she was beyond caring that the covers were kicked askew to the bottom. It felt good to be back in her own bed and to smell her husband's scent on his pillow, even though he was not there. She lay down, closed her eyes, and knew nothing until early morning.

Even without setting the alarm clock Hope awoke and showered before the sun rose. Dressed in a comfortable pantsuit, she searched the kitchen for breakfast foods. There wasn't much to pick from except stale cereal. She decided to find the hospital cafeteria instead and, later, a grocery store on the way home.

Hope arrived at ICU five minutes before 8:00. On the hour she was the first visitor through the door. Mark's bed was empty! For an instant she stood frozen, then raced toward the nurses' station. "Where's my husband?" she cried.

"Your husband is—?" the clerk asked.

"Mark Lancaster. Where is he?"

"Oh." She smiled. "We moved him out to the floor just a few minutes ago. He's doing much better."

Weakness softened Hope's knees. The breath she hadn't known she was holding came out in a long sigh.

"I'm sorry we frightened you, ma'am," the clerk said. "I was just about to call your home. He's in room 818. He's doing a lot better."

Turning to leave, Hope steadied herself against the wall for a moment.

"Are you OK?" a passing nurse inquired with concern.

"I'll . . . I'll be OK. I just had a bit of a scare. Which way is room 818?"

"Turn right out the door and take a left at the cross hall to the elevators."

~ ~ ~

Other than being a little weak and still having some rattles in his chest, Mark felt pretty good. But his breakfast tray sat undisturbed on the narrow table that extended over his bed.

"Not hungry?" Hope asked sympathetically.

"I don't know what restaurant this came from, but I bet it goes out of business soon," he grumbled.

"I doubt that'll happen," Hope said with a laugh. "They've got captive customers."

"Not for long if I have any say in the matter," Mark grumped as he lifted the rounded metal cover over his plate. "Just look at this stuff! I wonder if they'll let me go see Jennifer."

Hope eyed him warily. "All you'll be able to do is talk to her on the phone."

"I know. But I want to see her. Why did this have to happen?" he complained.

"I'm as shocked about it as you are. Do you feel up to walking that far?"

"Sure," he answered. "Question is Will they let me?"

Hope spent several minutes at the nurses' station before anyone could answer the question. "Only in a wheelchair" was their declaration. So they found one, and she pushed.

"How's my girl feeling this morning?" Mark asked when Jennifer picked up her phone.

"I'm OK. I miss you, Daddy. Can't you get me out of here? I feel like I'm in jail," she cried.

"Wait just a minute, doll. Your mom's getting dressed so she can come in and see you. She'll be there in just a couple minutes."

"OK," Jennifer answered glumly. "I'm feeling better. I want to go home."

"We'll spring you from here as soon as Dr. McCormick says it's OK. I promise." Mark spoke with all the confidence his strained confidence could muster. "Has he been in to see you yet today?"

"No." She grinned at him through the glass wall. "Yesterday

he told me that I might have my first zero count today."

"That would be wonderful! So why are you upset?" Despite her smile, Mark could see tears tracing his daughter's cheeks.

"I'm afraid."

"What are you afraid of?"

"That the count won't be zero and I won't be able to get out of here and . . . and . . . and that I won't get well."

Her sad voice was more than Mark could take. Tears sprang to his eyes. "Listen, Jennifer. Your mom's about to come in there. Talk to her about it, OK, sweetheart?"

"OK. I love you, Daddy."

"I love you, too, Jennifer." They both hung up their phones.

Hope slid her hands into a pair of the gloves just like those that had nearly killed Mark two days before. After a final check from the nurse she pushed open the door. Mark watched from outside as his wife and daughter embraced and began sharing words he could not hear. He reached down and released the wheel lock on the wheelchair. Turning it around, he threaded his way down the hall to the window at the end. It was there that Hope found him 30 minutes later, staring into space with tears tracing his cheeks and a particular set to his jaw.

"What's wrong?" she asked tenderly.

No reply.

"Mark. Mark? What's wrong?"

He stared, as if mesmerized, at the rain streaking the window glass. Hope looked around, found a chair, and brought it close so they could talk quietly. She laid a hand on his arm, only to have it pulled back.

"Do you want to talk about it?"

"Talk about what?" he snapped back.

"Whatever is bothering you. This isn't like you. Can you tell me about it?" she asked softly.

"It just isn't fair!"

"What's not fair?"

He turned to her, his face an angry mask of pain. "It's not fair that Jennifer's in there suffering from leukemia. Maybe even dying. What kind of God lets that happen to an innocent, beautiful child?"

Hope started to say something, then stopped.

"It's not fair," Mark repeated. "Why does it have to be her instead of you? Or me? Why *her*? What did she do wrong to deserve to be so sick?"

Hope took a deep breath and let it out slowly. "She didn't do anything."

"Well, I'll tell you what," Mark declared, "I just don't know about a God that would do that to an innocent child. I just don't know how to love a God who would do that."

"You're angry at God! That's not right, Mark. God loves us. We'd be nowhere, we'd have nothing, if Jesus hadn't died to save us. So how can you be angry at God over Jennifer's being ill?"

"How can I *not* be angry?" Mark yelled. With a swift turn of his wrists he jerked the wheelchair around and started back down the hall. Nearing the isolation unit telephone, he slowed as if he might pick it up, but instead wheeled beyond it at an even faster pace. Hope had to walk quickly to keep up as Mark wordlessly spun the large wheels back toward his room.

He brought the chair to a skidding stop right against his bed. Sweat covered his face. His breath came in hoarse gulps.

"Mark, can I pray with you? Let's pray for God to give us understanding," Hope suggested.

"Pray all you want," he snapped, and indeed, something had snapped inside him. He felt engulfed by the emotion and fear he'd kept buried the long weeks he'd been on his own with Jennifer.

He spun the chair around to look at his wife. "Right now I'm having a really hard time believing God even cares anymore. First you start traveling all over the place, and when Jennifer gets sick I'm the one who's home taking care of her. Then you hike yourself off globetrotting and almost getting yourself killed. Meanwhile, I'm stuck here at home without a job. I don't think you even cared how loaded down I was, worrying if my wife was going to survive a war zone, and if my daughter—my only child—was going to live or die."

He coughed, gasped, coughed again, and continued. "And on top of all that we've got this huge health insurance bill to pay for the time between when my insurance ran out and yours started. Then I had that stupid latex reaction, so now I can't even go in to see my daughter. All I can do is talk to her on a phone and look at her through a window!"

Hope put her hand on his shoulder. He jerked away. She took a step backward. "But she's getting better, Mark! She's getting better. You saw her cell count chart. It's going down."

"So she gets better. What happens in a few weeks or a few months when she gets sick again? Does she lose just her hair again? Or does she lose her life?"

Someone knocked at the door. "May I come in?" Dr. McCormick requested.

"Do come in!" Hope answered, relieved to stop their conversation. "What news do you have for us?"

"Well, it's good. I wish it were better, though it's not unusual. I really thought we might see our first zero count this morning. It's still going down," he reassured them, "but it may be another day or two before we see that magic number. I'll let you know as soon as I have the test results."

Husband and wife looked at each other, then at the oncologist. They both were exhausted. There seemed nothing more to say.

He asked for their questions and reassured them the best he could. The problem was that although he felt confident, he could make no promises. Then he was gone. Mark and Hope sat in silence as the clocked ticked away their lives.

"See what I mean?" Mark said at last. "It just goes on forever. You tell me how a caring God can do that to an innocent child. She wants out of isolation so badly!

"I just can't believe in a loving God anymore if He lets a child suffer like that. It doesn't end. It just goes on and on and on . . ." His voice broke into sobs.

TWENTY-SEVEN

Mark was released from the hospital the next day and sent home with doctor's orders to throw out every piece of underwear in his dresser that had an elastic waistband and replace them with boxer shorts that tied with a drawstring. He was also given an appointment with an allergist to see if his immune system could be desensitized to latex. Last—but very important—he was given an Epi-Pen, the emergency epinephrine injector to use in case of another allergic attack. If he had an allergic reaction, the Epi-Pen could buy him enough time to get him safely to a hospital emergency room and further medical care.

Two days later Jennifer was moved from the isolation unit to a regular room on the pediatric oncology unit. Still, visits were limited to the immediate family until her immune system strengthened and she was able to fight infections. She seized on the relocation to participate in every activity available to the kids on that floor.

"I don't know where this girl got all her energy, but I wish she'd share some of it with me about now," a nurse observed to Hope one afternoon toward the end of her shift.

~ ~ ~

The next Sunday morning Hope decided she needed to go to church. She debated, hating to miss even a few hours with Jennifer. When the unit's social director told her that cartoons were planned for Sunday morning, Hope talked it over with Jennifer and decided to go.

It felt good to walk through the church doorway into the

foyer. Friends greeted her warmly; others regarded her at a distance. She felt stares from more than one and actually slipped into the restroom to see if she had smudged her makeup or spilled part of her breakfast on her dress. *H'mm, no lipstick on my teeth,* she thought. *No stains on my dress. My makeup is perfect. Hair's OK.* She added a layer of lip gloss and went on out to join the Sunday school.

"Hi, Lisa," she greeted the discussion leader upon entering the room where her class met.

"Hi, Hope! It's great to have you home."

"Oh, it feels great to be home!"

"How's Jennifer doing?" Lisa wanted to know.

It felt wonderful to have good news. "She's doing well. She's out of isolation and should be home in a few days."

Within a couple of minutes the circle of chairs had filled with friends and visitors. "I thought it would be good if we went back and reviewed the scriptural evidence behind some of the major Christian doctrines in which we believe," Lisa began. She sat in a chair, too, her open Bible on her lap. "As I thought about it this week, wondering where to start, I decided that—with all the things that have been happening lately—it might be good if we began our study by looking at the Secret Rapture."

"Good pick," someone said.

"Yes!" said another. "Timely topic."

I wonder what led her to that topic, Hope pondered.

"After all, Jesus warned us to be aware of the time in which we live so we could be ready to meet Him when He comes to take the redeemed to heaven," Lisa continued. "Let's start our study in Matthew 24. What signs of Jesus' return do we find in these first few verses?"

"False christs will come," one observed.

"Wars and rumors of wars," another answered.

"Persecution of believers," said a third.

"False prophets," Hope added.

"The luf of many waxin' cawld. I guess dat means believuhs fallin' away," drawled an elderly woman they all called Miss Charlotte, who sat just across the circle. Her face was a patchwork of wrinkles, but her bright eyes shown with intensity.

"You are all correct," Lisa continued. "But many observers

say that this first part of the chapter is talking about the warnings of the fall of Jerusalem that happened in the year A.D. 70. *That* was a time of terrible upheaval too. But when we get to verse 27, it sounds like Jesus has shifted gears and is talking about His own return. Somebody read verse 27."

"'For as the lightning cometh out of the east, and shineth even unto the west; so shall also the coming of the Son of man be,'" a woman two chairs to Hope's left read aloud.

"Now, we believe that when the Rapture happens it will be very visible to those who are taken away," Lisa said. "That is what's happening here in verse 27. Then we see verse 29 talking about a time of tribulation. Going on to verses 30 and 31, we see Jesus returning the final time to take home those who have been converted during the Tribulation."

A dozen thoughts fluttered through Hope's mind as she listened to Lisa and followed along in her Bible. Should she say anything? Did Lisa know how her viewpoint had changed? Was Lisa pointing a finger at Hope, or was this just a logical coincidence? And most of all—should she say something in rebuttal?

In the lull that followed Lisa's words, Hope held up her hand to be recognized. "I have a problem with some of what you said."

"What's that?" Lisa queried.

"You said that verse 27 speaks of the Rapture being visible to those who are taken away. But verse 27 talks about whatever is happening—I believe it is Christ's return—as being as visible as the lightning flashing across the sky."

"Well, yes . . ."

"But, you see—"

"We believe that . . ."

Several people spoke at once. Lisa raised her hand to quiet them and asked Hope to continue her thought.

"Well, have you encountered lightning that was visible to some people who stood where you were but not visible to others there in the same place? Jesus is the one speaking," she went on. "The words are in red in my Bible."

Others nodded, and murmured. They had a red-letter Bible too.

"Christ doesn't say that His return will be visible only to the redeemed. It says it will be visible to everybody."

Lisa nodded, considering Hope's words. "Well, yes, we believe that the visible coming will be at the end of the Tribulation seven years after the Rapture. Only the believers will see the Rapture. Everybody who is alive later will be able to see His coming."

"Can you show me where the Bible says there will be two different comings—or that one of them will be secret?" Hope countered. "I sincerely want to see it. Over the past few weeks—starting before I went to Jerusalem—I've read the entire New Testament through several times. I've found places like further on here in chapter 24 where Jesus talks about some being taken and the others left behind as a warning for us to be ready all the time. And I've found a lot of places here and through the rest of the New Testament that talk about visible events when Jesus comes—the elements melting with great heat and the mountains falling into the sea, for example. But nowhere do I find anything that says Jesus' return will be secret or that He will come twice before the destruction of the wicked."

"What about the warning over here in verses 37 to 39 about it being like the time of Noah?" someone asked

Hope looked at the man with a smile. "I had that question, too. But if you go back to Genesis where it talks about Noah and the Flood, it was the *wicked* who were taken away by the Flood. They were destroyed. Noah and his family were *left behind*—in the ark—and they were saved."

She was leafing through her Bible to the book of Genesis. "But we take that text and turn it around as if the people who are taken away will be saved, and the people who are left behind will be lost."

"Well, what about all the texts that talk about the time of tribulation?" a woman at the opposite side of the circle countered. "Won't the Temple in Jerusalem be rebuilt and 144,000 of the Jews be redeemed at that time?"

"Yeah! What about that?" someone echoed.

Hope looked at Lisa. Lisa shrugged as if to say, "Go ahead."

"Well, I've got some major problems with that," Hope answered. "First of all, we've believed that the Temple is going to be rebuilt before the Rapture happens and the Tribulation begins, right?"

Heads nodded.

"If the Rapture is about to happen now, then we can expect

that the construction of the Temple is going to begin pretty soon, right?"

More heads nodded.

Hope shook her head. "There's a big problem. Since the bomb that exploded over it, it's not possible to rebuild the Temple. The Temple Mount is so radioactive that no one can visit for more than a few minutes at a time, much less build anything on it. Scientists say it will be heavily radioactive for the next 2,000 years."

At that, people turned to each other and to Lisa for help. There seemed no way to dispute the problem. "We have a major problem with our time line of what's going to happen," Hope concluded. "I learned about the Rapture about the same time I started eating solid food. It's all I've ever believed." She looked at Lisa almost pleadingly, then around the circle. "It seems to me that things are turning out different than we've been expecting."

"I dawn't believe it," Miss Charlotte drawled. "I grew up be-lievin' in the Rapture, an' I'll die believin' in it, an' anybody who don' believe it's jes plain lost."

"If God can create this world by speaking, then He can wipe away a little radioactivity, too," someone observed.

Lisa held up her hand to quell the murmur rumbling through the group. "This is very interesting, and I'd like to make a point." She flipped through her Bible back to Matthew 24. "It's one thing to *say* you believe something. It's quite another to be-lieve something"—she paused, drawing a deep breath—"because the Bible says it is so. If we're *not* believing something because the Bible says so, then how can we be sure we're saved?"

"Well, here's something to think about," Hope interjected. "A moment ago someone brought up the 144,000 in Revelation 14. You know, the Bible doesn't say they're converted Jews. It actu-ally says that they're virgins. And if it means literal virgins—which I don't think it does; I think it's symbolic—that puts a whole different slant on the topic."

"You know, it seems like a lot of the world events and signs of the end aren't happening in the way we've always expected them to do," a woman who'd not spoken before observed. She was young, dressed in a stylish gray suit with perfect accessories. Hope didn't recognize her. "My whole family is without work, and my parents, in Missouri, were without electricity for more than a month because of that levee that broke wherever it was on the Mississippi. And then I saw you, Hope"—she nodded at Hope with a smile—"reporting from Jerusalem about a nuclear bomb going off over the Temple Mount and making it uninhabitable."

The woman leafed through the gold-edged pages of her Bible with a frown. "I'm afraid that I'm with Hope on this. I'm starting to ask some of the same questions she's asking. I've been reading my Bible a lot more lately, and I'm wondering if what we believe is going to happen is actually going to happen the way we believe."

"It *will!*" another woman declared. "It will!"

"But what if there's a little difference?" another asked. "Would it matter? Not that I think that there is," she added quickly.

Again class members turned to each other, some with quiet intensity, others raising their voices. Lisa let them go for half a minute, then called them back to order. "Jill," she addressed the woman who'd been speaking, "I don't think you were finished."

Jill nodded her thanks and continued. "As I was saying, with all that's going on I've really been digging into my Bible, and so help me, I can't find *anything* that directly says Jesus' return will be secret. In fact"—she held up her Bible to read from it— "in Matthew 24:23 Jesus says, 'Then if any man shall say unto you, "Lo, here is Christ, or there; believe it not."' I understand that as Jesus Himself telling us not to believe it if someone says that when He returns it will be to a secret place somewhere."

"Thass anothuh sign uv the end," the elderly woman declared. She shook her head, looking sad. "People leavin' the faith. Now we have *two* heretics in our class."

~ ~ ~

Aubrey Morris wiped his hands against the inside of his front pants pockets for the umpteenth time as the members of the board of elders entered the church conference room and took their seats around the large polished table.

"I'm glad we're having the meeting tonight instead of last night, or I'd be missing Monday night football," one elder joked to another.

"Me, too," another echoed, while a third chuckled agreement before exchanging handshakes.

Richard Johnson, the head elder, a gentleman with salt-and-pepper hair and expanded belly, called the meeting to order. Then the men divided into groups of three or four to pray for each other and for God's guidance in what they'd come to discuss.

Johnson cleared his throat to get everyone's attention. "We're here tonight—under the bylaws of our congregation—to reaffirm with Pastor Morris that he is solid in his belief in the teachings of the church. This became an issue two weeks ago when his daughter Hope, on the MBS morning show, declared that she no longer believed in the Secret Rapture. Board members almost rung my phone off the wall in the next couple of days, calling to ask what I knew about it—which I knew nothing at all—and worryin' that since our pastor's daughter has rejected her belief in the Secret Rapture, is it possible that Pastor Morris has, too?"

Heads around the room nodded their concern. Aubrey Morris felt the knot in his stomach grow larger.

"After all," Johnson continued, "it wouldn't be proper to have someone preaching in the pulpit if we weren't 100 percent confident that he believed every one of the truths the church teaches."

Again heads nodded, accompanied by audible murmurs of agreement.

"So, Rev. Morris, in the presence of God and this board, I ask you to answer the question Do you believe in the Secret Rapture?"

In the quiet that followed, Aubrey Morris scraped back his chair and rose to his feet. "Gentlemen," he began. "Thank you for giving me this opportunity to respond." A light flush covered his face. He felt himself sweating under the arms. It occurred to him that a man who'd just had a heart attack shouldn't be in this position at all. He took a deep breath and continued.

"You men are my friends. You know me. We've worked together for the Lord for years on end. And I assure you that I have not wavered one iota in my belief in what the Bible teaches—including the Secret Rapture. In all honesty, I will tell you that my daughter is challenging me to go back and study this great truth again, and I can do that with confidence."

He mopped his head with a large handkerchief. "It is my prayer that in the near future she'll repent of this heresy." Tears filled his eyes. "If I may paraphrase a text, sharper than a serpent's tooth is a daughter who turns away from the teachings of her childhood. With everything happening in the world today, I look for the Rapture any time now."

He looked around the table from one face to the other. "Gentlemen, I'll sit down now. That's all I have to say."

"Amen! *Amen.*"

"Thank you, Reverend."

"God bless you, brother."

"May God have mercy on your daughter."

For the first time in days, it seemed, Aubrey Morris let himself relax. *Dear Lord, thank You for getting me through that,* he prayed, momentarily closing his eyes. Now, again he assumed his role of leadership. "Gentlemen, now that we've settled that important question, let me turn it around and ask each of you: Do you—each of you—still uphold the Secret Rapture? "Richard?" he questioned.

Richard Johnson nodded. "Yes, Pastor. I do."

"John?"

Another affirmative.

"Danny. What about you?"

"Yes, sir," came the firm reply.

"Kyle?"

A nod.

"Jerry?"

Jerry Smith's glance darted around the table.

"Jerry, it isn't like you to be so slow answering. Is something wrong?" Johnson asked.

The young man took a deep breath. "Yes, I guess there is," he replied, turning to the pastor as a ripple of surprise ran around the table.

"My wife was in the same Sunday school class that your daughter attended yesterday, and she came home with a lot of questions about Bible prophecy and the Rapture. I don't mind telling you that we spent all afternoon and evening studying our Bibles. That's why I missed the evening service. Robin and I were on our knees praying about what we were learning."

"And what did you learn?" Johnson asked, as if he could not believe what he was hearing.

Jerry reddened. "That the teaching of the Secret Rapture is not supported by Scripture."

A bomb would have made a lot more noise, but it could not have surprised the men more.

"Jerry! I've always respected you as a thoughtful, even serious student of the Bible," Aubrey declared. "How could you come to such a conclusion on a topic that we've believed and taught all our lives?"

"Because, sir, it isn't in the Bible." He opened the manila folder in front of him and began passing sheets around the table. "I had a feeling that this might come up this evening, so I brought something to share with you. On the top half of the page is a list of texts that we typically use to prove the Rapture. I challenge you to look over this list and tell me if any of them directly say that Jesus will return in secret. Believe me, Robin and I have been over this list a dozen times." His voice rose. "Can you possibly think that we *wanted* to come to this conclusion?"

He paused, waiting until every man there held a sheet in his hands. "Now, some of the texts talk about the need to be ready for when Jesus comes, but none, not a single one, talks about His returning secretly.

"On the bottom half of the page is a list of texts that speak of the *manner* of Jesus' return. I beg you to go home and look them up. See if you find in any one of them Jesus or His disciples saying that Christ's return will be anything but very visible and earthshaking.

"We put the texts together and mix them up, and somehow come out with the conclusion that Jesus is going to snatch away His followers secretly so they can avoid the Tribulation." He leaned forward, almost pleading. "Friends, I didn't look for this. It's there! And I challenge you to find a plain statement in *any* of these texts that truly supports the Rapture."

"That's heresy! You've gone and made yourself a heretic—just like the pastor's daughter!" an angry voice snarled from across the table.

"Call me a heretic if you wish," Jerry answered kindly. "I stand on the Word of God. I have no other foundation." He stood up, almost unconsciously. "Can you think that I want to separate from my good friends, from the people who came to my wedding and wept with me when our first child was stillborn?"

He paused, waiting for some response. He saw heads shaking in sorrow. He saw angry scowls. And heard more than one voice saying, "Dear God, have mercy on his soul."

"Robin and I expected it would come to this," he told them, turning to the board chair. "Brother Johnson, I won't make you ask for my resignation. I must resign from this board because I can no longer in good conscience serve as a leader in a church that teaches something I cannot find in the Bible. And so, gentlemen, I bid you good night."

With that he picked up his Bible and the manila envelope, pushed back his chair, and walked out of the room.

Shocked silence reigned for a minute.

Aubrey Morris fanned himself with the sheet of texts. "Jerry Smith!" he exclaimed. "Of all the people in this church, he's the last one I would've expected to turn against us. But you know, the Bible tells us that in the last days there'll come a delusion so strong that—if possible—it will deceive the very elect." He shook his head, still in shock "I guess poor Jerry's just not one of God's elect. Well, not anymore."

'm not sure what's gotten into your dad lately, but he's been spending an unusual amount of time alone studying his Bible and his religion books," Susan complained to her daughter. "I wish he'd do more around the house. I used to be able to count on him to load the dishwasher and keep the floors vacuumed. But now every time I turn around he's back in his study with his nose in a book."

"Maybe that's not all bad," Hope mused, wondering herself what was going on. Taking advantage of Jennifer's nap, she'd gone to sit on one of the benches placed just outside the hospital lobby and use her cell phone. With Jennifer feeling almost like her old self, she wanted her mother with her all the time. They watched videos, read to each other, and otherwise kept Jennifer occupied. She was well enough to go to the play room and enjoy other kids, too, but the hospital wanted an adult with them at all times.

"At least it's the Bible that he's studying," Hope replied. "Do you have any idea what triggered this?"

Susan sighed "Not really. Who knows what goes on in a man's mind!

"He came home from the meeting with the board of elders greatly relieved that he'd been reinstated, but muttering something about one of the men being a heretic. Maybe it has to do with that. He's been on the phone at great length with someone, and I know that Thursday evening he and two of the elders are going to visit whoever this is. Maybe he's studying up on how to deliver a biblical call to repentance."

"Sounds pretty serious."

"Well, your father's treating it seriously."

"I wish he'd at least talk to me, and stop giving me the silent treatment," Hope said a moment later. She pulled her jacket up around her neck. Today's sun was warm and felt good to her face, but the wind was chilly.

"I wish he would too," Susan sputtered. "It's just not right for a father to call his daughter a heretic and stop speaking to her. It's plain crazy. As my grandma always said, 'blood is thicker than water.' You just don't turn your back on your own flesh and blood! I just wish I could persuade him to change his mind about you."

"Well, listen, Mama, I called to give you some good news. Jennifer's coming home tomorrow. That's the big Christmas present at our home."

"Oh, that's wonderful! Oh, I can't wait to share that with your dad!" Susan squealed. "Praise the Lord! Oh, God is good." She was almost singing. "What are you getting Jennifer for Christmas?"

"You know, we haven't decided," she said. "I know! Christmas is Monday, and we haven't done any shopping yet. Well, money's tight, and we've spent so much time at the hospital we've hardly even thought about Christmas shopping." Her joyful laugh rang like holiday bells. "I mean, the house is barely decorated on the inside, and we've not hung a single light outside. We put up a Christmas tree only just yesterday. We debated waiting till Jennifer got home, but decided that with everything else going on, it would be better to have the tree waiting for her."

Susan couldn't keep her secret any longer. *"We're getting her a bicycle."*

"Oh, Mom! That'll be great! I'm sure she'll enjoy that a lot. I know we'll get her some clothes—she likes new clothes, and things are so big on her right now—and a game or two. I've been thinking about a set of actual kid cookware."

"Huh?"

"These educational stores carry it. It's child-size, but can actually be used in a real stove. Jennifer's really into tea parties, and I was thinking that could be fun for her—to have her own baking things for making tiny cakes and cookies."

Susan laughed. "That child is the love of my life, you know. Not that I'd want the other grandkids to know it. I guess"—her voice dropped—"I guess because we almost lost her."

"Yeah. I know," Hope whispered.

"You know what Jennifer told me the other day?" she asked Susan.

"No telling."

"You're right there! She said that she wanted a baby brother for Christmas."

"Well, of all things—"

"I know," Hope laughed. She stood up and went through the automatic door back into the lobby. The wind had gotten a little too strong. "You know, Mom," she said, talking quietly right into the phone, "for the past two or three years Mark and I have hoped we'd have another child or two, but God just hasn't given them to us. Right before Jennifer got sick we were talking about seeing a fertility specialist. Of course, too, Mark had just lost his job." Her voice trailed off. "Mom . . . no one could ever have told me how difficult real life truly is."

Susan struggled to know how to reply. Their family didn't generally confide such personal details. "God knows best, sweetheart," she said by way of comfort. "And no one could be as sweet as Jennifer."

"Yeah, I know." Hope wasn't ready to give up the subject. "I've been reading about what they call secondary infertility—when you can't get pregnant a second time."

By now Susan had recovered her usual take-charge competence. "You know, we have a little money tucked away," she said. "After the holidays, why don't you look into just how much it would cost to see a fertility specialist."

Hope laughed again. "Oh, Mom. It just helps to tell someone. That's all. We have enough to deal with right now. You can just help me get through Christmas first." She looked at her watch. "Jennifer's probably awake. I promised her we'd go to the play room, so I'll talk to you later."

"Wait a sec. Can you all come early Christmas morning? I'd like to get everybody here early enough to have breakfast after we open presents," Susan said.

"Sounds great to me. I'll tell Mark and Jennifer."

~ ~ ~

305

Once home, Jennifer made a beeline for her bedroom to put away her clothes and find homes for the dozens of little gifts that family members and friends had brought to her at the hospital. A half hour later she appeared in the den wearing a Sunday dress and with her blond wig carefully brushed and tied back with a colorful ribbon.

"What are you all dressed up for?" Mark inquired.

"Don't you look grand!" Hope added to the chorus.

"I just wanted to," Jennifer declared, twirling so that her full skirt flared wide. "Whee!" She twirled close to where her father sat in his recliner and collapsed across his lap.

He responded with a tickle and a shake. "You know what? I'm so happy to have you home that I could just tickle you."

"Me too, me too, me too," she giggled.

"Stand there and let me look at you for a second," Hope commanded. She surveyed Jennifer up and down. "The last time you wore that dress I thought you were growing out of it. You've lost more weight than I realized."

"Does this mean I can be a fashion model?" Jennifer teased.

"Maybe when you're grown up!" Mark declared.

~ ~ ~

Without her parents knowing it, when she went to bed Christmas Eve Jennifer set her clock radio for 5:30. She awoke quickly, shut off the radio, and got dressed using only the glow from her night-light. Then she slipped downstairs and turned on the coffeemaker. Precisely at 6:00 she delivered her parents each a steaming mug with the right amounts of cream and sugar.

Mark and Hope eyed their daughter through sleep-laden eyelids and grunted a response to her cheery "Merry Christmas! It's time to get up and go to Grandma and Grampa's house!"

"A bit ago I dreamed that someone was singing 'Grandma Got Run Over by a Reindeer,'" Hope said sleepily.

"Me too," Mark grunted. "But I went back to sleep."

"Then I dreamed a blond-haired daughter brought us each a mug of fresh-brewed coffee," Hope said as she pushed herself up against the headboard and reached for her favorite mug on the tray Jennifer held out. "Thank you, pet. This is awfully sweet of you. By the way, what time is it?"

"It's time to get up and go to Grandma and Grampa's house."

Hope looked at the clock on her bedside stand. "6:02! You got us up this early? Jennifer! You really *are* eager to go, aren't you?"

Jennifer nodded. "Are you mad?"

"No, just sleepy. I guess this is as good a time as any to get up on Christmas morning, isn't it? You want to get in bed with us?"

The parents held their mugs carefully as they made room between them. "Are you going to read the Christmas story from the Bible like you do every year?" Jennifer asked.

"I guess so." Mark yawned. *If you can't beat 'em, join 'em, and besides—Jennifer's home!* He reached over to his bedside stand for his Bible. It had been a long time since he'd picked it up. Hope didn't mention that she'd had to dust it thoroughly when she'd cleaned the room.

"That's in the book of Luke, isn't it, hon, or is it Matthew?" He turned pages for a few seconds. "Here it is. Luke. Chapter 2.

"'And it came to pass in those days, that there went out a decree from Caesar Augustus, that all the world should be taxed,'" he began.

Jennifer snuggled close to her father and wrapped her hands around his arm. Mark continued reading. "'And there were in the same country shepherds abiding in the field, keeping watch over their flock by night.'"

Pausing, Mark looked down at his daughter. After only a few verses she had fallen fast asleep.

"Boy! If that's not turning the tables!" Mark chuckled. "She brings us the coffee to wake us up, and then she's the one who falls asleep."

~ ~ ~

Right at 8:00 the Lancasters arrived at the Morris home. "Merry Christmas!" Susan called from her cinnamon-scented kitchen, hurrying toward them for hugs and kisses. "The others will be here shortly."

Jennifer ran to her grandfather for a pickup hug and twirl around. "Merry Christmas, Grampa!"

"Merry Christmas to you, too. I just got my very best Christmas present of all."

"What was it?"

"Seeing you getting well," Aubrey declared. "If I get nothing else for Christmas, I'm still happy." He gave her another squeeze before putting her down.

The sight of her dad and her daughter almost brought tears to Hope's eyes. Christmas was a time of healing. Everything was going to be OK, and she walked toward him with open arms.

"Hello, heretic," he said coldly as he turned away.

"What's wrong, Daddy?" Hope asked, feeling crushed on this morning of mornings.

"You're leading people astray, that's what."

"Dad, if my studying the Bible is leading people astray, then what are you teaching?" Hope countered.

"You're teaching things different from what we believe. You've gone on national TV saying that you don't believe the truths you've been taught since you were little—that's no less than calling me a liar!" His face reddened. The veins in his neck and forehead grew more pronounced as an unfamiliar sharpness entered his words.

His narrowed eyes latched fixed firmly on Hope's eyes. "I'll put up with you being here today because I don't want a scene with the rest of the family," he said in a hoarse whisper, "but I'm serving you notice right now that until you repent and return to the truth, you're not welcome in this house."

Shocked into silence, Hope and Mark could do no more than stare. It seemed an eternity before he turned his back on them and walked away. "I'm just thankful Jennifer's in the living room with the tree," Hope managed, tears in her eyes and voice.

Mark shook his head. "I can't believe this."

"Hope, dear, will you help me set the table?" Susan called from the kitchen. "I'm about ready to take things out of the oven."

Hope's feet seemed glued to the floor and her mouth braced open.

"What's wrong?" Susan asked, coming into the entrance.

"I . . . I can't believe what I just heard from Daddy," Hope choked.

"What? What did he say?"

"I . . . uh . . . he just told me that after today he doesn't want me in the house again until I've repented."

"Repented? Hope! You've done nothing that he could demand you repent of, have you? That's ludicrous."

Hope shook her head, searching her coat pockets for a tissue. "It's this whole rapture thing. I've come to believe differently because of what I've read in the Bible. Daddy's demanding that I repent of it. I can't do it, Mom. How can you repent of something you read in the Bible that you believe is true? I can't do it. If Daddy's taught me one thing my whole life, it's to follow Jesus and the Bible no matter what. And now he's demanding that I do different."

Anger flared in Susan's eyes. "I'm going to have some words with my husband." She turned with quick steps into the living room where Aubrey was playing with Jennifer. She grabbed him firmly by the arm and took him down the hall toward their bedroom. When they reappeared several minutes later it was obvious that she'd delivered a tearful chastisement.

Susan made a beeline for Hope. "It's OK for now. I've laid down the law. He's *not* going to say another word about it today. He *is* going to be nice to you today, tomorrow, and *any* time *my daughter* wants to come visit."

Despite Susan's attempt to smooth things over, tension was thick at the breakfast table. "What's between you and Daddy?" Allison asked Hope after breakfast.

"I'd rather not talk about it right now."

"It's not Jennifer, is it? She's OK, huh?"

"She's fine. For now." Hope's voice held infinite sadness. Her daughter's illness . . . the struggle to understand biblical prophecy . . . her decision . . . and now being disowned by her dad.

"Does this have something to do with your not believing in the Rapture anymore?" Allison whispered as they walked toward the living room to distribute and open presents.

Hope nodded.

"Well, for what it's worth, after what you said on TV I felt as angry as Dad. But I've been studying my Bible backwards and forwards, and Hope," Allison whispered, *"I'm* starting to believe the same way."

The sisters eyed each other in surprise. "Well, don't look so shocked," Allison whispered, sitting down on the couch next to

Hope. "When we study the Bible we're supposed to learn things, right?"

"Ho, ho, ho! Merry Christmas!" called a red stocking-capped gentleman from the living room doorway.

"Grandpa!" Jennifer giggled.

"Gwampa," the toddlers echoed.

"I've got a package here for my blond granddaughter!" Susan announced as she delivered a brightly wrapped box to where Jennifer had sat down on her daddy's lap.

Hope smiled as she absorbed the joy on her daughter's face, then let her eyes move to the right to include her father's face. Hard lines reappeared around his eyes as their gaze met, erasing the smile he'd had for Jennifer and the other children.

~ ~ ~

"I'm brokenhearted, Hope. Your dad says he will not talk to you so long as you're a heretic," Susan confessed the next after-noon in Hope's kitchen. They sat at the kitchen table, sipping herbal tea while Jennifer amused herself with a coloring book and crayons. "It's killing me, Hope, to see him act this way. In all the years we've been married and all the years we've had you kids, he's never been vindictive like this."

"I wish there were some way to change his mind," Hope an-swered. Two weeks had passed since that happy-sad Christmas Day. True to his word, Aubrey had all but disowned his daugh-ter. He didn't try to stop his wife from contact, but he said that as a pastor of the Word he could not have Hope in his home.

"Listen, Mom, Daddy's OK about you staying here with Jennifer, isn't he?"

"Oh, of course. She's the light of his life! Not that he doesn't love the other grandbabies, and Carla's new one is such a sweetie." Susan nibbled a shortbread cookie. "I guess it's because Jennifer's been so ill. I think we're all a little partial to her."

Hope drained the last of her cup. "Then we're set. I'm flying to Missouri this evening." Susan listened with half an ear as her daughter explained—again—that she'd be away several days, working on a one-hour network special. "It's about how people are putting their lives back together now that the river disaster is over. You've got my cell number, right?"

Susan eyed the bulletin board above the kitchen phone. "Got it right here, and I've got it in my purse."

Hope flew around the kitchen, stowing clean dishes, opening drawers. "Mama, I'm already second-guessing this trip," she confessed.

"I know, sweetheart. But it's OK."

Hope reminded her—again—that there were casseroles in the freezer and a list of suggested menus. I've bought everything you'll need, except the fresh stuff, of course."

"Hope!" her mother laughed.

They both laughed. "I know. I'm going nuts!" Hope told her. "Listen, Mark and I have explained to Jennifer how long I'll be gone. She has a special calender to mark off the days—if she wants to." She paused, one hand on the refrigerator door. "You know, I think she's excited about your staying with her. Daddy's promised to take her to the zoo and places"—she frowned—"if the weather's not too bad."

"Your dad will have a ball with her."

"You know," Hope went on, "I have a feeling things are going to work out. Daddy just needs time to work through how he feels about all this. After all, when you've grown up believing something is going to happen one way and it turns out another, that's pretty upsetting."

"You've got that right. But what's really making it hard for him is how many people in the church are suddenly outright rejecting the Rapture." Susan bit her lip. "I've never seen such apostasy in my life. I never imagined it could happen."

"Is that apostasy? Or is God revealing truth to His people?" Hope asked softly.

Susan paused, searching for the right words. "You know, the other night in my Bible study group someone asked the same question, and I didn't open my mouth. You would have been proud of me, I think." She poured hot water over a new tea bag. "I just listened. And do you know what I heard?"

"What?"

"People are studying their Bibles like they never have before. One lady—Karen Tipton—said that what started her studying was realizing that there were too many things about the Rapture and the Tribulation that just didn't add up. She said that it seemed that the recent major disasters and economic collapse are on a scale that shouldn't happen until the Tribulation." She added a spoonful of sugar to the cup and stirred it in. "And then that part about the Temple Mount being too radioactive to rebuild the Temple for more than 2,000 years. She said *that* was the real kicker for her."

"You see where I'm coming from now, don't you?" Hope asked carefully. "Do you still believe in the Rapture?"

"Oh, child," Susan laughed, "I haven't decided yet. I'm still studying it. You know, it's pretty hard to give up something you've been taught to believe for more than 50 years."

~ ~ ~

The floods resulting from the levee breaks on the Mississippi River had scoured and changed much of the landscape of southeastern Missouri. River channels twisted and turned across the gently sloped land. In one place the awning above the gas pumps in front of a convenience store were the only evidence that busy paved roads had once crossed there. The building—including its foundation—were gone. The only evidence of a road was a mud-encrusted stop sign on a post twisted slightly by the current.

"This is where my store was. Or where I think it was," Howard Graham told Hope as they walked westward into the afternoon sun.

"Do you want to rebuild?" she asked.

The man took a deep breath and let it out slowly. "Do I want to run a convenience store on a busy corner where there's lots of customers? Of course. That's what I did for the past nine years—until a couple months ago. Do I want to do it here? No way. I may own the ground, but there's no road, no building, no customers."

"Did you have flood insurance?"

Howard shook his head. "I'm wiped out."

"So how are you going to restart?" Hope asked.

"Well, I've got a disaster loan from the federal government that'll cover the cost of buying a new site and putting up a building and like that. That's the easy part."

"What's the hard part?"

"Doing it without my wife." Howard's eyes misted up, and

his voice broke. "She was in the store when the flood came. She never had a chance to get out. Rescue workers found her body a week later 28 miles from here."

~ ~ ~

"You know what amazes me?" Hope observed to her crew as they found their way along a rutted dirt track leading back to the nearest paved road. "That we still have cell phone service in the middle of this area that's been totally devastated. I mean, you can drive for miles out here without seeing a building, without being on a road, and your cell phone still works!"

"That's not amazing," the technician answered. "The cell phone towers were all put on the highest ground around, so they didn't get washed away. Plus, most of 'em have solar panels and the capacity to operate on batteries, and they're linked by fiber-optic cables that didn't get washed away."

"I just wish they'd built the roads as well," the cameraman remarked as he jerked the four-wheel drive SUV around another rut. "Too bad the network won't let us use a helicopter out here."

"Well, you know about the budget cuts at the network with the economy down and ad revenues falling," came the answer from the technician in the back seat.

The first traffic light the trio reached was not working. The electricity still had not been restored to the small town. A few vehicles were around as property owners set about the task of recovering from the disaster. A handful of merchants prepared to serve what customers would return.

Hope's cell phone played its lilting ring tone. She dug among the gear strewn around her feet and pulled it from her purse. "Hello."

"Hope?" It was Mark. The tone of his voice jerked her to full focus.

"What's wrong?"

"How soon can you be home?"

"Uh, maybe tomorrow. What's wrong?"

"Your dad. He's had a major heart attack. He's in the coronary intensive-care unit at Memorial Hospital. The doctor says it's really serious and suggested that we get the family together."

The cameraman saw the color drain from Hope's face. "What's wrong?" he mouthed.

Her mouth opened; no words came out. She swallowed, tried again. "A heart attack? When?"

"Early this morning," Mark told her. "I've been trying to get you since about 10:00. Where are you?"

"I'm about 40 miles north of New Madrid, I guess. Listen, Mark. I've got to figure out how to get out of here, but it'll be as soon as I possibly can. I'll let you know as soon as I have something figured out, OK?"

"OK." A pause. "Love you, sweetheart. Try not to worry too much."

"Yeah, right," she said with a sob. "Love you too."

What am I going to do? What . . . One after another, thoughts tumbled through her mind, colliding, bouncing away into nothingness. "Brandon," she said cautiously. "I'm sorry. It's my dad."

"I heard. Listen, don't worry about it. Family comes first, even in this business. We'll just call someone else—or wait till you're available, depending on how things go for you" was his answer. "You just get yourself on home."

Tears filled her eyes. If Brandon only knew . . . *What if he dies without forgiving me? How can I live with that?*

"I've got an idea," the camera guy announced. "All your stuff's at the motel, right?"

Hope nodded.

"And there's an airport over at Sikeston. During the first flood, didn't you do a story about a group of pilots that parked their planes over there to save them from the flood?"

"Yes, I did," Hope answered, her mind already back in Memphis.

"Well, what if we grab your things from the motel, then go to Sikeston and hire one of those guys to fly you down to Memphis? You'll be home in a couple hours." He looked up at the low cloud cover with an afterthought: "I hope you don't get airsick."

~ ~ ~

Three hours later the single-engine Cessna touched down at Memphis International Airport and taxied through the darkness past the gigantic Federal Express terminal to the general aviation ramp. Outside the service building Hope hailed a cab to take her to the parking lot where she transferred her luggage into her SUV, then headed directly for the hospital.

"What room is Aubrey Morris in?" she asked the Red Cross volunteer at the front desk.

"That's M-O-R-R-I-S," the volunteer confirmed.

"Yes. Aubrey Morris. Well, which way to the coronary ICU?"

The volunteer studied the computer screen and looked up. "Are you a member of the immediate family?"

Hope's heart sank toward her feet. "I'm his daughter," she said, her voice desperate. "What's wrong?"

The man looked Hope directly in the eye. His voice was kind. "Ma'am, I'm terribly sorry to tell you this, but your father passed away about two hours ago. His body's already been taken to the funeral home."

Hope grasped the counter as strength drained from her legs. A pink lady standing nearby wrapped an arm around her shoulders and guided her toward a chair. Someone pushed a packet of tissues into her hand.

"I'm terribly sorry, ma'am. Is there anyone I can call for you?" the man asked.

Hope shook her head as her shoulders shuddered and tears flowed as if they'd never stop. Clutching tissues in both hands, she covered her face and wept. *It's not possible. Words don't make it so. I don't believe it. I won't believe it!* Hope, the competent career woman, the international reporter, cried like a heartbroken child. Slumped forward, her face in her hands, she periodically dropped a soaked tissue onto the floor and pulled a fresh one from the packet. *How could God let him die without making peace with me?* Then, strangely, it seemed she had no more tears. Her eyes burned. She blew her nose, letting that tissue, too, drop to the floor. Looking up, she saw the pink lady sitting across from her, a spare packet of tissues in her hand and a sympathetic look on her face.

"Can I get you something?" the woman asked.

"No. Nothing."

"Do you feel as though you can drive safely?" the volunteer inquired gently. "Should I call someone to come get you?"

"I . . . I think I can drive," Hope whispered. She pushed herself up from the chair. "Thank you. Thank you."

Somehow Hope found her way to the parking garage. *I can do this. I can . . .* Speaking aloud, she talked herself through turning the ignition, putting the car in gear, and driving out of the parking garage. Outside on the streets, nothing looked familiar. It was as if she drove through a fog. Not a literal fog; perhaps a dream fog. "Turn here," she instructed herself. "Go to the next light and . . ."

Inside the kitchen door she melted into Mark's arms and again dissolved in sobs. "I just can't believe it, I can't believe it," she repeated between sobs. "It's not right. It's wrong, it's . . ."

"Sweetheart, I can't believe it either," Mark said, still holding her close. "It killed me to tell Jennifer, but of course she knew something was wrong. I just knew it was going to break her heart, but there was no way to keep it from her."

"She's in bed?"

"She went about an hour ago. Cried herself to sleep. I checked on her right before you got here. She was whimpering in her sleep."

~ ~ ~

By agreement, the family met at the funeral home the next morning. They'd go in together—supporting their mom—to see their dad. Hope's younger brother, David, had helped Susan choose a casket—a deep rich walnut. The family spray of winter flowers bloomed at its foot. Pink-tinted lights, tastefully positioned around the room, gave a rosy glow to the otherwise-somber setting. A few bouquets had already arrived and were placed on each side of the casket.

It was difficult to walk through the doorway. Seeing him lying there, eyes closed, in his best suit and tie—not quite looking like himself—sent each one back into their own private grief. Susan wept, sobs shaking her body, as she stroked his cold hand and murmured endearments. Hope bit her lip; her hands trembled. Mark drew her close, tears in his own eyes. Jennifer was with Aunt Allison, examining each bouquet and reading the condolence cards.

David stood by Susan a long while. Just stood there, not saying much. He didn't know how Susan would get by now. His dad—in his late 50s—was too young to die. It didn't make sense, but then death didn't make sense. He was glad that Carla hadn't come. The baby was still very small, still nursing on demand. They'd get a babysitter for their two, and she'd be at the viewing. With their large, active church family the room would be packed.

David turned to Allison, who'd taken a brief look at each bouquet. "I think they've made him look really good," he said.

She sighed. "Yeah. He looks asleep, doesn't he?"

"Hardly any gray in his hair."

"He looks like he's taking a nap," Jennifer observed. "Daddy, when will Jesus wake up Grampa?"

"When Jesus comes in the clouds of glory He's going to call out to all the dead people who died loving Him. He'll tell them, 'Wake up! Time to get up. I'm here!'" Mark told her. "Then He's going to take them all to heaven, where they won't ever get sick again."

"And they won't die again, right?" Jennifer asked.

"That's right," Mark declared.

Jennifer wriggled between the adults, then stood on her tip-toes to look into the coffin. She gazed at her grandfather's face for a long time, then turned to Susan and slipped her arms around her waist. At the gesture Susan cried softly. They stood together for a long minute; then Jennifer kissed her grandma's waist and slipped aside to find Mark.

"I want go outside," she told him. "I don't like it in here with all the flowers and stuff. Everybody's crying too much." She looked up, her face puzzled. If Jesus is going to wake Grampa up and Jesus is coming *soon,* why is everybody so sad?"

Mark smiled at his daughter and headed for the door. "Girl, you have an amazing way of asking the hardest questions to answer!"

~ ~ ~ *

The next three days were a series of private family times remembering their father, meeting with friends and relatives during viewing hours, and preparing for the funeral. So many bouquets arrived that finally word was sent to all the area floral shops to keep the cards but deliver the flowers to area nursing homes for the residents to enjoy. The families' mailboxes were filled each day with sympathy cards from friends far and near.

Six church deacons carried the casket holding Aubrey Morris to the front of the church, placing it on a gurney just below the pulpit from which he'd delivered so many sermons during his ministry at Fifth Street Baptist Church. As the family filed into their reserved pews at the front, Hope turned and took a quick look around the sanctuary. It was packed to capacity clear into the balcony. "More than a thousand people," she said quietly to herself. "Thank You, Lord, for Dad's loving influence and for so many caring friends."

The funeral service was filled with uplifting songs, happy re-membrances, and Scripture readings reminding of God's love. Then the six deacons again strode to the front and carried their pastor out for the drive to the cemetery. As the procession wound through city streets, cars stopped to wait, and men on the sidewalk took off their hats in respect. After several miles they turned into the vast lawn speckled with regularly spaced bronze markers set into the grass. The hearse halted a few yards from a canopy raised by an open grave. The black-suited and somber-faced funeral directors guided the family members to the rows of cloth-covered chairs next to the grave.

Jennifer turned in fright and wrapped her arms around her father's waist. From that vantage point she watched everything out of the corner of her eye, her head pressed against her father's waist. Mark covered Hope's hands with his as they lis-tened to the minister. He was a young man—an up-and-coming speaker—who'd been trained by Aubrey Morris. He closed his quiet words of comfort with Revelation 21:1-4, and the promise of the new earth fell like music on Hope's mind.

Then came the awful pronouncement of "from ashes to ashes and from dust to dust" and a closing prayer.

It took some minutes for the crowd to say goodbye to their pastor's family, but gradually they went to their cars and drove away. Skillfully, one of the funeral directors guided the family to a spot away from the grave site before the casket was lowered into the ground and the vault lid put in place. Despite being re-moved from the scene, the group watched from where they stood. Two men removed the canopy, and a tractor pulled a small trailer beside the grave, where it dumped its load of dirt into the cavity. A second man used a shovel, then a rake, to smooth the dirt, and the pair covered the dirt with a mat of sod. Then the bouquets of flowers were arranged across the top of the grave.

"Let's go," Susan told her family. "I may want to come back this evening, but right now the women of the church have prepared a nice lunch for us at the fellowship hall."

Jennifer took Aunt Allison's hand, and they went to her car. David, looking back for his mother, heard her ask Mark if she could ride with them.

"Sure. Come along," Mark said. "Anyone else coming?"

"No," Susan told them. "I sent Jennifer with Allison. I want a private moment with Hope." Once settled, she reached into her purse, extracted an envelope, and handed it to her daughter. "I found this in your father's study this morning."

Her eyes on the legal-size envelope, Hope's hands trembled. The handwriting was her father's. What message was in it? Gripped by fear, she shook her head.

"Go ahead. Open it," Susan encouraged.

Hesitantly Hope pulled open the flap and extracted the sheet. She could see that he'd pecked out the letter on his old typewriter. Tears filled her eyes at the distinctive type and her dad's typos and extra spaces between words. Her heart would be broken if—

Her eyes fell on the first words. "Dearest Daughter," she read aloud. *Dearest Daughter! Thank You, precious God.*

"It is not easy for me to admit that I have been wrong. Neither is it easy for me to ask your forgiveness. Yet I must admit my wrongness and ask forgiveness for the way I have been treating you lately. I treasure your presence in my life, and I do not want this division between us to continue any longer.

"Remember that day when you were on the morning show and you said that you no longer believed in the Rapture because of what you'd been reading in the Bible and what you'd seen in Jerusalem? I'll never forget it. Not for what you said, but for the anger and hurt I felt hearing you reject something I've taught you as gospel truth since you were a small child. Your words were like a slap in the face. Yet it challenged me to once again pick up my Bible and study what we teach about the Rapture.

"Hope, it was more than just your words that drove me back

319

to the Word. It was also the calls I started getting from church members sharing what they were discovering as they studied. So many others were questioning and rejecting the Rapture teaching; it was like a fire I couldn't put out. No matter how I protested and argued that it was what our church taught, more and more rejected it.

"Then you asked me if what I believed and what the Bible taught were the same thing. When you asked that, I knew what was happening was either a major deception by Satan or the work of the Holy Spirit. I had to know which it was. Old man as I am, I had to know the truth.

"Since then I have studied every text in the Bible that talks about how Jesus will return and every verse that we use to prove the Rapture. I've gone over them time and again. After all that study I must tell you—I no longer believe that Jesus will return secretly and snatch away His followers. Too many texts say that when Jesus returns it will be a visible event that destroys the world and kills the wicked.

"One thing I believe has not changed: that all the prophetic signs are telling us that the day of Jesus' return is in our very near future. I look forward to living to see Him coming in the clouds of glory to take all of us home with Him.

"I hope you will find it in your heart to forgive me so that we can be united in our love for Jesus. And yes, do come back to my home. I miss you.

"Love,
"Dad"

Tears flowed freely down Hope's cheeks, but she smiled as she folded the letter and put it back in the envelope.

"Is everything all right?" Susan asked.

Hope nodded. "Oh, yes, Mom. Everything is very, very right."